Match Games

A Lukas Novak Investigation

The HemiHelix Effect Episode 3

Bea ScS # 44/50

by Bea Schirmer

Published by Kinder Press 2015

In human psychology The HemiHelix Effect is
the individual's realisation that one has the ability
to change direction, whatever the circumstances

Introduction

He leans in the doorway holding a bottle. His fingers absent-mindedly peel away its label. His stomach tight, he watches the bodies twisting on the bed. The room is pretty dark, so he can't see too much detail. And he can't hear too much either as the music is deafening. The one who calls him matey is beckoning for him to come over to the bed; teeth glistening an eerie white as the man grins and shouts and waves at him. One of the girls looks up; the whites of her eyes strangely illuminated too. Her make-up is smeared and she is definitely not smiling. She mouths something at him. He drops the bottle, turns and walks from the room.

Prologue

'In theory all football is fixed. Be it that you won't pass to your colleague because you've had words at training or he's nicked your girl, or be it that you keep fouling that player who kicked the shit out of your teammate in the first leg. Or maybe someone is paying you a lot of money to miss that sitter…

You observe, you think about it and you decide for yourself.' GameWithoutFrontiers@wordpress.com

Chapter 1

Of all the bus routes in Greater Manchester Lukas hates the 86 most. Especially that stretch down Bonsall Street. You were never quite sure whether you were about to lose your lunch or the use of your spine. Why do they call this wreck the Magic Bus? Is it because despite its lack of suspension and handling it still has the ability to deliver you to the right place sort of in time?

At the old tollgate the bus bounces across the intersection of the four districts of Old Trafford, Whalley Range, Hulme and Moss Side, often cited the most notorious crossroads in the country by his colleagues. Through the heavy December rain he regards the squalor to his right – a row of shop fronts that used to be one of the most fashionable in Manchester. Years ago, after the demolition of the old and the building of the new Moss Side, the shops were taken over by barbers, tattooists, third-rate takeaways and betting shops, where those already hard up gamble it all away for the cheap thrill of an occasional win and a pint or five in the Whalley across the junction.

His 86 limps on, further along Upper Chorlton Road. It passes a number of reclaimed furniture stores and his old Caribbean mate Vic's tatty thirties semi; Vic, who still raises chickens in the front yard and does a bit of voodoo on the side in the back at weekends.

As the bus mounts the kerb on the left bend towards Chorlton Lukas curses the young Polish driver who treats the bus as his own private vehicle of vengeance; the youngster's way of getting back at the economic circumstances responsible for him finding himself here in this country. A country he has no respect for, because these stupid English buggers don't know how much worse things are at home, or at least used to be, before Sterling went bad.

Lukas gets off the bus one stop before his normal stop, and as recommended by the recent posters in every bus shelter. The campaign's logo reminds him of a bunch of dancing jelly babies. To him, the idea of walking an extra stop to put an end to the country's obesity problem is absurd; producing healthier food might help, but manufacturers would make less profit and profit is all that matters these days, profit, profit and more profit.

Those kids are hanging around outside his house again. Well, on the next corner, which is close enough to his front door to make him edgy. It seems impossible to pass them without overhearing some stupid comment or another. He should be more grown up about situations like this but once you've been on the receiving end it's hard to ignore the jibes, however immature they might be. He watches the kids watching him cross the road. Have they no homes to go to, no hobbies? What are their parents thinking, having them roam the streets at all hours? And why do kids dress like these do? To Lukas the boys look like drowned rats in their shiny, black tracksuits with barbed wire designs printed on their tops, their baseball caps askew on their almost completely shaven heads. He'll never understand why you would want to shave your head so uni-generationally and then, when you've grown out of it, you find that you've gone bald. He himself has always worn his thick reddish-blonde curls just as they wanted to grow and his nicknames have been varied. The real problem is that his hair won't succumb to any cut or form; he used to try to coax it into shape, in his youth, and had given up when the ridicule got worse. Later, when the ridicule no longer mattered to him as much, his mop suddenly became fashionable. But fashion still matters little to him. Fashion always parades itself with an inflated ego attached. Even in his youth Lukas disliked arrogance more than anything else; people full of themselves, or rather full of how they wanted others to see them. Parading their ego. Constantly. Unlike actors, who at least stop acting when the curtain closes and the lights go up, in theory, anyway.

Lukas holds the stare of the boy in charge as he walks past the group. The girls giggle as one boy whispers something. It is the girls he seriously worries about. It might not be the first time in history that mini-skirts are in fashion, but this time they are worn with much less purpose and dignity. The motivation behind wearing a short skirt today, he believes, is much different from in the sixties, when the mini-skirt was almost a political statement. Today, in his view, the girls are dressed like little tarts aiming to pull the boys, who seem so much younger than their female counterparts, to get laid, to get married, to prove to themselves that they are attractive, desirable, grown up or whatever.

He often wonders about the difference in the outfits: the girls really mean to impress while the boys mostly look like they sleep in theirs. One similarity though remains: both sexes' clothes are cheap and trashy, if not in price, then certainly in appearance. As far as Lukas is concerned, the popular magazines are to blame for the girls' dress code: meet the stars, footballers' wives. It's OK to be trashy these days, just look at this week's favourite gossip columns; a vision of what is allegedly important in life. To Lukas all this feels unbearably empty and ultimately cheap. It reminds him uncomfortably of the battle he is fighting with his daughter, Lilian, who too, suddenly, at the age of sixteen, is mesmerised by all this image nonsense and has started attending school covered in what Lukas deems to be more make-up than your average transvestite wears for the opening night of the carnival in Rio. To him, though, it comes as no surprise that she is turning out that way, since Lilian lives with her mum, who in turn blames him for everything under the sun since their divorce three years ago. At least Pavel is out of the family home and safely in digs studying IT at Manchester University.

As he unlocks his front door Lukas wonders if the kids on his corner have any hope of ever making a positive contribution to society. He frowns and immediately dismisses the thought as one flaw, if not the one fundamental attitude, that is keeping the generations apart.

Chapter 2

The pile of mail on the table looks huge. Lukas eyes it apprehensively, puts down his coffee and tears at the only envelope worth opening in today's delivery. He recognises the typeset and logo.

Lukas and Vladimir go back a long way, all the way back to the peculiar Polish drafting system that had them both serve their twenty-four months of basic training near Katowice. Plucked out of college at eighteen, they sweated in a country that neither of them knew well or could make themselves understood in. They both learned quickly, the language as well as that the best way to live through the gruelling training was to do the training. Both were soon transferred to a different department, where their English and German language skills were used in minor spy tasks and to translate paperwork, as well as quite a few episodes of *Derrick* and *Monty Python's Flying Circus*.

After their return to Britain and the completion of their studies Vladimir joined *The Mail* to get his foot in the door of journalism. Lukas, at that time, already despised the British papers' way of reporting and decided to try a freelance career. But as is the case with most freelance work, opportunities tend to come and go; Lukas has had considerable success but has also gone through some real droughts, part of the reason his wife decided to find someone new to supply her with a lifestyle more in keeping with what she had in mind when she married him for the potential of worldwide journalistic fame.

Vladimir left *The Mail* after a few fruitful years there with his conscience virtually intact, a suitcase full of useful contacts and quite a bit of cash. He set up his own publishing business and is now one of Lukas's main employers, that is, if Lukas has a story, which he doesn't at the moment.

Vladimir's letter holds encouraging words for his old pal and a small royalties cheque, but also contains a virtual kick up Lukas's backside, with a reminder that his last great piece of reasonably paid work – a report about the abysmal conditions in some pet kennels in the UK – is over twelve months old. Lukas's most successful work was a piece about the influence of the weather on the New England autumn colours. The report was published in *The New Yorker* to highest acclaim and won him a few minor prizes and a much fatter cheque than he is holding right now.

In his final paragraph Vladimir calls Lukas a miserable, moaning bastard and encourages him to get in touch. Lukas smiles and lets the letter float onto the table. His smile turns to a frown as he opens the first broadsheet. Several headlines had jumped out at him in the shop, hints at another alleged scandal at Mancunia FC. A sceptic at heart he is very aware that allegations involving big football clubs sell copies, whereas serious journalistic investigations into social issues often get shrugged aside.

The first article he reads accuses some first team players of throwing an early Christmas party, which through the night allegedly developed into a bit of an orgy. The party took place a couple of days ago at one of the city's most expensive hotels, where the team had booked the whole top floor to amuse themselves.

With a sigh Lukas picks up another paper, reads a similar story, slightly less objective and more conservative than the previous paper's tale. The third paper takes the "boys will be boys" approach. The rest he just scans, convinced that this is once again the beginning of a long debate, the tip of an iceberg. By the time tomorrow's papers roll off the press several new factions will have jumped on the bandwagon, all with their own agenda on the story, for their personal gain.

With dread he is aware that he is already turning the story over in his head, illuminating it from different angles. He really does not want to contemplate investigating such a can of worms. How could one ever get to the bottom of, or to the truth of, such a story? If something improper has gone on everybody would lie: the club to save its image, the players to maintain their integrity, the hotel to preserve its status and to ensure that the next party again takes place on their premises, and any ladies involved because they might be famous. Everybody's palms would have been thoroughly greased anyway, to ensure that the event took place without a hitch and more so, without anybody sticking their nose into a private affair. And if the party was just a boring old party and what the papers are now dreaming up a lie, then there wouldn't be anything to investigate anyway.

No, he must not touch it. He is not interested in suggested filth, however much it smells. However, it wouldn't hurt to take some notes. Maybe there is more to the story. And if there is, whoever is responsible must be found. He promised all those years ago that he would do his very best.

An hour later Lukas puts his notepad down, peels his change out of his jeans pocket and counts it. He dials Vladimir's number and leaves a message on his answerphone.

Chapter 3

A horizontal gale sweeps down from the Pennines through the dark streets of the rain-sodden Windy City. Lukas pulls his hoodie over his head and runs the two hundred yards to the corner onto Manchester Road. The weather is bad enough to have scared the corner kids away to some drier meeting place.

Vladimir sits at the bar, watching the front door as Lukas is blown into the pub. They shake hands.

'Of all the places in the world to live.'

'Wet? I got your message. Krombacher please, love. Two pints. What have you got for me, Shakespeare?'

'Don't call me that!' Lukas sits down next to Vladimir and looks at him sternly. 'Seriously.'

'OK.' Vladimir grins back.

Lukas lifts his pint. 'I might have an idea. Though I don't really want to touch it.'

'Why is that?' Vladimir raises his glass and clunks Lukas's.

'Because it's predictably messy.'

'That could be of advantage or disadvantage.' Vladimir swigs on his beer, then looks at the glass. 'I wish they would at least try to pull this stuff properly.'

'No chance. That would involve a learning curve. They don't even have the right glasses. What do you think, Krombacher Breweries sending over a big, blonde German beer instructress from Bavaria to give an introductory course in how to pull a proper Pils?' Lukas drinks deeply. 'I tell you what, all the Brits would be shouting about the head and the time it takes to pull a pint. They'd think they'd be short changed in beer, though the breweries have made the glasses bigger and moved the line to compensate for a proper head.'

'So is this what you're going to write your latest dissertation about? Or are you just fantasising about Bavarian waitresses again? Don't expect me to publish it. Go to *The Observer. Food Monthly*.'

Lukas laughs.

'Seriously, you should. You drink enough of the stuff to be an expert. Another?'

As the next two pints arrive Vladimir regards his friend inquisitively. 'So what are you thinking about?' His double chin resting on his palm, his coat's sleeve soaking up beer from the bar, Vladimir looks at Lukas over the rim of his glasses.

'It's a stupid idea and I should bin it. Just want to hear it from you. It's all over the papers.'

Vladimir raises an enormous eyebrow. 'It's that footballers' party thing, isn't it? Forget it! You'll get crucified.' Vladimir has pushed himself back on his stool, hands on the bar. 'It'd have to be bullet-proof for me to publish anything that dicey.'

Lukas studies his fingernails, then looks up abruptly. 'I thought you'd react the same as me. I've taken the liberty to leaf through the rags to compile facts anyway.'

Vladimir leans against him. 'But they are not facts, my friend, don't you see? Half of it, if not all, is pure fabrication.'

'Could still be interesting to probe a bit. Maybe once it's all died down a bit.'

'That's a possibility. I know you're not going to rush into anything stupid and you're always thorough. Possibly the German in you,' Vladimir says. Lukas laughs. Vladimir looks at him sternly. 'If you were to have a closer look, where would you start?'

'I'd try and find a way to speak to someone connected to the club.'

Vladimir raises his eyebrows again. 'Mancunia FC? You're going to ring up Moses and ask for an audience? Might as well be asking to see the Pope on Christmas Day. And what exactly are you going to ask him? Whether his players have been shagging underage pussy lately? He's going to be laughing all the way to court where he'll have you for slander.'

'There might be other ways of finding a way in, apart from Bradshaw. As I said, I haven't really got my heart set on the story anyway.' Lukas finishes his pint.

'Glad to hear it, mein Freundchen.' Vladimir guffaws and changes the subject. 'What's in store for you at Christmas, the festival of love and oblivion? Seeing the family?'

Lukas shakes his head resolutely. 'There's no point, Vladi. The little one is being turned against me by her mum as we speak. I'm not stepping into the bull ring at this time of the year. I sent some CDs. I'll be meeting Pavel though, on Christmas day for a pint. Care to join us?'

'Maybe. I'll let you know. Need to be back at barracks for tea. Her whole family's coming to meet me for the first time. Do you think I'm presentable?'

'Absolutely not, you old fool. It'll be a case of damage limitation. Don't even open your mouth if you can help it.'

'I'm afraid that won't be possible. A man's got to eat. So, you won't get too lonely, will you?'

'I'll have a look at what the papers come up with over the next few days. I'll compile some more info to keep myself amused.'

'You'd be better off using the time to find yourself a better story, my friend.'

Chapter 4

The Sun tops it all, having unearthed a girl who has sold her story to the newspaper for allegedly more money than Lukas earned last year. She is on the front page, in tears. The language of the article is despicable.

Lukas opens *The Independent*. Here, the story does not even feature until the comment page, where one of his colleagues preaches from a very tall pulpit about a crumbling society, the corruption of youth and the damage to innocence caused by today's media. Lukas smiles, not only because he wholeheartedly agrees, but because the last time he saw the comment's author was in the Press Club at 4.15am one morning, the old boy comatose, with his hands and spit all over a lady of the night far too old to be dressing like an eighteen-year-old.

Lukas switches on the kettle and the TV. A press conference preceding the afternoon's match is being shown on *Sky News*. Moses Bradshaw, manager of Mancunia FC, talks about the club's new signing, Jason Entwistle, a young goalkeeper from Bolton.

'The lad's keen and I may just give him the opportunity to play part of the match this afternoon.' Bradshaw's West Country accent makes him sound as if he has been on the cider. Next to him the new signing looks about fifteen years old and rather sheepish. The boy wears a suit but Lukas immediately puts him in the hoodie brigade.

'Today's game is important and the lad should get a taste of the action straight away. I believe we can win despite Halifax Ranger's recent form,' Bradshaw concludes.

Lukas picks up the phone. 'Are you up yet, son?'

'Just.'

'Fancy watching the game today? I've just seen Moses saying they're going to win.'

'Funny he should say that. I've just emailed you a link. You're still on the lookout for unusual stories, aren't you?'

'Always.'

'Take a look at what I sent, Dad. I'd like to watch the match, but do we have to go to the Hare?'

''Fraid so, son. Sky Sports.'

'You know I hate the beer in there, and the locals.'

'You'll be fine, let's just go. We're there for the football.'

'Along with the rest of scrotesville. I'll come round to yours at one.'

'Just make sure you wear the right jersey.'

'A red one?'

'That'll do.'

Lukas boots up his ancient laptop, checks emails, deletes all spam and opens Pavel's post. It consists of only a blue, underlined link. Lukas clicks it and reads: '*Think about it: which fouls are predictable, which goals would have been stoppable, which player goes down again and again in the area? Who's the ref who did not see a player being kicked in the lower back although he was only three feet away? It all becomes predictable after a while; so you should be looking at constellations on the pitch not in the stars and hopefully after a few months you'll be rich. GameWithoutFrontiers@wordpress.com*'

Chapter 5

'Did you look at that link I sent?' Pavel asks.

Pavel and Lukas are walking towards Chorlton Green. The wind blows leaves off the tarmac and into the air, in wet and filthy mini tornadoes. Lukas wears long johns for the first time this year and his old, furry Polish army hat.

'I did. He sounds a bit mad, that blogger.'

'Did you read the latest post, the one after the press conference?'

'No.'

'If you think he's weird wait until you read this.' Pavel pulls a printout from his pocket and hands it to his father. The wind catches hold of the paper. Lukas is in danger of losing it.

'It's getting on my nerves, this bloody weather. I'll read it when we get inside.'

The Hare and Hounds near the Green was once a real ale pub with a reputation well beyond Chorlton. But in recent years the pub has gone from bad to worse. The new landlord is said to attract the wrong clientele, some even go as far as suggesting that he has been put in there by the brewery to run the place down. Or maybe the pub's demise is just a sign of the times. Lukas silently agrees with Pavel; occasionally he too feels uncomfortable in there, though he would not admit to it. It is the only place in Chorlton with Sky Sports that's not completely packed on match day.

A large group of men smoke and drink by the front door, ignoring the No Alcohol sign on the nearby lamp post.

'See what I mean?' Pavel slows down.

'The force is with you, son.'

'Yeah, but the spirit has been with this lot for quite a few hours longer.'

'We'll be alright in the snug. You don't mind the small telly?'

'Teletext would be cool with me.'

'You Emo or Goth, Nosering?' a red-faced drinker shouts. His mates roar with laughter.

Lukas pushes Pavel towards the door. 'Serves you right, looking like a corpse.'

'And you look like a Viking. Let's wear T-shirts only next time, OK?'

'OK, I'll make a note of that. In you go.'

They push their way through the drunken mob; Lukas avoids making eye contact. He used to stand out here himself when he still smoked, and remembers meaningful conversations with some of the men he now chooses to ignore. They sit down with two pints of bitter in the crowded snug on some partially slashed seats that spill out foam filling. The match preamble is in full flow. This morning's press conference is repeated.

'You should read the printout,' Pavel urges.

Lukas pulls the crumpled page out of his jacket pocket, straightens it out on the table and reads.

'Hohoho! It's Christmas. Be merry, the bookies are. Hark the voice from the sky, the voice of a great prophet. Listen to the prophet for his voice tells you the future. He knows, because he's controlling it. Like the parting of the Red Sea. And what a Red Sea parting it will be. Pie in the sky, it's written in the stars. Hohoho! The result? Email me a tenner to my PayPal account (which you'll find in my profile…) and you shall know. Hohoho and a prosperous Christmas!
GameWithoutFrontiers@wordpress.com'

'The guy likes the sound of his own voice.'

'And tries to make a quick buck.'

'You're not honestly suggesting he's to be taken seriously, are you?'

'He's making serious allegations.'

'Which are?'

'That Moses knows the outcome of the game. And controls it somehow.'

'Come off it, Pavel. Conspiracy theories.'

'The reference to the bookies. He suggests they know the score in advance.'

'How? Match-fixing allegations are as old as the game. There's too many people on the pitch for one person to steer it. Bradshaw got his name 'cos he saved so many clubs from relegation, not because he can perform miracles.'

'Dad, please keep your voice down and put that paper away. Do you have any idea what the odds are on Mancunia winning this game?'

'Nope. Oy!' Lukas addresses an old gentleman in the corner who is reading *Racing Post*. 'What are the odds on FC winning?'

'Don't you oy me, you wee gobshite! What the fuck do I care what the odds are on a game of football? I'm a horses man. Bunch of poofs, footballers. Can't have a quiet pint anywhere.' The old guy gets up with difficulty and makes his way to the door, clearing his path with the vigorous help of his walking stick. His exit is accompanied by cajoling.

'Come on, Bill, stay and watch the footy.'

'Ey, Billy, horses have longer legs.'

Lukas and Pavel look at each other and smirk.

'Excuse me.' The man sitting to their left leans across. 'Odds are 4–3 in Mancunia's favour. They weren't until Bradshaw let it all hang out so confidently earlier. After all, Halifax have won their last five matches and Rudolpho is injured.'

Pavel looks at Lukas. 'See?'

'See what?'

'He's swung the odds.'

'Bollocks, Pavel, he's just done a pep talk like any manager would.'

'Except his pep talk swung the odds. Someone is listening to him.'

Lukas pauses and takes a long drink. Then he gets up. 'Let's watch the match and see what happens. I'll get us another pint.'

'We was robbed.'

'He brought that Wallace on.'

'I suppose he thought the young lad had proved himself.'

'I suppose so. But when Wallace came on the goals started going in.'

'But that wasn't Wallace's fault. Shoddy defending. Callaway was all over the place. Don't know why he brought him on too. Stevens looked fine to me.'

'Don't you pay attention? He's carrying a metatarsal injury. Bloody hurts, that.'

Lukas turns away from the conversation. They have repaired to the Globe for a post-match pint. Mancunia's clear defeat by Halifax had put the frustrated crowd in the Hare in a confrontational mood which both of them wanted to avoid.

'So?'

'So what?'

'Your analysis of the match?'

'We lost.'

'Deliberately?'

'I don't know.' Pavel drinks, and looks into the distance. 'Are you going to follow this up?'

'Maybe. I still think the blogger's a lunatic who wants to attract attention and make a fast buck.'

'I'd like to help. Let me have a look at betting swings during the match.'

'How will you do that?'

'Leave that to me. There'll be statistics somewhere.'

'I forgot, you have ways of unearthing information.'

'I'm not doing anything illegal, Dad.'

'I bloody well hope not.' Lukas looks at him sternly.

Pavel hesitates. 'Dad, will I see you Christmas Day? I need to go and see Mum now. She wants me to help her get the tree up.'

'She's putting the tree up late?'

'She's holding on to your tradition, for our sake.'

'Don't make me laugh. What does *he* have to say about that?'

'He understands.' Pavel drags the last word out.

'Oh yes, I forgot, he's a new man, as well as stinking rich.' Lukas narrows his eyes. 'Is she feeding him sauerkraut tomorrow?'

They both laugh as they get up and leave the pub.

Chapter 6

'Wallace Gromits it.'

Lukas smirks at *The Post's* headline. Below it is a detailed and one-sided analysis about how hard done by Mancunia were in yesterday's match. Substitutions, goals and refereeing decisions are listed on a timeline showing how the game tipped against Mancunia's favour. The game had been an entertaining one, fair in Lukas's opinion, heated at times, which was to be expected in a match between two teams whose history was as loaded as Mancunia's and Halifax's. After all, at the beginning of last season, James Moses Bradshaw had still been at Calder Park, had made some tough decisions at the club and got rid of several key players and board members; some of them he had single-handedly fired while others resigned due to irreconcilable differences. Bradshaw's reign tore through the club like a hurricane. Not that Halifax's game needed shaping up at the time. They were doing well in the Premiership, had won the title a few seasons before. But there was bickering. Between players, between management. Bradshaw uprooted everything. Nothing was exposed, no scandals, just assumptions of mismanagement and dissent in the squad. Rumours were quickly quashed and nobody involved spilled any beans. Maybe there were no beans to spill. Maybe the whole of Bradshaw's reign at Halifax was just a bit of a gardening exercise.

Lukas closes *The Post* and looks out at the rain. Bradshaw had left of his own accord, handed in his notice, at the beginning of the summer break. The Rangers didn't need him any more, he announced. The club didn't really comment. Bradshaw moved on to Mancunia after two months holiday in the Caribbean. By then speculation about his leaving Halifax had fizzled out. During his absence the media explained it away with Mancunia offering more money – an undisclosed sum, of course.

Lukas carries his coffee to the small table in the kitchen corner and boots up the computer.

Since joining Mancunia Bradshaw has been uncharacteristically quiet. No upheavals, no sackings. He seems to be getting on well with players and management alike. He has made a few unusual signings, but these have paid off, like the efforts of promising, young Entwistle yesterday.

He sits down and navigates to the blog. Today's post consists of a single sentence. '*I told you so, did you go out to bet and put it all on red?*' Lukas forwards a link to Pavel's email address. Then he leans back in his chair, crosses his arms behind his head and exhales deeply, his eyes still on the screen.

His mind is racing ahead – planning, exploring avenues. He hasn't instructed it to do so. It takes on a mind of its own. It runs off without him, calculating and assessing. It doubles back when it has found a dead end and makes a mental note when it stumbles over an obstacle. All the while he stares at the screen. His eyes are not observing any more, all his concentration has been rooted to his subconscious, which is directing his mind in its exploration. This is what happens every time.

His unconscious mind decides when an idea becomes real. It has nothing to do with him. Sometimes his mind runs around for ages, checking, moving data, only to overthrow the idea in the end. This doesn't leave him disappointed, just a bit bemused at the closure that his mind manages to achieve. Other times it decides that it cannot let go. Like now. Somewhere, something is happening. There are pieces of a puzzle that need to be matched and it is him who should try to find them and match them. Now his mind is relentless, analytical. It won't leave a stone unturned, driving him on. It nags that there is something he is supposed to find and he knows it will not let go until he gets as near to the bottom of the story as he can. It was the same with the cattery story. Now his mind is sending him the same signals.

And then his mind is silent. It waits for him to take action. It will come up with a plan. He cannot force it. It is as if it is not up to him.

Chapter 7

The Christmas tree has been out in the yard since he bought it a few days ago, wrapped in a piece of thick plastic to keep it dry. He unwraps it, lifts it out of the bucket and carries it into the kitchen. It makes a little puddle on the kitchen floor and he realises that his hands are covered in resin. Should have done this the other way round. Should have got the stand, then the gloves, then the tree. Anyway. He cleans his hands the best he can and retrieves the Christmas tree stand from the cupboard under the stairs. He also lifts out the box with the Christmas paraphernalia. He puts the tree trunk into the stand, tightens the screws and pushes in the wedges, then stands up to assess the straightness of the tree. When he is satisfied, he carries the tree into the bay in the kitchen, points its best side into the room and fills the stand with water. Then he steps back and frowns at the result of his handiwork.

His hi-fi system is ancient but state of the art. He added a CD player when CDs became the recording standard. Since his system is made up of individual components and he managed to get a CD player in the same width and colour, it is hard to tell that the unit is a later addition. Lukas switches the stereo on and inserts a CD. The original vinyl record had been played and scratched often, before Pavel ripped the record onto CD for himself and copied it for Lukas. The recording is from the sixties and features some provincial choir and small orchestra performing popular and some more eclectic Polish and German Christmas carols. The instrumentation includes cornemuses and recorders, lending the sound an ancient, rural feel that transports him back to his childhood Christmases.

Lukas opens the box of decorations and hangs stars and glass balls, angels and candleholders on the tree. There are some of last year's candles in the box too. At 3 o'clock he packs everything away, switches off the hi-fi and puts on his coat.

The building is a glorified Portakabin with modern stained glass windows. Outside, the pastor shakes hands with his flock. His wife hands out cardboard disks with a hole in the middle. Lukas takes a candle from a box by the church's inner door and pushes it into the hole.

It has taken him thirty minutes to walk here from Chorlton. He likes attending the afternoon service. It features a Christmas play, acted out by the smaller members of the congregation. He loves children, before they turn into the strange creatures whose habitat is the corner outside his house.

The service is in German. After the play and the Christmas readings the candles are lit by passing the flame from one person to the next. Eventually, the church lights are extinguished. The final hymn is as always "O du fröhliche", Lukas's favourite. He is close to tears with serenity and content. Happy, for no particular reason other than it is Christmas and he always feels like this on Christmas Eve. Even two years ago when he brought that Maggie here. God knows what had possessed him. If there ever had been a transitional relationship it had been with her. He'd convinced himself it was the real deal at the time, had even cried during "O du fröhliche" in front of her, as he squeezed her hand. Last year he had been here on his own and he much preferred it that way.

On the way out he shakes the pastor's hand and wishes him a Happy Christmas. He walks back to Chorlton, past the Globe, glancing at his mates inside, drinking. He has no desire to join them, not tonight.

Back at the house Lukas puts the CD back on, peels four potatoes and puts them on a high heat. He chops some smoked belly and places it in a frying pan along with some onions. When the pork has browned and given up most of its fat Lukas transfers it into a pot, opens a jar of sauerkraut and adds it to the pork. He fries the sausage, which comes in a big ring, in butter. It is a Christmas speciality from the Polish delicatessen down the road. Then he lights the candles on the tree, mashes the potatoes, seasons the sauerkraut, pours himself a DAB and sits down to his meal.

Later he boots up the laptop and opens his email. Pavel has sent several links to recent newspaper articles as well as an electronic Christmas card. Lukas frowns, gets out his mobile and texts a Christmas message to each of his children. Then he clicks through Pavel's links and learns that at the time of writing the FA are investigating several matches as a result of one or two major bookmakers refusing to take any more bets on the games in question. The bookies had recorded irregular betting patterns which could point to illegal activity. Lukas learns that it is illegal for anyone involved at a particular club to bet on any of the club's matches, or on any matches in the competition the club is competing in. Lukas thinks about a club associate not being allowed to bet on his club's matches. He gets out his notepad and writes. *Supposing you're a goalie and you told your best mate that you're going to let at least three in the net on Saturday afternoon and after that your mate goes to the bookies and puts a lot of money on your team losing.* He places three question marks behind his note. Could it really be that simple? He continues to write. *Where do the betting swings come from? Surely a bookie is not just going to refuse bets because the goalie's mate is on the way to making a killing. It would have to involve many attempted bets and a lot of money to make a bookmaker close.*

Lukas puts the pen down and navigates back to the blog. He scans today's post again, frowns, and decides to delve deeper into the blog. He starts with the archives. He wonders how many people are reading this blog every week, and how many take it seriously enough to subscribe or even pay for more in-depth info. Lukas picks up his pen again and adds *betting syndicates, spread betting* and *betting patterns/swings* to his notes. Then he sits back and crosses his arms behind his head.

Chapter 8

'Is this guy for real?' Vladi has joined them in the Globe. His nose is very red. It could be the weather or the red wine he is drinking just because it is Christmas.

'Dad doesn't think so, do you Dad? You think he's crazy and just trying to make himself more important than he is.' Pavel looks at Lukas quizzically.

'I read a lot of the blog last night. And your links. The blogger sounds like he has some inside knowledge.'

'So you do believe he's for real?' Vladimir leans forward and pushes his glasses up.

'I don't know. But if I decide to look into the matter further I need to start believing him, otherwise there's no point following the matter up.' Lukas sits back. 'I don't even know what I'm looking for, really.'

'What have you got so far?' Vladimir asks.

'I have a guy who writes a blog about football. Although he never says so directly he implies that he knows the outcome of matches in advance.'

'Who supplies the information?'

'And who benefits?' Pavel butts in.

'The information comes from inside the footballing world. Who benefits? Ideally everybody.' Lukas reaches into his pocket and unfolds the piece of paper with his unsolved questions. 'Someone gives him a tip. Someone inside. He puts it on the blog. His subscribers read it. Those who are serious can subscribe further by paying a tenner and getting more detailed information, presumably more exact match results or whatever, to place a more accurate bet and win more. The blogger will be doing the same thing. And whoever supplied the info in the first place will get paid by someone placing a bet for him. Maybe the blogger even pays him for the info. Who knows? And this is where it gets tricky.'

'Hang on. Let's get this right.' Vladimir fills his glass from his bottle of Rioja. 'Why and how would someone inside a club leak match results? How can you know a result beforehand?'

Lukas smiles. 'Quite. Knowing the exact outcome is an extreme scenario. The scenario where a match is actually fixed outright.

Remember that World Cup semi-final in the 80's where both teams were prancing about doing nothing? Then one team scored by trundling the ball into the net and both teams went back to passing the ball to and fro until the ninety minutes were up. That match was fixed. Everyone watching it knew it. They made some kind of a deal to let the winning team go through to the final. What I'm talking about here is not just the outright fix, but the suggested fix. Which team is going to win, but not the exact score.'

'Like the day before yesterday's match,' Pavel suggests.

'Possibly. Those links you sent me mention things like releasing team news, player fitness and so on ahead of official time. This would then influence public opinion about club morale or player stats, and if the chances of the team winning are reduced and so on. The betting pattern can swing rapidly as a result, if I understand correctly.'

Pavel continues. 'And when those swings happen, often in the lead up to a match, without any reason, as the swings happen before the relevant information is officially released, they call it irregular betting patterns.'

'The information is in the public domain before the club has released it,' Vladimir summarises. 'And people are betting on it. And because there's no official news yet, the bookie smells a rat. If it happens too often he stops taking bets.'

'Exactly.' Lukas drains his pint. Pavel gets up to get another round in.

'Must be an awful lot of people betting to scare the bookmakers so much.'

'That's another thing I need to look up; betting syndicates. He mentions them in the blog. I haven't had time to research it yet.'

Chapter 9

'Seasons' greetings, all you footballers' wives. Are you having a lovely Christmas while your husbands are out playing? The goods are plenty in Leonard Louis's posh shop and not as dear as you may think. How much do you think they cost? Anything at all if the payout could just be a house in Alderley Edge and your picture on the front page of a magazine? You all started somewhere didn't you?

And we all like to gamble. Did you see the headlines? It could be you, you just need to buy your ticket.'

Lukas is not sure how to start. Maybe he is trying to email a complete lunatic. After five minutes of chewing on a pencil he types.

'Dear Blogger, I've been reading your posts with interest. I am not a punter. I'm an investigative journalist putting together material for a possible article regarding match fixing in sports (again). I would like to talk to you about some of the points you make in your blog. Your personal details and sources would never be disclosed. You do make some tall claims. I'm curious and would like to talk to you further. Merry Christmas. Yours sincerely, Lukas Novak, Investigative Journalist'

He gets up to make coffee. As he fills the kettle his laptop pings, informing him that he has a new message. He sits back down and looks at the screen incredulously.

'A very Merry Christmas to you too, Luke. Of course you're curious, but you can't talk to those who don't exist.
Yours truly, X'

Lukas clears his throat and types
'Dear X, What a boring pseudonym. The fact that you reply means you do exist. What is the point of your blog if not disclosure?
Luke'

'Luke, oh Luke, The only thing I disclose is the truth and my motivation is cash. Why don't you buy yourself a ticket? Y?
PS because you're curious?'

'Y? Maybe you don't agree with match fixing? What about the footballers' wives thing? You're referring to the Christmas party, aren't you?
Luke PS I'm not a gambling man'

'Dear Saint Luke, I wouldn't call it match fixing, more match making. Whether I agree with it or not is irrelevant. It is paying the mortgage.
Yours truly, The MatchMaker
PS The footballers' wives thing is just my own personal bitch'

'Dear MatchMaker, Can I therefore assume that you're involved in what you refer to as the "making" and I refer to as the "fixing"

process? Do you have more information than the papers about the second allegations?
Luke
PS Nobody is untraceable, especially not with a mortgage'

'Dear Saint Luke, Yes I am in the "making" process, the money making process. I don't like the way you probe. Why don't you buy yourself a ticket and bugger off?
MM
PS the mortgage bit was hypothetical'

'Dear MM, As I told you, I don't gamble. And I especially don't throw my money away to dubious con-artists like you.
Luke'

'Luke, Ouch. I have many rich customers as a result of the data I supply.
MM'

'MM, Where's the proof?
Luke'

'Dear Saint Luke, Belief should be right down your street. Do try me with a tenner.
MM'

'MM, OK, I will. Who do I make the cheque out to?
Luke'

'Dear Saint Luke, I never thought I'd see you fall so low. Nice joke by the way. PayPal only. matchmaker@wordpress.com You'll receive your goods once I've received mine.
Soon to be richer,
MM'

Chapter 10

Mancunia FC's training ground in Ashton-under-Lyne is partly covered in snow when Lukas arrives in Vladimir's's battered SAAB 900i. The busy car park resembles an ice rink, but the SAAB's ABS system, designed for six months of Swedish winter, lets Lukas safely manoeuvre to a stop just outside the main entrance. The building reminds him more of a social club than the training headquarters of one of Great Britain's most successful football teams. His perception changes as soon as he enters the foyer and notices the new development being constructed at the back of the clubhouse. He now remembers reading about the extra funding the club received after Bradshaw's appointment.

When he rang yesterday, asking for an interview about the club's famed education programme he was invited to join today's education session at the training ground. After introducing himself at reception he is met by Simon O'Neill, Mancunia's education director, who removes a glove to shake Lukas's hand warmly. 'Ready for a run-about, Mr Novak?'

'Call me Lukas, please.' Lukas nods in reluctant agreement. His own trainers are ancient and he is wearing the washed-out pair of tracksuit bottoms he usually lazes about the house in on rainy afternoons.

O'Neill leads him out onto the training ground where a group of ten-to eleven-year-olds are putting out mini-cones for dribbling practice. 'These are kids from Crumpsall and Audenshaw. They're training alongside the first team over there. The session's a kind of Christmas present from the club to the less privileged communities in Manchester.' He points across to the main football pitch. 'The kids do the same exercises as the players, then they have a little match when the players take a break. Of course they'll be cheering the kiddies on and some of them might even join in. Later the youngsters will have a chance to watch the team play a ten-minute mock game with lots of goals. Then we take them inside and give them a healthy lunch, and some of the younger players will join them.'

Lukas nods and smiles, watching the children, who are now divided into two teams, dribble a ball around the cones, racing each other. Across the field the Mancunia A-team players are doing the same exercise. He recognises Steven Shaw, the reliable midfielder and Niall Keenan, the Irish-born left winger, lead the two teams. Ashley Rigby, who has recently joined from Halifax Rangers, dribbles around the cones for the red team. He is only a few yards ahead of Thomas Klein, Mancunia's gigantic German striker, who is in his fourteenth season with the club and speaks the strangest German–Mancunian accent.

Lukas turns back to the coach. 'Do the players enjoy getting involved?'

'Yes, they do! Heck, most of them are only kids themselves. For some of them it's almost as if their younger brothers and sisters are joining in. They love playing with the kids.'

They watch silently for a moment then O'Neill clears his throat. 'I'm sorry, Lukas, but can I leave you for a bit? I need to attend to some bits and piece. Please feel free to look around. Are you going to take pictures?'

Lukas smiles. 'I'm not a photographer.'

'Good. Unfortunately, these days you need to ask the parents and get clearance and all that. I know it's insane – '

Lukas continues to smile. 'I won't take any pictures and yes, the world has become a strange place.'

Simon O'Neill laughs and nods. 'I'll see you in a while. Look around, OK? Speak to the players, too.' He jogs off.

Lukas looks around. Speak to the players? He hadn't expected it would be so easy. Surely he can't just march over and interrupt the training. O'Neill has jogged over to speak to a tall man who Lukas recognises as defender Leroy Callaway. O'Neill points over at Lukas. The tall man nods and makes a thumbs up gesture in Lukas's direction.

It is time for the mini match and a handful of Mancunia players come over to mingle with the children, who hop up and down excitedly. Their young coach encourages two children, a boy and a girl, to pick their teams. Mancunia's players get picked first, amid a lot of shouting and jostling. Finally, both teams take their sides and the match begins. The professional players play clumsily, missing the ball and falling over a lot. The children take the match very seriously, shouting for the ball and venting their frustration on the FC players.

'He dived. Again.'

'Useless.'

'Come on, ref!'

There are red faces and tears of frustration among the children. Things are about to get out of hand, when suddenly the Mancunia players start to play for real; not just among themselves, but with the children, as a team, at their level. The game changes and tears turn to eagerness and utter enjoyment.

'Jumpers for goalposts, ey?'

Lukas turns round to see Leroy Callaway's outstretched hand. He shakes it. The man has a warm, confident handshake and smiles straight at him. One gold tooth in two rows of perfect, white pearls.

'You're Lukas, right? Simon said – ' Leroy points a thumb over his shoulder.

Lukas smiles a little shyly. 'You're Mr Callaway, if I'm not mistaken?'

Leroy chortles. 'Call me Leroy. You're here for the education thing?' The man giggles like a girl.

'Yes,' Lukas says, still slightly tongue-tied. 'I'm very interested in how sports education has changed. So many institutions are now running excellent education programmes, theatres, galleries, symphony orchestras.'

Leroy nods. 'Yeah, I hear there's great stuff going on in a lot of places.'

'How do you choose the youngsters? Do they apply?'

'That's generally how it works. Through the communities.' Leroy looks about. 'Walk with me.' He starts to walk towards the main training pitch.

'So these are all underprivileged, or students from rough areas?'

'Hey, Lukas, I grew up in a really shitty place and look at me now. We work with everyone, man. We even foot the bill if they can't afford it.'

'Do you ever spot talent in any of these sessions?' Lukas looks at Leroy from the side, hands crossed behind his back, walking slowly.

'Sure, we do. There's always surprises.' Leroy looks into the distance towards the Pennines.

'And do you think lads from a less privileged background or from rougher areas are more talented? Maybe they have more time to practise in the streets, I mean look at the talent coming from Brazil. Do you think race plays a role?' Leroy looks at him and stops walking. Lukas continues. 'Please don't get me wrong, Leroy, it's a touchy subject to talk about these days – '

Leroy looks straight at him. 'You're right there, too much rubbish in the media, right? Hey, I suppose you're one of them?' he chortles.

Lukas laughs with him. 'No, not at all, exactly the opposite. I left newspaper work for exactly that reason. I like to write about reality, not the perceived truth.' Leroy nods. Lukas continues. 'Football has had it quite tough recently, hasn't it? First that racism case and now those alleged parties – that must affect you personally? I'm sorry, I don't mean to pry, neither of those subjects is why I'm here – '

'Don't worry.' Leroy looks into the distance, his jaws working. 'Both those issues have affected me. When things get taken out of context and blown up out of proportion, that's not right nor fair to anybody. It makes a good story though. I guess that's why stuff gets published that way. Sells more papers.'

'Do you find you can't be yourself any more?'

'Yeah, man, totally. There's this public persona that everybody thinks you are and then there's you yourself and only you know what you're like.'

'Does it affect you?'

'Course it does, man, it infuriates me. I want to tell the world, hey look, it's me, not the bad boy you read about in the papers.' Leroy walks faster, strutting.

'Do you think you have a bad boy image, Leroy?'

'Nah, I just said that. White as milk, me. Ha, what am I saying? To a journalist? I must be crazy. White as milk, from a black guy, would that be racist?' He chortles.

Lukas smiles. 'No, I don't think it's racism that way round.'

'I think we'd better change the subject.' Leroy rolls his eyes and shows all his teeth.

Lukas smiles back at him. 'Yes, I think we better had. So you reckon they're making your involvement in the parties up just to get a good story?'

Leroy keeps smiling. 'I'm the social secretary, man. I organise leisure time. Did we not just speak about the papers exaggerating the facts?'

'Yes we did and they are, undoubtedly. Here comes your boss.' Lukas nods in the direction of the approaching manager. Bradshaw nods at him, then looks at Leroy.

'Hey boss, this is Lukas Novel—'

'Novak,' Lukas interrupts.

'Lukas Novak, journalist, but one of the good guys. He's here to watch our education session.'

Bradshaw holds out his hand. The man is slightly cross-eyed. 'Pleased to meet you, Mr Novak. I hope you're suitably impressed.'

Lukas shakes his hand, enthusiastically. 'It's been an interesting morning so far. Sorry about my attire. I don't really do sports.'

Bradshaw returns the smile. 'Don't worry, I've seen worse. Maybe we can kit you out with some of our gear. Leroy, what do you think?'

'Sure, boss, right away.' He clicks his fingers and waves. 'Oy, Jayz, come over here a sec.' The young goalie comes trotting over, looking glum. Incredibly gangly, he towers a full head above Lukas. 'Ey Jayz, why the long face? We've guests.' Leroy elbows the young man playfully.

'Hi.' Jason squints down at Lukas through a sweaty fringe spilling out from under his beanie. Black eyes.

Leroy slaps his back. 'Sorry 'bout him, we're still educating him too. He's only just joined. This is a reporter, Jayz, r-e-p-o-r-t-e-r.' The young man looks embarrassed.

Lukas feels sorry for him and smiles broadly. 'Do you enjoy working with the children, Mr Entwistle?'

Entwistle looks away. 'Yeah, I do,' he eventually says, barely audible.

'Wow, he speaks!' Leroy laughs. 'Jayz, be a good lad, get Mr Novak a full kit, size XXXL, I assume?'

'Correct.' Lukas smiles and bows slightly. 'Thank you, Mr Entwistle.' The boy blushes, mumbles something and leaves.

Bradshaw laughs sympathetically. 'Isn't he cute? So shy, but you should see him going for the ball when someone comes running at him.'

'I saw the last match. The lad did well, very well. Shame you didn't keep him on. What do you think happened?'

Bradshaw frowns. 'I gave the boys a good telling off. The performance wasn't up to our usual standard. Are you interested in football, or do you just write about education?'

Lukas smiles politely. 'I watch the odd match or two, in the pub. It's ages since I played. Can I ask you something?' Bradshaw nods. Lukas clears his throat. 'My son came across this blog the other day, that seems to indicate that outcomes of some matches can be predicted. What's your opinion on this? Do you think it could be true?'

Bradshaw turns to him abruptly and laughs. 'And how do you think this would work, Mr Novak? The constellation of the stars? There are a lot of people talking a lot of nonsense.' He shakes his head vigorously.

'I know.' Lukas rolls his eyes. 'It's just, you wouldn't believe it, but these guys take money to give tips, implying they have inside knowledge about the result – I'm sorry, I came to talk about education, and I've already put my foot in it discussing racism with Mr Callaway, and now – I suppose, were it true, something like this, you would call it match fixing? I really don't mean to imply–'

Leroy laughs.

Bradshaw briefly glances up at the defender before his eyes return to Lukas. 'Now, Mr Novak, were something like this going on anywhere in the Premiership, I would know about it. And I shall forget at once that you've mentioned it here, on Mancunia FC's training ground. Mentioning it to me means that you suspect we fix our matches, don't you, Mr Novak?'

'No, I didn't – '

Bradshaw raises his hand. 'I'm disappointed. I believed your intentions were honourable. I don't have any more time for this.' He turns away and bumps into young Jason's midriff; the boy is standing right behind him with Lukas's kit in a Mancunia FC carrier bag.

'I shouldn't let you have this. You don't deserve to wear our strip.' He tears the bag from Entwistle's hand and swings it behind him, hitting Lukas in the chest. Bradshaw pulls out his phone, his back turned.

Leroy turns to Lukas, and points a finger. 'Man, I thought you were for real. You just came here pretending you cared about the kids. Really, you only want some dirt – ' He kicks the ground.

Bradshaw holds his phone to his ear. Lukas hasn't seen him dial. 'I'm very sorry, Mr Callaway. I didn't mean to imply anything goes on here, at Mancunia. I just wanted an opinion. I think your boss' — he gestures towards Bradshaw — 'is over-reacting, but I understand he's a busy man, and certainly the most successful manager in the Premiership. Of course he doesn't have to concern himself with issues that don't further the club. Have *you* heard about the blog though? Who could be supplying tips to an outfit like that? In the general football world, I mean, not here – what's your opinion?'

'No idea about any blog or tips, man. We play football. You lot dig up dirt where there isn't any.'

'What about the allegations about what went on at your Christmas party?'

Bradshaw turns abruptly. The scowl on his face is the one he is famous for. 'Enough. This has gone too far, Mr Novak. I appreciate your curiosity, it's part of your profession, I understand. These allegations are nothing but hearsay and I will not comment any further on either subject, be it connected with Mancunia, any of my players or football in this country in general. You're just doing your job, I know, and now I will do mine. You're always welcome at this ground as long as you report objectively and factually. But for now I must ask you to leave or I'll have you escorted from the premises. And if you decide to publish any of these allegations I'll see you in court.'

Lukas smiles. 'That won't be necessary, thankfully. I never publish unconfirmed rumours. Your reaction though has taught me that you're as concerned about these delicate subjects as I am. Thank you for the interview and for the kit – ' Lukas holds out his hand. Bradshaw shakes it, forcing the wryest of smiles.

'Entwistle will see you out,' Bradshaw says.

Lukas turns to Leroy and offers his hand. 'Man – Jeez.' Leroy twists and squirms, and finally brushes Lukas's fingertips and sulks away.

Jason Entwistle, a picture of embarrassment, his hands deep in his tracksuit pockets, stands by Lukas's side.

'Come on then, young man, you heard what the boss said, throw me out. By the way, I think you're going to be the regular first team goalie in no time.'

The kid squints down to him. 'You reckon?'

'I do. You played great the other day. It's a shame you weren't allowed to stay on for the full ninety minutes. You'd have done a lot better than Wallace, I'm convinced.' Entwistle does not respond. 'Come on, Wallace could have saved a few, don't you think?'

'Yeah, well – ' The kid walks faster now.

Lukas continues as if he hasn't noticed. 'Mind you, the defence wasn't much good either. Looked like Callaway and Wallace had been out partying the night before, both as bad as each other, ey?' Lukas laughs out loud. Entwistle does not answer. As they arrive at the clubhouse Lukas grabs the young man by the elbow. 'Hey, Jason.' Entwistle turns around and looks him in the eye. Black eyes. Markus's eyes. 'You're going to be a great goalie. Hell, you are already. Don't let anyone tell you otherwise. And don't let anything get in the way of it either. You've worked hard enough for it, I bet.'

'All my life,' Entwistle says.

'It's a beautiful game. Enjoy it. You won't be playing it for long.'

'What do you mean?' The boy looks frightened.

'I mean that most footballers' careers are over after fifteen years; goalies last a bit longer.' Lukas winks up at the kid.

'Yeah – I see – '

'Thanks for the kit.' Lukas lifts the bag. 'And thanks for the chat. Nice to meet you.' He holds out his hand. The boy has a handshake like a wet fish. Hard to believe he is a goalkeeper in real life.

'Nice to meet you, too,' the boy mutters. Lukas can barely hear him. Could he possibly be any shyer? He raises his hand and walks into the building, leaving Entwistle standing outside, in the drizzle.

Interlude

'Dick, Jim here. Just had a visit from a journalist. Pole, name of Lukas Novak. He was asking questions about our education programme. And he mentioned the Christmas party.'

'Anything in particular?'

'Just what's in the papers,' Bradshaw says.

'Heresay.'

'Absolutely. Leroy was there by the way.'

'Leroy's problem, then. If there is a problem.'

'What the boys do in their spare time has nothing to do with the club.'

'Of course not, but the public might see it differently. What can I do for you?'

'He also mentioned that blog, the one about match fixing. Novak seems to think it might be a good idea to investigate further.'

'So Novak is looking for a story and he comes to you to stir up a bit of muck.'

'Looks that way.'

'You want me to keep an eye out?'

'I didn't say that.'

'Of course you didn't.'

'Thanks, Dick.'

Detective Chief Inspector Richard Briggs puts the phone back in its cradle. He leans back in his chair and puts the tips of his stubby fingers together. The archetypal policeman to his colleagues, painstakingly methodical, sullen and controlling, he has led his department of Greater Manchester Police for twenty-two years, holding all the strings, and with an excellent track record. His dull grey eyes rarely betray life or recognition and only once or twice in his long career has he displayed genuine emotion. Slightly overweight and balding he suffers from an incurable pasty addiction, chronic bad breath and the onset of heart disease.

He leans forward and jots Lukas's name down on a piece of paper.

Chapter 11

'Is it possible to find the whereabouts of someone through their email?' Lukas and Pavel are walking through a wintry Whitworth Park towards the gallery. It's been snowing.

'You mean if you don't know their name? Like the blogger?'

'Correct.'

'It depends how ethical you want to be about it. Electoral register isn't an option without a name.'

'People leave traces on the internet, don't they?'

'Yes, every time you go online, you leave traces.'

'So how do you find people?'

'The more you know about IT the better. That's where we get on dodgy territory – data protection, hacking and all that. That's ultimately how people get found and convicted of web crime.'

'And paedophilia?'

'Yes, and fraud, financial as well as copyright. Companies selling miracle weight-loss pills or the ever present male member enlargement nonsense. To cut a long story short, you'll end up having to cancel your cards.'

'You're speaking from experience?' Lukas says with a smirk. Pavel looks startled. 'If so I apologise for my genes.' Lukas looks down at himself.

'Don't be ridiculous, Dad. I just know about internet scams. There's hundreds of sites leading to the same selling site and to the same product.'

'And is that illegal?'

'No, but it's highly annoying if you're looking for a genuine product or a genuine piece of information.'

'So if you wanted to find a no-name you'd start with the IP address or with any payment they receive online? What exactly do I do?' Lukas bites off a huge chunk of chocolate cake.

Pavel explains the procedure. Five minutes later Lukas scratches his nose. 'You're beginning to lose me now.'

Pavel has scribbled a great many numbers and links onto a napkin. 'OK, Dad. Just do what I told you. I don't think he's untraceable. Nobody is.'

'Maybe he's careless and full of himself.'

'Let's hope so.' Pavel smiles. 'Do you think you'll be alright with this?'

'I'll give it a go.' Lukas wipes his mouth. 'Can I email stuff to you to double-check? He tends to email and post Tuesdays and Fridays.'

'He does what?'

Pre-match?' Lukas raises his eyebrows.

'Possibly.' Pavel pauses. 'He is a blogger, right? Takes himself seriously, you say. Talks a lot?'

'Yes. Are you saying he can't be online all the time?'

'Maybe he doesn't have continuous access. It's possible he uses internet cafes, Wi-Fi. Send me his stuff. I'll have a look.'

'And if this fails, can you still help me find him?'

'Theoretically, yes.'

'What do you mean, theoretically?'

'It means that I support you in your quest, but the means needed may be beyond what I can or am prepared to do.'

Lukas looks at him for a while. 'Illegal,' he finally says.

'Dodgy, yes.'

'You're talking about proper hacking.'

'Yes, I am.'

They sit for a while, then Lukas pays the bill. Outside it has started to snow again. They turn up their collars and walk through the park towards Pavel's digs.

'I won't come in, keen to get back.'

'Going to the Globe?'

'No. Want to do some thinking.' Lukas waves, turns and walks off towards the nearest 86 bus stop.

Chapter 12

'Bloody hell!' Lukas slams his fist onto the table making his coffee cup jump. He stares at the screen in disbelief then rings Vladimir. 'I need to borrow your car.'

'Hello, my friend, again?' Vladi sounds like he has had a few.

'Where are you? In the Globe? Are you parked round the corner? You're not going to drive home, are you?'

'I will, unless you get that Polish arse of yours over here and prevent me from doing so.'

'Krombacher, please,' Lukas says, halfway through the door.

He finds Vladimir tipsy but not beyond conversation. In fact, he has never experienced Vladi drunk enough not to be able to argue his point. As usual he has one elbow on the bar and a mischievous glint in his eye.

'How far are you to putting an end to match fixing? Or have you gone the other way and decided to cash in on your internet mate's expertise?'

'Put a sock in it. I need to talk to you seriously.' Lukas drinks deeply.

'Seriously? In here? With all these nutters about?'

Fifteen minutes later Lukas has updated Vladi about his email exchange and the resulting online search for the blogger. 'I researched the IP addresses of his email trail and forwarded them to Pavel so he can double-check. The blogger is definitely in the Manchester area. The email address he mails through, which is the same as the one he uses for people to contact him through the blog, is sort of anonymous. He uses The MatchMaker as his name. I ran a Google search and there are hundreds of mentions, mainly on betting sites and blogs. But he also seems to crop up on the Ibiza clubbing circuit. I haven't had time to research further, but while I was surfing I got another email from him.' Vladi leans forward. 'He says it's his final attempt at converting me to the evil ways of betting. Urges me to subscribe to his tips. Says there's a big game on Sunday, and that it's been fixed.'

'But he didn't tell you which way.'

'No, he tells me I need to sign up.' Lukas leans back.

'And did you?'

'Yes I did..' Lukas smirks.

'What happened? Virus? Crash?' Vladimir almost falls off his stool with curiosity. His bloodshot eyes bulge as he looks at Lukas over the top of his glasses.

'Nothing like that.' Lukas laughs. 'I got an automated response with a tip. But just before that, when I got to PayPal to subscribe, it listed an invoice email address with a a proper name. Franklin Staines. I looked him up in the phone book. There's only one in Manchester. In Cheetham Hill.'

'You beauty!' Vladi slaps the bar. 'Have you told Pavel?'

'No, came straight here. More?' Lukas drains his beer.

'Absolutely. What will you do now?'

'Pay him a visit.' Lukas smiles.

'Do something else before you do that,' Vladi says. Lukas raises his eyebrows. 'Make bloody sure you place a bet.'

Chapter 13

Lukas parks the car two corners away, effectively behind the house he intends to visit. The neighbourhood is run down. Many of the council houses have been painted red by their inhabitants in a vain attempt to make the street look more presentable than it is. The house he is going to is no exception. Its small front yard has been paved sometime in the past, but now weeds grow in the cracks between the paving slabs. A few empty plastic flowerpots along a rickety fence complete a picture that is duplicated along the length of the street.

Lukas walks through the open gate and knocks on the door. He has been wondering what the blogger calling himself the MatchMaker looks like. He imagines a young man, with an interest in politics and current affairs, but also someone slightly eccentric. The thought that maybe he should have taken Vladi with him for a second opinion has also crossed his mind. Since he has no official reason to be here he has thought up a cover story.

The man who opens the door looks to be in his seventies and supports himself on a crutch.

Lukas smiles broadly. Stale, nicotine-filled air escapes from the inside of the house. The man looks at him quizzically. 'Good afternoon, sir, my name is Lukas Novak. I'm an investigative journalist conducting a survey about neighbourhood safety in your area. Would you be able to spare a few minutes for a chat?'

'You got ID?' The man looks up at him suspiciously. Lukas produces his old press pass, covering the expiry date with his thumb.

'You'd better come in then. Close the door behind you.' The man turns, reaches for his second crutch and shuffles off down the corridor.

Lukas bends over some mail on the floor and quickly reads the name on the top envelope from Manchester City Library. Mr D. Staines. Not F. 'Do you want me to pick these up for you, Mr Staines?'

'Put them on the sill.'

The man moves into the kitchen. Lukas follows him, mail in hand and places the envelopes on top a pile of post on the window sill. Propped up next to it is a photo of Staines in work clothes, wearing a flat cap, smiling. Taken on his last day at work, Lukas guesses.

'Brew?' The man supports himself on the worktop, and twists round awkwardly to look at Lukas.

'Please.' Lukas surveys the kitchen. The house is unaired and run down but tidy.

'Please sit down.' Lukas sits. 'I've had a hip replacement three weeks ago. I'm a bit slow.'

Lukas jumps up. 'Can I help you with that?'

'You can help by asking your questions.'

'May I start by asking how long you've lived here?'

Twenty minutes later Lukas has left the old man, convinced he has met the wrong person. The conversation had been slow. Staines feels safe in the neighbourhood, a fact that Lukas had deducted as soon as the man had opened the door to him. There is a neighbourhood watch scheme in place, though the area does not seem like a neighbourhood where a watch scheme would be successful in deterring the kind of criminals and gangs that the *Manchester Evening News* and *Metro* so often reported about. Staines eventually slipped into the conversation that the area is being controlled by one of north Manchester's most notorious gangs, the Ryleys.

On his way back to Chorlton he's placed a modest bet at a bookies, already deeming it a waste of money, his belief in the MatchMaker waning.

Now Lukas sits in the Globe, on his own, jotting down his observations on his crumpled notepad. The address had been right, but the man he'd met is surely not the right Mr Staines? A D Staines was the addressee on the mail he moved. Couldn't it be that the Franklin Staines he was looking for lives elsewhere, maybe in the Cheshire commuter belt, the middle of Shropshire or not in the UK at all? He could be a relative or even the landlord of the old man. Staines had a frailty about him, something not immediately noticeable, but there had been a moment when he almost fell, causing one of the crutches to drop to the floor. Lukas had picked it up for him.

Why has he assumed that the blogger lives in or near Manchester? Just because the email IP addresses had been in the Manchester area, as far as he can tell, and Pavel says this is how you find people? Frustrated, Lukas puts down his pen and stirs his coffee absent-mindedly.

He hadn't wanted to pry into the old man's life any more than necessary, having gained entry by false pretences. It would have been different if he had met someone who matched more the picture of the blogger he had in his mind. Faced with the old man he'd felt a fraud and an intruder and could not wait to get out of the bleak house. Before he'd left he had briefly excused himself to go to the toilet, out of necessity rather than curiosity. A quick look into the two bedrooms hadn't revealed any high-tech electronic or computer equipment. An old transistor radio sat by a bed and on his way down past the living room he saw an early stereo system, probably from the 70s.

As he made to leave, he had asked if the old man had any day to day help. The man insisted that he was fine on his own and the crutches were only the last reminder of his hip replacement. When Lukas was already halfway down the path Mr Staines had said something else. About being helped. At this moment a police car had roared past, drowning out the old man's voice.

Vladi's entrance, early for his second daily appointment with his beloved Spanish red or the odd pint or five of German lager, interrupts Lukas's thought process.

Lukas fills Vladi in about the afternoon's visit to Cheetham Hill and the fact that he thinks he has drawn a blank. That he needs to cast his net wider. He excuses himself just after 7 o'clock, hungry and keen to finish his notes. The thought that was with him before he was joined by Vladi nags him; the feeling of having missed something at the old man's house. And his mind tells him that despite everything he is somehow on the right track.

Interlude

As always the neon strip light in his kitchen flickers as he operates the switch. He hates with a vengeance the cold light he has lived with for so long and is angry with himself for never changing it. He breaks some eggs into the frying pan and adds a couple of rashers of bacon. It takes no time at all until he sits down at the kitchen table to eat his simple meal.

The rap on the front door disturbs him. It went dark more than two hours ago and at night he is not so confident to open the door if he isn't expecting anyone. But he hears someone shout his name through the letterbox. He sighs, pushes himself up, grabs one crutch and shuffles down the corridor.

'Did you forget something?' he asks as he opens the door.

With the street light behind them their faces are in shadow, but he is convinced that he has never seen the two young men before.

Chapter 14

Lukas sits at the kitchen table with a cup of tea poring over his notes. The problem with Vladi is that he can never get away from him and the pub. Once they've finished talking shop, or politics, or religion, the conversation moves on to lighter subjects. Fuelled by several jars and egged on by other regulars Lukas often ends up outstaying his welcome.

Tonight a bowl of spaghetti bolognese and several strong cups of tea have restored his ability to focus. He turns his memory back to the moment he left the old man's house. The old man had said something, which was drowned out by the police car passing. On a whim Lukas picks up the phone and calls Pavel.

'I was just about to call you.' Pavel is chewing. 'Did you find out more after I emailed you?'

Lukas is impatient. He wants to tell Pavel about the email address on the PayPal site and about his visit to the old man, which has turned out to be a bit of a waste of time. That there is no way the old man could be the same person receiving money for tips and calling himself the the MatchMaker.

' – which he does from libraries. Hence the time brackets during which he posts,' concludes Pavel.

'Can you repeat that? My mind's been wandering – ' Lukas has jumped up from his chair. Even before Pavel has a chance to repeat himself Lukas has grasped the meaning of what his son is saying and its connection to what he had forgotten earlier.

'The blogger posts from libraries, namely Wythenshawe on Tuesdays and Chorlton on Fridays.' Pavel sounds triumphant.

Lukas is almost shouting. 'He mentioned he's being helped.'

'He's being helped – by who?'

'Someone helps him with the paperwork. There's not a single book in the house and he doesn't read his mail, but he has a library account so he can book a computer terminal to post match-fixing blogs online.' Lukas slaps the table hard with his fist. 'Pavel, you're a genius!'

'I don't quite follow you, Dad. Who's helping who?'

'How did you find out? Tell me later. I'll ring you back, son. Got to go back.'

Cheetham Hill looks even bleaker in the evening sleet. For the second time today Lukas is unsure if it is a good idea to go to the old man's house on his own. The sudden urge to ask further questions has disappeared. What is he going to ask the man? Permission to look at his mail? Lukas drives on, racking his brain about a possible angle of questioning that would not arouse suspicion. The conversation earlier has instilled trust in the old man, he tells himself as he turns into the street, opting to park at the front of the house at this hour.

The street outside the old man's house is cordoned off with blue and white tape. Several police cars are parked on the kerb, lights flashing. A group of police officers are talking to a small crowd of people gathered on the pavement opposite.

One of the officers spots Lukas's car and walks over talking into his radio. Lukas winds down the window. Sleety rain blows into the car. 'You can't pass through here. Turn around!' The officer points back towards the main road.

'What's happened?' Lukas squints at the officer, then remembers the three pints he had earlier. He feels as sober as he has ever been.

'Suspected burglary. Are you a resident?'

'At number 46?'

'Yes, how do you know?'

'I visited there earlier.'

The officer bends back and speaks into his radio, then he puts both his hands onto the car roof and leans inside. 'Sir, I'm going to have to ask you to step out of your vehicle and accompany me to one of our cars. There's a few questions we need to ask you.' The officer opens the car door. Lukas puts on the hand brake, gets out and locks the car carefully.

The inside of the police Range Rover is invitingly warm. Lukas is ushered into the back seat. The front passenger seat is occupied by a stocky man in a wet trench coat. He turns to face Lukas. 'I'm Detective Chief Inspector Briggs and I'm in charge of this investigation. PC Johnson tells me you visited the victim earlier today.'

The smell emanating from the inspector nearly knocks Lukas out. He'd be surprised if this man had seen a dentist in years. Immediately he feels a strong aversion towards the inspector, a reaction not just triggered by the stink of halitosis, but by the man's cold, impenetrable black eyes.

Lukas clears his throat. 'Who's the victim?' Despite the warmth of the idling car's heating system he feels cold.

'Staines, the guy at 46.' Briggs stares at him.

'What's happened to him?' Lukas coughs.

'Normally I ask the questions but since you've visited him I suppose you've a right to ask. He's been badly done over in a violent burglary.'

'Is he dead?'

'Nearly. When did you visit?'

'This afternoon.'

'Are you two friends?'

Lukas clears his throat again. 'I'm conducting a survey about neighbourhood safety. I interviewed him. I'm a journalist.'

'Who else did you interview in the area?'

'No one yet. He was my first interviewee.'

'Who do you write for?'

'I'm independent.' Lukas crosses his arms.

Briggs still stares at him, his expression unreadable. 'And he seemed alright to you then? What time did you say you saw him?'

'About three. He was fine, I think.'

'You think? I'm afraid you'll have to come to the station once we're done here. What did you say your name was?'

Chapter 15

He'd phoned Pavel. And Vladi, who wanted to be updated as soon as Lukas was out. Then he'd followed the police van to Bootle Street police station. Pavel had met him there and driven Vladi's car back to Chorlton.

Lukas had always wondered what it would be like to be assisting the police with their enquiries. After being fingerprinted and photographed he now sits in the reception area waiting to be processed and feels guilty though he has done nothing wrong. His main concern is with what happened to the old man.

A young officer finally leads him into the interrogation room. Does he want a cuppa? He declines. Twenty minutes later he regrets not having taken up the offer; he is being kept waiting. Just as he is about to ask for a drink and the toilet DCI Briggs enters the room, accompanied by the young officer. Briggs switches on a tape recorder, sits down and starts the interview. After stating the names of those present he gets straight to the point.

Later Lukas walks past the Central Library and down Oxford Road to catch the 86 outside the BBC. He is on the phone to Vladi, summarising his interview. Briggs is no stranger to Vladi, as Vladi covered much of the gang trials that Briggs was heavily involved in, and he knows Briggs to be a very astute interrogator, and not someone who is easily pleased. The interview had lasted nearly ninety minutes and Lukas had been concerned that his responses had been building a picture of involvement beyond his short visit. Briggs's questions had at times been leading, looking for answers that Lukas could not deliver. A guilty man could easily stumble into a trap by this kind of questioning. Lukas, at times, had wondered if he wasn't being forced to talk himself into trouble.

Briggs hadn't been pleased that Lukas could not produce further interviewees for his assumed research project. And Lukas had been careful not to give away the real reason for his visit to the house. By then the news was received that the old man was stable. Lukas had asked Briggs if he could visit him but Briggs had said no.

'Am I being considered a suspect?' Lukas had asked jokingly.

'Yes, you are,' Briggs had replied, without any trace of emotion in his voice.

Pavel sits at the kitchen table. 'What's been happening, Dad?' He switches on the kettle.

Lukas quickly summarises the events of the day, the police interview and his impression of his interrogator.

'He seems like a real piece of work.' They sit, cupping their mugs.

'Old school, straight out of the movies,' Lukas says, smiling. 'I haven't done anything wrong, you know.'

'I know. But *I've* done something that's not legit.' Pavel pauses. 'You know that info I gave you earlier? Well, this mate of mine, Mitchell, he hacked the library computer. Don't ask me how, but we were talking about your searches online and he said piece of piss. Half an hour later he'd traced the IPs to Wythenshawe and Chorlton libraries, got the guy's library card number, his address, date of birth, everything.'

'What's his date of birth?'

Pavel opens his laptop. 'He's on my course, Mitchell, though I met him on Facebook.' Pavel laughs and logs on. He scrolls around and opens an email. 'Thirteenth September 1941. Frank Staines.'

'Frank Staines? You sure?' Lukas looks at the screen.

'Yes, Frank.'

'The mail at his house was addressed to D Staines.'

'Maybe that's the helper you mentioned earlier.'

Lukas leans forward. 'This is what's going on: the helper does the paperwork. Maybe they're related, maybe D is just using Franklin's surname. And receives his own mail at Franklin's house. He also uses it as a business address and proof of residence. And if anyone comes looking for him he's not there.'

'But old Staines is.' Pavel pauses. 'Who'd put their relative or friend in that position?'

'Especially when you're involved in writing blogs that might piss people off.'

'Maybe he's not a relative, then,' Pavel muses.

Lukas nods. 'And the old bugger wouldn't know any better since he can't read so well and never opens his mail. I wonder where they met.'

'Or how D picked Franklin. Social services?'

'Maybe. We'll have to jot down some professions that would bring someone like D in contact with someone like Franklin.' Lukas digs out his notepad and taps it with his pen. 'David, Daniel, Dexter, Dean – '

'Maybe they just met in the pub,' Pavel suggests.

'What kind of a person is our blogger? Staines doesn't seem like someone who's got out of Cheetham Hill a lot.'

'Unless he was in the merchant navy or the army.'

'I didn't see any tattoos.'

'Do you know what he did for a living?'

'No, I couldn't wait to away. I was there under false pretences. And I didn't ask enough questions.' Lukas scratches his head.

'With hindsight, Dad.'

'Yes. Who'd expect the old bugger to be attacked.'

'Did they take anything?'

'No idea. That DCI's like a block of ice. He wasn't volunteering anything apart from the fact that the old man was beaten up.'

'Maybe a burglary?'

'There was nothing in the house worth taking, visibly at least. And according to Frank the whole neighbourhood is protected by the Ryleys. Would be a huge risk for an outsider.' Lukas writes down the name of the gang on his pad.

'An inside job then? Did he piss them off?'

'Possible, but unlikely. He didn't say much but he didn't feel threatened. He opened the door to me, at his age and in his condition.' Lukas suddenly feels exhausted. 'I've got to sleep on this, son. I can't think straight. Apparently, I'm a suspect in a bloody assault case.'

'They're just doing their work, Dad. Eliminating you from the investigation.'

'Sure.'

'I'll leave you to it. I'm buying Mitch a pint. Well done for finding that PayPal address.'

'Cheers, son. I'll speak to you tomorrow. It's been a long day.' Lukas smiles and lifts his hand. With Pavel gone he boots up his laptop, opens his email program and begins to type.

Chapter 16

'Dear MM or shall I call you Dean, or Dan, or Dave? Your friend Franklin was attacked tonight. He's in a bad way at North Manchester General. Maybe you should watch your back? Luke PS: I did subscribe to you earlier. Congrats on your "instant" access activation! I placed a bet based on your blog suspicions for the FC – Birmingham match tomorrow. Will you still be trading after today?'

Lukas is about to close the laptop but changes his mind. He opens up the settings for his email account, changes his password to a string of random letters and numbers and jots these down on his notepad. He tears off the top page and stuffs it into his wallet.

He briefly contemplates the pub and decides against it at almost closing time. In bed, he thinks about the blogger. Has he taunted him enough to provoke a reaction? The vibration of his mobile on the bedside table jerks him out of a fitful slumber.

'What time do you call this?' he says, yawning.

'Time to wake up I should say.' Vladi sounds genuinely excited. 'Listen to me,' he whispers into his handset. 'I'm at the Midland casino.'

'How wonderful for you.'

'Shut up. Guess who's here?'

'No idea. I can hardly hear you.'

'OK. That Leroy Callaway. From Mancunia. And guess who he's talking to?'

'Some bird?'

'Some jailbird all right. The very inspector that questioned you earlier.'

'Briggs?' Lukas sits up in bed.

'I know him. From the gang thing. He's in here a lot. His breath stinks.'

'I know'

'Callaway and a few other faces were gambling near me at the blackjack table when the copper came in. Callaway immediately walked over to him, called him by his name. That's when I put two and two together.' Vladi giggles. 'They huddled up in a corner like two luvvies. I mean, I'm pretty drunk, but there's something going on here. And with you having just been down to Mancunia to talk to Moses. You talked to him, didn't you, to Callaway?'

'Yes.'

'They got really worked up, talking.' Vladi giggles again. 'And my view of them was excellent, so I took a couple of piccies.' Lukas laughs nervously. 'I did a panorama of the whole casino for you and another in zoom – a close-up of the footballer and the inspector. Thought you'd appreciate that.'

'I do, Vladi, but get to the point.'

'I'm telling you the point, my dear. Listen, it gets better. So that boz-eyed Magyar of a bouncer, one of a twin pack, comes up to me, calls me a polack and tells me to stop taking pictures. I say, hey, I'm here all the time, etcetera, and he winks and says not to do it again. All the while I'm not sure who he's looking at.' Vladi laughs. 'You still there?'

'Yes, Vlad,' Lukas says impatiently.

'And then they get up.'

'Callaway and Briggs?'

'Yes. Walk right past me. And guess what?'

'What, Vladi?'

Vladi whispers. 'I heard the P word again.'

'The P word.'

'P, for polack.'

'They said polack?'

'Briggs did, yes,' Vladi says. Lukas's mind is racing. Vladi breathes heavily. 'You still there?'

'Yes. I need to go. Thanks, Vlad. Don't do anything stupid. I'll be in touch.'

Lukas packs his rucksack. Mobile phone and charger, passport, hat, gloves and a raincoat. The footballer and the inspector. Having a heart to heart about polacks. Lukas checks the cash situation, less than ideal at just over fifty pounds. He pulls on a black hoodie, combats and trainers. His bicycle tyres were flat when he checked them after Vladi's call. He's pumped them up and now the bike is hidden behind the hedge of the sheltered accommdation backing onto his house. He doesn't use the bike that much these days; used it more when he still went cycling with the kids. Now it might come in handy.

Chapter 17

At 3 o'clock Lukas wakes with a start and a sore jaw. He's been grinding his teeth through a terrible dream, being chased around Cheetham Hill by the Ryley gang. He'd run into Frank's house to hide. Frank wasn't in. In the dream Lukas kept telling himself that Frank was in hospital. Nevertheless he searched the house looking for the old man for an eternity before the banging on the door started. Now he sits straight upright in bed. The banging is real. Someone shouts. 'This is the police. Open up!'

He can't believe his hunch has proved right. He gets up, fully dressed. The bedroom window is unlocked and slightly ajar. He swings the rucksack onto his back and opens the window, invisible from the alleyway behind the house, where he expects an officer to be waiting for him to make his escape.

He climbs out of the window onto the flat roof of the kitchen and pulls the bedroom window shut behind him. It closes with a slight click. As he crouches in a corner under the window, his left knee pops. Hastily he puts his hood up; his hair must be like a beacon. The banging at the front door continues. No doubt they'll put the door through any second. Crackling noise from a radio confirms the presence of an officer in the alleyway, and Lukas overhears that the officers at the front of the house are going in. He hears wood splintering and sees the beams of at least two torches light up his bedroom ceiling.

He forces himself to move. It has always annoyed him that teenagers and drunks keep throwing bottles onto his flat roof. Now he silently thanks them as he grabs one and lobs it over the head of the officer at the back, towards the main road. It crashes noisily on the cobbles. His action has the desired effect; the officer spins around and takes a few steps away from him, his torch beam searching the alleyway.

Slipping down the side of the kitchen extension his feet find the wall as the officer, still facing away, says something into his radio. Then he hears sirens and wonders if this could be back-up already. He jumps off the wall expecting to lose his footing or twist his ankle on the old cobbles. But he lands safely, catching his weight by bending his knees, and immediately runs towards the hidden bicycle. Maybe the officer has noticed him despite the sirens. Maybe he has observed a shadow moving behind him out of the corner of his eye; he says something into the walkie-talkie, more urgent this time, his voice slightly raised.

Lukas does not look round as he grabs his bike and pushes it further onto the sheltered accommodation property. The gardens are lawned and he half carries, half pushes the bike diagonally across the grass, towards the road. He lifts the bike over the boundary wall, gets on and immediately jumps off as the back tyre has lost all air. He swears under his breath, leans the bike against the wall and walks speedily down the road. He turns right and left into the next alleyway and speeds up to a slow jog, his heart and feet pounding and the sirens of two police cars sounding closer. Panic grabs him, reminiscent of the dream he woke up from less than ten minutes ago. Finally, he reaches Oswald Road.

Turning right, he stays close to the hedges, then crosses over another road. The sirens seem further away now. Would they notice that the bedroom window had been opened? Though the self-locking mechanism had clicked shut the handle will still be turned to "open". If they find it will they connect the abandoned bicycle to his escape, and what will the officer behind his house conclude? Did he really notice anything?

He reaches the end of Oswald Road, turns left by some allotments and is joining the footpath past the primary school when a dull, thudding sound fills the air. A wave of nausea washes over him as he identifies the sound of a helicopter. It passes overhead and heads north, towards Manchester. He has never been on the run, only when playing cops and robbers as a child. Then, the fear had been exciting. Now he asks himself if he is completely insane to try and evade arrest. They have nothing on him, so why should he be afraid?

Yet a previously unknown, primeval survival instinct has kicked in, an intuition that has made him run, a suspicion made stronger by Vladi's observations at the casino. He does not want to put himself in the hands of the man Briggs; something feels not right, a gut feeling tells him he needs to find out more. Why would a high ranking police officer sit privately in a casino with a soccer player? A player who he himself recently interviewed and who laughed in his face in front of his manager when asked about match fixing in football. And a police inspector who earlier had questioned him about an assault on a mistaken identity, who happens to be a possible acquaintance of a blogger who rants about match fixing in football and subsequent betting scams.

There has to be a link somewhere. But why the heavy-handedness of the police? Is he being paranoid or has he really stirred something up?

The chopper gone, he still hears sirens. They wouldn't send a chopper out if they weren't absolutely sure that he was running. Then he hears it again. The distant vibration of rotating blades. Across the meadows the tall trees of Longford Park loom in the dark. He runs quickly, but stops halfway across to look back at the helicopter hovering over the approximate location of his house. Sweat runs down his neck. What a brilliant idea this is, to run away. He should have more trust in the British legal system. Paralysed with fear he stares at the chopper widening its circles above the area.

He forces himself to a jog until he reaches the other side of the meadow. No chance of evading a chopper when standing frozen with fear in an open field. The Mersey. Is that a good idea?

There's plenty of cover. But also plenty of open space. And leafy cover is no good, since they have those thermal imaging devices. Nevertheless he turns down towards the river. His mind scans the route ahead for possible hiding places, his ears pricked to the ever-changing hum of the chopper.

At Stretford Bridge he takes a left onto the canal. The chopper sounds closer and he ducks under the bridge. The chopper passes over, its beam illuminating the towpath. Presumably they will be scanning the undergrowth for warmth, as documented on those ever-repeating police camera programmes. Should he turn round, head away from the direction the chopper is taking? He is too confused to think straight. Heading into town seems a dangerous idea and too far; he is exhausted already and the wilderness of the Mersey attracts him. He knows his way down there; he goes for long walks a couple of times a week, and has always wanted to go all the way to Stockport. Maybe now is his chance. He follows the direction the chopper has taken, towards Sale. It is still visible in the sky, lights flashing somewhere over the water park.

He moves quickly along the towpath, towards the boathouse near the cemetery. Here he leaves the canal, and turns left onto the unadopted road which passes under the canal. To his right are two further arches; the first a horse-riding track, in bad repair, obviously rarely used or maintained; the second a footpath, overgrown and impassable. He chooses the latter, pushing himself into the undergrowth. The feet of the arch pillars are slightly wider and form a crumbling shelf. He climbs onto it and sits against the wall, his arms wrapped around him, as he tries to calm down in the cold. After a while the sound of the helicopter fades and eventually stops altogether.

Interlude

The Ryleys. There, on a notepad on the kitchen table. Briggs picks it up and puts it into an evidence bag. Possible links to organised crime in the Cheetham Hill area. One more piece of jigsaw puzzle, apart from Frank Staines. Survey, my arse. Briggs turns round. Another table. Printer, scanner cables, desktop computer, laptop. Another notepad. Quite a few houseplants for a guy living on his own. Tidy, too. Spag bol last night, the only plate that's dirty. He'd washed up the pan. Reheated dinner rather than cooked from scratch, after the interview. Two mugs, a late visitor. Briggs bags the mugs for fingerprints and DNA. The areas either side of the fireplace, once part of the range, now are shelves with books, CDs, vinyl and cassette tapes. Likes to read, likes to listen. Taste in music mainly classical, Mahler, Strauss, some opera. His reading more diverse. Research material. Dictionaries, reference stuff. More CDs on a shelf above the computer table. Computer software. Nothing exciting, nothing illegal, no games. Old papers, cut-outs on the side. More interesting. Articles about match fixing, footballers' parties. Briggs leafs through them. The collection goes back to just before

Christmas. No need for him to take any of this; it's all in the public domain. He picks up a second notepad, and runs his thumb through it. He tears off the first page and holds it against the light. He smiles. He would come back on his own, at a sensible hour.

The early morning raid had been necessary, though a waste of time, as far as his colleagues were concerned. The bird had not been there. No trace of him when they knocked on the door. No need to mention to his colleagues that the bed had been warm when he'd slipped his hand in seconds after they had broken the door down. Only he knows the bird had flown. The chopper had been in the area chasing some drug dealers. He had asked it to do a few extra loops for reconnaissance. As far as the other officers were aware Lukas Novak might as well be on holiday.

Chapter 18

He stays in his uncomfortable position until sunrise. By now the trams are running and he hears occasional voices and footsteps on the towpath above him. Stiff with cold he gets off the shelf and wrestles through the thicket, his legs like lead after last night's exercise. He grunts and continues his journey towards Urmston.

During his tense rest he has constructed a plan. With the police, and especially Briggs, after him he has limited options. He would surely be arrested if found, even if it is only for evading arrest. They must have come to bring him in earlier; one does not have the police kick one's door in at 3am just to have a polite conversation. How Briggs has arrived at the conclusion that he could be Frank Staines's attacker is a mystery to Lukas. Briggs would need evidence for an arrest and he can't for the hell of him think how he might have implicated himself. What did he touch in the old man's house? A mug. The toilet flush. The man's mail. Maybe the front door.

How many resources are being used to find him? The use of the chopper is surely expensive. They must have been certain he was in the house. Is he really such a great danger to society that they call a helicopter out to help catch him? After all, the charge, if he were proved guilty, would be GBH, not attempted murder. Has Frank's condition worsened? Who attacked the old man in the first place? And why? Was it just a random attack or is it to do with the mysterious relationship between D, the blogger and Frank Staines?

As he approaches Urmston station, he tells himself to stop guessing. Since he is unsure of how much police power has been deployed to find him he is extremely cautious. Scanning the area for any police presence he quickly walks up to the station and looks up the next train west. The first service to Liverpool Lime Street has already gone through; if they are monitoring trains he hopes they would have searched the first one. His escape is more than four hours old. Are they expecting him to have remained closer or travelled further afield by now?

The next train is due to leave for Liverpool in nine minutes. There are two ticket machines on the platform. He buys a return ticket to Warrington Central from the machine at the rear, then waits for the train by the side of the machine, invisible to anyone stepping onto the platform. Occasionally he looks round the corner to check for fellow travellers. As his train pulls into the station he scans the interior for uniforms. Few people are travelling so early, so he chooses a forward facing seat which will allow him to check the next station's platforms as the train pulls in.

His short journey is uneventful though tense; he is joined by a group of what he guesses to be six-formers, all girls. They remind him of Lilian; made up to the nines, though naturally beautiful. So unsure of themselves that they strive to be somebody else; beautiful young women, behaving like children after a night on the tiles.

He feels a sudden pang. How long has it been since he spent time with Lilian? He has no idea what is going on in her life, he doesn't see her often enough. And she is changing into a young woman, who he doesn't know any more.

Warrington has been blessed with a new shopping centre since he last visited. Now the town centre looks as anonymous as anywhere else in the UK. He buys a sandwich for his growling stomach. First things first. He hates being hungry, it makes him irritable and fuzzy in the head. A few days ago he had checked his bank account; this month's alimony had not been drawn yet, and now Liz would have to do without it. He finds a cash machine, inserts his debit card and enters his PIN. The machine bleeps. A message on the screen informs him that his request has been denied. The machine keeps his card. He looks at the cash machine, numbly. Surely not.

'Are you done, mate?' A twitchy youth behind him wants to know.

'Yeah, yeah,' he stammers. What now? Joint account? The account that the alimony goes into. He queues up again. The youth finishes his withdrawal and eyes him suspiciously as he turns and stuffs some notes down his jeans' pocket. Lukas inserts the joint account cash card. He cannot recall the PIN. Something with nines and zeros. The correct PIN is stored in his phone under his daughter's name. They would know where he is if he switched it on. Heck, they know anyway, since the machine has just swallowed his card.

He takes off his rucksack and digs for the phone. The cash machine spits out the card and bleeps. Evidently he is taking too long. A small queue has started to form behind him. He takes the card, steps out of the line and smiles apologetically at the lady behind him. Rucksack in one hand, phone and card in the other, he walks round the corner. The whole situation suddenly seems ridiculously like a scene from a movie. On the run, with helicopters after him and his cards cancelled. What exactly had he done? Obviously more than he understands.

He finds another cash till, here he'd have to walk inside for withdrawals, through one of those electric doors, activated by the clients' cash cards. Too risky, he decides. He could get himself trapped inside if the joint account is blocked too. He walks a few hundred yards to another machine. He inserts his card and enters his PIN. The machine bleeps and keeps his card. He breaks out in a hot sweat. He looks about and behind him. He knows it's irrational. This is not Hollywood and his movie is longer than ninety minutes. Nevertheless. He walks. Back to the station. He forces himself to breathe deeply. To put some miles between his last traceable appearance and himself.

At 11.22 he boards a train to Manchester Piccadilly, getting off again at Urmston, which is as far as his ticket allows him to travel. He must not risk staying on the train all the way to Manchester, though Piccadilly would give him more travel options and place him further away from his home. He crosses the road and walks into a pharmacy to make the purchases he did not dare make in Warrington. One of his favourite movie characters has always been Dr Richard Kimble. He enjoyed the television series as well as the film version; Harrison Ford especially made a brilliant fugitive. Though Harrison's Kimble had the advantage over him at the start of the chase; he had sported a huge, unkempt beard. Easy to shave off and change appearance. Lukas has not shaved for a few days, but his efforts are not as impressive as Ford's beard; the little that has grown on his cheeks and chin is blond, or maybe greyish white.

The public toilets near Urmston station are not very savoury, but at least they are open. He shaves dry and by feel inside a cubicle, leaving a goatee. Then he mixes the dye on the toilet cistern and smears it over his beard and hair. He waits fifteen minutes as instructed on the leaflet, during which he hears several people using the toilets.

Once the coast is clear he emerges from the cubicle and quickly rinses his hair and face in the sink. The amount of colour draining out alarms him. It does not seem to want to stop, so eventually he pulls his towel out of his bag and dries himself off, staining the towel a mucky dark brown. He smoothes back his wet hair with gel and pulls on a knitted hat then checks his appearance in the broken mirror above the sink. A stranger looks back at him, a rough-looking, sturdy, middle-aged man. He puts the used toiletries back into the plastic bag and throws it into the bin outside, then makes his way back to the station, following signs for trains to Manchester Piccadilly.

The train arrives at Piccadilly on Platform 13, a through platform away from the main station building, which is perfect. He checks the departures on the monitor. The next train leaves for Hadfield on in four minutes. Ideal. He runs towards the connecting bridge.

'Sorry, mate,' he shouts at the guard trying to read his ticket. The man is making moves to stop him so Lukas pushes his ticket into his hands. 'Got to run, sorry.'

'OK.' The guard is no longer interested.

He jogs across the bridge above the platforms and just makes it onto the Hadfield train before the whistle blows. He sits down on the empty train, picks up a copy of *Metro* from the seat opposite and exhales.

Interlude

Manchester Metro News, Sunday supplement

Burglary leaves pensioner hospitalised
(Picture of Frank Staines in flat cap, smiling)
'Another cowardly attack has left a defenceless pensioner hospitalised.

Frank Staines (71) was attacked and robbed on Saturday evening by thugs wearing hooded jackets at his home in the Cheetham Hill area of north Manchester. Frank, a retired bricklayer, who is unable to read and write, lives on his own. Neighbours did not notice anything unusual until Frank was spotted lying on his doorstep at around 8pm. Frank is believed to have had a visitor in the late afternoon. The police want to speak to a man in connection with the visit.

'We believe we have a good lead,' says DCI Richard Briggs. 'It just goes to show what kind of a society we live in when criminals prey on the weakest of the weak. We want to speak to this man at his earliest convenience.

'The suspect's name is Lukas Novak, of Chorlton-cum-Hardy. He is of Polish descent, tall, heavy built, with curly blond hair. Please contact DCI Briggs at Bootle Street police station if you have any information.'

There is a recent photo of Lukas at the bottom of the article.

Chapter 19

Lukas is still in shock when he arrives at Glossop station. A sign on the platform welcomes him to the Gateway of the Peak. The railway viaducts crossed during the journey and the majestic hills to the east have all but escaped him as he was staring at his picture in the paper.

He forces himself to step off the train purposefully, to trust in his disguise. Nevertheless he feels people are looking at him suspiciously. But then this is a small town, and a stranger easily catches people's eyes, he tells himself.

On the station square, there are several pubs. The Star to the left, the George ahead and the Norfolk right on the main A57, which, beyond Glossop, turns into the Snake Pass to Sheffield. Lukas is hungry. There's a Co-op next door with a coffee shop. He doesn't think it's wise to sit down and be ogled by the locals, so he chooses a filled baguette from the sandwich rack instead. The *Glossop Advertiser* catches his eye. He picks up a copy, puts it on the counter and places his sandwich on top. He pays quickly and avoids the checkout girl's eye.

The small park just down the road looks inviting and quiet. He sits down on a bench, opens the paper and finds the accommodation section. Few B & Bs advertise. Maybe they don't have to; this area is known to be a walker's paradise. An advert for one catches his eye, on High Street East. The address spans ten house numbers, a fairly big place, perfect for his needs, nothing too personal. He puts the paper in his backpack, unwraps the baguette, bins the wrapper and walks towards the high street. He eats on the move and reaches The Ridges B & B in ten minutes.

His instinct was right. This is accommodation for labourers who stay a few weeks and then move on; not the kind of place families or walkers would choose for their spring term holiday. His entry into the shabby foyer is announced by a bell.

A young woman in her twenties appears almost instantly, clouded in cigarette smoke. 'You want a room?' she asks, disinterestedly, and pulls a notebook towards her. He tells her it's just for one night. A small child is getting excitable in the adjacent room.

She looks at him up and down with big, blank eyes. 'You're not a grafter?' Her face is pale but attractive. A piercing adorns her lower lip.

'No, just a day's walking.'

'Aren't you a bit late in the day for that?'

'Spur of the moment decision.'

'OK.' She seems satisfied, and focuses her attention on the register. Then she hands him the key to a room and looks at him with big eyes. Not inquisitively, just blank. 'They're all twenty-five quid. We prefer cash.'

'Cash it is.' Lukas fumbles in his pocket, puts two tenners and change onto the counter. Now he is almost broke. He calculates quickly that his remaining funds must be about fifteen pounds, which will buy dinner and two or three pints. Dinner is going to have to be on the cheap side.

'Sign here.' She points at the book with heavily manicured fingernails. He signs his name as Peter Blackley. She reads. The child wails loudly in the back room.

'OK, Peter Blackley, you can hear I'm wanted. Have a nice hike.' She disappears into the adjacent room, closes the door and starts to shout.

Chapter 20

'Y'alright, mate?' It's not a real enquiry, more a query of whether the bar stool next to Lukas is taken. The man looks at him inquisitively. Lukas gestures vaguely at the stool, trying to avoid the man's eyes. He is unsure if the man is grinning out of one corner of his mouth or snarling out of the other. Under his furrowed brow his eyes are the blackest Lukas has ever seen since DCI Briggs's. 'Cheers, mate.' Vaguely Scouse. The man leans on the bar, and puts down a pint of Fosters.

Lukas does not want to get drawn into a conversation, neither does he want to arouse suspicion by leaving abruptly. So he stares hard at the TV screen on the wall opposite. Mancunia vs Birmingham Town. 0– 0.

The Scouser looks at him briefly, and takes another swig of beer. 'Tried the Chinese?' Lukas nods. 'All you can eat, my arse. And they mean it.' The man laughs. 'Haven't seen you here before. Or in any of the other boozers. Passing through?' Out of the corner of his eye Lukas sees the man grin.

'Sort of.' Lukas swirls the dregs of beer in the bottom of the glass.

'How can you be sort of passing through? You're either passing through or you're not.'

Lukas turns to him. 'I've only just arrived. Not sure how long I'll stay.'

The Scouser holds his stare, too long for Lukas to bear. His black eyes burn holes into the back of Lukas's retinas.

A howl from the football-watching few. Appeals for a penalty. Lukas glances at the screen and just catches sight of Leroy Callaway sliding into the Birmingham striker inside the area. No sign of any ball contact.

'He's going home.' The Scouser briefly looks over his shoulder. 'Cheating bastard! Come on, ref!' The referee has awarded a penalty to Birmingham; he points at the spot and gives Callaway a warning.

'Send him off! He's got to go. Foul in the area. Bent referee!' Several men have jumped up and shake their fists at the screen.

'B & B down the road?' The Scouser has turned towards Lukas again.

'What?' Lukas stares at the screen, then at the Scouser, then back at the screen and again at the Scouser. 'Yes.'

The fouled Birmingham striker takes a run at the penalty spot, puts the ball straight at Entwistle, who fumbles and drops it. The ball slowly trundles towards goal. The young goalie makes to jump on top of it but misses it completely.

Birmingham have scored. The crowd roar. Lukas laughs loudly. First goal a dodgy penalty. The MatchMaker had been right.

'Is it OK? I've heard mixed reports. The B & B.' The Scouser looks at Lukas, who reluctantly shifts his gaze away from the match. The man continues. 'Planning on doing some walking, see the planes?'

Lukas is convinced the man is trying to pick him up. 'Maybe.' Without a clue what planes the man is referring to, he is not about to ask. He feels increasingly uncomfortable in the man's presence and in this pub. He is not a homophobe, but he doesn't want to make a fuss and get noticed on his first night here. He looks around the pub and scans the clientele. All fairly hard-looking men, grafters, most of them. Crew cuts. Not a woman in sight, apart from the restaurant staff.

Just now a group of younger, dapper looking men enter. The Scouser suddenly grabs Lukas's arm. Hard. It hurts.

Before Lukas can react the man has pulled him close. 'Go! Now! Out the door, turn right, up the hill. Queen's Arms. Ten minutes. Coppers. Go – and keep your head down!' The Scouser pushes him off the stool and has already vanished out of the back door by the time Lukas has steadied himself and turned around.

Chapter 21

The Scouser waits for him in a corner of the busy Queen's Arms, two pints on the table in front of him. He half gets up, stretches out his hand. 'Mark. Nice to meet you.' He smiles and scowls.

Lukas hesitates, but finally shakes Mark's hand. 'Pete. Nice to meet you too.' He sits down at the impossibly low table and bangs his knee.

Mark tilts his head. 'Pete, ey?' He raises his eyebrows. 'Been stepping on a few toes recently, have we?'

'I got to go. Thanks for the drink.' Lukas makes a move to get up. The man is drunk and Lukas can't read him. Situations like these easily turn unpleasant. Better give him the slip now before he gets in too deep.

'Sit down, mate.' Mark makes an appeasing gesture. 'Shall we start again?' He gets up, stretches out his hand and bows. 'Mark, nice to meet you. To which you reply'—he turns round and bows again—'Lukas, how do you do, nice to meet you too.' The Scouser sits down.

'What did you say?'

'You got it tattooed right there on your forehead.' Mark drinks.

'I'm going.' Lukas gets up again.

'Sit down!' the Scouser demands. 'You're the guy from the front page. I recognised you straight away,' he says very quietly.

'Bad disguise.' Lukas sits down slowly.

'It is to me,' Mark still speaks quietly, then leans back and drinks.

Lukas looks at the floor. 'Are you after me?'

'No, but every other copper in the country is. That's why I got you out of Glossop's number one copper pub, you twit,' he says scowling.

'You're police?'

'Have been. Never again. Disgraced. Thank fuck.' Mark finishes his pint. 'Get them in then,' he says. Lukas hasn't touched his beer. 'What's wrong with you?' Mark frowns.

Lukas thinks. He's almost broke. And this man is either a lunatic, a complete drunk or alarmingly honest. 'Were you looking for me?'

'No, I stumbled over you by accident. I walked in and there you sat in my local and me thinks, it's that face from the paper, the one Ol' Stinky's looking for. Right here on my pad.'

'Ol' Stinky? You mean Briggs?'

Mark spits on the ground. 'Don't you mention his fucking name in front of me.'

Lukas finally drinks. 'What's he to you?'

'He's nothing to me. He just had me framed and kicked out of the service.'

Lukas signals towards the bar for two more pints. 'Why are you telling me this?'

Mark leans across the table, tilting it. 'Because I'm a bit pissed and I saw you and thought, ay ay, it's that's unlucky chap that Stinky wants. Likelihood he's being set up. So I decided to help you. I hate him!'

'Why?' Lukas puts down the pints.

'Why I hate him or why I want to help you?'

'Both.'

'What he did to me is too long a story for tonight. I want to help you because virtually everything that twat does is dodgy. Not obviously, but his motive is always a different one from the one he claims it is.'

'So in my case?'

'We're about to find out.' Mark leans back, smiling and scowling.

'Ask yourself, why did you run?'

'When my mate rang from the casino, I got a really bad feeling. I didn't give them anything during the interview, apart from my supposed research in Cheetham Hill.'

'So someone guessed a connection, just like you did. A possible link between Ol' Stinky and Leroy. But you haven't figured out what it is yet.'

'They could just be two local celebs gambling together.'

'What did your mate say? "It clicked; I put two and two together." Maybe it's time you started using your little grey cells, you twit.'

They are still in the Queen's. Post match the pub is heaving. FC eventually won 2–1, which doesn't concern Lukas; he's placed his bet right. He looks around the pub furtively. No one is paying them any attention. He feels safer now in the presence of the Scouser. The man argues intelligently, despite the amount of lager he has – they both have – consumed. Nevertheless he feels strangely sober. The conversation is reassuring, keeping his senses alert and adrenaline is once again surging through his body. This morning he had woken up under a canal bridge.

He had made a failed attempt to disguise his movements, his physique, and more so the location of his cash card usage. But he'd been figured out. Someone had been quicker.

'I'm an investigative journalist. I don't stab around in the dark. I need hard evidence. I'm the victim of a case of mistaken identity.' Lukas crosses his arms.

'How much evidence do you need? Put two and two together like your casino mate, will you?' Mark laughs. 'For a journalist you're pretty thick. Usually your lot take no time jumping to conclusions.'

'That's why I don't work for the papers. I like to present proper evidence.'

'Yeah, I thought that once. Try presenting hard evidence from inside a fucking concrete cell.' Mark finishes yet another pint. 'Or from the morgue.'

'You were inside?'

'No, I'm talking about you. You will be soon if you don't start thinking a bit quicker. Your mug shot is already in the news. You go see Moses and Callaway. You put all your cards on the table like a really clever dick. "Could you please tell me what's going on at those parties? And what do you think about that blog? Oh yes, and by the way, I think you or one of your players is involved in match fixing." Why didn't you pull down your pants in front of them as well? You could have had your arse slapped right there and then. Jesus!' Mark starts on another lager.

'I tried to provoke a response.'

'You certainly succeeded. 'Cos what happens next? Old Joe, whatever his name is, ends up in hospital. Just after you visited him. How's that? Come on, Sherlock, talk me through it.'

'His name's Frank. I thought he was the blogger.'

'And?'

'He's not.'

'And?'

'His nephew, or whatever friend or relative, is.'

'Possibly so. And?'

'And what?'

Mark exhales noisily. 'Why did he get beaten up? Coincidence?'

'Maybe.'

'Come on, Luke, you mistook him for someone else. Why not somebody else making the same mistake?'

'You think I was followed. I don't think so.'

'Maybe not directly. But you found the blogger chap online—'

'And his address. Someone else could have traced him too.'

'Ah finally, behold! They got to him after you did. Luckily for you. You could've been dead and framed for murder at the same time.'

'Seems that's what you're implying I'm being pursued for anyway.'

'They'd have a lot more on you if you *had* stumbled into a fresh crime scene, spreading yourself about like you'd have undoubtedly done, my friend.' Mark slaps him on the shoulder. He suddenly seems sober and gets to his feet. 'Sorry to be a party pooper. I've a job on in the morning and I've had far too much. And you spent the night under a bridge. You undoubtedly showered off the tramp earlier but you still look like shit to me.'

Lukas is dog tired, all of a sudden. 'Can I ask a favour, Mark?'

'Thought you never would, darling. How much?'

'Twenty quid?'

Mark digs out his wallet, which is full of twenty-pound notes. He pulls one out. 'Meet me at the Prince of Wales at fourish. It's opposite the Commercial.'

'I'll be there.'

'And don't you touch that internet! Or your phone.' Mark points at him, frowns, and walks away.

Chapter 22

Manor Park looks glorious in the sunshine, with a few daffodils already showing their green tips, and the air smells fresh and clear. Lukas is in good spirits. He walks up towards the Queen's and follows the river past a steelworks factory, an eyesore in this beautiful landscape. Moments later a stunning valley opens up in front of him. The scenery takes his breath away. Sheep bleat expectantly in the morning sunshine. First a jogger, then a cyclist pass him. An old man tends to his garden. He says hello. Everybody smiles.

Pavel would love it out here. He needs to get in touch. And he needs to find a bookie's. Yesterday he just had enough funds to pay for one night's B & B and he's checked out this morning, in case his hypothetical winnings wouldn't cover a further night. He did not meet the owners, guessing that the girl at reception was an employee. Luckily not a very bright one as she never asked for his ID. Maybe the fractious child in the back room had sidetracked her enough to forget. Maybe she just couldn't be bothered.

The bridge invites him to lean on its railing. Young trout play in the peaty water below. So he met an eventually likeable stranger in the pub, who seems to know an awful lot about the officer who is pursuing him. Coincidence? Fate? Or carefully planned stalking, hidden behind an alcoholic smokescreen.

Nevertheless, Lukas trusts the Scouser, and is looking forward to learning more about Briggs – a police officer who late at night socialises in casinos with footballers who are implicated in organising sex orgies with allegedly underage girls, and who Lukas could've sworn got away with a tackle in the area just last night. A tackle that resulted in a penalty but not a sending off. Refereeing error? That's what the papers say. It happens.

Lukas stares into the water, watches a young trout struggle against the current, upstream. Who said it was going to be easy and straightforward? And who said it was going to be obvious? Two and two equalling four? Surely, that would be too simple. There has be a catch. He'll find out what it is. To do so he needs to trust people. But not all the way, and not first time.

He walks back towards the town centre, goes into a betting shop and collects his handsome winnings.

The library is located near a pretty millstone church. Virtually everything here is made from Derbyshire millstone. Even the cobbles. He welcomes cobbles. One doesn't see them too often these days.

The lady in charge looks at him sternly over the top of her glasses as she takes his Manchester Central Library card and scans it. 'We don't normally do this. You really need to be a resident.'

Lukas smiles broadly and looks at her badge. 'I'm thinking about becoming one, Gladys. Your town is so friendly. I've been looking for a cybercafe in vain.'

She turns her nose up at his remark. 'We don't have one. No demand. People come here to the library.' She types something on her keyboard. 'I'm making an exception. You're not supposed to go to naughty sites. You're also advised not to do internet banking. For your safety. You never know who's looking over your shoulder.' She hands him a card. 'Most people use the interweb for information and for email.' She directs him to a terminal. 'You have it for one hour.'

'Thank you so much for making an exception.' He bows slightly. She gives him a sweet and sour smile and puts his library card into a wooden box.

He sits down at the terminal and navigates to his email supplier's website. Taking the note with his new password out of his wallet he keys it in with one finger, double-checking the unfamiliar string of letters and numbers after each entry.

There are emails from Vladi and Pavel, voicing concern, urging him to get in touch. Of course they've seen his photograph in the papers. Lil and Liz, both sounding worried and accusing at the same time; why doesn't he pick up his phone?

And finally an email from the MatchMaker's account. The missing link. No message. Just a time – and a location.

Chapter 23

Lukas gets off at Guide Bridge station in Audenshaw, a network hub where several rail lines interlink towards Manchester Piccadilly. He turns left out of the station and walks through the drizzle towards a newsagent, the suggested location in the MatchMaker's email.

Lukas is early.

Fifteen minutes to the appointed time.

Fifteen minutes until he will know the MatchMaker's identity.

Fifteen minutes until he will know why D wants to see him. Surely not just to congratulate him on subscribing to his blog.

He stays in the shadow of the railway bridge diagonally opposite and fifty yards from the newsagent. Near perfectly concealed in a recess and behind a telephone exchange box Lukas is pretty sure he'll get a good glimpse of D before he himself is seen.

A black Jaguar passes under the bridge, and parks on the cobbles halfway between Lukas and the newsagent, facing away. A couple cross the street, arguing, walk past him towards the station. Another train pulls in overhead. Another dark car parks further up the street, a hundred yards away from the Jag and on Lukas's side of the street, facing him.

Lukas feels tense. No one has got out of either car. If one car contains the blogger who is in the other?

A minute from the appointed time two men walk past him on the opposite side of the street. Stocky. Shaven heads, black knitted hats. Hands in pockets. They look this way and that, and over in his direction, but don't seem to notice him. They disappear into the newsagent.

Then the Jag moves slowly forward until parallel with the other car, which Lukas now believes to be a Toyota sports model. The Jag's side window opens and an elbow pokes out. Lukas sees machinery, but the car is too far away and his eyesight is too poor to distinguish what it is. He should have written down the Jag's number plate when he had the chance.

The two men come out of the newsagent and walk across directly towards him, still scanning the road. Lukas presses himself into the gap, hoping he is out of view and the men approaching are not here for him. Then tyres squeal in the distance. Not the Jag, but the Toyota. Nought to seventy in four to six seconds. Maximum twelve seconds to be level with him under the bridge.

The heavies approach steadily. A bicycle bell behind him. Lukas twists round. A woman on a mountain bike, on the wrong side of the road. No Lycra, no helmet. Jeans and canvas jacket. The heavies look at her and stop. Lukas twists right to attempt an escape and looks straight into the headlights of the Toyota. The car swerves, presumably to avoid the heavies who are more than halfway across the street. Then it mounts the kerb, heads straight towards him, missing the exchange box, and with the low bumper scraping the kerb.

Lukas crouches and watches in terror as the car slides towards the cyclist in slow motion. The woman screams, eyes and mouth wide open. She brakes hard and locks the back wheel. Her front wheel hits the kerb, sending her flying over the handlebars. She lands, hands first, on the pavement next to Lukas as the Toyota crushes her bicycle beneath its heavy chassis, dragging it along for a few yards before disappearing round the corner, tyres sqealing.

Lukas instinctively leans over the woman to check her out. Then the two heavies are on top of him, pulling him off the woman, and dragging him to his feet.

'Where the fuck is he?' one of the heavies hisses into Lukas's face. The other man stands behind his mate, grinning.

'Don't know what you're talking about.' Lukas holds the man's piggy-eyed stare. The heavy looks round at his mate, who just nods. Piggy-eyes pushes Lukas backwards. He stumbles and falls over something. The exchange box breaks his fall and he hits his head against the brick wall. His world goes black.

When he comes to, Lukas hears punching and grunting. He opens his eyes and sees the injured woman, bleeding from her face and still on the floor, kicking out hard at Piggy's friend. The man swears, bends down and punches her in the stomach twice. She groans and doubles up in the foetal position. Then the man kicks her in the kidneys.

Lukas struggles to his feet, outraged, a strange kind of war cry escaping from his throat, but he instantly collapses to the floor. The pain kicks in after he hits the cobbles. He's been dead-legged. Piggy laughs, and bends over him. Lukas kicks out with his good leg, and hears a satisfying grunt. A split second later he is rewarded with a kick in the ribs. All air leaves his body. His head hits the pavement. He sees stars as the woman screams and something crunches. Piggy's mate pulls her to her knees. Her jeans have ripped in the fall, blood stains the faded fabric. The man holds her in a vice grip. Then he pushes her forward. She yelps helplessly.

Lukas is sandwiched between the wall and the exchange box as the woman falls towards him. He braces himself. She lands on top of him, winding him once more. Piggy puts a Doc Marten boot onto the small of the woman's back and laughs as she whimpers and squirms.

Another engine roars, Lukas cranes his neck to look up. The Toyota is back. It creeps towards them, but the roaring comes from elsewhere. A black BMW. It cuts up the Toyota, sliding sideways so fast that it is bound to crash into the side of the kerb and ultimately, into their scuffle. The driver's door flies open halfway through a vicious handbrake turn, hits Piggy's friend directly in the midriff and knocks him to the ground. The open door narrowly misses Lukas's head.

Piggy takes his boot off the woman's back and turns towards the BMW and his mate on the floor. Lukas kicks Piggy's legs from under him, struggles up and kicks the man again, this time where it hurts most.

Chapter 24

'Get the fuck in!' The BMW's rear door flings open. Lukas glances inside. Mark pulls the ski mask up to briefly reveal his face. 'Now,' he screams.

Lukas grabs the woman, who struggles and stumbles, and pushes her onto the back seat. He jumps in after her. Mark takes off. Lukas's feet still hang out of the open door, and he feels himself sliding backwards. Mark turns right abruptly which flings Lukas back into the BMW's interior and slams the door shut behind him.

'What the fuck are you doing?' Mark screams, head turned back, his face scarlet with anger. His fist flies towards Lukas but instead hits the seat, twice, hard. 'You fucking twonk. I told you not to go online, and what do you idiot do? Go straight to the library and bloody well log on!' Mark, still facing backwards, his left arm behind the passenger seat, fist clenched, only looks at the road for split seconds at a time. 'Who the fuck is *she*?'

Lukas is stuck in the BMW's foot space. The woman whimpers on the back seat.

'See to her, for fuck's sake!' Mark gestures at her, then turns forward and slams his fist on the wheel.

Lukas hoists himself halfway onto the seat and glances at her. She moans and stares at him wide eyed. Lukas looks out of the back window. The Toyota is yards behind them, swerving wildly from side to side, trying to overtake on the right. 'Mark, watch out!' Lukas croaks.

Mark pulls onto the opposite side of the road, forcing the Toyota to brake, then immediately turns left then left again. Two-way traffic now. Mark jumps a red light and passes two waiting cars on the inside. Horns blare at them. They join the M60 in the Stockport direction. Lukas looks back. The Toyota is still behind them; they've only gained fifty yards.

'He's still there.'

'I see that, thanks, Sherlock.' Mark glares at Lukas in the mirror. 'I can't believe it, you know. I tell you not to do something and you go straight out and do the very thing.' Mark shakes his head. 'Didn't even notice me stood ten feet behind you, did you. You might have finished your internet session, but you never logged out of your mail account. All I had to do was open it and voila: all your emails.'

Lukas groans. 'I'm sorry, Mark. I didn't think all this would happen.' He looks down at the injured woman, feeling utterly helpless.

'Well, it's a tough old world. You arrange to meet someone after someone else has already tried to top them and you're surprised they try again? They know who you are by now and in hacker-kid's absence they have a go at you. Blogger must've smelled a rat not to turn up. So you pick up this bird instead. Nice work! As if we're not in enough shit already. How is she anyway?'

Lukas checks the woman. 'I think she's in shock or something.'

She moans quietly and turns her head away. Her face is cut and she holds her arm below the abrasions from her fall. 'Hello, love.' She doesn't reply. He says it again, gently, and pats the woman's arm. She moans. 'What's your name, love?'

With great effort the woman looks at him and opens her eyes a little. 'Luke, I'm Dannii – ' she says and passes out.

Chapter 25

'Fuck me!' Mark stares into the rear view mirror. He swears again. Then he just drives. Lukas watches the woman come round. They sit on the motorway at ninety for a while. 'Listen, love,'—Mark turns round, calmer—'No idea if you can hear me or not; don't matter one way or another. I've absolutely no idea how you fit into this mess we're in. We're the good guys, you hear me. But there're some bad guys after us, or rather after you, as it seems, so I'm getting us out of here. So the schtummer you can keep, the longer we'll be friends, kapish? Mate, make sure she doesn't bleed to death, will you?'

Lukas fusses helplessly over Dannii, dabbing at her cuts as carefully as he can. She no longer moans and her eyes are half closed. Lukas suspects she is out for the count.

Mark weaves in and out of the traffic, exceeding considerably the fifty mile an hour limit before Stockport. As the distance between the BMW and the Toyota grows marginally, Lukas touches his own wounds; his side hurts where he's been kicked, his ribs are bruised but not broken. He is short of breath and his head hurts; he touches his face carefully. Pink pus rather than blood. The back of his right hand is scratched and bleeding, where it had scraped the wall. How he'll walk after the dead leg remains to be seen; he's not stood up since he was kicked. He looks down at Dannii and swallows hard. It's his fault she's here on the back seat, bleeding. He saw her come off the bike and hit the ground, witnessed her get punched in the stomach several times, saw the vice crunch that probably dislocated her shoulder. She'd been pushed to the ground hard at least twice. She'd been stomped upon. Who would do such a thing? As far as he recalls she wasn't kicked in the abdomen, which minimises the risk of internal bleeding. Lukas still checks the inside of her mouth, and notices a trickle of light-coloured blood, possibly from the punches she received. Her face is cut and scraped in a few places but she's not bringing up blood. 'Looks like she could be concussed. Hit her head quite hard,' he observes.

'Make sure she doesn't choke on her own vomit.'

Lukas looks back. 'Still there.'

Mark swears under his breath, drops a gear and accelerates through thick traffic. ''Bout time we lost them and got some peace.'

He leaves the M60 via the M56 link and turns off immediately towards Sharston, overtaking a bus and several cars against traffic, before turning left into a council estate. The Toyota has caught up and screeches round the corner behind them. Mark makes a hard right into a boarded up cul-de-sac. The Toyota follows. Mark speeds down the deserted street, then slams on the brakes, turning the BMW by 180 degrees, so it faces the Toyota. The driver of the Toyota spins his car to come to a stop in front of the BMW, at right angles, blocking them in.

'Shit!' Lukas exclaims.

Mark laughs and floors the accelerator. The BMW lurches and pushes its nose into the Toyota's driver's door with a slow crunch. Dannii comes to, sits up and screams. Mark is already out of the car and on the Toyota's bonnet. Something glints briefly in his hand before he smashes it down through the Toyota's windscreen. Only now does Lukas notice Mark's black leather gloves. The windscreen implodes into a million tiny, bejewelled cubes. Through the broken screen and the steering wheel Mark grabs the driver's collar and pulls and smashes the man's head hard against the wheel, again and again. The driver's nose squashes to pulp and through the blood and glass Lukas watches as the man's brow splits open.

Dannii opens the door with her good arm and vomits. Mark hollers at the driver, like a lunatic. Finally, he slams him back into his seat and punches him in the face. The man slumps. Mark fumbles through the man's pockets, pulls his head forward onto the horn and leaves it there. He slides off the bonnet, back into the BMW and throws the man's effects into Lukas's lap. Lukas jumps at the sight of the gun. Mark reverses the BMW, then slams it into first.

The first hoodies appear as they turn out of the cul-de-sac, attracted by the jammed car horn. No one pays any attention to the speeding BMW leaving the estate.

Chapter 26

Still on the road, Mark has zigzagged them all over Cheshire, up and down the M6. Now they are on top of Thelwall Viaduct, going north, having stopped at a shop for food and water. The damage to the BMW's front is minimal, one light out, a few dents. Lukas cleans their scratches with water and covers them with plasters from the car's first aid kit, and puts Dannii's arm in a makeshift sling. She now sits up in the back seat, behind Mark and cradles her shoulder. Lukas sits beside her and offers her some chocolate.

'Did you know them, love?' Lukas turns toward Dannii, grimacing with the pain from his ribs.

She shakes her head. 'No,' she mouths and starts to sob quietly.

'Never seen them before? What about the driver of the Toyota?'

Dannii shakes her head. Lukas looks at Mark in the mirror.

Mark turns off the M6 and onto the M62 towards Liverpool. 'Listen, Princess, if you know anything, if you have any idea why you're being targeted, you need to tell us. We're risking our necks here, trying to extract you from this giant shit-hole you seem to be submerged in, so open your mouth!'

Lukas glares at Mark, then turns back to Dannii. 'Sorry, love, that was Scouse for polite. Why is someone so concerned about you and me meeting?'

'They think I'll spill the beans, I guess.' Dannii blinks at him through tangled blonde hair.

'What beans could you spill?'

'About who's in the fixing scam.'

'Who's responsible?'

'Yes, and who's organising it.'

'And you know who?'

'It reaches further than you think.'

'Do you have proof, names?'

'No hard proof. I get phone calls and texts.' She straightens up, groaning.

'Someone contacts you with the results?'

'Someone gives me hints, rarely complete results. They want me to continue, don't you see? They don't want you to investigate and stop me passing on tips. That's why they want to stop you talking to me. Everyone's making big money. But they don't want you to spread what else I'm writing. They want the tips to go out, but they also want to control what I write. See, I don't just pass on tips, I also spill beans; they don't like that.'

'Why not just spread the tips? Wouldn't that make you a wealthy woman? What are you in it for?'

Dannii looks out of the window. She starts to sob again. 'Can we do something about my shoulder, please? I'm in agony.'

'Soon, princess, soon.' They leave the M62 at IKEA Warrington.

'Fame. You want to be famous. The one in the know? Is that what it is?' Mark sneers.

She suddenly looks hard, and her jaw juts forward. 'I hate what these bastards do to the game. It's not sincere any more. No one can tell if a game's been messed with, at least not generally. It's getting like American wrestling, all show.'

'Excuse me for butting in again, love, but what does a nice girl like you know about footy, the beautiful game? Wouldn't you be better off tending to the kitchen sink? You see what it leads to sticking your pretty little turned-up nose into other people's business. Bent refs, bent players, bent everyone. You go out, get them, love.' Mark snarls in the mirror.

'Where did you pick up this homophobic poof, Luke? If he weren't driving at this moment I'd hit him.' Dannii kicks the back of Mark's seat.

'Whoo-hoo, girl, bring it on! Give us a good scratching,' Mark hollers and slaps the steering wheel.

'Leave it out!' Lukas hisses and turns to Dannii. 'So you write your blog to get at those responsible for bastardising the sport and hope that someone will do something about it. And you still keep on taking tips and passing them on. Isn't that a bit of a contradiction?'

Dannii shifts. 'I'm putting my life on the line.'

'And ours. Listen to this arrogant bitch!'

'I'm putting my life on the line, spilling the beans, moron. This is why I only give access to certain areas of the blog to paying subscribers; in case something happens to me, so someone will be able to figure out who had access to the real dirt. Why d'you think I'm of no fixed abode, have no credit card? So they can't get me. That's why I don't think they're after me, but they rather wanted to prevent you from talking to me, Luke.'

'A tart writing about football. What's the world coming to?' Mark shakes his head.

'Twat,' Dannii says and looks out of the window.

'Do you know how I found your address?'

'No,' says Dannii, defiantly.

'The email address on your payment site at PayPal. One look in the phone book, there's only one Franklin Staines in Manchester. Such an unusual name, Franklin. But you don't live at the address in the book, only old Frank lives there. And he gets beaten up in your place. Someone you've conned into believing you're a relative? Are you proud?'

Dannii shakes her head. 'That all wasn't supposed to happen. The address thing, yes, I should've though. I didn't realise PayPal would disclose a private, physical email address in the payment process. I took one out in Uncle Frank's name, at his house. There's a modem somewhere in the house, not connected. And Frank loved me visiting. No, I'm not proud. I did help him with his mail. He's so fond of me. Terrible neighbourhood he lives in. I felt sick when I read your email. I never wanted anyone to come to harm, least of all him. Someone mistook him for me.'

'Yes, how is that possible? We've been wondering, sweetheart.'

Dannii tuts. 'Must've been a right thicko. Frank's too old to be a blogger. And they couldn't have known what I look like.'

'Nor known that you're a girl,' Lukas says and smiles at her.

'Police are trying to pin it on this twirp here.'

'Why?' Dannii looks puzzled.

Lukas fills her in on his visit to Frank's house.

'It's not the same guys today that attacked the old codger, I don't think,' Mark chips in.

'How's that?'

'These are professionals. Security. Organised.'

'Not police?'

'But that stinking bastard Briggs hired them to stage this little private party for you and Miss Minogue back there, that's my guess. He was sat in the Jag taking pictures.'

'Is that what I saw – a camera lens? He's watching us meet, but can't get involved. He's cleaning something up. Or he's got something to hide. He might well be working for someone else.' Lukas runs his hand across his face. 'It's all connected. The blog, the attack on Frank, the attack on us earlier. We just can't see the common thread yet. For example, Briggs meeting Leroy Callaway in the casino the night they came for me – was that coincidence?'

'He's on my books,' Dannii says quietly.

'Who? Briggs? He gets tips off you?' Lukas says, stunned. 'But that doesn't make sense. For a while I thought that maybe the likes of Bradshaw and Callaway are trying to get to her through me, like I was followed—'

'Which you probably were, by someone,' Mark interjects.

'But if Briggs is mates with Leroy and is her customer as well, then why use me? My theory must be wrong.'

'Not necessarily. Maybe Stinky can't be seen to be involved directly.'

'Yes, as I said earlier. Maybe Stinky has more than one agenda.' Lukas pulls out a small notepad and starts jotting down some thoughts. He stops suddenly and looks at Mark in the mirror. 'I am an idiot. I know how he found us, how he knew of my meeting with Dannii. It's Briggs alright. I changed my password before they tried to arrest me; had a funny feeling something was going to happen. And'—he pulls the crumpled note from his pocket—'I wrote down the new password on a notepad, in biro.' Lukas hits the back of the passenger seat.

'And Briggs spotted the pad at your place, saw the biro marks on the pad and got hold of a pencil. Far more complicated than me just standing behind you waiting till you vacate the terminal. You've done it twice, you moron. Why don't you put it in the *Evening News* next time!'

'Might as well, ey?' Lukas laughs.

'Fucking hell, mate, what a private detective you are.' Mark sniggers.

'I don't think it's very funny,' Dannii pipes up from the back. 'You almost got us all killed!'

'Ey, twirpy, it's you who's getting us killed and it is funny, OK? And by the way, it's time we turned the tables on these bastards.'

Chapter 27

'What have we got?'

'We've a gun, a mobile phone and a wallet. The last two both goldmines, hopefully.'

Dannii is stretched out on Mark's worn couch, half asleep, full of painkillers. They left the Warrington compound, where Mark's business associates store their vehicles and supplies, an hour ago. Lukas and Dannii are kitted out in new tracksuits, their torn and soiled clothes discarded. The Toyota driver's effects are on a small Formica table.

Mark opens the wallet. 'Driver's licence. Our friend's name is Colin MacFarlane, born 1976, which makes him thirty-five. Overweight, all muscle, of course. Typical bouncer, dodgy security. Brown hair, blue eyes, apparently. Lives in Ashton, almost a local then. Hundred and eighty and hang on, two quid and shrapnel. Here you go, Lukas, you're a bit short aren't you?'

'Not any more.' Lukas glances at Dannii and grins. She strains to return his smile.

'Oh, yes, I forgot. You found a bookies, then? In Glossop, the hottest place for gambling and other vices in the High Peak? Anyway, cash card, Visa. Nothing else. He's careful. What about the mobile?'

Lukas scrolls through the entries. 'Only four numbers, one landline, likely to be the work phone for this job. I've written the numbers down, here.' Lukas rotates the notepad. 'Ring any bells?'

Mark studies the pad. 'Not immediately. Names?'

'Initials.' Lukas jots them down next to the numbers.

'DIB. Guess who?'

'Let's assume that it is for now.'

'The other two are likely to be the two gorillas that attacked you. But the landline?'

'City centre number. Bootle Street?'

'Maybe, we'll check it later. Question is, why has nobody missed him? Why has nobody phoned that bloody phone? Status update on our well-being?'

'It's a bit late by now.' Lukas sits back in his chair.

'Yeah, it is now, but how about half an hour after I slapped him up? They didn't miss him?'

'Maybe there was no "they". He was on his own.'

'Answerable only to—?'

'DIB, DIB, DIB!' They say simultaneously.

'Ey, that's another seven happy years together, luvvie!'

'Shut up. There's no texts, no answerphone.'

'Did Stinky call him?'

'Yes, yesterday morning. The only incoming call that's listed.'

'When did you email Lukas, love?'

Dannii groans on the couch. Mark hadn't been too gentle when examining her shoulder back at the compound. Lukas suspects that there might be more to Mark's background than just a failed career as a set-up police officer.

'Got his mail first thing in the morning and replied straight away.'

Lukas looks down at Dannii. 'Why did you want to speak to me?'

'*You* wanted to speak to *me*. I'm freaked out about Frank too, more than ever after today.'

'You weren't put up to it by Briggs, by any chance, one of your clients?' Lukas asks Dannii. Mark looks up sharply, first at Lukas, then at Dannii. Lukas continues. 'How long has he been your client?'

Dannii shakes her head. 'It's not like that, no. He's been a client for about a year.'

Mark gets up. 'If you've led this creep to us I'll kill you.'

'I didn't. He did me in too, can't you see. He wanted me!'

'He doesn't give a fuck about you. Those arseholes didn't have any scruples about beating up boy or girl. Mind you, they probably didn't work out who you were, thought you were just a passer-by that got in the way, which could work in our favour. Still, no manners. Stinky wanted to stop Lukas learning more. Best way to do that is to shut you up, you stupid cow! Did he hire you to lead him to Lukas?' Mark glowers over Dannii who cringes on the couch.

'Mark,' Lukas says gently and takes his arm. 'It's the opposite way round. I led Briggs to Dannii, I'm convinced. Briggs wants her for someone else. Maybe they ultimately want to shut me up; I'm probably a greater risk to them than a seemingly two-faced bloggess. And you're right, Mark, Briggs might not even know that Dannii's a girl. If Briggs has been subscribing to the blog for a year, he's most likely been monitoring Dannii before he knew of my existence and certainly before I knew of Dannii's. He could've found and acted upon the PayPal email address before us. Maybe he did look for Frank's home address, maybe he didn't, but he certainly didn't follow it up if he found it. Not until I arrived on the scene. Which makes me think that I'm the threat, not Dannii. And maybe he initially just subscribed to the blog because he likes to gamble, though I'd like to believe his motivation was to spy on her.'

'I never had any contact with him, online or anywhere else. I wouldn't have mentioned he's a client if he'd hired me, would I?' Dannii says, defiantly.

'If I find out you're playing us I'll have you dead as a dodo,' Mark says scowling.

'So, where does this leave us? Briggs is probably still waiting for MacFarlane to return. This phone will ring at some point, unless MacFarlane contacts Briggs some other way, if he still can. We can safely assume that MacFarlane has by now sought medical treatment,' Lukas summarises. 'Did he call the other two numbers?'

Mark flicks through the phone. 'Yes, this morning.'

'So MacFarlane is in charge of the two men who attacked us and Briggs is in charge of MacFarlane. We need to find out if the attack on Frank Staines was orchestrated by the same people. Mark, tomorrow morning, I suggest you go and visit Frank in hospital.'

Chapter 28

Half an hour later Lukas has purchased five pay as you go SIM cards, jotted down their numbers and allocated one each to himself, Vladi, Pavel, Mark and Dannii. He inserts his into his mobile and stores the others' numbers. Then he posts two envelopes Special Delivery and places the remaining SIM cards in his wallet.

Back at the flat he hands Dannii one of the SIMs. She groans as she struggles off the couch, digs around in her rucksack and gets out a tatty looking phone. 'My spare. For family calls,' she says, apologetically. She changes the SIM card and puts the old one in her purse. 'Ring me.'

Lukas presses the call button. After a few seconds Dannii's phone rings. Then MacFarlane's mobile rings, like an electric shock cutting through the silence. Lukas walks over slowly to it and looks at the flashing screen.

'Aren't you going to pick it up? Dannii asks. She sits on the edge of the couch, cradling her mug.

Lukas shakes his head, and lets the phone ring out. He looks at Dannii and smiles. 'It'll ring again. Who do you think it is?'

Dannii frowns. 'Whoever hired him. You should've answered it.'

The phone rings again. At the same time the door opens noisily. Mark looks at Lukas, looks at Dannii, looks at the phone. 'What are you two luvvies doing, holding hands? Come on, you twirp, pick it up!'

Lukas lifts the phone and presses the green button. He hears breathing. Then a voice booms down the line like thunder. 'This is not your phone.'

Lukas looks up at Mark and nods. Mark makes a fist and mouths yes. Lukas ends the call and switches off MacFarlane's mobile.

'Pub,' Mark says and turns on his heels.

'Count me out.' Dannii sighs and curls up on the couch.

Lukas hesitates. 'Are you hungry, love?' he asks. Dannii mumbles something to the positive.

'You coming, mate?' Mark asks, halfway through the door.

'I'm going for a quick pint. I'll fix something later, OK?' Lukas says to her. Dannii grunts. He closes the door behind him gently.

'Same number?'

'Same number. Saved it to my phone. By the way, I could smell him through the receiver.' They laugh. Lukas drinks deeply.

'We got him. Bloody hell, am I relieved!' Mark slaps Lukas's shoulder.

Lukas nods. 'We can now definitely link him to the attack on Dannii and myself. It was clearly his voice on the phone. And the phone number shows up as DIB in MacFarlane's caller ID. What I still don't get is why he wants to get at Dannii. He's one of her customers.'

'My guess is he's doing that bit for someone else, and the betting for himself. What about cyber girlfriend, then? Got anything useful out of her?'

Lukas frowns at him. 'Not really. I didn't want to stress her more. We both needed to relax. We drank tea.'

Mark smirks. 'You drank tea. How lovey-dovey.' Mark wags a finger at Lukas.

'Cut it out!' He feels himself blush.

Mark whoops. 'Oh, in love, are we? Why didn't she come along? Wouldn't mind getting to know her a bit better myself, y'know what I mean?' Mark winks theatrically. 'A bit of the old "how's your father".' He rotates his hips.

Lukas rolls his eyes. 'Cut it out. Couldn't you see she needs some rest.'

Mark sniffs. 'Guess we're going to have to take her shopping, you and me, for the New Year's Eve party tomorrow. Plus we can't be having a bird in tracksuit bottoms lazing about the flat.'

'Why not?' Lukas looks at him quizzically.

'She's supposed to adorn the place; she's a girl.'

'Adorn the place? What century do you live in, you wally?' Lukas finishes his pint. 'I want to get back. She needs checking out and I need feeding. What are the sleeping arrangements, by the way?'

Mark grins. 'Did you use the toilet?'

'Yes.'

'Then you saw the bed. She can have that. You'll have the couch. I need to get back to Warrington tonight.'

Lukas squints. 'You sure you should be driving?'

'I'll get picked up later. Got some business to attend to.'

'What, tonight?'

'Yep.'

'You still going to see Frank in the morning?'

'Yes, mate, I will.' Mark reaches into his pocket and passes his keys over.

The shop at the bottom of Manor Park Road stocks all the ingredients Lukas needs for his spaghetti bolognese. He is surprised to find a decent bottle of red with a screw top in the shop's off licence section and also picks up a two-litre bottle of mineral water.

Dannii is sleeping when he returns. He sets the shopping down carefully and looks for cooking utensils. He ends up cutting the vegetables on a plate and is glad to have bought a pull-ring tin of tomatoes, in the absence of a tin opener. Mark owns a two-ring electric cooker but only one pan. Bolognese first. The spaghetti will have to wait until the sauce is done. Lukas opens the wine. He stirs the sauce occasionally and watches the traffic on High Street East. Puddles mirror the street lights above, lending a timelessness to the evening; it is his stomach growling, reacting to the smell of food, that wakes him from his reverie.

He takes a sip of wine and turns to check on Dannii. She looks at him through a tassel of hair, motionless. For a split second he is panicked. Then she blows the strand away from her forehead.

'How long have you been awake, love?' He makes a move to walk over but stops.

'It smells delicious,' she croaks.

He smiles. 'Only spag bol,' he tells her. She asks him for some water and he moves quickly to pour some into a mug. She struggles to sit up. He takes one step towards her and passes her the mug. Her hand shakes a little as she drinks greedily. 'How's your arm?' He wants to sit down next to her but pulls up a chair instead.

'What've you got there? Wine? Can I have some?'

He fetches the bottle and pours. She takes a deep sip and groans. 'Hm, that's good.' She looks at him and lifts the mug a little. 'Arm is instantly better.'

'Seriously.'

'Seriously.' She smiles.

'Good.' He nods.

'How long is food going to be?' She holds out her mug.

'How long does it take to boil up some spaghetti?' He smiles and gives her a refill.

'Long enough for me to have a fag. D'you mind?' She pulls out a pouch of tobacco.

'Not at all. I used to. Reformed.' He laughs and looks at the bottle. 'At this rate I'd better get another. Won't be long.'

'I'll put the spag on.' She struggles to get off the couch.

He takes her elbow gently and helps her to her feet.

'How much did you win?'

'Two hundred and fifty quid.'

'You should've put more on.'

'I would've put more on. I was broke. Accounts locked, cards swallowed.' He passes her a plate of food.

'Crap,' she says and takes it, greedily spooning a forkful of pasta into her mouth. 'This is good.' She nods.

'Thanks. 'Bout the only thing I cook with confidence.'

She looks at him and chuckles, her mouth full. He grins back. 'So you don't gamble?'

'I tend to lose.' He twists pasta round his fork.

'You won't lose any more. You'll have an eighty per cent success rate.'

'Only eighty?' He chews and looks at her.

'Human error.'

'What? The chess pieces not performing as they should?'

'Yep, and the bloody ball being round and all that.'

He laughs. 'Can't get the staff these days, ey?'

'Precisely. Someone always moves the goalposts.' She pushes the plate away. 'Luke, I got to hit the sack.'

'Of course. You must be shattered.'

'Literally.' She rolls her eyes.

Lukas notices with a pang that he finds her utterly charming and her company delightful. He instantly dismisses his realisation as an indulgence and, ultimately, delusion. He gets up and looks around the room, then asks if he can get her anything else or help her. She shakes her head and looks at him.

He moves towards the middle room. 'Mark says you have his bed.' He pulls the curtain aside that separates the two rooms.

'Where is he sleeping?'

'He's gone to Warrington for a job.'

'Now? What does he do?'

'No idea. You saw the compound.'

She walks through into the bedroom. She pulls off her top. Lukas looks at her back, the abrasions on her shoulder and elbow. 'I feared it was dislocated, you know.'

She turns to him. 'So did I. Now do you mind?'

'Sorry.' He feels himself blush. He asks if she needs anything for the cuts and points vaguely at her.

'I'll be fine.'

Lukas nods. 'I'll get you some more water.'

'That would be nice,' she says as he walks out.

He sits by the window and mulls over the day. Then he finishes the wine and looks at the couch. A few stains where her wounds have left faint marks. He runs his hand over the fabric then looks around for a blanket. To go to the bathroom he needs to walk past her. He pulls the curtain aside carefully and sneaks to the door at the other end of the room. He takes extra care coming back, having just flushed the toilet.

'Luke,' she whispers.

His heart misses a beat. 'Hm?'

'Thanks for looking after me today.'

'It's OK,' he whispers.

'Night, night.'

'Night, night.' He waits a brief moment, then tiptoes back to the living room.

Chapter 29

'So it could be today or tomorrow the SIMs are delivered.' Mark stirs his coffee. No milk, five sugars.

'If the Special Delivery do their jobs over the bank holiday.'

'Did you put your number on their cards?'

'No. Didn't know how to.' Lukas leans against the wall.

'Better this way anyway.' Dannii chews while she speaks.

'And why is this then, Miss Brains?' Mark points his fork at her and squints.

Dannii stops chewing and glares at him. ''Cos then Luke can call them whenever it's convenient for him and not—'

'And not halfway through something else,' Mark says then laughs.

'She's right, Mark. Pavel will be concerned but put two and two together. If my number was on the SIM he'd call immediately and we could indeed be caught up in something else.'

'Like what, Sherlock? Playing internet detective and leaving your cyber pawprints all over the world wide web and a few notepads to boot?' Mark scowls and shakes his head.

'I wish you'd let it lie. I know I made mistakes. We actually had some breaks from it, didn't we?'

'Like almost ending up in hospital.' Dannii frowns, still chewing.

Mark leans forward towards her. 'Not me, love. I'm your prince, your knight in shining armour, here to the rescue.'

Dannii pushes her plate away. 'More likely the frog, waiting to be kissed,' she says. Lukas laughs out loud.

'Oh, you're going to kiss me, are you? Fabulous. I can't wait, hear that?' Mark turns to Lukas. 'I told you, didn't I?'

'Yes, you did.' Lukas looks down at him.

Dannii makes to get up. 'Yes, you did what?' she asks and steadies herself on the table.

Mark smiles broadly and leans towards her. 'I told him you fancy a shag, love.'

Dannii pulls the table top up sharply. Mark ends up on the floor with his breakfast in his lap. 'Bloody idiot.' Dannii grabs her jacket and rucksack from the sofa and storms out of the flat.

'Bloody idiot, she's right,' Lukas shouts and runs after her.

'That bloke has serious issues.' Dannii marches ahead into Manor Park.

Lukas struggles to keep up with her. 'We both know that, can you not just – hey, can you please slow down? We've an agreement.'

Dannii stops and stomps. 'That agreement does not include me being verbally abused by a deranged, homophobic, Scouser ex-cop with a chip the size of Liverpool on his shoulder. Why don't you keep him under control?'

Lukas catches up. 'You're doing quite well on your own, love. You just decked him,' he says. Dannii shrugs. 'He doesn't mean it. He's just a bit, well, weird. His background has helped us enormously so far.'

'As has his violence and complete lack of self-awareness. He could've killed that MacFarlane bloke.' She slows down and stuffs her hands in her pockets.

'I agree. His methods aren't very politically correct; that's why I think he wasn't just police.'

She turns to him quickly, her eyes narrowed. 'I thought security. Are you thinking more Special Branch?'

'Definitely special training. He knows a lot of inside stuff and has a great memory for cases and places.'

She kicks a stone, dithering like a little girl. Lukas smiles. She is fiery. 'I need some clothes,' she says, defiantly, pulling at her tracksuit bottoms.

Lukas scratches his nose. 'The only shops I've seen are charity shops.'

'Oh, great.' She rolls her eyes.

'You shouldn't have any problem finding something nice there, love, size-wise, your figure being sort of middle of the road.'

'Middle of the road!' she explodes in his face. 'You two balloons really know how to treat a woman. Where are they?'

Lukas steps back. 'What?'

'The shops! And I need money.'

Lukas pulls a wad of notes out of his trouser pocket. She snatches the cash and slaps half of it back into his palm.

'That way,' Lukas stutters and points towards the high street.

Dannii turns and marches off.

He rings Mark. 'I've lost her.'

'You what?'

'You heard.'

'You bloody knob!' Lukas hears Mark bashing his mobile repeatedly on something and holds the handset away from his ear until Mark talks again. 'Well, she's no great loss to us. She's got a screw loose anyway. And, was it all worth it? What did we learn?'

'We got some background.'

'Great. I'm so happy for us. Why am I hanging out with you anyway?'

'I've no idea. You found me.'

'What's the plan now?'

'I'll try the mobiles tomorrow.'

'I'm going for a pint. It is New Year's Eve.'

'Lunchtime. Suit yourself.'

'I will, thanks. You think she'll be back?'

Lukas finishes the call without answering.

'How badly pissed are you?' Lukas says when he joins Mark in the Commercial at nine o'clock. 'And why here, the cop pub?'

'They're all on duty, mate. Heard from Ursula Andress?'

'Fuck off,' Lukas says and takes the pint Mark offers him.

'Pissed on your chips there.' Mark laughs.

'Thanks to you, who set her up.' Lukas necks half the drink.

'Why? What did I do?'

'Enough to end up on the floor.' Lukas finishes his pint.

'I've had worse. Anyways, I've been thinking about match fixing. Isn't that supposed to happen in the lower leagues only, or am I missing something?' Mark turns towards the bar and signals for two more pints.

Lukas tries to snap out of it. Today he's spent too much time fretting and walking around. It's New Year's Eve. Time to make some resolutions. He clears his throat. 'That's what I initially thought, too. But there's got to be a link with Mancunia. This whole nonsense started after I spoke to Moses Bradshaw. Anyway, your turn. What happened at the hospital? Did you speak to Franklin?'

'Of course I did. The old bugger isn't exactly happy.'

'What did he say?'

'Hang on! Let me start from the beginning.' Mark takes the top of his fresh pint. 'I figured Franky to be the victim of mistaken identity. The police may think so too, and that's not just Stinky, but the whole of CID. Our mate Stinky has to report to someone too, has to run things properly, at least on paper. So I figured that Frank will have some kind of protection in case the bastards try again. An officer outside his door for example. From Stinky's point of view this kills two birds with one stone: he's following protocol by having the victim protected and at the same time he might get lucky and catch you trying to sneak in to find out about the real attackers. Thus proving your innocence by stupidly visiting the old bugger in person. So he's going to put a copper that's loyal to him outside Frank's door. Someone who'll report back to him first. Someone who can keep a secret. I figure from her highness's rantings that the old bugger doesn't have too many friends or family. So anyone visiting could be a potential link to either you or to the people behind the attack. And this is where the waters are becoming murky: did Stinky ever talk to you about anything else but a burglary?'

Lukas thinks. 'No. I was questioned about my conversation with Frank. I was told that what happened later was a violent burglary.'

'What was taken?' Mark narrows his eyes.

'No idea if anything *was* taken. Does it matter?'

'It matters hugely. First, if you were questioned in connection with a burglary then you can't be done for GBH or attempted murder or manslaughter or the likes. And why should the burglar, or plural, come back and attack Frank again? Surely what they were after was at the house. And only Stinky knows if anything was taken.'

Lukas nods. 'That means the officer is standing there, waiting for me to prove my innocence.'

'Quite. And again only Stinky knows that. These guys went to Cheetham Hill to do the blogger over and nothing else and they got the wrong person. There was no computer equipment at Frank's house and the guy's whole profile is wrong. He's far too old and comes across as far too simple to be an international blogger. They might be thugs but they're amateurs; they were sent by someone else. They reported back to whoever sent them, got a bollocking for beating up an old age pensioner and put back in whatever cage they're kept in.'

'Not the same people as yesterday.'

'Absolutely not! Yesterday's attack was a proper outfit, as we established. And my visit to Frank proves it if you only stopped butting in and let me continue with my story. Your round, by the way. So I figure there's no easy way into Frank's room. And assuming there's a copper stood outside, there's no safe way in as a civilian. You'd have to be family, medical staff or the law. Family's out. Medical? No good at bluffing. I was always the good copper.' Mark laughs. 'So there's only one disguise I know and one disguise I have: the bloody uniform that's hung at the back of the wardrobe.'

'Didn't you have to give that back?'

'I didn't bother. Thought it would come in handy.'

'Isn't it out of date? And what about ID?'

'There's always ways, mate. Anyway, I puts the thing on again, pull the cap down deep and set off. You and cyber-girlfriend still blissfully asleep, no doubt. I gets to the hospital just after breakfast, all hands busy. Copper outside the door alright. He's sipping a coffee. I figure he's been there all night, waiting to be relieved. He's got to be tired. He sees me, almost jumps up, smiles, thinks I'm going to put him out of his misery. Then he realises I'm a superior, so his smile sinks and he sits down again. Then he thinks he'd better get up 'cos I'm a superior. So he puts down the coffee, gets up and almost salutes. I tells him I'm from Bolton CID and that we may have a vested interest in the attacker, that he's on our database. The copper nods, looks puzzled but lets me through. I reckon it's not going to be long before he rings someone for confirmation of the rubbish I've just told him. So I got to be quick.

'Frank's in a bad way, black eyes, broken arm. Bloody bastards. He smiles at me. I ask him how he is. He likes that, smiles a bit more. Tells me he's mending. I tell him where I'm from and ask him to tell me about the muggers. Muggers, I says. Not burglars. They was right scrotes, he says. Plural. Skinheads. Young. Them tattoos on their necks. Boxer tattoos, like that Mike Tyson has on his face, but on their necks, he says. Old bugger points to the right side of his neck. Both of them? I asks. Yes, he says. He says they told him to stop pointing fingers at people. Says he had no idea what they were on about. They knocked him out after that and he woke up in hospital. I asked him about you. You were a nice man he says, although personally I'm not sure where he got that impression from. Anyways, Frank carries on, says you do this thing for the community, so they can all be safer, though if you'd ask the old bugger, you're wasting your time. Ryleys protect us, he says. Where were they? I asks. No idea, come to think of it, he says. But them kids are not with them? I asks. He says he's never seen them before, that they were probably from up my way, or Rochdale. Lucky me hip didn't pop back out, he says. Nothing broken, apart from your arm? I ask him. I'm tough, he says. He laughs. I thank him for talking to me and tell him he was a great help. I try and get away before someone gets onto me. Then he tells me that the other officer hadn't been very nice – he smelt bad. I got fidgety then. He tells me that he'd asked why they didn't look for the two scrotes but the officer wasn't even listening. I tell him to look after himself then I'm off out the door. The copper outside is on the phone. I wave to him. I could've been four minutes max. I go down the service stairs. Left my rucksack behind a bit of shrubbery. Pull off the shoes and uniform, got me sweats on underneath. Trainers on, off I go. One minute max. I jump over the fence to the roundabout. Police car pulls off the roundabout to my left into the hospital grounds. Coppers don't see me, which is lucky and damn close. I hail a cab to the station and here I am.'

Lukas smiles. 'Good work.' He feels adventurous after three pints. 'What's next?'

Mark leans forward and whispers across the table. 'We're going to pay two visits very soon.'

'Who to? Mancunia again?' Lukas rubs his hands.

'No, you twirp. We're going to visit the Ryleys. And then we're going to find out who those two tattooed scrotes belong to.'

At midnight, and with some difficulty, Lukas sends a text to Dannii's SIM card, wishing her a Happy New Year. By now he finds it hard to focus on the little screen. He checks the mobile every five minutes for a while then forgets about it over an unnecessary round of Jäger Bombs. When his phone beeps at 3am he is fast asleep on Mark's couch. Since he has forgotten to plug in the handset, the mobile switches itself off at about 4.30.

Chapter 30

Mark guides the BMW slowly and deliberately through Cheetham Hill, the rough end. Part high-rise, part two-up, two-downs. All council. Dog dirt, battered shopping trolleys. No pride in the famous British front garden here and maybe no point in trying to maintain one.

Mark's eyes scan the alleyways. His right elbow pokes out of the open window. Lukas is in the backseat scanning the rear. Five kids in black hoodies are following them on BMX bikes. One of them throws something which hits the car. Sounds like a half-empty soda bottle. Another pulls up next to the car and spits on Lukas's window.

Mark breaks abruptly. He reaches out of his window and grabs the kid by the front of his hoodie, pulling him right off his bike. The bike clatters against the car and onto the road. He puts his face right up the kid's. 'Ryleys,' he hisses at the boy through clenched teeth.

The other hoodies pull up. Multi-racial, thirteen to seventeen years of age. One or two make threatening noises, shaking their wrists rapper style. The rest look vaguely alarmed. Big mouth and nothing to show for it, Lukas thinks. But probably all carrying. The kid on the end of Mark's grip is wide-eyed but silent.

'Ryleys!' Mark shouts and head-butts the kid. The kid's nose starts to ooze blood and snot.

One of the older boys steps forward. 'Yo man, 'e's only fourteen. Your mother never told you not to pick on someone littler?' The boy sounds bright, but bored.

Lukas pushes down the lock on his door carefully. The hoodies are far too focused on Mark to notice him in the back seat.

Mark tosses the bloody-nosed boy into the gutter. The kid lands awkwardly. He doubles up in agony and starts to cry. The older boy looks at him briefly, concerned. 'Come on!' Mark hollers.

The whole gang jumps. Lukas too. He hits his head against the car roof. He sees the barrel of the gun. Its grip must be in Mark's left hand. He must have pulled it out from under the driver's seat. He taps the barrel on the window casing. The boys stare at it wide-eyed and motionless.

'The Junction,' the older boy says. He cocks his head. Puts his hands in his hoodie pockets. Mark tenses. The boy grins. 'What d'you want from Ryley anyway? He's going to rip your shrivelled balls off.' The boys laugh, and exchange hi-fives.

'Information,' Mark says calmly. The barrel of the gun has disappeared.

'Yeah?' The older boy struts. 'Why don't you ask us?'

'I tried, but your stupid mates are more intent on getting themselves hurt.'

The boy shoots daggers. 'You're in the wrong hood.'

'What about the old man the other day?'

The gang comes to life. 'Yo, that wasn't us.' The older boy steps up to the window. 'Old Frank nevva did anyone no harm, y'understand? And we didn't harm him. Protected him we did, looked out for him.' The boy jabs at Mark, and looks into the back as if to rally Lukas's support. The other boys step closer. They mutter that Frank is one of the hood. One of them. Protected.

'Who was it then?'

The boy turns to his mates for support. 'Not from here, ya? Nevva seen 'em before –'

The other boys shake their heads and look at the pavement.

'So you saw them?' Mark lights a cigarette. Lukas doesn't recall him smoke before. He offers one to the boy. The boy takes a few cigarettes with one hand and hands them out to his mates. He takes one for himself and allows Mark to give him a light.

'Saw them, yeah.' The boy turns round and checks with his mates.

'Saw them where?' Mark drums his fingers impatiently on the side of the car, and checks the rear mirror. This is taking too long. 'Come on, son, we haven't got all day.'

The boy shrugs. 'By the Co-op. They was dropped off. Walked the last bit.'

'Did you follow them?'

'Yeah. We wasn't sure who they was or if there was more in more cars. We was going to give them a hidin' but we needed to check.'

'With who?'

'Ryley.'

'And?'

The boy drops his cigarette on the ground and stubs it out. He blows his last smoke into the car. 'They got to Frank's first.'

Mark reaches for the boy's hoodie front. The boy shrinks back. 'You saw it?'

The boy looks round at his mates. They all study the floor and nod. 'Yeah, we did.' The boy looks sheepish. 'They was too quick. They was picked up again at the next corner. There was no time to get there.'

'And you didn't report it?'

'Ryley said not to.'

'Why not?'

The boy looks defiant. 'Ask Ryley.'

'What's your name, son?' Mark's voice has gone soft.

The boy shrinks back further. 'Who wants to know?'

'Just call me the big, bad monster from outer space. And if anyone's ever prosecuted over the attack on Frank and you don't open your fucking mouth you'll be done as accessory to attempted fucking murder.'

The other boys guffaw and elbow each other.

The older boy frowns. 'You going to speak to Ryley now?'

'You bet your ass,' Mark says in an American accent. 'Which one do I want?' Mark's hand is in his breast pocket.

'You want big Sean. Tell him Flea Blue sent you.'

'Flea Blue?'

'The Cheetham Hill Blue Boyz.' Flea smiles broadly.

Mark stretches out his hand at Flea. Between his middle and index finger he holds some red bank notes. Flea's eyes bulge but he keeps his cool, takes the notes and stuffs them into his jeans's crotch pocket, which is somewhere on his middle thigh. 'Yo.' Flea shakes Mark's hand fingers up. 'Anything else you want to know, bro?'

Mark shakes his head. 'Nah,' he says, and moves the car forward. The injured kid stands close. Mark smiles at him and pats him on the arm.

Chapter 31

The Junction pub is just round the corner. They park up and walk towards it. Both look round to check the damage the kid's bike has done to the car. Bit of street-cred. They glance up to see the Blue Boyz turn the corner.

Mark marches straight in. Lukas is unsure if he still has the gun. There appears to be only one person in the pub. Big Sean. A giant, as well as very obese. Mark walks right up to him. Lukas makes it about halfway, then two heavies in black block his way. Lukas looks from one to the other and tries to remember why the two should seem familiar to him. Both men are cross-eyed and identical.

Mark looks back at Lukas, smiles and looks the two bouncers up and down. Then more heavies, most of them heads completely shaven, appear from everywhere. Lukas counts eight. Nine including Big Sean.

'Sean, happy New Year.' Mark stretches out his hand. Big Sean looks up at him, his hands folded over his enormous belly. 'Flea sends me.' Mark takes a further step forward and widens his smile.

Big Sean groans and leans forward. He shakes Mark's finger tips and cranes his neck to look at Lukas. The heavies blocking Lukas step aside to clear the view. Sean looks back up at Mark. 'Why does he send you?' His voice is high and penetrating.

'Because I asked for you.'

'And he just volunteered my whereabouts?'

'Eventually, yes.' Mark smiles. 'Nice kid,' he says. Big Sean sits back. 'Frank Staines, Sean.'

'Are you the law?'

'No, we're at the receiving end too.' Lukas steps through the gap between the two bouncers. They let him pass. Big Sean looks him up and down and says nothing. Lukas continues forward. 'We think that the attack on Frank was a case of mistaken identity.'

'Yeah, and we want to find out who did it to pay them back,' Mark adds. 'We're mates with Frank's niece, the one who stays there occasionally.'

'Pretty face.' Big Sean is a man of few words.

'We –' Lukas starts, but Mark coughs discreetly.

'We just haven't got a clue where to start looking for them. And since this is your turf—'

Big Sean leans forward and interrupts. 'Yes, this is my turf. I do payback here.'

'Do you know who sent them then?'

'What are you saying?' Big Sean frowns. His heavies stir.

'I'm saying that Flea and his sorry lot saw the attack and you told them not to report it to the law. Were you turning a blind eye or were you paid off?'

Lukas looks at Mark. Surely he's not going to take on this whole lot. Big Sean says nothing. The heavies move closer. Then Big Sean starts to laugh. A short, stabby chuckle. He holds his gigantic belly. The heavies join in the laughter and eventually Mark does too. Lukas only manages a tense smile.

Then the room goes silent and the giant man speaks, serious again. 'Listen, you morons, this is my turf. No one does business here without my knowing about it. I don't know who this lot were, but if I find out, their arses are toast. We don't need the law here, like the other night, the place swarming and stinking of pigs.'

'Don't you want to get to the bottom of who did this?' Lukas says in disbelief.

Big Sean waves his hand. The heavies disappear into a backroom. Behind the bar the landlord wipes the pumps. 'What are you drinking?' asks the big man.

'Two pints of lager. Thought you'd never ask.'

'Three Stella and your own,' Big Sean orders the barman and gestures at the table.

Lukas and Mark pull up two chairs, then wait until the man has brought their drinks and returned to his place of duty. They drink in silence. Then Big Sean folds his hands as if in prayer. 'I'm not a bad man.' He looks at them ruefully.

Mark clears his throat. 'It must be hard to run a place like this.'

Sean nods. 'It is. People are hard up. The poor rip each other off. Everybody feeds off someone else. All the kids want to be gangsters. It's appalling.'

'And you're making sure people remain decent with each other.'

'I'm ruling with an iron fist. I got respect. For now. My family's always run the place, but times are changing.'

'They're after your throne.' Mark drinks.

'Everyone carries these days. It's only a matter of time. Might even be one of them.' Sean points behind him with his thumb. 'Et tu, Brute.'

'Latin, ey? I'm impressed.'

'A-level. I had good schooling.' Sean empties his pint and raises the glass towards the bar.

Lukas hangs on the edge of his chair. 'About these attackers —'

Sean looks at him as if noticing him for the first time. As if he is utterly superfluous. He turns to Mark. 'Who is he?'

'He's the one the cops are framing for the attack on Frank.'

Sean raises his eyebrows. 'Oh, a fellow victim. Welcome to Cheetham Hill.' He smiles at Lukas, who feels extremely uneasy.

'He's mates with Frank's niece,' Mark says.

Big Sean nods slowly. He takes a long time to make up his mind. 'We don't know who they are,' he finally admits. 'We 'aven't a clue.'

'Flea's gang saw them?'

'They might be able to identify them, yes.'

'But you don't know where to start looking.'

'Precisely.' Now the big man looks uncomfortable. Like he has been found out. Like he has lost face. Like he is not as influential as he would like to be after all. And having to admit this to strangers. He turns to Lukas. 'You're friends with Frank's niece, right? Part of the family. And family needs protecting. If you need me I'll help. But I really don't know who these guys are.'

'They had these tattoos—' Lukas starts.

Big Sean interrupts him, pulling a face. 'They all have them these days. Ugly.'

Lukas continues. 'These were quite distinctive. Like the one Mike Tyson has on his face. Except they had them on their necks.'

'Eddie!' Big Sean hollers. Immediately, another huge man enters from the back room. 'Sit down,' Sean orders. Eddie sits. The chair creaks under his weight. He must be twenty-five stone. 'Eddie,' Big Sean introduces him. 'My brother.' Eddie is different from Sean. Eddie has hair. Lots of it. Everywhere. 'Tell him,' Sean says to Lukas.

Lukas clears his throat. The man opposite him could kill him with a single blow. He is convinced of it. He has no neck. His completely round head sits like a balloon on his enormous shoulders. His eyes are as round as his head and completely black, as if he is wearing black contact lenses. There is no way of telling what goes on behind those eyes. The rest of Eddie is completely square. His hips are as wide as his broad shoulders. His arms and hands are huge, as are his legs. He looks like a man in a blow-up Santa costume. Except his bulk is not hot air and neither is it fat. Eddie Ryley is pure muscle.

'The two blokes who attacked Frank Staines,' Lukas begins.

Eddie twitches and looks at Big Sean sharply. Sean nods and smiles like a priest taking confession. 'Go on, son.'

Lukas looks from one giant to the other. 'The two blokes, they had tattoos on their necks. Here.' He points at the right side of his neck. 'Like the tattoo Mike Tyson has on his face?'

Eddie visibly tenses and looks at his brother. 'Can you two just go over there? Private chat.'

Lukas and Mark get up and walk away.

'Bingo,' whispers Mark out of the corner of his mouth.

'I saw it too.' Lukas nods. 'The tattoo rang a bell with Eddie.'

Mark smiles. They wait and watch the two big men arguing. Eddie points at them and Sean shakes his head, looking over repeatedly. Eventually Sean waves them back. 'My brother thinks we should kick your butts, but I explained that you know Frank.' He nods at Lukas. 'Also explained that the law wants you in connection with the attack. Just out of interest, were you there? Were you in the house? Just to get a complete picture.'

'I visited Frank earlier that day,' Lukas says. 'Checking up on the old bugger,' he lies.

Mark scowls.

Sean nods. 'Tell them what you told me, Eddie.'

Eddie shifts in his chair and clears his throat. 'Doesn't seem right to tell you, don't know you from Adam, but Seany says it's OK.' He pauses, gathering his thoughts, thinking slowly. 'I box, OK? I run a boxing club here for the lads, keeps them out of trouble. Gets rid of their aggression and all that testosterone. Used to be semi-professional, me. Did quite well for myself. Paid fights, etcetera.' Eddie pauses.

'Go on,' Lukas urges.

Eddie looks up at the ceiling. 'There was a chap – this is ten years ago – he had like a stable of fighters. From Bolton he was. Big Tony. Big Tony Jackson. Got himself into trouble.' Eddie pauses and looks at Sean as if to ask permission to carry on. Sean's hands are folded on his belly. He stares into the distance, smiling. Eddie continues, slowly. 'He had strong fighters. But he also paid people off.'

'He fixed the fights?' Lukas asks.

'They were big business. A lot of money involved. And Jackson, he was well scary. And yes, he paid people to win or lose. Good money.'

'Did everybody play ball?'

'No, they boxed.' Eddie looks confused.

'Did everybody take the bribes?'

'Of course not. I didn't. Some others didn't. But there were enough who did. 'Some people made a nice profit.'

'Were these fights legit?'

'Were they fuck. Just a bit of fun. Big money, though. Some well-known faces, too.'

'Ten years ago?'

'Give or take.'

'What happened to the guy?'

'Got told to stop fixing.'

'By who?'

Eddie looks sideways at his brother. Insecurely. Sean has woken from his reverie. 'The law, son, the law.'

Lukas perks up. 'Was he prosecuted?'

Mark puts his hand on Lukas's arm.

'No, it's OK,' Sean says. 'He was sent down for a while. Then he came back. Let my brother continue.'

Eddie clears his throat. 'He set up legit, boxing club in Bolton. No more paid fights. Just like me.' Eddie giggles girlishly. 'Called his joint Dolly Green Boxing Club. For the kids, you know. But it all caught up with him in the end. The fixing. Someone knifed him. Slashed his face. Bled to death allegedly. Never found out who did it. Nobody was sad to see him gone. Was a nasty piece of work.'

'What happened to the club?'

'Still going strong. His nephew took it over after the end of his career. Got too fat and boozy to fight any more. Got his ego dented in Vegas too.'

Lukas's stomach lurches. Mark butts in. He whispers loudly, 'Stan Entwistle.'

Eddie looks at Mark. Then he shakes his head and continues. 'Correct. And he runs it well.' He leans towards Lukas, as if to confide in him. 'The kids at the club, some of them have those tattoos, here, on their necks.' Eddie repeatedly points at the space where his neck should be, staring at Mark, frowning.

Mark gets up. Lukas looks up at him, astonished. 'We got to go. We'll be in touch. Thank you.'

Eddie raises a hand. 'Hang on, I was going to ask you something.'

Mark doesn't hesitate. 'It'll have to wait. We'll be back.' He walks away quickly. Lukas follows him but turns round before he gets halfway across the room. 'Just one final thing, who felt Jackson's collar?'

'Same pig that was snooping around Frank's house couple of days ago. Goes by the name of Briggs.' Sean spits on the carpet.

Chapter 32

'They're either too stupid to ask the Ryleys for permission or they don't know who's running the area. My guess is they don't know, which makes them non-gang related. It means that someone hired them to do a dirty when they aren't really used to doing dirties. Little inside knowledge. So this excludes Stinky; he knows the Ryleys. He put Sean behind bars over that kiddie sex thing. Of course, Sean doesn't know that we know that. Otherwise he wouldn't have volunteered the name. Strictly speaking it wasn't kiddie sex either. The boy was fifteen and Sean's half-brother. Boy would've never have reported it himself, of course, but his older sister did. She'd got out of the area years ago; she wasn't family. She came back to visit and he told her in strictest confidence. She went to the police. Sean went inside for four years. Out after two and a half. Rumour has it the lad hasn't slept since. He's grown up to be Sean's right-hand man on the streets. Has more pull with the kids although he's twenty-four now. He's also got a serious heroin habit.'

'And the sister?'

'She got it every which way, courtesy of Eddie and his mates. Ended up in hospital. Will never have kids. Didn't press charges. I guess Eddie made himself clear.'

'And how d'you know all this?' Lukas looks at Mark inquisitively.

'I was around then.' Mark holds Lukas's stare. Lukas looks away first.

They drive in silence.

Eventually Lukas stirs. 'They're thick. They should have suspected there's protection in Cheetham Hill and you don't just barge in like that.'

'Probably thought they could get away with it.'

'And so far they have. If we hadn't started asking questions Big Sean would probably have let it lie. He seems too bothered about losing face to admit he hasn't a clue.'

Chapter 33

'Vladi. It's me, Lukas.'

'Bloody hell! Britain's most wanted criminal. Where are you? How are you? What did you do to deserve this? I've worked out your little phone scam. Clever me, of course, but it only could've been from you, the great Houdini.'

Vladi has had a few, Lukas can tell. 'Excellent! What's happened in the last few days is a long story which I'll tell you some time, but not now.'

'Why not? I've all the time in the world,' Vladi cackles.

'Yeah, but I don't. I need your help. That night you rang me from the casino, the photos you took?'

'What, the snaps of the copper and the manky Manc?'

'Can you message them to me? I'll set up a new email account ASAP. For god's sake, don't send anything to the old one, it's been hacked.'

'Will do. What are you going to do with them? Buy yourself a get out of jail card?'

Lukas smiles. 'Don't think the photos alone are incriminating, at least not at the moment, but it'd be useful to have them anyway, just in case—'

Vladi butts in impatiently. 'How's the investigation going then, Monsieur Poirot? What amazing revelations have you unveiled? Murder, mystery, suspense?'

Lukas imagines Vladi's mocking grin. 'Certainly mystery and suspense. I can't say any more now, sorry Vlad. I got to go. Speak soon, send the photos.'

'Right away. And you must phone Pavel. He's been calling. Sounds worried.'

'OK. Now go away!'

'Ay ay, Kemo sabe.' Vladi rings off with a chuckle.

'Now what?' Mark looks up at him from his pint and paper.

Lukas pulls up a chair and drapes his jacket over the back. 'I just spoke to Pavel – something's wrong with my daughter. He didn't say what, just that she's withdrawn and gets touchy when asked if she's OK.'

'Bloke trouble.' Mark looks back down at the paper.

'Oy!' Lukas raises his voice. 'This is my daughter you're being dismissive about. She doesn't do bloke trouble.'

'How d'you know?' Mark squints at Lukas.

'She's my daughter.'

When did you last speak to her?'

Lukas thinks. 'It's been a while, a few weeks maybe.'

'So you basically haven't got a clue what's going on in her life. You've got every reason to be embarrassed.' Mark returns to the paper.

'Hey! Don't you lecture me about something you haven't got a clue about.'

'What's that?'

'Fatherhood.' Lukas shouts.

'Oh, you reckon?' Mark scans the page.

Lukas hesitates. 'You're a father?'

'Two lovely children, a boy and a girl.'

'I don't believe you,' Lukas says quietly.

'Mitchell and Sue,' Mark replies, just as quietly. Lukas's mind stirs. 'What's her name?'

'Lilian.'

Mark leans forward. 'What d'you think is going on with her?'

'No idea. I should speak to her.'

'Yes, you should. Send her one of them SIM cards.'

'Maybe meet her for a coffee.'

'Good idea.'

'Trouble is, she doesn't like me any more,' Lukas says.

Mark sighs. 'Why not?'

'Her mum told her all sorts of nonsense about me. Poisoned her, though that's a harsh word.' Mark just looks at him. Lukas continues. 'Lilian holds me responsible for her adolescent problems. Thinks they're to blame on me not being there, regardless of the fact that it was Liz who walked out.'

'Liz, the bitch.' Mark smirks.

'Just Liz, Liz Taylor.' Lukas smiles wryly.

'You're joking.' Mark guffaws. 'And by the way, mate, where does the "not any more" come into Lilian not liking you?'

'She's my little girl. We used to be close. She was always a daddy's girl.'

'Then you'd better get your finger out and become her best friend again, you twirp. All I see is you dithering. The fact that you haven't seen much of her recently won't exactly have enamoured her to you. You're the grown-up here, mate, now go and act like one. You're her father, for Christ's sake!' Lukas doesn't reply. 'And don't you start blubbing on me – you look like you're about to.'

'Don't be ridiculous!' Lukas snaps.

'OK, that's sorted then. So d'you think you could go and get us another pint now?'

'Idiot,' Lukas says under his breath and gets up to go to the bar.

'You got a message, by the way.'

Lukas brightens up and sits down. 'You'll like this! It's from Vladi,' he opens the SMS. '*Happy New Year to you too, lucky Luke. XXX*' He reads and swallows hard.

Much to Lukas's surprise Vladi's images display without problem. He shows the phone to Mark, who grins and scowls. 'Lovely. What a beautiful couple. Useful, me thinks, somewhere down the line.'

'I think so too.' Lukas smiles.

'Any sign of Miss Congeniality?'

'Nope,' Lukas lies. Shocked at having completely forgotten he'd texted her last night he is still digesting her reply. She had finished her text with "xxx". 'You think Briggs knows who she is?' he asks eventually.

'Why don't you ask her? You've got her number. New approach. Call the woman.' Mark turns back to the paper.

Lukas fiddles with the mobile. He texts '*Do you think Briggs knows who you are?*' He sends the SMS in reply to Dannii's text. And waits. The answer comes quickly.

Mark grins as the phone pings.

'*Do they heck! Just an innocent girl on a bicycle. Blogger never showed as far as they're concerned. Got to get back to business. Want any more tips? Like Mancunia to win 3–2 tonight? Yours truly, MM x*'

Lukas smiles and puts the mobile into his pocket, his heart beating hard.

'What?'

'She doesn't think so.'

'Is that all she says?'

'Pretty much. Any idea if the bookies are open today?'

Mark laughs. ''Course they are. It's match day. Here.' He digs a ten-pound note out of his jeans pocket. 'Put that on whatever she recommends, you cheeky git.'

Chapter 34

'Bloody hell! Did you see that? What a stonking save.' Mark jumps out of his seat, pointing at the TV.

'Sit down, you gobshite!'

'Wrong team.'

The Star is obviously a Rovers pub. Mancunia FC vs Manchester Rovers. The north Manchester Derby.

Mark turns round to face the hecklers. 'Ey, calm down! I'm a Liverbird, me. All I'm saying is not a bad save for a Manc shite.' Mark turns to Lukas. 'He's good, the kid. You said you spoke to him?' Mark drinks.

'Yes. Told you the story first night.'

'Tell me again.'

'Why?'

''Cos we might've missed something.'

'Like what?'

'Like why he's so brilliant and then he messed up that dodgy penalty the other day. Remember? First goal a dodgy penalty, the lady said. And wasn't it just.'

'I remember. You can read stuff into things, you know.'

'But you're investigating alleged match fixing. You told them to their faces. Why did you do that?'

'To provoke a reaction.'

'And? Did you get one? Apart from pissing them off so much you'll never have a cat in hell's chance of conducting another interview at FC.'

'Not so sure about that,' Lukas mutters.

'What? Anyway, tell me about young Entwistle again.'

'He's extremely shy. Handshake like a fish. Not like a goalie's, more like a flounder's,' Lukas says. Mark cackles. 'He's also extremely tall, but stoops as if he wants to disappear off the face of the earth. And he doesn't look you in the eye easily, but when he does all you see is a bottomless pit.

'What are you saying? He's on drugs?'

'Don't be ridiculous! No, there's something about him, and it's not just insecurity. Something's not right, as if he's experienced something that he can't digest.'

Mark leans forward. 'Aren't you being a bit too deep here. I mean you've talked to the kid for, what, two minutes?'

Lukas crosses his arms and shakes his head. 'I know that look.'

'You know that look, really? Sigmund Freud as well as Sherlock Holmes, ey?'

'Someone very close to me used to look like that,' Lukas says, quietly.

Mark leans back. 'Who, mate?'

Lukas's mobile rings. 'Pavel, hi.'

'Hang on, Dad, I'll pass you on.' Rustling at the end of the line. 'Here you go.'

'Hi, Dad.'

Lukas jumps up. 'Lilian? Shouldn't you be in bed? It's half past eleven.'

Mark's eyebrows couldn't be raised any higher and his lips silently whisper the word twat. His right forefinger repeatedly stabs his forehead.

'Lilian, love, you still there?' Lukas pauses, and paces. 'Lilian, sweetheart, are you crying? I'm sorry –'

'Dad –' she sobs quietly.

'Yes, Lil, sweetie, what is it?'

'Dad, did you hurt that old man?' She sniffles at the end of the line.

'Lilian, no!' Lukas runs his hand through his hair. 'No, darling, I didn't. I swear. I was there before. I was seen –' he peters out.

'It's just that—' she starts.

'Tell him. Tell him what you told me, Lil!' Pavel urges in the background.

'Gaby says you did it.'

Lukas is confused. 'Who's Gaby, Lil? You've never mentioned her before.'

'She's in my year. We hang out.'

Hang out. Like the kids outside his house. Lukas rolls his eyes. Patience. 'OK, how does Gaby know, darling? Did she read the paper?'

'Don't know if she did, but her dad told her. Please Daddy, don't be mad –'

Lukas grimaces. 'Darling, how could I be mad at you? I love you. Gaby's dad told Gaby that I hurt Frank Staines? Everybody thinks I did. It was all over the papers.'

'No, Dad. Gaby's dad knows. He's with the police.'

Lukas sits down. He stares at Mark, who stares back, mouths a silent "what?"

'Lil,' Lukas says quietly. 'Do you know what Gaby's surname is, sweetheart?

'Yes, Dad, she's Gaby Briggs. Her dad's a chief inspector or something.' She sounds scared.

Lukas stares hard at Mark. 'Don't worry, darling, they're just following procedure. D'you know Gaby's dad, Lil?'

'No. I don't know Gaby that well either. We just hang, you know?'

'Yes, I know.' He clears his throat. 'Sweetheart, I haven't seen you for ages. I'd like to take you out for a cuppa sometime, catch up, how does that sound?' He stares, waits for the reply.

'OK. Where?'

'It's your choice.'

'Blackpool, like the old days?'

Lukas laughs. 'Of course! One condition – you have to meet me en route, you know, now that the cops are after me.'

Lilian laughs. 'Are you serious?'

'Deadly!'

'Where?'

'Somewhere you don't normally go.'

'I'm coming with you.' Mark butts in.

'No you don't!' Lukas mouths. Mark scowls at him. Lukas shows him two fingers.

'Dad?'

'Yes, love, have you thought of somewhere?'

'Who's there with you?' She sounds hesitant.

'No one, just another customer.'

'Are you in the pub?'

'Yes, Lil. Have you thought of a place to meet?'

'I'm driving you. Make it somewhere quiet,' Mark hisses.

'Dad, what's he saying? Who is he?'

Lukas sighs. 'He's a friend. He's offering to drive us.'

'Oh, ok. Is he cool?'

Lukas laughs. 'I would not exactly describe him as cool.'

Mark raises his eyebrows and shows two fingers in return.

'Has he got a nice car?'

'Since when are you into cars, Lil?'

'This friend of mine – I'll tell you all about it when I see you,' she finishes quickly.

She asks if they will stay over. Lukas tells her to bring an overnight bag and they arrange to pick her up on Saturday morning. 'Don't tell your mother, Lil,' Lukas tells her. She says that she'll say she's going shopping with him and going by bus.

'You won't believe this but she says she goes to school with a girl called Gaby. She "hangs" with her.'

'Yeah, great,' Mark tuts.

'You'll never guess Gaby's surname.'

'Come on, mate, stop stringing me along.' Mark scowls.

'Would it help your imagination if I told you that Gaby's dad told Gaby that Lilian's dad, aka me, has beaten up an old age pensioner, just like it says in the papers?'

Mark stares at him. 'No,' he says slowly. 'You're fucking kidding me!' He jumps up. 'You're joking!'

'Coincidence?' Lukas asks.

Mark sits back down. 'Too much, mate. Ask yourself, why you?'

Lukas suddenly feels very cold. 'It's not a set up. It can't be. I've never done anything wrong.'

'You've gone probing.'

'Yes, but before? It must be coincidence. It's a big school, thousands of kids. Any idea where Briggs lives?'

'No idea, but I could find out.'

Lukas shakes his head. 'No, not now. Let's meet Lilian. I accept your offer of a lift. We'll see what she has to say. There was something she wasn't telling me.'

'A secret?' Mark leans forward.

'Something she wasn't happy to tell me over the phone.'

'Do you want another pint? I'm buying.'

'Yes, and a double Grouse, I need it.'

'Coming right up. Pint and Grouse tonight, Dolly Green tomorrow, then a weekend in Blackpool with daughter in distress and join AA first thing Monday morning.' Mark laughs and saunters up to the bar.

Chapter 35

'What are we going to say when we get asked why we're here?' Lukas looks over at Mark.

They are on their way to Dolly Green Boxing Club. It is snowing heavily, but not sticking. The wipers are doing overtime.

Mark is scowling. 'You tell me. You're the brains of the operation.'

'Twit!'

'Apparently.'

'I could pretend to do the education thing again. If young Entwistle told his big brother about my visit to FC, it would tie in nicely.'

Mark nods slowly. 'Makes perfect sense.'

'So who are you and why are you with me?'

'Im not with you. I'm going in to enquire on behalf of my son, who's about to start his studies in Manchester. I want him back boxing. He's getting a bit too soft.'

'Mitchell?'

Mark looks over. 'No, you blurt, my hypothetical son, Declan. Honestly!' He tuts. 'Can't go waltzing in there together like a pair of big poofs, just to enquire about their education opportunities. It's a boxing club, for flip's sake.'

Absent-mindedly, Lukas watches Mark punch the stirring wheel. 'And are you going to sign him up, your imaginary son?'

'I might just do that. Gives us a reason to come back in the future, if necessary.'

Lukas clears his throat. 'So, just to recap, we think someone has hired the thugs that beat up Frank and that due to their tattoos they might be connected to Dolly Green, Eddie says.'

'Correct.'

'Do we suspect anyone in particular? I mean, do we think Briggs is involved?'

Mark doesn't answer. Lukas glances at him. Mark's jaw muscles are working overtime. He looks over. 'What makes you think that?'

'We touched on this before. He's in the car taking pictures but he doesn't do the dirty work himself; he hires MacFarlane. Why couldn't it be the same thing with Frank? Him hiring someone else to do his dirty work? He lets me go, but then he comes back at night presumably to arrest me? I run, there's a chopper in the sky, all my cards are cancelled, I really get the heebie-jeebies and end up in Glossop. If he wants me to lead him to the blogger, how can I do this when I'm out here, in hiding? Why the heavy hand on one hand, so to speak?'

Mark is silent.

Lukas carries on. 'I remember Dannii saying how they wanted her to continue spreading tips, but not rumours. Briggs wants it to continue, the tips, the fixing. As she says, she's sure he profits from it himself, so why should it stop? So for Briggs, me out of the way and not leading him to the blogger is ideal; he can justify to those who want the blogger that the only lead to the blogger, me, is unobtainable. And he's in the clear. All he has to do is chase me a bit, hire the odd heavy hand. Watch my family, most probably. Create confusion. Wait until I resurface. In the meantime, he's cashing in.'

'You sound like you're getting the drift. Carry on.'

'Who wants the blogger to stop giving tips?'

'No one.'

'Exactly. They just want the blogger to stop telling the truth about all the other nonsense.'

'Correct.'

'So who sent the thugs to Frank's house?'

Mark pulls up. 'We're here. Here's the keys. Wait five minutes.' He gets out and starts to walk towards the old church.

Lukas opens the door a crack. 'What are we hoping to find?'

Mark turns, spreads his arms, grinning, then scowls.

The building is imposing. For a boxing club, anyway. Lukas expected some crummy sixties concrete prefab Portakabin, like his little church in Stretford. But this is, or rather has been, a proper Edwardian beauty. Neglected, maybe, the car park showing signs of wear and tear, chewing gum, litter, broken fencing. Lined up against the walls of the church are three Portaloos, which suggest a lack of plumbing inside. On closer inspection the church windows are covered in mesh, the original stained glass long gone. To the left-hand side of the massive wooden door is an outdoor ashtray, the ground beneath it covered in sleet and cigarette butts.

He opens the door. A musky church aroma mingles with many years' smell of leathered fists on sweating bodies. Three boxing rings, the largest one central, a smaller one to either side, temporary training rings, to be taken down for fight night. Facing the main ring some more permanent seating, which would make any Health and Safety representative reach for his telephone. He also notes several makeshift compartments, an office and rudimentary changing rooms. On the walls posters depict famous boxers, others advertise future fights. Patterned carpet covers the floor, mouldy at the edges and in need of a clean.

A few water dispensers are situated near the rings and several portable gas heaters glow in the corners. The lack of permanent heating and ventilation explains the musky odour. Lukas wrinkles his nose. Hardly the establishment he expected the former featherweight champion of the world to run. More like a seedy Bronx club.

By one of the rings Mark is in conversation with a hefty man in his thirties. The man wears a beanie hat and fingerless gloves.

Lukas walks the other way, towards the offices. Through one of the open doors he sees a monitor and keyboard which is being operated by a woman, judging from the stockinged legs below the table. He clears his throat as he steps up to the door.

'Hiya,' she shouts, before he can say anything. 'You're here with the permit, love?' She gets up from her desk and onto her impossibly high heels. Mini-skirt, low-cut blouse. A wide, gappy-toothed smile. Lukas puts her at about sixty. She adjusts the skirt downwards, wiggles towards him and stretches out her hand. 'Hiya, I'm Linda.'

He shakes her hand. 'Lukas. Lukas Novak.'

She keeps her hand in his and and giggles. 'The permit, love?'

He smiles back. 'I'm sorry, love, I haven't got the permit.'

She withdraws her hand and looks genuinely shocked. 'Why not? They said it were going to be delivered today. Stan won't be happy.' She puts her fists on her hips and pouts.

Lukas laughs. 'I'm sorry, love, I meant I'm not the permit man.'

She looks aghast. Then suspicious. 'Well, who are you then?'

Before Lukas can reply, the hefty man shouts over. 'Make us a cup of tea, will you, love? Two sugars each. Warm us up a bit.'

She giggles. 'Alright, Carl.'

Carl and Mark walk towards them. Linda hesitates and squints. Then she points a finger and starts to scream. 'It's – it's you!' She's jumps up and down. 'It's him. It's Bill.'

Carl looks at Mark, then looks at her.

Mark smiles at her. 'Hi, love, I'm Mark.' He stretches out his hand. 'Here to enrol my son. He's gone a bit soft, you know.'

'No!' She shakes her head vigorously. 'You're not having me on. Not again. You're him, I can tell.' She stomps her foot.

'Look, love, you've got me confused with someone else.' He turns to Carl. 'She's got me confused with someone else, mate.'

'No,' she screams. 'You're Billy the Bullet, I should know. We went out, remember, you paid for these.' She lifts her ample breasts with both hands.

Mark laughs. 'Seriously, love, I don't know what –'

Lukas watches Carl taking Mark by the elbow. Carl is very serious. 'Billy the Bullet?' he asks. 'You don't look like the Bullet to me—'

Linda shouts, 'No, he's done something to his face, but his eyes are almost the same, and his voice, and the way he walks and all.' She turns to Lukas. 'You recognise him, don't you?'

Lukas smiles, apologetically, and looks at Mark, who stares back raising his eyebrows. 'I'm sorry, love, I don't know the gentleman in question.'

Mark rolls his eyes. 'The gentleman in question used to be a semi-pro boxer. She's got me confused with him.'

'No I haven't.' She stomps. 'And to think that we used to go out.' She looks him up and down. 'You always was a bully, never a sodding gentleman.' She walks up to Mark and slaps him in the face.

'Hey, love!' Lukas steps forward, and takes her by the arm.

She pushes him away. 'Don't you start. I still don't know who you are – you with him?' She points at Mark.

'No, I'm an independent journalist—

'The press? Ha!' she cries. 'That's all we need round here. Why don't you write about this, the resurrection of Billy the Bullet, after we all thought he was dead.'

'I'm not with the papers, love. I wanted to have a word with Mr Entwistle about—'

'Well, I don't think he'll welcome you with open arms after he's learned you came here with him.' She points a finger at Mark again.

'I'm not with him –' Lukas, too, points at Mark.

Carl still looks at Mark. He shakes Mark lightly by the elbow. 'I'm confused here. Our Linda says you're the Bullet and you say you're not. Now, I've never met the man, before my time, but our Linda's not daft.'

'You could've fooled me,' Mark says, under his breath.

Carl shakes him a bit more. 'You watch what you say, sunshine. D'you know the Bullet?'

'I know of him, but like yourself, I've never met him.'

'D'you box?'

'Do I heck.'

'He's lying!' she screams. 'Used to be the best boxer in the club. Massacred the lot of them, he did.'

The front door opens. Two youths walk towards them. Carl still holds Mark by the elbow as Linda shakes a fist at him.

'Oy, what's going on here?' The older of the two youths, hands in pockets, swaggers right up to their little group and looks them in the eye. Lukas puts the lad into the rat category. Bad teeth, bad skin, small pupils, smells of weed. The usual black, shiny shell suit, baseball cap, hoodie. The other youth looks identical, but smaller, younger and not quite as streetwise, yet.

Carl lets go of Mark. 'It's OK, Dean, just a misunderstanding.'

'Yeah? You sure? Who are these?' He nods at Mark and Lukas.

'I'm here to sign up my son, so he can become your best mate,' Mark replies, his smile turning to a scowl.

Dean laughs. The other lad joins in. 'Let's see what he's made of first, if he's hard enough.' Dean says. The youths share a rapper's handshake.

'Don't you worry, lad, he's well hard for you.'

The lad turns and frowns at Mark.

'Don't you listen to him, Dean, he's a bloody liar!' Linda screams.

Dean steps forward towards Mark. He takes his hood down and unzips his jacket. 'What was that?' he hisses. 'What've you done to upset our Linda?' He is right in Mark's face. The right side of his neck sports a large tattoo, similar to the one that Mike Tyson has on his left temple. Mark swings his head back for purchase and headbutts the youth right on the nose.

Lukas hears the crunch of bone. Linda screams. The kid falls to the ground, blood shooting out of his nostrils. Carl grabs Mark by the shoulders. Mark elbows him in the throat. Carl goes down.

Lukas holds on to Linda, who screams and kicks. Mark, blood running down his face, goes up to the other kid, and pulls his hoodie down. He looks at the right side of the boy's neck, then pushes the boy backwards.

Linda screeches. 'Run, our Darren, he's mental!'

The kid stumbles away, further into the building. Mark runs to the door and disappears. Lukas lets go of Linda. She is crying. So is Dean. Carl gets up slowly, holding his neck.

Lukas clears his throat. 'I'm sorry – what a maniac! I'll come back another day.' He hesitates. 'Is there anything I can do for you?'

Carl crouches down by Dean's side. 'It's alright mate, we'll look after this. You better not have anything to do with him though.' He nods towards the door. 'Whether he's the Bullet or not.'

Lukas smiles and raises a hand. 'You!' Linda walks up to him and shakes a fist. She glares up at him through a curtain of mascara and tears. 'I'll tell our Stan, all of it. And Mr T'll be wanting a word, too. He'll have you!' She kicks Lukas in the shin.

He stumbles with surprise. 'Love, honestly, I—'

'Get out!' She points a finger at the door. 'Just get out, you and your mate. He *is* the Bullet and you're not kidding me.'

Lukas retreats quickly and hobbles towards the door.

Chapter 36

No sign of him. No sign of the bloody idiot. At least the Beemer is still there. He looks around. No one following. No one here at all. Still snowing but not sticking. He presses the button on the remote key. The car flashes its lights and bleeps twice. He gets in the the driver's seat. Can't find the wipers. Never driven one of these before. Luckily it's automatic. Still manages to make it lurch somehow.

Two hundred yards down the road he spots him. He must have run quite a bit to get so far. Idiot. He pulls up beside him.

Mark gets into the car. 'Drive.' Lukas accelerates away. Mark looks at him. Lukas stares straight ahead. Mark looks out of the side window, then turns to Lukas again. 'Was it something I said?'

'No, something you fucking did.' Lukas hits the steering wheel hard. 'Are you going to tell me what the fuck is going on? Billy the Bullet?'

Mark shrugs. 'What do you want to know?'

'Whatever the fuck it is you're not telling me, you twirp.' Lukas swerves into a sleety lay-by and stops the car. He gets out and paces up and down.

Mark opens the door and swings his legs out. 'Do you really want to have this conversation here on the hard shoulder of the A58 in the fucking snow or would you rather have it in a warm, civilised manner, in the pub?'

Lukas steps up to the car, and bends down to Mark. 'I want to know what I've been missing. Seems to be rather a lot, so a rough summary will suffice for now. And you have blood on your face.'

Mark pulls his handkerchief out of the ocket of his trillby and dabs at his nose.

'A bit higher.' Lukas says. Mark dabs a bit higher. Lukas nods. Mark then tosses the handkerchief into the road. He squints up at Lukas through the snow. 'And? What d'you want to know?'

'Are you who they say you are, the Bullet?'

'I was, but now I'm not.'

What's that supposed to mean?'

Mark gets out of the car. 'I was undercover.'

'Doing what?'

'Undercover police work.'

Lukas turns to face him. 'Don't get fucking smart with me!'

Mark frowns. 'I was undercover as a boxer at Tony Jackson's boxing club.'

'Why?'

'Because he was fixing fights, you blurt. Eddie Ryley told you so himself, remember. I was investigating.'

Lukas stands, hands in pockets. 'You must have been very successful to have paid for your girlfriend's boob job.'

Mark rolls his eyes. 'It was all part of the character. And yes, I was good.'

'And well paid, obviously. An excellent horse in Tony Jackson's stable.'

'What are you getting at?' Mark squints.

'All the time we were sat at the Ryleys' you knew all about Eddie Ryley and Jackson and that Dick Briggs sent Jackson down, yet you feigned surprise at every corner. Pretending to discover, with me, all these fantastic revelations; how everything was staring to fit together –' Lukas shakes his head.

'There's more,' Mark says quietly.

'I'm not sure I want to know any more. I asked you if I could trust you. Hell, I even put a good word in for you with Dannii, who wouldn't trust you as far as she could throw you. Yet you played me right from the start.'

Mark smiles. 'As I said before, Sherlock, you're not the brightest button in the box.'

Lukas grabs him by the collar. 'I trusted you, because you convinced me that I should. You made me believe we were on the same trail.'

Mark grabs Lukas's hands, and tries to prise them off. 'We are, mate, don't you see? It's Briggs's trail we're on.'

'Are we?' Lukas lets go of Mark's collar. 'I don't think I understand anything any more.' He looks around. A bus stop in the distance. He turns to Mark. 'At least have the decency to give me a few hours to clear out of your flat.' Mark nods. Lukas turns away and walks towards the bus stop.

He posts the keys through the letter box. On his way from the station he's bought some provisions and checked back into The Ridges. Now he heads through the park in the direction of the valley that leads up towards the Pennine Way.

'Come to see the planes?' the girl at the B & B had asked. She seemed to have no recollection of having met him before, just a few days ago. The child had been crying again in the back room. He assumes that the aforementioned planes would be up on the fells, above Glossop.

Beyond the factory, at the start of Doctor's Gate bridleway, a signpost to the Snake Pass Inn points east. He knows the pub from family outings over to Sheffield and the Derwent and Ladybower reservoirs. The bridleway gently winds its way up along a stream. Highland cattle and scruffy horses stand side by side in the winter mud. He passes a couple of neglected houses and workshops. In the distance he notices his possible ascent, too much of a hike maybe for a wintry day like today, but he promises himself to return at a more suitable time of year. For now he keeps walking towards the farm past the next gate.

He must cancel, postpone or change the date with Lilian tomorrow, as he has no transport.

His phone beeps. '*Where are you?*' the text message reads. He squints at the little screen in the sunshine. It's from Dannii.

He stops. '*I'm in Glossop,*' he texts back.

She replies instantly, '*So am I.*'

Lukas dials her number. She picks up immediately. 'Hiya,' she chirps.

'Hiya, love, what are you doing back in Glossop?' He's already turned around and is walking fast, back towards the factory.

'I forgot something,' she says.

'I've got bad news for you. I've just posted the keys to the flat back through the letter box.'

'Oh no! What's happened? You two haven't had a little tiff, have you?'

Lukas frowns. 'We've had a big one. He's played me after all.'

'No,' she says, dragging out the "o".

'I'm afraid so. You were right. Woman's intuition.'

'You said it, not me,' she says laughing. 'Where are you?'

'I'm on a walk, though I haven't come very far.'

'That sounds lovely. Where?'

'Up in Old Glossop, by the factory.'

'Can I join you?'

'Of course you can.'

Lukas hears her talk to someone, and say OK.

'I'll jump in a cab and see you in a mo.'

'OK,' Lukas says and puts the phone back in his pocket.

She gets out of the taxi minutes later. She looks radiant. Until now he'd never really noticed how beautiful she is. It's as if he's never looked at her before, properly. She smiles and her hair flows in the wind. As the taxi drives off she walks towards him in slow motion. Then she is close to him and she puts her arms around him and kisses him.

He can't move. 'What did you forget?' he asks, breathless.

She smiles. 'I forgot I left you here.'

Chapter 37

'I've had a good think. That's why I have to talk to you.'

'What about?' Lukas can't take his eyes off her. They walk up Doctor's Gate, together, the sun shining on a winter wonderland.

'What happened to Uncle Frank is my fault. Indirectly.'

'You used him as a base, yes. But they mistook him for you. It's their stupidity that's to blame, not you.'

'I led them to him, Luke.'

He laughs. 'That's exactly what I said about me.'

They walk. He fills her in on the events at Dolly Green Boxing Club and the subsequent fallout with Mark without divulging all the details. He is still digesting them himself. The scenery changes slowly along the farm track. Now the distant, lush mountains seem much more rugged than he had imagined. Close up, they seem hostile.

'I've a possible plan of action.'

He looks at her and smiles. 'You sound determined. What is it?'

'An action plan for getting you your story, if you're still interested.'

'Of course I'm still interested, love. I'm currently just not quite sure what story I'm supposed to be writing. I set off to investigate match fixing in football and have now got caught up in what looks like a personal vendetta of an ex-undercover copper who masqueraded as a semi-pro boxer.'

'And to top it all, the subject of his vendetta is the very DCI that wants you in a GBH case of mistaken identity, which made you go on the run to Glossop. And now you're walking up Doctor's Gate with the very blogger you tried to find in the first place. Exciting stuff.'

He turns to her. The wind tugs at her hair. She could do with wearing a hat; it's cold enough. She smiles at him as he carefully brushes a strand of hair off her face.

'Tell me your story,' Lukas says.

They are sitting in the Royal Oak on Sheffield Road. She'd wanted to call in for a drink saying she was parched. He said he needed one after the day's events. They both sip on pints of Guinness and port, as a winter warmer.

'I always wanted to be a boy,' she starts. 'Don't know why, but I think my dad wanted me to be one, too. I had only boys' toys; mind you, I wasn't interested in dolls. My dad took me to football matches when I was tiny. That's when he was still fond of me, when I was small and cute and he could show me off. I used to sit on his shoulders so I could see better.' She takes a sip of her drink then continues. 'I started playing football when I was seven, made it through school and into the youth teams. Got the piss taken out of me by the boys initially, but I fought back. I broke a boy's jaw once, though I'm not proud of it. He started it but I almost got expelled. Funny old world, isn't it?'

'Unjust. Did you play in an all boys' team? How did you fare?'

'I was better than most boys on the pitch, but I was going nowhere when I got to mid-teens. I wanted to play at top level, but that wasn't possible as a woman, still isn't today. So I quit. I learned trombone, and joined the National Youth Orchestra,'

'Wow, you like classical music?'

'Yes. Then I took up horse-riding and won a few competitions.'

'You're starting to impress me. You don't have to, you know.'

'That's not all. I even won a national art competition. Don't you see, I grew bored quickly and as soon as I'd succeeded, and proved myself, I went on to the next thing. My friends and classmates got fed up with me being so bloody good at everything. I tried not to be pig-headed, but at the same time I couldn't let anyone else win if I could beat them. That would've been dishonest, wouldn't it?'

'Of course, but I bet you didn't have many friends,'

She laughs. 'No, I didn't. I only ever socialised with the people who were into the same thing as me. When I moved on to something new I didn't keep in touch with my previous mates and they didn't either.'

'Presumably because for them it had been such a pain in the bottom that you were always so bloody good.'

'Presumably.'

'I'm fairly intimidated myself.' Lukas takes a sip.

She laughs and slaps him on the back. 'You're not serious, Luke. Anyway, once it got to picking A-level subjects I ended up with more than anyone else in the school. I was just interested in so many things. All my other stuff went out the window. I was studying all the time and now I had to prove to myself that I could have my cake and eat it. At this point I was working a lot with boys. I was taking economics, politics and maths, subjects considered male subjects. The boys I studied with were bright and I went out with a few of them. I also took up running to clear my head and go over my revision.'

'When did you sleep?'

'I always thought I'd sleep when I'd made it.'

'And did you make it? What came after school?'

'It all changed when I went to Oxford after a year off travelling in south-east Asia.' She finishes her pint and asks Lukas if he wants another, then orders the same round again.

'How on earth did you fund Oxford?'

'Scholarship.'

'And you studied politics and economics? I think I'll get me coat –'

'Actually, Luke, I found it too easy and too dry.' She looks straight at him. 'It was all bullshit. There was no challenge. Student nightlife was great and I got sucked into it. I seriously got into trance music and clubbing. I didn't agree with the DJ's choices so I bought a pair of decks and started spinning myself.'

'Naturally,' he says.

'Everybody loved me. I was the first female DJ spinning in mainstream clubs. And I was posh. I made quite a bit of money and I stuck quite a bit of it up my nose.' She pauses. 'Does that shock you?'

'No,' he lies. 'We've all done stuff,'

'It was a fantastic time and a crazy lifestyle. I didn't sleep. I had lots of partners and loved it. All the seriousness was gone and I was enjoying life. I felt free. Success and drugs made me believe the hype I was living. For the first time in my life I was happy and fulfilled, and not tempted to move onto something else. I got a record deal, remixed some tracks, you know, the Fat Boy Slim way. I was released on a small label only, but online my stuff went viral.'

He looks at her for a while. She holds his gaze, eyebrows raised. He clears his throat. 'Love, I'm stuck for words. I am in the presence of Wonder Woman.'

She shakes her head. 'I believed I could sustain the pace, but I paid for it later. I eventually had to put the degree on hold, because I got invited to do Ibiza. I did four seasons, then I was finished. Burned out.' She leans back. 'Four summers on virtually no sleep, little food and lots of sex and drugs. In winter I was catching up on my fan base in the UK. It was crazy. I didn't even attempt to see my family, and lost contact with nearly all my friends. I didn't have proper relationships with anybody. I was as thin as a rake and seriously unhealthy. I chain-smoked. I was 23, sleeping with 17-year-old airheads.' She pauses. 'Sorry.'

He smiles. 'It's OK, Dannii, go on,'

'One morning on a downer I watched some lads play football on the beach. I can do that, I thought and joined in. They found it hilarious that I kept falling over in the sand. I thought it was too until I realised they were laughing at me, not with me. I was an embarrassment, staggering around mid-morning, high as a kite, with a fag on the go, pretending to be cool, which I definitely wasn't any more.'

'I'm sorry.'

'Don't be! It was my own fault. And I want you to know. I hate secrets.' Lukas swallows on the lump in his throat. 'I returned to Oxford. Slept an awful lot. Went for walks. Depression struck. I dragged myself through it somehow. Tried to be strong. Started running again.'

'I want to tell you about my brother, sometime,' Lukas says quietly.

She nods and pauses. 'In the autumn I picked up my studies again. I had an awful lot of explaining to do to be allowed back in. I tried to make up with my dad who'd shunned me for my DJ lifestyle. Apparently, I was an embarrassment and had to prove myself before he'd accept me back into the family fold. He shunned me just like he shunned Uncle Frank for not having a "proper" education. He's a bloody tyrant. That's why my mum left him and is now happily farming sheep in New Zealand. She basically ran away from him.'

They sip their drinks. Lukas listens.

'I don't blame her. He'd been carrying on with this wannabe posh woman called Gaynor for a while. My mum's more a Linda McCartney type, and Gaynor convinced him he could do better than eating veggie sausages with a woman dressed in dungarees. My mum literally got wind of it because she smelled Gaynor's loud perfume on him.'

'Oh, love, you've had it hard. I can't believe you're such a balanced person.'

'I'm not balanced at all inside. I'm quite insecure. That's why I pretend to be a male blogger and hide behind an old man.'

'Go easy on yourself, love. Are you in touch with your mum?'

'Not much. I was so little when she left. She's explained that she needed to leave it all behind, which made me feel bad because "all" included me. But then I realised I didn't really miss her, so I told myself to stop feeling sorry for myself. Be tough.'

'And that's what you've been doing ever since.'

'Story of my life –'

'Tell me about Frank.'

'Gaynor made it quite clear who was boss and which direction the family was going to take from now. She considers herself upper class, so fur coat and no knickers we went. My dad's an architect, a strange and ambitious choice of career for a working-class lad. He did well for himself and had no problems fitting into the class upgrade Gaynor had in mind for us. But Uncle Frank, his brother, didn't fit at all and was swiftly struck off the Christmas card list. Not that he was ever able to read Christmas cards, being illiterate and all.'

'Unbelievable. Family is such an important unit.'

'Yep. Mine was ripped apart so early, there wasn't much hope for unity. I was in the way of their new life with two small children, seven and eight years my junior. They were glad when I was out, so they happily paid for the football and the weeks away with the youth orchestras. And I didn't mind missing out on their family holidays.'

'And your father hasn't changed his mind to this very day?'

She shakes her head. 'He's very unforgiving and doesn't really want me in the family fold. A DJ, for Christ's sake!'

'So what then?'

'When it was time to start life after Oxford I was at a loss. Real life, for the first time. I was still groggy from my exploits, with no idea what I really wanted to do. Teacher? Politician? No way. I wanted to travel again. I was running away from the responsibility of making a decision for my life. And I'm bloody starving now. Do you think we could get something to eat?'

'I'm told there's a great Sri Lankan down the High Street.'

'Have you been?' he asks as they walk towards the centre of town. They both have their hands buried deeply in their coat pockets on this cold evening. 'Sri Lanka, I mean, not the restaurant.'

She laughs and shakes her head. 'No, but I've always wanted to go.'

'Me too. See the elephants.' He smiles at her.

She smiles back. 'And the Tamil Tigers.'

He laughs. She is fast. She takes his arm. His heart misses a beat.

Chapter 38

They order after the recommendation of the beautiful Sri Lankan waitress. A set dinner for two, with a wide variety of specialities from the mouthwatering menu. Lukas is starving. He has chosen a bottle of Pinot Grigio and some water. He pours her wine. They clink glasses.

'In Germany they "prost" each other, you know. You're not allowed to drink before you've done that.'

She smiles. 'What do I do?'

He holds his glass up. 'You raise your glass like this.' She copies him. 'Then you look each other deeply in the eye and say "Prost".' She looks straight at him. He tries not to blink. Her smile widens as she holds his stare. 'It means good health. Pro sit, from the Latin.' He tries to look enigmatic. The mocking look disappears from her eyes and he sees something softer enter her expression. 'Prost.' He breathes, not at all Germanic, then raises his glass and sips.

'Prost, yourself, you old romantic.' She smiles and sips, too.

His heart stumbles again. He knows he's blushing. She doesn't speak, just continues to look at him. He is relieved when the food arrives; his body is in disarray, over one extended look. Is he cut out for this, as much as he wants to be near her? She dishes out the starter, meticulously. He watches her concentrate, feeling a sudden painful pang in his chest. It's ridiculous to react so strongly to little things like noticing how long her eyelashes are, even without make-up. Does she even wear make-up? He can't remember. The food smells delicious, unknown oriental aromas penetrate his nose, making his mouth water. She licks her lips in anticipation and his whole body goes into turmoil. He almost spills his wine as he reaches for his glass and drinks deeply.

'Dig in,' she says. 'Or is there a German ritual we need to follow first?'

Stuck for words, he shakes his head. Suddenly he isn't hungry any more. He wants to say something, something to explain himself. Fork in hand he stares at her.

'Luke, you OK?'

He nods and looks at her. She smiles. 'Yes, yes.' He snaps out of it. He spears a prawn and pushes it between his teeth. Unknown flavours explode in his mouth. Delicious nuances of herbs and spices he loves from Indian and Thai food mingle with vast amounts of black pepper, garlic and the zest of many lemons. 'Wow!' he growls. 'This is extraordinary.' He looks at her.

She is positively stuffing her face. 'Amazing,' she mumbles through a mouthful of bean sprouts.

Six different small main courses arrive, accompanied by mildly flavoured rice and a variety of small naan-style breads. Lukas has forgotten what he wanted to say to her, what he needs to say so badly that it robbed him of his appetite just a minute ago. They both go through the food as if there is no tomorrow. He observes her bashfully, watching her feed, her greed almost animalistic. The way she devours rather than savours stirs him in a deeply carnal way, awakening an overpowering desire to do to her as she does to her food, devour her completely. As he gulps his wine she looks up at him, innocently, smiling. He returns to his plate and attacks his food, swallowing large forkfuls whole, following her example.

'So you went travelling again. Where did you go?'

She wipes her mouth. 'Again, I ended up travelling around south-east Asia for twelve months; Japan, Korea, Hong Kong. I still had some money from the DJ-ing, and the albums were bringing in a modest stream of not so hard earned cash. Nevertheless, I travelled on a budget.

I don't like being stuck in some five-star, looking at life from above, drinking a twenty-dollar G and T.'

'I'd be the same. Is this where you encountered gambling?'

She nods. 'What really struck me in these countries was the fondness of virtually everybody I met, from small child to pensioners, for gambling in every shape or form. I don't gamble – I'm far too afraid of potential addiction – but I was fascinated by the amount of gambling that was going on. So I started going to the races, the casinos, the card dens. I watched the little gambling tables on the streets and the soothsayers on every corner.'

'I know what you mean. I've been to Hong Kong – more wine?'

'Only if you promise to carry me to bed –' She grins at him and flutters her lashes mockingly. He almost drops both his glass and his jaw. She laughs. 'Only if I can't walk any more, I mean.'

'You'll have me under the table before you can't walk any more–'

She leans forward. 'I'll have you anywhere, Luke.'

He can't help himself but laugh out loud. The wine has subdued his awkwardness and he gestures to the waitress for another bottle.

'What also struck me was the presence of western ball games, predominantly the popularity of European football. Gamblers were betting on games, not just on straight results, but on offsides, fouls, yellow and red cards. The odds offered were sometimes outrageous and I asked myself how anybody could bet on strange circumstances like an own goal or a sending off and get the result right. People must be spending an awful lot of money. But then I'd watched ordinary people place thousand-dollar bets on individual numbers at the roulette tables.

'One day, in Hong Kong, I bought a nice dress and went to the New World Hotel rooftop casino. For the sake of not being mistaken for a prostitute I even gambled a little. I felt like a fish out of water. Maybe I should have one of the free drinks, I was thinking. Or maybe this wasn't the place I was looking for.

I took a taxi to the Sandringham, just round the corner and famous for its cream teas. And for its casino, which isn't as in your face as at the one at the New World, more like a gentlemen's club off Fleet Street. Quite small really. I sat down on a leather settee and ordered a G and T. I pretended to read the complimentary broadsheets. In a corner, behind some shrubbery, I could see monitors showing horse racing. In contrast to the relaxed atmosphere of the main casino the room in the corner was positively buzzing. Well shaded by drapes and mirrors, there was a lot of movement, human as well as digital. I was intrigued. I moved closer and pretended to watch the tables. Maybe I'd got a little close in my curiosity. The door opened and two boisterous Chinese men in their fifties spilled out.

'Hello, lovely lady.' They laughed and waved and stood right in front of me with wrinkly, half-moon eyes. I couldn't help but join in the laughter.

'Come, have bet, have drink.' One of them took my elbow. 'You like football, lady? Chelsea? Liverpool? You never walk alone?' he sang.

'Mancunia, actually,' I said as they ushered me into the room.

'Ah, Manchester. Good club, good team. United and City, too. Much money.' One of them steers me. The other jostles with a chair. Their friends cheer. 'Hello, lady, welcome!'

'Lovely lady, you wanna drink?'

'You wanna bet? Lucky lady, we make you very happy.'

I sat down. Betting sheets were put in front of me. I had no idea what I was supposed to do. The screens showed ball sports. Soccer. American football. Golf.'

'You want champagne? You try!' Another man had appeared next to me with a tray full of glasses. 'Champagne. Lovely, lucky lady,' he shouted and everybody cheered.

There were other women too, waitresses maybe or betting assistants. No hookers; this was the Sandringham.

The men cheered and clinked glasses with me. One of them leaned towards me, his face scarred from adolescent acne. 'Beautiful lady is lucky for us. Helps good omen. Big betting today. Your team, Mancunia.' he whispers conspiratorially. 'With you we win much money. Good omen.'

'What time is kick-off?' I was intrigued to say the least.

'Midnight, ghost hour.' He laughed a ghostly laugh. Of course everybody else joined in. This could be fun.

I gulped champagne and glanced at the clocks on the wall. 23:13 local time, 15:13 GMT. Time to pace myself. Food came out. Frogs' legs, chicken feet and locusts. More champagne. Some men ordered more food. Fillet steaks and Burgundy. Betting slips everywhere. In the food, on the floor. Chips and money all over the place. American and Hong Kong dollars. More men joined. I was introduced and complimented. Several matches were underway and being betted on. Mobile phones rang constantly.

A smart, young man had been sitting by my side for a while, his eyes fixed on the screens. Now he turned to me. 'You must bet. You can't lose. We get good tips. You wanna tip?'

'Would you like some champagne?' I took a bottle and glass.

'No, no, I must do this.' He took the bottle from me and cupped my glass-holding hand with his. 'You very beautiful lady.' He poured the drink. 'You will bring us luck.' He looked deeply into my eyes.

I smiled back. 'I thought you had good tip. Do you still need good luck?'

'Always need good luck of beautiful lady.'

We drank. Nice to flirt. No harm in it. I took his shoulder and leaned conspiratorially towards him. 'What's your tip?'

He looked at me with fire in his eyes. 'Tip? Your team? You wanna know?' I nodded impatiently. 'Red card. Just before break. Penalty for other team. 1–0 at break. Certain.'

I shook my head in disbelief. 'How can you be so certain? How do you know?'

He nodded towards a big mirror. 'They know. They tell us.'

As the game was about to begin the malt whisky came out. The proper stuff. Everyone cheered. Malt. I could do that. The men were pretty drunk now. Drunk with whisky and drunk with anticipation. The game was underway. Bets were still being taken. Mancunia did well until just before half-time when they fouled the opposition in the area. One of the players saw red. The resulting penalty was converted. The room went ballistic. And I wanted to know how all this worked.

I must have stared at the mysterious mirror a fraction too long. A door opened and a portly man in his sixties emerged. He was greeted enthusiastically by the crowd. He shook hands. Then he made his way over to me and bowed. 'Mr Li. Welcome, Miss –?' He stretched out his hand.

'Danielle.' Best to sound posh.

'Miss Danielle, what a wonderful name. You bring my customers luck. You bet yourself?' He showed several gold teeth.

I played bashful. 'I don't trust myself with betting –'

He laughed heartily. 'That's very wise. So you can't lose. Will you join me for coffee?'

Uh, oh. Suddenly I had a funny feeling about the situation. 'Sure,' I said. 'I think I had enough to drink.'

'You carry it well, not like my other customers here. Please follow me.' He led me into the room beyond the mirror. The other men slapped his back and shouted as we left the room. Chinese is not one of my languages.

He closed the door behind me and gestured at a chair by a big desk. 'Please.'

I sat down. The room was dark except for a desk lamp. Li clicked his fingers. A boy appeared through a hidden door. Li barked something. The boy bowed and disappeared. Li folded his hands on the desk and looked at me. The door opened and the boy was back with a tray. Coffee and Cognac. He poured the coffee and disappeared. Li uncorked the Cognac and raised the bottle towards me, like a question.

'A little.' Surely it was rude to decline.

Li poured generous measures into two heavy, cut crystal glasses. 'Cheers!' He lifted his glass. 'You have been travelling long?'

I talked about my travels through Asia. He asked how I liked it. I expressed my respect for Asian culture, especially Chinese, and how I was fascinated by the country and its people.

'And now you're in my casino, but you don't bet.'

I couldn't work out what this was all about. Rather than telling him fibs when I wasn't sure what he was getting at I decided to put my cards on the table. I explained that I was fascinated by the Chinese obsession with betting.

He laughed heartily. 'Yes, we enjoy betting a lot. We like to believe in good fortune.' He became more serious. 'Tell me, Miss Danielle, have you done much travelling elsewhere, to Spain, maybe, to Ibiza?' I seriously jumped. And wished myself far away from here. This man knew something about me, when only two hours ago I had walked into his casino, purely by chance. He smiled. 'Have I surprised you?'

'Why Ibiza?' Best not to give any more away.

He laughed. I reached for the Cognac. Li was serious again, his hands folded on the table. 'Miss Danielle, I have a proposition to make. Would you like to hear it?' I said yes, I would. 'Come back tomorrow morning. Ten o'clock. Meet me here. I will tell you my proposition.'

'Why not now?'

'Sleep on it. If you change your mind, don't come.'

'How can I change my mind if I don't know what it is?'

Li just smiled enigmatically. He stretched out his hand. 'See you tomorrow hopefully, Miss Danielle. Sleep well. And please leave this way.' He clicked his fingers and the boy reappeared. I followed him through the back door.

This is where I get jumped and taken away, if this is Hollywood, I thought as I followed the boy to the service lift. He never said a word as he led me out of the building.

Outside a limousine was waiting. The boy opened the door for me. 'Your hotel, ma'am.'

'Park Inn,' I replied, perplexed. They knew about Ibiza, but not where I was staying tonight. Interesting.

I spent the night pondering. My cash was getting low and it was about time to return home and make a decision about what to do with my life. Maybe one last adventure wouldn't be such a bad idea, providing it didn't go pear-shaped. Next morning I wasn't at all surprised to see the limo hovering outside. I got in and was taken back to the Sandringham, met by the boy and ushered upstairs .

Li's smile was broad. 'Miss Danielle. I knew you would return. Please.' He gestured for me to sit down. Coffee and croissants appeared. Li cleared his throat. 'Miss Danielle, I must apologise to you for being vague last night. I needed to make certain arrangements.' Here it comes, I thought. He pushed an envelope across the table. 'This envelope contains a one-way open air ticket to Paris and ten thousand pounds Sterling, for your troubles. You will receive another ten thousand upon delivery.'

'Delivery of what?'

'Yourself, Miss Danielle, yourself.'

'Myself? I don't understand –'

'There is someone who has an interest in you.'

'In Paris? An interest in me to do what?'

'I cannot tell you this, Miss Danielle, because I do not know.'

'How do they know I am here?'

Li reached under the table. A moment later a curtain slid back, revealing several monitors on the wall.

'Video feeds. Audio too, I guess. And whoever is taking an interest in me watches these. In Paris.'

'I see you understand now, Miss Danielle.' Li smiled.

'And what am I supposed to do there, in Paris?'

'I do not know this, Miss Danielle. But will you go?'

'If I don't know why, it's kind of hard to make a decision.'

Li's smile couldn't get any broader. 'It's a first-class ticket.' He paused. 'And it will get you back, closer to home.' This was of course true. And I could do with the cash. 'You don't have to make your mind up straight away, Miss Danielle. The ticket is valid for three months. There are two phone numbers with your ticket. When you decide to go, you must ring the first number to arrange your flight. You will also ring the second number and leave a message when you will be travelling.'

'So I can be met at the other end?'

'And receive a further ten thousand pounds Sterling, yes.'

'OK,' I said. I reached for the envelope and put it in my bag.

Li held out his hand. I shook it. 'It was wonderful to meet you, Miss Danielle. Have a good trip. Let me give you tip.' He was still holding my hand. 'Always look and dress your very best. Look glamorous. Beauty is your special asset. Now go.' He let go of my hand and bowed. The boy showed me down.

Two nights later I flew Cathay Pacific to Paris. I turned left when boarding the plane, a welcome change from budget long-haul travel.

Why I was being sent to Paris and who might want to see me there was still a mystery. I didn't really know anyone French, except some party revellers in Ibiza. And since Ibiza had been mentioned I assumed that's where the connection was.

And then I remembered Jean-Pierre. Surely not! Hazily, I remembered the yacht and his friends. It had lasted one night. He'd been the perfect gentleman. It was me who'd bolted. Despite modest fame, that kind of lifestyle freaks me out. He understood. Called me his butterfly. Said he would always honour the memory of me. That I was always going to remain part of him. That we should be friends. It had to be him. He was French. He was loaded. And there was a football connection. I readied myself to meet Jean-Pierre again.

And he looked just the same. A more handsome Depardieu. Ageless. It was just like before, in Ibiza. The clothes, the car, the sunshine. And the instant magnetism. I had taken Li's advice. I looked my best. And Jean-Pierre noticed, I could tell. 'Why am I here?' I asked as soon as we got into the car. He laughed. Told me to enjoy the ride. I did. How could I not, in a sixties open-top Mercedes cabriolet.

Paris was behind us. We drove for an hour. He asked about my travels. I kept talking, avoiding the questions I needed to ask.

His house, a dream of modern architecture. Tennis courts. Swimming pool. A lake, for Christ's sake. A butler and a cook. And a PA assistant.

Jean-Pierre showed me my room with a view of the rest of France. Then he invited me for a swim. Dinner was served outside, of course. Champagne, aperitifs, red Burgundy with the Chateaubriand. Jean-Pierre was charming but not flirtatious. A total gentleman. I forgave myself for once spending the night with him. An easy mistake to make. But it wouldn't happen again. All this wealth, this lifestyle, was well beyond me. We went for a stroll in the grounds. At a beautiful spot overlooking the lake he stopped. 'Dannielle,' he said, softly.

'Uh oh,' I thought out loud.

He laughed. 'Why so nervous?'

I explained that I wasn't nervous, which was a lie, but that I'd like to know why I was here.Then I stupidly mentioned money.

'Oh, Dannielle.' He looked disappointed. 'Do you not trust me to honour our deal?' He shook his head.

I explained that we might well have a deal but that I didn't know what it entailed. All I knew was that I was somewhere in the French countryside with a man I'd met only once before, when I'd been in somewhat of a haze, who owed me an explanation why he'd extracted me from Hong Kong and dragged me halfway round the world for twenty thousand pounds in cash, thank you very much. Jean-Pierre seemed to find this absolutely hysterical. He even slapped my back, which I found inappropriate, at this moment.

Then he turned serious and took my arm. 'Let's walk a little more. You have some questions.'

'Yes,' I said. 'How and why did you find me? You saw me on those screens at the casino, didn't you? How? Were you there?'

He smiled. 'Many questions. But I will tell you. I have video feeds sent to me from casinos all over the world. Important feeds. When things are different, you know, out of the ordinary.'

'You saw me?'

'Yes,' he replied and squeezed my arm. I ignored him.

'A western woman.'

'The only other women who go there apart from the waitresses are women of a certain persuasion, you understand. It was quite obvious you were not one of these.'

'Oh, thanks for noticing.' I squeezed his arm in return. 'You don't want hookers in there as it distracts the punters from the main objective, the gambling.'

'Exactly, Dannielle. You understand perfectly.'

'So was it coincidence that you saw me?'

'Yes. There are many images I look at, but I recognised you instantly. I said I would never forget you.'

He squeezed my arm again. This time I squeezed back. I had to win him over, because the next question was going to be the big one. I cleared my throat. 'So, most of the betting in that room was on detailed results of UK and European football matches.'

'Correct. We have special arrangements in certain casinos for this type of betting and we supply, you might say, the right atmosphere for our clients: good food, no distractions, etcetera.'

'You also supply something even more vital, don't you?'

'Yes. We supply a special subscription service for members only. For a modest monthly subscription we give out dedicated match information that has proved to be highly successful in its conversion rate.'

'And where do you get this dedicated information from?'

He smiled. 'I cannot tell you this, Dannielle. I would never reveal my sources.'

'Is it legal?'

He turned to me. 'I believe it is legal for me to pass on this information. My sources have to make up their own minds as to how ethical their choices are.'

'Everyone makes a lot of money?'

'Yes, Dannielle, everyone makes a lot of money. And almost everyone is happy.'

'Who isn't happy?'

'The ones whose conscience complains.'

'And yours doesn't?'

'As I said, I only pass on information. And this is why you're here.'

'You want to involve me?'

'You love football. I remember this from our previous – soirée. You're beautiful. And you're so unlikely to be involved.'

'Why am I unlikely to be involved?'

'Because you know a lot about football. You would not want to do anything to harm the game you love, would you?'

'No, not really, but—'

'Here's your chance,' he whispered. 'To save the game from within.'

'How?' I whispered back.

He started walking again. 'I want you to be my distributor. I need you to be invisible. You must not exist. You must be untraceable. And you must disguise yourself. Be the opposite of what you are. Be mad. Create a stir. Confuse people. Give them a little bit of what you are but make sure they think you're crazy. Smoke and mirrors. People will only notice the obvious and visible.'

'Until I came along,' Lukas says.

'Until you came along,' Dannii replies.

'Give it up.' Lukas leans across and kisses her softly on the lips.

Chapter 39

They leave the restaurant eventually, and walk down the road tipsy and giggling, oblivious to the drizzle that has set in.

'I enjoyed your story,' Lukas says. 'Really. A bit like a Hollywood movie. It'll take me quite some time to digest.' Lukas puts his arm around her shoulders loosely, and pulls her coat shut with the other hand. She giggles. 'You're going to catch your death if you don't zip up; it was very hot in there.'

'It's hot in here too.' She rubs her stomach. 'Boy, was it spicy!'

'Absolutely fantastic.' He pulls her closer, kisses her hair and breathes in deeply. She still giggles, and smiles up at him. Then she puts her arm round his midriff. He sighs and looks up into the rain at the night.

'You OK?' She tugs at him.

'Yes, I'm happy.' He still smiles at the sky.

'You're drunk.' She tugs at him more.

He laughs. 'Yes, happy and drunk. Could it be any better?'

'Could it, Luke?' she asks, quietly.

Suddenly, he remembers what he meant to say to her when she took his breath away so badly that he'd briefly lost his appetite. He stops and turns to her, then brushes the stubborn strand of hair off her face.

'I've been meaning to tell you something, Dannii.'

She looks up at him. 'About your brother?'

'No, about me.'

He watches her swallow hard. 'Look, I don't know how to say this, so I'll say it straight out.'

She looks alarmed. He touches her face. She forces a smile. 'This is the time when one usually finds out about some horrid STD or a criminal record or some dormant cross dressing fetish –' her words peter out.

'This isn't "usually", Dannii.' He stays serious. 'I've thought long and hard for some time, and especially since all this started, about where I am in life. What I'm doing, why my marriage failed and so on. I don't seem to have been doing very much, I now realise. Don't get me wrong, it's not that I'm not driven. I hope you've noticed that.'

She nods. He has his hand on her cheek and strokes her with his thumb. 'But I need to get my act together. There's so much going on in the world and it seems to be passing me by. I'm sat in the pub, safe, talking tall, but life is actually happening out there, and often I don't feel part of it.'

'Aren't we all like that sometimes, looking from the inside out, thinking that everybody else is having a great time?'

'Yes, that's true, like a rock on an island.' He laughs. 'I'll tell you about how I arrived at where I am sometime, if you want to hear it.' She nods and moves her face against his hand. 'But for now it's important where I go from here. This situation has really shaken me up. I've never been arrested before, for Christ's sake! And strangely, despite all the trauma, I feel more alive than ever. What's more, I feel I'm making things happen, through action. Whether my – our – decisions will be the right ones only the future will tell. But to make them decisively, now, feels right and makes me feel strong. I'm not dwelling on the past – that's for another day – but I will not go on as I have.' She nods and smiles. 'Sorry, love, I'm rambling. Tell me to get to the point.'

'Get to the point,' she whispers and kisses his fingers.

His thumb lightly traces the outline of her bottom lip. 'You know, sometimes it's time to leave behind what we've believed in, what we've learned during our childhood and our upbringing to be right and proper, because it's no longer applicable and doesn't hold true any more for our lives.' Lukas pauses, struggling to keep his line of thought. 'I might not know entirely what I want,' he says quietly. 'But I do know what I don't want.' He looks up at the heavens opening, then back down at her.

'Do you understand, Dannii? I don't want to be pussyfooting about any more.' She smiles. Encouraged, he continues. 'I don't want to wait and guess and try to read between the lines like a teenager. I've done it all before and it's always painful. I don't want to ache and constantly be hungry for something that's slightly removed from my grasp. Nor do I want conflict, never have. I want harmony and peace; maybe that's why I withdraw, sit in the pub where I know what's what.'

'What are you saying?' she asks quietly.

He notices a slight quiver and her eyes are moist. He hopes it's just the wind and the rain. He takes her face in both hands and shakes his head vehemently. 'What I'm saying, sweet, is that I want you to be in that peaceful place, with me.' He takes her icy hands, lifts them to his face and kisses them. 'I want you and me, simply, in peace and harmony. I don't want to go chasing around, longing, fretting, playing games, losing sleep, wondering if you're seeing someone, eating myself up.' He kisses her hands again and rubs them to warm them up.

'I'm not seeing anyone,' she whispers.

'Thank god.' Welling up inside, he rests his forehead against hers. He feels her breath; she is so close, and he holds her shoulders. 'You're shaking.'

'I'm so cold, Luke.'

He puts his arm round her, noticing how wet her coat is. Chilled to the bone himself, he turns her in the direction of the B & B, only a few doors away. A fire roars in the common room, but it is full of visiting builders.

He takes her hand and leads her up two flights of stairs and hastily unlocks the room door, almost dropping the keys. She looks around the tiny, cold space.

'You can have the bed,' he says quickly and gestures at the queen-size. 'I'll sleep on the floor. I'll make tea.'

'Luke.' She stands by the door, arms wrapped around her. He stops and turns to her, kettle in hand. The lump in this throat is back. 'I need you to warm me up.'

He puts the kettle down and walks over to her quickly. He wraps his arms around her and pulls her close. Her head rests against his chest and she breathes hard. He rocks her and strokes her hair. Then he notices her sobbing. He takes her head in his hands and looks her in the eye. 'Why are you sobbing, sweet?'

She sniffs. 'I thought for a minute you were going to tell me you didn't want me around.'

'Whatever gave you that idea?'

'I don't know, maybe it's just me, it usually ends in tears –' She gives a little laugh. 'Sorry, paranoid.' She smiles. He smiles back and kisses her cheeks, kisses her tears away.

She sighs and sits down on the bed. He sits by her side and leans forward to light the gas fire by the bed. During his first visit he'd cursed it for the proximity of its heat, now he is glad it is so close. 'Let's take this off.' He helps her out of her wet coat and leans forward to hang it over the back of the only chair in the room. He shrugs off his fleece and throws it into the far corner. Then he drags the blanket off the bed and pulls it around them. He rubs her hands, blows on them and kisses them. She reaches out and strokes his face with icy fingers. He keeps still, holding her gaze, returning her smile, savouring her touch. Then he kisses her cheek softly. She doesn't pull back, so he does it again. Her damp hair tickles his nose as he moves closer. She smells overwhelmingly fantastic, he tells her in a low whisper. She asks if it could be the curry he's smelling. He laughs and brushes his lips against her ear, which makes her pull in her breath a little. He plants butterfly kisses on her neck, aware that her arms lock around his shoulders, her fingers caressing the back of his neck. He moans into the nape of hers.

'What you said earlier, about not wanting to fanny about any more'—she pulls his head up and looks him straight in the eye—'I don't want that either.'

He nods and flicks on the bedside table lamp. 'Get in.' He pulls the sheets up.

'With all my clothes on?'

'On or off, whichever you prefer, but I need to lie down and hold you now, immediately.'

She slips in obediently. He pulls off her shoes, her socks. She loosens her trousers and he pulls them off. He rolls in beside her, kicking off his shoes. Then he turns to her and takes her in his arms, pulling her to him. She snuggles up to him and pushes her hands under his jumper. She is still cold, so he kisses her, gently on the mouth. She sighs and returns his kiss, innocently at first, but as his hands start to wander up and down her back, she pushes her hips against him and he can't help but return the pressure. Her lips open against his and he tugs at them with his own until it is her that shyly licks first her own lips, then his. He draws a sharp breath as desire slices through him like a sharp knife. He senses her smile.

'Feels good?' she mutters.

He moans in agreement and kisses her deeper.

Chapter 40

His eyes have been fully adjusted to the dark for some time. Never in his life has he experienced such abandon as in the last few hours. He'd pinch himself if his arms weren't asleep, holding the woman he loves. His nose buried deeply in her hair, he smells her scent intermingled with his own. He must stop doubting. She excels at everything she does, but she has made poor choices in her life, just like him. And their mistakes combined culminated in the most passionate lovemaking he has ever experienced. What he doesn't understand is why she is here and with him in the first place. Why not someone else, someone younger, more attractive?

She has not mentioned relationships. Is she going to turn out to be just another of the many mistakes he makes so regularly? Will she think the same about him when she wakes up? Or is it all just lust? He has only just met her, really. Alcohol-induced romanticism and emotional swings, paranoia, he tells himself. At least he is still able to rationalise. Sort of, anyway. And until she wakes he is going to hold her and smell her and know that he loves and wants her more than he can ever remember loving and wanting someone. Shut up and enjoy. As he holds her, first light creeps through the curtains, a hint of a new day to come.

The biggest surprise in the last two days had been the beauty that now sleeps soundly in his arms flinging herself around his neck upon her return to Glossop. He'd not dared to allow himself to acknowledge his feelings for her. He'd fancied so many, yet so few had ever known about it, usually with disappointing results. Nowadays he waits, unwilling to risk rejection. 'Every pot fits a lid' his mum used to say. It was easy with Markus. Lukas didn't mind comforting his brother's heartbroken and rejected. But it had hardly been love. Compassion, maybe, or pity. At that age he couldn't have cared less, nor known what love was anyway. Is he certain he would recognise it now? All he knows at this moment is that his chest is ready to explode with happiness, his body heavy with satisfaction, and that he'll do anything to make her happy and make her stay. Anything to hold her like this. She moves in his arms and turns over, pressing herself against him. He feels himself stir instantly, yet just continues to hold her, to let her sleep.

The smell of bacon cooking somewhere penetrates Lukas's nostrils. He needs to get up, needs to go to the bathroom, needs to re-think, needs to speak to Lilian. Reluctantly, he slips away and leaves Dannii snoring softly. He tiptoes to the bathroom, closing the door carefully, so as not to wake her. Mounted on one wall is a full-length mirror that he can't avoid. He doesn't understand what she could possibly see in him. He never really had a lean physique, ever. Personality, maybe. That's what people say when someone is big. He's been told that he can carry it off, his weight. At least he is tall, very tall for this country. Not some podgy little Brit, but of proper Polish-German build, with broad shoulders and not afraid of a jumbo-sized pig's knuckle and a few litres of beer. But man breasts, for Christ's sake?

Maybe he should try hill walking – he seems to be in the right spot for it – and a few press-ups. They say that walking is the new jogging. Go up to them planes, wherever they are, when the weather gets better. He wonders if she'd come along. If she's still here when the weather gets better. If indeed he is still here.

He turns sideways and looks at himself in the mirror. He breathes in deeply and sucks in his stomach, then lets it out again with a sigh. Then he curls up one arm and tenses his biceps, then stretches to make his triceps bulge. Johnny Weissmuller he is not. Not even John Wayne. More like John Goodman. Tall and cuddly. He looks at the shower, yet decides to give it a miss for now. He still smells her on him, and doesn't want to wash her off just yet.

He uses the toilet and returns to the bedroom, where she is propped up on one elbow, smiling. He mumbles something about the bathroom, painfully aware that he stands in front of her stark naked. Painfully aware of how she is looking him up and down. He forces himself to smile.

She lifts the sheets. 'Are you coming back in? It's getting cold in here.'

He quickly slips back under the covers, relieved to hide himself from her view. She wraps herself around him, arms and legs, and kisses him on the mouth, urgently. He makes himself respond, willing himself to abandon his doubt and allow him just to be, with her. He pulls her close and on top of him. She writhes against him; they fuse together in the tightest embrace. He hears himself moan with relief, that she's still here with him, that she still wants him. He can't hold her close enough. His hands travel down her back, down her sides, until he reaches her buttocks. He cups her in his hands, follows her movement. He runs his hands along her thighs by his side. He returns to her torso and gently strokes the side of her breasts, pressed firmly against his chest.

She moans, breathing hard in his ear. He pulls her tightly against him and turns her over onto her back. He worries about squashing her and tries to keep his weight off her, but she wraps her legs high around his torso, her arms tightly around his neck and shoulders, pulling him down, pulling him in. And he allows himself to let go completely.

'May I have an extra rasher or two of bacon, please?' Dannii says to the girl. Then she winks at Lukas. He's convinced the girl has noticed.

'Cost ya?' she says, without expression

'How much?' He looks up at the girl, seriously, dabbing his mouth.

'50p a rasher – it's organic.'

'We'll have four extra rashers then, please.' Lukas returns to his cereal, his face creased. He daren't look up at Dannii.

'Four?' the girl questions.

Lukas nods vigorously. Dannii kicks his shin under the table. He laughs out loudly, and pretends he's stifling a cough with his napkin.

'Want a glass of water?' The girl is still at his side.

He shakes his head. 'Just four extra rashers of bacon.'

Dannii digs around in her bag, shoulders shaking.

'Weirdos,' the girl mutters as she walks away.

They look at each other, grinning.

'You're hysterical,' she says.

'You bring out the best in me,' he replies.

His mobile rings. The new one. He looks at the phone, then at her. 'Let me get that. It's him.' He routes the call to speaker. 'Mark.'

'Listen, mate, I'm really sorry, I've been a bit of a cunt, leading you on and all that. I just wanted you to know that.' Lukas doesn't reply, but still holds Dannii's gaze. 'Are you there, mate? Look, I just wanted you to know that I'm sorry and I'd like to be back on board. But hey, you can tell me to fuck off after yesterday. I wouldn't hold it against you. Are you there, Sherlock? Will you say something, please?'

Lukas clears his throat. 'I'm going to have to call you back,' he says and ends the call.

'We're going to have to make a decision.' Lukas refills their cups.

'He's been lying to you from the start,' Dannii insists, leaning forward, both hands on the table.

'I know.' Lukas drinks. 'But he's known Briggs like no other for ages.'

'Briggs?'

'After yesterday we know there's a definite connection between pretty much everything that's been happening. To summarise, we know that the youths who beat up your uncle are regulars at a boxing club run by Jason Entwistle's brother, Stan. You know, the boxer. Was world-champion once. So there's a connection with Mancunia. Also, Briggs hangs out with Leroy Callaway at an inner city casino, like they're the best of mates. I've got a photo, here. Briggs, hence, is connected to Mancunia.' He fumbles through his messages and hands her the phone. Dannii looks at the photo and nods. 'The copper that arrested Jackson, who fixed the boxing matches, who employed Mark aka Billy the Bullet – what a stupid name – was Briggs. Who ended Mark's career in the force? Briggs. Who arrests me for the alleged assault on Frank? Briggs. Who takes pictures of me waiting for the blogger at Guide Bridge? Briggs. And who rings the hit man's phone, after the hit on us backfired?'

'Briggs.' She sits back.

'And now, guess who tells my daughter at school that her dad's beaten up an old age pensioner and will go down for it?'

'Who?'

'Briggs's daughter, Gaby.'

'You're joking.' Dannii stands up and leans on the table. 'What on earth is going on?'

'I don't know. But I do know that Briggs holds an awful lot of strings that lead to some huge knot which needs undoing.'

'Nicely put. And he's on my books. Gambler. Wants me to stop digging up dirt but continue to give tips. Wants the best of both worlds.'

'It's very hard to both have your cake and eat it.'

'Impossible. There must be a loose end somewhere. Something he can't control.'

'That's exactly the one string we need to find, the one string that holds everything together. When pulled, the whole knot will unravel and everything will make sense.'

Dannii smiles, then walks up to him and puts her arms round his neck. 'You should let Mark back in. He knows too much to be left out in the rain.'

He pulls her close. 'Apart from that, he'd be a dangerous adversary to have.'

'Nah, he's just a pussycat – just keep the lagers coming. Not difficult.'

He phones Mark. 'No, not in the pub,' he tells him.

'Why not? It's the perfect meeting place,' Mark replies.

'It's time to sort this out, Mark. I'll meet you in the Curly Cornet in ten.'

'Spoilsport.'

'It's too early for a pint.'

'It's never too early for a pint, mate, but if you insist, cappuccino it is.'

Lukas has ordered coffees and biscuits. Mark looks sheepish when he walks in. He sits down, beanie in hand. 'Alright?'

Lukas nods.

Mark stretches out his hand. 'I'm sorry. I really am.'

Lukas looks him in the eye, takes his hand slowly and eventually shakes it. He leans forward and talks quietly. 'I don't want to talk about yesterday. What's done is done. Let me make that clear. I also don't need any more apologies from you. Neither do I want any more tall stories or surprises. Can we agree on that?'

Mark nods. 'Yes, we can agree on that.'

'Can we shake hands on that?'

'Yes we can.'

124

This time it's Lukas who stretches out his hand. Mark shakes it gingerly. 'Handshake like a wet fish,' Lukas jokes. Mark shrugs. 'Let me summarise: I got into this because I was looking for a story. I thought maybe having a look at match fixing might be a starting point. There was an interesting online blog talking tall and I thought speaking to the blogger might be a good idea. I was also following the parties thing in the papers. The blog touched on these too. There's a lot of cover up about the parties so there could be another story.' Mark nods. 'So, all I needed to do was prod a little at Mancunia and all hell breaks loose. The alleged blogger gets beaten up, though this turns out to be a case of mistaken identity, which leads to a boxing club that's run by the brother of a Mancunia player. I'm being framed for the attack by a copper who's friendly with another Mancunia player. I'm being driven out of my house and into hiding. My bank accounts are frozen. An attempt to meet with the blogger against all odds results in a wild goose chase around Cheshire followed by a deranged hit man and with an even more deranged ex-copper in shining armour coming to the rescue. The latter in the shape and form of an alcoholic Scouse bloke with a violent streak and a shady past, who I've met in a pub in my new exile only a couple of nights before, i.e. you.'

'I resent the alcoholic bit,' Mark says.

Lukas continues. 'The Scouser, i.e. you, seems to know an awful lot more about me than I'll ever know about him, and for the sake of repeating myself, has a chip the size of Liverpool on his shoulder about the copper, or shall we by now say the bent copper, who's trying to frame me at all costs for something I didn't do. Why? This knot we're looking at needs to start unravelling, rather than get tighter and it's time for it to start happening now, before we get in any deeper. I need to know who you are if I'm to allow you near my nearest and dearest.'

'If that means you'll still let me drive you tomorrow, then thank you for your trust.' Mark finishes his coffee and gets up.

'Mark, I need to know who you are, why you do what you do and how you got involved in this, with me, with the whole situation.'

'Listen, mate, I agree to play ball, and I stand by my word. But I can't do this here, in a fucking coffee shop. It's after lunch, it's time for a pint, focus my mind, OK? I'm going to the Queen's, nice and quiet there. You do what you got to do, sort stuff out for tomorrow, whatever, meet me there, OK? Food's good too, if you're into solids.'

'What's she doing here? I thought she'd left.' Two pints of lager on the table, one almost finished. Mark is eating from a packet of crisps.

'Hi, moron. Nice to see you again, too.' Dannii turns to Lukas. 'I'm getting them in. Veltins?' Lukas nods.

'When did she come back? I thought you two had fallen out. Remember –' Mark leans forward. 'She's at the centre of this, y'know. Everybody gets hurt around her. Wouldn't trust her as far as I could throw her. Just like Briggs, she wants it one way and the other.'

'She wants it which way?' Dannii returns with the lagers.

'I don't know which way you want it, darling, but I'm happy to give it to you either way,' Mark guffaws.

Lukas sits down. 'She came back yesterday. After I got back.' He looks Mark in the eye. Dannii sits down by his side and blows a strand of hair out of her face.

Mark looks at her, then at Lukas. 'No.' He looks at her again. 'No, you haven't. You can't have.' He laughs. 'You're kidding me. You managed to pull her?'

Dannii gets up. 'I'm going outside for a fag, before I kill him.'

Mark's gaze follows her. He lifts his pint in a toast. 'Bloody hell, mate, I didn't know you had it in you. Blimey, the blogger and the beast!'

Before he can control himself, Lukas grabs Mark's collar and drags him off his stool. He pulls Mark's face right up to his own. 'Listen, you,' he hisses. 'We had a deal. Stick to it or you're out. And bite your tongue with her or I'll kill you seconds before she does.' Lukas butts Mark lightly on the nose and pushes him back onto his stool. A trickle of blood oozes from Mark's left nostril.

'Bloody hell, I'm impressed.' Mark dabs at his nose with a napkin.

'OK, you two.' The landlord strides over. 'This is your first and final warning! If you didn't have a lady with you I'd bar you outright. Behave.'

Dannii returns. 'What's happened?'

Lukas rubs his forehead and Mark dabs at his nose, laughing. 'He's just saved your honour, love. Give him an extra one tonight, will you?'

'Oy.' the landlord shouts across. 'Pack it in, you. I mean it!'

Dannii looks at Lukas. 'You OK?' Lukas nods.

'Ey, what about me? I'm bleeding.' Mark points at his nose.

'You'll live.' Dannii downs most of her pint in one.

'Wow, did you see that? A girl after my own heart.' Mark laughs.

'If he weren't watching'—Dannii nods in the direction of the bar —'I'd let you have the rest of this down the front of your pants.' Mark finds this hysterical.

Lukas slaps the table, hard. 'Enough! Both of you. Let's calm down and get on an even keel here. Stop bickering and sort out our mess.'

Mark puts the bloody napkin on the table and sniffs.

'For god's sake.' Dannii picks it up and takes it to the toilet.

'Thanks, hon,' Mark remarks, as she returns.

She sticks two fingers up at him and returns to the bar. Lukas overhears her making their apologies to the landlord, something about him and Mark being schoolmates and the best of friends, more drinks and could they have a look at the menu, please.

She comes back with two more pints of lager though Lukas hasn't touched his first one yet, and three menus tucked under her arm.

Chapter 41

'Tell me the truth about you and Briggs, Mark.'

'OK. It's best you hear it from me. Don't want you accusing me of holding anything back or lying to you and the missus.' He nods in Dannii's direction and clears his throat. 'About ten years ago, when I was still in the force – I'll try and keep it short – I was involved in a case of something fairly nasty, a sex thing of the role-playing variety, to put it politely. It had got out of hand, just a bit, to say the least. There were several ladies of the night affected, and they were all pretty upset. There was talk about some really disgusting stuff, but they were cagey, not very forthcoming with the identity of the bastards who did it to them. I wasn't directly in charge but I was called in by Manchester CID to help with paperwork. Guess who was one of the bigwigs in charge of the investigation?'

'Briggs.'

'Exactly. I'd dealt with him a few times before, but not closely. He ran a tight ship, was well known for it, even then. Anyway, he was in charge of parts of it. He was dealing directly with the victims. Incidentally, the ladies didn't report the abuse themselves. One of their pimps mentioned something to a friendly copper who passed it on to his superiors. If it was bad enough for the pimp to be concerned it must have been serious, 'cos you know what they're like, they're allergic to anything in blue.

'So now the investigation's official; you can't just brush cockroaches back under the carpet. As I said, to cut a long story – was anybody ever prosecuted? No. Not a single arrest. Were the ladies interviewed? Yes, but the paper trail was too short. I genuinely don't think they said anything usable in the interviews, but I also believe that Briggs didn't actively pursue the leads from whatever little they did say. Do you remember that Hungarian striker, that baby-faced kid, Miklos Kovacs? He apparently had a wild imagination when it came to eroticism. He and his mates were well known for travelling great distances to visit prostitutes who'd accommodate them. After all, you don't want to tarnish your own soil, do you? There was also talk of some southern players coming up for male bonding sessions with their mates. There was talk that they enjoyed the company of some experienced professional ladies that would cater to their specialist tastes – and would keep their mouths shut. Still some of the allegations got into the papers, just like today, just like those parties you're so interested in, but this is one generation later –' He laughs. 'They called themselves The Clan, by the way. They were all bent and deprived. Anyway, in due course the papers had to take it all back, issue an apology. Nothing ever changes. The bastards always get away with it.'

'Money,' Lukas states.

'And someone who looks after them.'

'Correct.'

'Go on, ask me, love. And tell your man here to be patient.' Mark looks out of the window.

Dannii clears her throat. 'How were you involved?'

'As I said, I was on the investigation. Much smaller scale than Briggs, but I had access to the paperwork. And computer files. There was a kind of a network in place, even then. Bit like the internet, but internal, police only. I was disgusted by the whole thing, that these shites should get away with blue murder. And more to the point, that someone was looking after them, mopping up.' Mark pauses. He leans forward. 'Remember Tony Jackson, the guy with the illegal fights who got stabbed in the end, uncle of Stan and Jason Entwistle?'

'Yes, he tried to go legit or so he said, but someone got him for what he did previously. What about him?'

Mark leans back, and looks straight at Dannii. 'It's true, I was working for him.'

'As a boxer. Lukas mentioned it –'

'I was undercover. I was fighting his bleeding fights, taking money to lose.'

Lukas rises from his chair. 'So you turn out to be Billy the Bullet after all. I still don't get why you couldn't tell me earlier.' Lukas paces up and down.

'It's classified, that's why. Classified that I was undercover. Nobody knows. It's better that way.'

'But does it really matter, after all these years? Couldn't you have told me something, I mean, let something slip?'

Mark laughs. 'Well, you haven't exactly behaved like a super-spy. You keep making mistakes, not very professional. I didn't know how far I could rely on you not to make any more – or to blab.'

'You arrogant tosser! I'm trying to run a safe, thorough investigation, avoid making waves, and you accuse me of being an amateur?'

'No, mate, I don't. I just want to avoid you getting hurt. I know your heart's in the right place, but this situation did stretch far beyond my reach and I think it's still ongoing. I think The Clan still operates, though with different players. What I know is not for the faint-hearted. People have been killed for less.'

'Jackson?' Dannii asks.

'Maybe. I could never produce enough evidence to nail Briggs for involvement.'

'His involvement in what exactly?' Lukas leans on the table.

'He's a gambler as we know. Even on your missus's books here. Used to be hopelessly addicted. Got himself into a mess financially. Loved the dangerous bets, high stakes. In another life he'd have played Russian roulette.'

'He bet in those fights? I need another beer. Love?'

She nods and gets up.

'Me too, please, hon. Yes, he did, but never openly. On the contrary, officially he was only there on police business, checking that nothing dodgy was going on. What bollocks!'

Dannii returns with the pints.

'But Jackson knew he was betting?'

'Jackson was taking his bets. Said he was his best customer.'

'You're bloody joking! So why did Briggs send him down?'

'To make a point, of course, Sherlock. No one in their right mind would send down their excellent source of income, would they? He did it to make absolutely sure no one suspected him of any involvement. Probably felt some kind of heat after a while.'

Dannii interrupts. 'Mark, if you and Eddie Ryley were boxing at the same time, how come he didn't recognise you the other day?'

Mark scowls then grins. 'Boxing at the same time is one way of putting it. Eddie re-arranged my face so badly I was out for a very long time. During which I looked a bit closer at the pawprints Briggs was leaving all over the network. Files he'd accessed, added and removed. I was building a nice case against him and his mop-up operation, stuff to do with the Kovacs investigation, but also Sean Ryley's case and a few others that may or may not be related. But just like you, Sherlock, I left my own prints behind on the network. I know F-all about computers. Suddenly there was an investigation about me – not against me, I hasten to add, but about my role and involvement in such dubious circles as Tony Jackson's. Someone reckoned I'd been "affected" by it. That of course was Briggs's work. He was trying to get rid of me. It was perfectly legit for me to access case files in relation to the prostitution mess, but I guess Briggs didn't like it. So he constructed this yarn about me being partially "turned" by the underworld and not fit to be a copper. I was allegedly "emotionally unstable" and a danger to impartial police work.' Mark draws commas in the air. 'Again, some other department took all this over and didn't realise it was a sham. They took it seriously, had me psychologically profiled and questioned about my boozing and the fact that the drug tests turned out positive for dope and charlie. I mean, what were they expecting? I'd been working underground for two years. We wouldn't even put the gloves on without doing a few lines. I didn't have a habit, by the way. I was well in control.' He raises his glass towards Lukas. 'After all, all the alcoholics are in AA meetings, whereas we're in the pub.' He laughs and drinks.

'And at the same time you were involved in the Kovacs investigation?'

'Desk job, mate, during my time off. My official job undercover and when not at Tony's was supposedly supermarket shelf-stacker, out of the way, so to speak. In reality I was sat at home with a sirloin steak on my face most of the time. And the force thought I wasn't working hard enough.' Mark laughs. 'So anyway, the outcome was they placed me on the witness protection programme. I gave evidence against Jackson. I felt like a fucking traitor. But he needed to go down for the stuff he'd done. That wasn't the bother. I just hated that I was indirectly helping Briggs, giving evidence in this case. 'Cos he framed Jackson, using me. He even tried to buy me. I hate the bastard for that. And indirectly I feel responsible for Tony's death a few years later.'

'Do you think Briggs was involved in that? Surely that'd be going too far even for a bent copper.'

Mark shrugs. 'I really don't know. Could've been a number of reasons why he was topped. In my view Briggs's aim was to deflect any attention away from himself by getting Tony arrested, so I'd be surprised if he was involved in his murder after so much time, but then stranger things've happened.' He drinks.

'So you got witness protection –'

'And my P45 since I was "unstable". Cheers DCI Briggs. Since my fizzog was in such bad shape I managed to persuade them to pay for part of some remedial plastic surgery, darling, to make me look half human again. They did a good job – private, of course. Hence Eddie not recognising me. But Linda identified me despite my new face. Mind you, she got much closer to me than Eddie.' He laughs. 'I did look very different then, had about five stone more on me, was blonde and blue-eyed. Paid the rest of the surgery myself, courtesy of the payoff, ta very much.' Mark finishes his pint, raises his glass to the bar to signal for another. 'You not thirsty, Luke? Was it something I said?' He chuckles.

Lukas sips at his pint. 'Witness protection, you got relocated,' he says. Mark nods. 'And presumably you were give a new identity?'

'Correct.'

'So your name's not Mark.'

'Nope,' Mark says and laughs.

'So what's your real name?' Lukas growls.

'Does it really matter? I've almost forgotten it myself, by the way. It's Joseph.'

'Does Briggs know you're a Mark now?'

'I'm only Mark to you, and to you, love.' He nods in Dannii's direction. 'My "real " protected name is classified, full stop. And it's best it stays that way. But I imagine Stinky's managed to look it up. I'm too dangerous to him.'

'Would he recognise you?'

'I'd have to assume he would.'

'Does he know you're in Glossop?'

'I'm not in Glossop.'

'The flat – is not yours?'

'Glossop Furniture Project. For the disadvantaged.'

'Where do you normally live?'

'Closer to where the Beemer parks. Lymm.'

'Why are you in Glossop?'

'Because of you, mate.'

Lukas sits down heavily. 'You didn't see my face in the paper, did you?'

'No.' Mark smiles smugly.

Lukas turns to Dannii. 'I'm going to kill him. He's still playing me.'

Dannii puts a hand on his arm. 'Luke, we wanted cards on the table. We're in the process of that. There's bound to be surprises.'

Lukas gets up again and paces. 'Dannii, don't you tell me you knew – not you, too. Please don't say –'

'Now you're really being paranoid, mate.' Mark finishes his pint. 'More?' He lifts his glass.

'Fuck off with your beer. You should be in the Priory.'

'I'll have another,' Dannii says.

'Good girl.' Mark goes to the bar.

'Promise? That you don't know him?' Lukas frowns at her.

'I promise I didn't know him before he dragged me into his car at Guide Bridge, cross my heart.' She kisses him quickly.

'Thank god for that.' Lukas breathes out heavily. 'For a moment I thought—'

'You must be joking.'

'He's back.'

'Doesn't even slur his words.' She giggles like a girl.

'Remember Mitchell?'

'Mitchell?'

'My son, you dork. I mentioned him twice. You still haven't made the connection.' Mark rolls his eyes.

Lukas thinks hard. He looks up at Mark. 'Pavel has a mate—'

Mark slaps the table. 'Finally!' He rolls his eyes. 'Fantastic powers of observation.'

'It bloody well is easy to spot, when you've orchestrated it yourself,' Lukas shouts. 'Mitchells, there must be dozens at Manchester University. How could I have known? I thought it was a coincidence.'

'No, you didn't spot it.' Mark leans back.

Lukas looks at Dannii out of the corner of his eye. She smiles encouragingly. He leans back and sighs. 'Pavel's mate from uni. The hacker. Found Dannii's or rather Frank's address, date of birth etcetera and the fact that you log on from Chorlton and Wythenshawe libraries. Which gave me the idea to log on from Glossop. Only I didn't realise I was leaving traces. But then even you did, Ms Wordpress.' Lukas slaps Dannii's thigh.

Dannii squeezes his hand. 'I don't think it's possible to do anything online without leaving traces.'

'Will you two stop, or I'm going to puke. I'm sure my son doesn't leave traces.'

'Let's hope he didn't and Briggs doesn't make the connection, otherwise we'll have to book another room for him at The Ridges.' Lukas relishes Mark's alarmed look.

'That's not going to happen, Luke. I'm sure Stinky won't dig that deep.'

Lukas has never seen Mark look so worried. He smiles. 'Tell me how you found me, through Mitchell? Did he hack me too? Maybe he hacked me and Briggs hacked him?'

'Look, I'll tell you, but only if you stop freaking me out. Bloody conspiracies. You can read too much stuff into stuff, you know.'

He waves his empty glass about, but Dannii is already on her way to the bar.

'Speak,' Lukas demands.

'Your son told my son, over a pint, good lads, that his dad is looking for this blogger, who talks about match fixing. His dad is interested in shedding more light on the footballers' parties and the scandal around them, possibly in order to write a new piece. And that seemingly unconnected his dad gets almost arrested and is on the run. Pavel mentioned this vile smelling police officer, at which point Mitch twigs and links the football connection with, it seems, the same officer who lost his dad, yours truly, his job six years ago. Mitch, clever boy, at the age of fourteen, remembers overhearing me shouting at the missus about this smelly copper being connected to the footballers somehow. That I couldn't prove anything, the copper was bullet-proof and that he'd tried to buy me. Which I'd refused, of course. And that was the beginning of the end of Mitchell's dad's CID career.

'Mitch phones me immediately, eager for old scores to be settled, and I've no trouble finding you in your local boozer, the same that the boys go to when they're out on the razz in Chorlton, and where you are, this and any other evening, drinking with that other pissed polack. I follow you home and tail your escape later that night. I wait for you outside the toilets at Urmston and sit on the train to Glossop right behind you. I see you read the paper and later watch you check into The Ridges. I'm guessing which pub you're going to go to, i.e. the closest one, which is the cop shop, which of course you don't spot. There I make your acquaintance.' Mark sits back and smiles.

'The flat?'

'Next morning I had plenty of time to organise some digs for meself and make them look authentically lived in with the help of a charity shop.'

'You make it sound so easy.'

'It is, when you've orchestrated it yourself.'

Lukas sits back. 'I think I'll have another pint. And a short. And make it a double, please.'

For the second time in a short while Lukas feels like everything he has taken for real has suddenly changed and the goal posts have been moved. He is glad Dannii is with him. His head spins as they walk back to the B & B. He tries to summarise mentally how his reality has been turned upside down again, another U-turn in a short space of time. It's almost enough to make him feel like he is losing control. And there is something else he remembers, something to do with her, some unanswered question. He is relieved she is still by his side, and looks forward to being inside, safe with her tonight. He unlocks the door to the B & B, and then to their room. He suddenly remembers, being back in the same place that the original conversation took place. He turns to her and touches her shoulders. 'Talking of tying up loose ends, what were you going to suggest to me yesterday, your possible plan of action? You never told me.'

'That's because we stopped talking, remember?'

'I remember clearly.'

Dannii giggles. Then she looks him in the eye, her face serious. 'I want you to speak to Jean-Pierre.'

'What will that achieve?'

'Nothing about this little investigation of yours, but it might help you get your story. Tell him what you know. Leave the police out of it. Tell him you love football and about your disgust about match fixing. Make something up – once this is all over.'

'And you would sort this for me?'

'I sure would.' She looks him up and down. 'Is there anything else that needs sorting?' Lukas smiles as she unbuttons his shirt.

Chapter 42

'So you think she's got a problem?'

'She didn't sound right on the phone.' Lukas wipes his mouth. 'It's ages since she's talked to me. She was upset about what Gaby Briggs said to her.'

'Understandably.' Dannii spears one of Lukas's mushrooms.

He pushes his plate towards her. 'But it's not just that. She basically used to blame me for everything she deemed wrong with her life, 'cos I wasn't there.'

'That's childish. Surely she'll grow out of that.'

'One would hope so. Liz probably stirs it too, that I'm not good enough or something.'

Dannii laughs. 'Sounds familiar. So your wife had a class upgrade as well?'

'She certainly did. The new hubby works in real estate, UK and Florida. Don't really know much about his business, but it does sound a bit shady in places. It's called Taylor-Made Estates. I don't know how much Liz knows about the business side of things, but she's certainly happy with the lifestyle. Lil embraces it too. Pavel is more sceptical, I think. Mind you, he's a Goth, so labels aren't high on his agenda.'

'So, let me wind back, your ex is Liz Taylor now?' Dannii grins.

'She certainly is.' Lukas smirks. 'Do you want to go for a quick walk before the drunk picks me up?'

She laughs. 'OK.'

With the weather brighter, sunshine turns the snow to slush. They walk briskly across Manor Park but the Doctor's Gate track has turned into a small river.

'Apart from the Gaby Briggs incident, did Lilian sound troubled?'

'Well, there was something in her voice, something I hadn't noticed before. An urgency, something wanting to come out. But the fact that she hasn't talked to me for so long and now she's confiding about Gaby, even agreeing to see me, makes me hope that maybe she's growing up and out of it.'

'Or maybe she can't relate to anyone at home?'

Lukas nods. 'That's crossed my mind, too.' He takes her hand.

'And wanting to go to Blackpool? It's like she wants to go back to her childhood.'

Lukas pulls her to him and adjusts her hat. 'You're very perceptive, you know.' He kisses her on the nose.

She gives him the biggest smile. 'I know. But do you realise the Pleasure Beach is shut at this time of year?'

'Is it? Bugger, she won't like that.' Lukas frowns.

'There's a traditional Christmas market and an ice rink, though. The grotto will be shut by now, I guess.' She smiles.

'She's probably a bit big for the grotto, at sixteen, don't you think? Do you want to come along?'

'And get the Scouser off your back?'

He smiles. 'To have a perceptive woman present might be useful.'

She laughs. 'You just want me to take care of Mark.' She beats his chest.

Lukas pulls her closer. 'No, I just want you with me.' He kisses her quickly. 'I just couldn't bear not having you near me.'

'OK. I'll come. We'd better get back, he'll be here in ten.'

'He'll be here in five, knowing him.'

'What's been keeping you? Been picking flowers in the park?' Mark drums his fingers on the car roof.

'Moron,' Dannii hisses. She gets in the front.

'What do you think you're doing, love?' Mark jumps behind the wheel and scowls at her.

'What does it look like?'

'It looks like you're sitting in the front seat of my car.'

'Well observed.' She smiles at Mark.

Lukas squeezes himself into the back, behind Mark.

Mark looks into the mirror. 'Tell me she's not coming, mate.'

'She's coming, Mark. We could do with some female intuition.'

Mark tuts. He puts the car in gear and pulls away from the kerb.

'You two hairy-arsed ruffians could well scare a young, impressionable girl,' Dannii says.

Mark leans towards her. 'Don't you be talking about my arse. Talk about Sherlock's as much as you want but you're not getting anywhere near mine, love.' Lukas laughs out loud. Mark looks in the mirror again. 'What's got you in such a good mood? Got some last night?'

Dannii hits his leg.

Lukas grins. 'Got plenty last night. Thanks for asking.'

'OK, OK!' Mark slaps the steering wheel. 'Too much information.'

Dannii leans towards him, smiling. 'We hardly had any sleep.'

'Shhh!' Mark hisses. 'Behave yourself.'

'It got really hot and sweaty, didn't it, sweetheart?' She turns round to wink at Lukas.

'Oy!' Marks shouts. 'You're getting out in a bit. No way for a lady to talk.'

'Oh, I'm a lady all of a sudden?'

Mark grimaces. 'No, love, just the same gender as a lady.' Dannii shows him two fingers. 'Same to you, love.'

'Do you know where you're going, Mark?'

'Didsbury, then Blackpool, though god knows why.'

'You offered, mate.'

'So, Kingsway, and then?'

'School Lane. Big Catholic church.'

'I know it.'

'There she is!' Lukas exclaims and points. 'God, she's grown.'

Lilian stands by the side of the road clutching a rucksack.

'She has your height,' Dannii observes.

'Fortunately for her she hasn't got your girth,' Mark adds and pulls in.

Lukas ignores him and opens the door. 'Lil,' he shouts. 'Get in.' Lilian is frowning as she looks in the front of the car. 'Come on, love,' Lukas urges.

She gets in. 'Who's this, Dad? And what do you look like?'

Mark takes off.

Lukas leans over to kiss her but she shies away from him, clutching the door handle. 'Lil, this here is Mark. I told you he'd be driving us.'

Mark turns around and beams. 'Hi, hon.'

'Nice car.' Lilian says.

'And this is Dannii, a friend of both of us.'

Dannii turns around and gives Lilian a big smile. Lilian grimaces.

'So love, how are you?' Lukas asks.

'I don't know –' Lilian says. 'I didn't expect –'

'It's OK, love. These two have been helping me the last few days.' He nods towards the front seat. 'Shall we just see how things go?' He tries to catch her eye.

She looks up at him. 'OK,' she whispers.

'So, Blackpool, ey? Fancy the Big One?' Mark turns round.

She pulls a face. 'Erm, no –'

'Please yourself,' Mark mutters. 'Women.'

Lukas pushes his knee further into the back of Mark's seat.

'Ouch!' Mark yelps. 'Mind where you put that.'

Lilian looks Lukas in the eye. 'Is he always like that?'

'Yes,' Dannii answers. 'A total charmer.'

'Okay –' Lilian draws the word out in the American way.

'He's fine,' Lukas says.

'So you don't fancy the Big One, love?' Mark looks back, eyebrows raised. 'I thought all kids liked rollercoasters.'

'I'm not a kid, you weirdo. I'm, like, sixteen.' Lilian scowls.

Mark laughs. He turns to Dannii. 'What about you, love? Fancy a go? Fancy getting chucked about a bit with me?' He blows a kiss in her direction. The car is doing 90 up the M61.

'The Pleasure Beach isn't open this time of year, moron. And will you keep your eyes on the road! Narrow lanes, keep your distance.'

'Are you telling me I can't drive?'

'I'm telling you, you drive like a maniac.'

Lukas does the knee thing again.

'OK, Sherlock. I'll shut up. Keep my eyes on the road. I won't even ask you about the Big One, which is shut anyway, 'cos you won't fit in the car.'

'Leave Dad alone!' Lilian sits up.

'OK, love. I meant he wouldn't fit in a car with me and all.' He holds up both hands, laughs and puts them back on the wheel quickly.

'Yeah, whatever. Don't impress me.' Lilian mutters. A smile forms on Lukas's lips. In the mirror Dannii grins at him. Lilian frowns at Lukas. 'What does she mean, the beach isn't open, Dad?'

'It's shut in winter. There's a German market though, and an ice rink.' Lukas omits mentioning the grotto. 'Will that do? You like skating, don't you?'

Lilian looks out of the window. 'S'pose so,' she says.

Blackpool is Blackpool. Arguably the most famous British seaside resort. Lukas has never fully understood the attraction. To him the place is the essence of what is wrong with this country. He has seen similarly grubby resorts elsewhere in the world, but unlike Blackpool these were on the decline, almost out of business, and certainly out of favour with the general public. But not Blackpool. Blackpool is going strong. The masses still queue along the motorway for a dose of the typical British seaside. The place scares Lukas. There is an undercurrent that he doesn't savour. Something that's just waiting to erupt. He likes a drink, but not out of plastic at 10am. He *is* probably overweight, but compared to what waddles around here he feels like Mr Universe. He is also not fond of football colours. Especially not that many different ones together in one place, and in every pub. Red faces, hollering, swearing at each other already, as last night's vomit dries on the pavement.

Mark looks like he is loving every minute of it. He strides round the vintage fairground excitedly, eating a German bratwurst and swigging from a plastic pint pot with flat lager. His third. He has already stuffed down a burger and chips, a pork pie and some Blackpool rock, the remains of which stick out of his back pocket. Lukas spots the collar of his Merseyside jersey sticking out from under his sweater. 'There it is. The Big One. My life's aspiration. And it's shut and in darkness. But there's an ancient Waltzer over there. You wait and watch me go!' Mark gulps down his beer in one and strides off in the direction of the vintage ride. They follow him slowly to the queue for one of the few traditional rides on the fair. 'Best have an ice cream, while we wait.' Mark laughs.

'While *you* wait, fat copper.' Dannii says.

'You're the one to talk.' Mark laughs again and nods in Lukas's direction. Dannii elbows him in the side.

'Do you fancy an ice cream, love?' Lukas asks his daughter.

'Can we go to the Ice Paradise, Dad? My friends go there when they come to Blackpool. It's by the ice rink, over there.' They walk towards the spidery outline of the closed rides on the Pleasure Beach.

'Bring me a 99, Luke. I'm gasping here!' Marks shouts after them.

'I'll get him something,' Dannii says. 'You go ahead.' She shoos father and daughter away.

'So your friends come here a lot?' Lukas looks down at her as they walk.

'Well, not a lot, but when they do, they go to the Ice Paradise. It's got Koffeeworld.'

'Oh, great.' Lukas sighs.

'Don't you like Koffeeworld?' She shoots him a questioning glance.

'I just don't like paying three quid for a coffee, love.'

'But everybody goes there!' she says.

'I'm not telling you not to use Koffeeworld. It's just not my scene.'

'I like it.'

Lukas puts his arm around her shoulder and shakes her a bit. 'And you continue liking it, love. I'm not telling you what to do.'

'You're not?'

'I haven't seen you in ages, my fault entirely! Who am I to now tell you what you can or can't do?'

She smiles at him. 'Mum said you would forbid me things.'

'Like what?'

They have reached the Ice Paradise and Lukas holds the door open for her.

'Like what things, love?'

She turns to him, excitedly. 'Can I have a Latte Mocha-chino?'

'Of course, love. Is that what you recommend?'

She nods.

'Then I'll have that too.' He orders two Latte Mocha-chinos from the spotty-faced youth behind the counter. These days, barista, apparently, is the most desirable job in the country for youngsters, he read recently. Most kids prefer it to entering into an apprenticeship. Making overpriced coffee for the rest of your life, or until the coffee fad of recent years has come to an end.

'Large, full fat?' The barista asks.

'Normal size. Full fat?' Lukas frowns.

'He wants to know if you want skimmed, semi-skimmed of full fat milk, dad.' Lilian rolls her eyes at the boy.

'Chocolate?' The boy smiles so widely at Lilian that Lukas fears the young barista's pimples might burst.

'Yes please.' She says, coyly.

'You want any cookies or cake? I recommend the choc chip brownies.' The boy suggests.

Lilian chooses a giant brownie. Lukas needs something more savoury and picks a sandwich.

'That's £11.55. Pay over there. Drinks'll be at the end of the counter,' the boy addresses Lukas flatly.

Lukas looks at the boy incredulously. The barista just shrugs and turns to the next customer. Lilian takes Lukas's sleeve and drags him to the cash register. 'Keep the change, you've robbed me already,' he says to the cashier.

'Ta, love,' she chirps and drops the change in the tip box.

'Come on, Dad.' Lilian still has him by the sleeve. She drags him to the end of the counter where their drinks and food are waiting. They find a table and sit down. Lukas bites off half his sandwich in one. 'Starving,' he states with his mouth full.

'I can see that.' Lilian pulls a funny face.

Maybe he should play the fool more often.

'You'd better come and have a look at your mate,' Dannii says behind him.

Lukas turns round. 'You look annoyed,' he mutters through his sandwich.

'Pissed off is the expression I would use,' Dannii says. Lilian giggles.

Lukas wipes his mouth and gets up. 'Come on, love. Take your coffee,' he says to Lilian then turns to Dannii. 'What's happened?'

She twists her mouth. 'Shall we just say the glutton has burst.' Lukas looks at her, quizzically.

'Oh no, Dad, I know what she means –' Lilian falls behind.

Mark is outside, holding on to a lamp post, his sweater covered in sick.

'Gross!' Lilian turns away.

Mark bends over and throws up again. A small crowd has gathered and watches in disgust.

'Apparently he erupted after only a few laps. He was definitely not Mister Popular at the end of the ride. Especially not with the parents.' Dannii says.

Lukas's face has turned to stone. He marches over and takes Mark by the elbow. 'Come,' he says, drags Mark to the toilets by the ice rink and pushes him through the door. 'Clean yourself up,' he orders.

'You're not coming in?' Mark looks green.

'You must be joking.' Lukas slams the door. 'Jesus,' he mutters under his breath.

The door opens and a drunk forty-something in a Mancunia shirt staggers towards him. 'Bloody hell!' He shouts and bumps into Lukas. 'Is that your mate, mate?' He points his thumb back over his shoulder and sways.

'Sorry.' Lukas mutters and steadies the man, who burps sour beer in his face.

'What a fucking mess. What a swine!' The drunk staggers off.

Lukas swallows down bile.

Dannii touches his arm. She smiles. 'No surprises there then,' she says. Lukas shakes his head, squints at her and tries a wry smile. 'What now?' she wants to know.

He clears his throat, feeling pretty sick, by proxy. 'You go. Take Lilian. Are you OK with that?' She nods. 'Find a B & B, or even better, a Travelodge. I don't want some nosey landlady sniffing us out.'

'No, that wouldn't be a good idea.' She smiles wryly back.

'Get a double and two singles. If they haven't got singles, get three doubles. Sod the money, nobody's sharing with him tonight.' Lukas nods in the direction of the gents. Dannii squeezes his arm and turns. 'Sweet –' She hesitates. 'You'll probably need a card –' He lifts his shoulders in apology.

'Don't worry, I'll sort it somehow. Where's Lil?'

Lukas nods over to the Ice Paradise. Lilian stands by the entrance, texting and chewing her hair. Neither a child nor a grown up, he thinks, as he walks over to her. 'Lil.'

She looks up, from a world of her own, then reluctantly mooches towards him, looking at her phone. She stands close to him and scans the area. 'Where is he?' She wrinkles her nose.

Lukas nods at the gents. 'Still inside.'

'Gross, Dad,' she repeats. She looks peaky.

'I'm feeling pretty sick myself. You go with Dannii now. Find us a hotel somewhere.'

She mooches off in Dannii's direction, texting.

Dannii smiles at him.

'Where's Lilian?'

'Downstairs, playing a game on her phone.'

Dannii walks up to him, takes his hand. 'She's got a boyfriend.'

'No!'

'She told me when I asked.' She strokes his arm.

He shakes his head vigorously, then looks her in the eye. 'Do you think they're –' He stares at her, waiting for a reaction.

She shakes her head. 'I don't think so.'

'What makes you so sure?' he says frowning.

'She didn't talk about him in that secretive, admiring way, the way girls talk about boys when they physically fancy them.'

'Which way is that then?' He still watches her, not wanting to miss a hint that his, and any father's, worst nightmare had come true.

'You know, hush-hush, giggle-giggle, furtively.' He frowns. 'Have you ever noticed girls in huddles giggling on the streets, Luke?' He shrugs. 'What do you think they're talking about?'

'Justin Bieber?'

'Ha, possibly! Having sex with Justin Bieber, to be more precise.'

He looks at her absent-mindedly. 'And she didn't giggle.'

'Who?'

'Lil, for Christ's sake!' he thunders.

She hushes to calm him down. 'No she didn't,' she says quietly.

He grabs her by the shoulders, shouting down at her, 'Don't you hush me! It's my daughter's – for fuck's sake – virginity we're talking about. Do you think she's still – ?'

Her arms remain loose by her side. 'I don't know if she's still a virgin, Luke, but I'm pretty sure she's not thinking about *this* boy in that way,' Dannii says quietly.

He shakes her, gently. 'What are you saying? That there might have been others?'

She cups her hands round his face. 'I'm not saying that. Not at all, sweet. But there could have been, let's face it.' She strokes his five-day-old beard.

'You're so beautiful,' he whispers and leans towards her. His right hand moves from her shoulder to her face.

'Do you love me, Lukas?'

'I think I do. I still don't know you that well.'

She smiles. 'But do you like what you know?'

He is lost in her eyes. 'Yes, I do, despite everything,' he says. Her smile broadens. 'Your smile –' he whispers and kisses her ever so softly.

'How does it feel?' she mutters against his skin.

He breathes hard. 'It feels like I can't go much longer without making love to you again.' He kisses her neck and nuzzles her ear.

'And how do you feel?' she whispers.

He doesn't stop. 'In heaven.' He breathes.

'Happy?'

'Ecstatic,' he groans.

She pushes him back with some effort and smiles. He breathes hard and looks at her, his eyes dark.

'And would you deny your beloved daughter the same happiness?'

He stares, blankly. He wants to hit something. Then he says softly, 'She's sixteen.' He moves closer, and she pulls him to her until their foreheads touch.

'When did you lose your virginity, Luke?' He tries to kiss her. She wriggles. 'When?'

'Fourteen,' he mutters.

'How?'

'My brother's cast-offs. I was fat. They wanted to be near him.'

She grabs him by the beard. 'You didn't even love them, plural? And you're freaked at the prospect of her feeling something real?'

He tries to turn away. 'She's a girl.'

'She deserves to desire, to love.'

'She'll only be taken advantage of.' He tries to struggle free.

She holds on to him, despite his size. 'Whose daughter is she? Whose values does she have? Who does she take after?' She shakes him. 'You're not all bad.'

'Who?'

'Blokes. Supposedly taking advantage of Lil. Even that twat downstairs, he's not bad.'

Lukas stands, like a pillar. 'Some are evil.'

'Yes. Others are stupid and ignorant, but not all blokes are bad. Most people want the same things in life, male and female alike. Love, respect, warmth, community, a place to belong.'

He swallows hard. 'What's her fellow like?'

'She seems fond of him, but concerned.'

He looks at her. 'Who is he?'

'I don't know, Luke, but he seems to be, well, in the public eye. She didn't say precisely, just that he was under constraints.'

'Is that what she said?'

'She said he had a brief to work to.'

'A brief?'

'She was rather enigmatic, I admit.'

Lukas sits down on the bed and rubs his face. 'A crook on bail or a celeb, ha! Or someone with a family –'

'He seems young and shy.' She sits down by his side and puts her arm round his shoulders.

He looks at her. 'What does she say?'

'That she likes him and that she's concerned. She says she'd love to like him more, but there's something about him, like he's so lonely and lost and it's in his eyes.' She takes his chin and turns him towards her. And he remembers. He remembers that look. Markus had it. And young Entwistle, too.

He shakes his head. 'I am so tired,' he says. 'I don't know what to think.'

She kisses him. 'You've got to talk to her.' He nods, eyes closed. He rubs his face against hers. She embraces him and rocks him to and fro.

He'd escorted Mark to his room and dumped him there, stinking of sick. He'd gone on and on about wanting to watch the match at four. Lukas couldn't wait to get rid of him. Dannii had booked three rooms in a Travelodge-type chain hotel and this is where Lukas sits and drinks instant. She's gone out to buy provisions, water, fruit and whatever else. He could do with water now; he's got the coffee shakes. He takes the instant to the bathroom and throws it down the sink. Then he drinks deeply from the tap, leans on the sink and looks himself in the eye in the mirror.

His daughter has a boyfriend, but apparently not in that way. She likes him, but there is something not right about him. Something sad, something that makes him think of Markus. But that's just him interpreting things. There's a rap on the door. He prays it won't be Mark as he opens it.

'Dad.' She looks around the room.

'Hi, darling.' He hugs her, surprised that she lets him.

'Where is he?' She frowns up at him.

'In his room for all I care.' He lets go of her. 'Cuppa?' She nods and asks for hot chocolate.

'Sorry the day started so disgracefully, love.'

She shrugs and blows on her drink. 'It's not your fault, Dad.'

'Please understand, love, I'm in a bit of a mess. He helped me.'

'Who is he?'

'I don't really know, but he saved my bacon.' She shakes her head and frowns. 'I was being followed. Someone wanted to get me.'

'The police? Gaby said you're wanted by the police.'

'Lil, I've already been questioned by the police. All this other stuff happened after I ran.'

'Why did you run?'

'I had a hunch that someone was coming for me.'

'Who?'

'That's what I don't know, love. But someone chased me and Dannii in a car. They almost ran us over, then two men beat us up. Mark rescued us.'

'Dad, I don't understand.'

'Come on, love, let's go for a walk on the beach. I'll tell you from the start.'

'Can we get fish and chips later?'

'What else would we have when we're in Blackpool?'

Lukas texts Dannii. Then he takes his daughter for a long walk on Blackpool beach. Past the rock shops and the resilient British sun worshippers, even in winter, to the deserted, windswept sands to the north. And he tells her his story. The one she needs to know. His story, minus his visit to Mancunia, minus the blog and the blogger, minus the sex parties, minus the possibly wider DCI Briggs connection.

He tells her nothing about Mark and Briggs's previous history. Nothing about the Ryleys or Dolly Green Boxing Club. He invents a hospital visit to old Frank without mentioning that himself turning up would've been too much of a risk. He invents a story that during that visit he met Dannii, Frank's niece. That him and Dannii talked, sharing concern for Frank, and subsequently walked down the street to the station, where they were attacked. That Mark was supposed to pick him up at Guide Bridge station and that Mark witnessed the attack and helped them escape. He makes a mental note to inform Mark and Dannii of Lilian's version of the story.

'Were you badly hurt?'

'We both had cuts and bruises. Dannii almost dislocated her shoulder. Mark treated it for her. He has some medical background,' Lukas lies.

She nods. She seems to believe him. 'What will you do next?' she asks. 'After you get back, like tomorrow?'

'I am, or rather we are, going to try and figure out who's behind all this, who's responsible for attacking us.'

'Can't you go to the police? Can't you speak to Gaby's dad again? He believed you, didn't he?'

Lukas turns to her. She looks at him quizzically. 'What's your hunch, Lil?'

'My hunch?'

'You need to learn to trust your gut feeling. It's your best guide through life. What's your gut feeling about me confiding in Gaby's dad?'

She thinks for a moment. 'Possibly not a good idea?'

He smiles. 'And what makes you think that?'

'The way Gaby spoke about you. Like you're some criminal.'

'That wasn't her opinion, was it?'

Lilian shakes her hear. 'It's what her dad told her.'

'And what did she do with that information?'

She suddenly looks embarrassed. 'She made me look stupid. You're not a criminal.'

Lukas laughs and puts his arm round her shoulders. 'Gut feeling?'

'No,' she says. 'Fact.'

When it starts to drizzle they turn back.

'Are you and Gaby good mates?'

She thinks. 'No. She's bossy. She tells everybody what to do.'

'Is she one of those people that always knows best?'

'Yes, but everybody wants to be like her. She's so mature.'

'And how does her maturity manifest itself?'

'Dad! You ask too many questions.' Lilian pauses. 'She was the first to have a boyfriend.'

'Did you meet him?'

'No, she talked about him.'

'So you didn't really know if he existed? She could've made him up to impress you.'

Lilian pulls a face. 'But now she's going out with someone really important. I'm not supposed to tell.'

'Why not?' he asks naively. 'Is it a secret?'

'Yes,' she whispers. 'He's very well known.'

'Can't be that famous if she won't let people know,' he teases. 'Who is it?' he asks conspiratorially.

'I can whisper, so the wind doesn't take it away?'

'Go on!' He leans over to her and she whispers in his ear.

He feels the blood rushing to his head. Rarely has he been this alarmed. He needs to speak to someone urgently, even Mark would do, but a mile out of Blackpool on the beach with Lilian, he needs to manage on his own. What had Dannii said about Lil's boyfriend? He can't quite grasp it. What was the word she'd used? He'd been so angry and lost in his feelings for her. Hadn't Dannii mentioned that Lilian's boyfriend was in the public eye? A thought forms in his head, a thought he can't bear to follow, but can't let go either. But this isn't the time and place to probe. He needs to keep calm and focused. Make her feel at ease. So he laughs. 'Really?' he says. 'Wow! I'm impressed.' He daren't ask Gaby's age, maybe she's exaggerated by a year or two. 'Have you met him too?' he asks, a lump in his throat.

'Yes, once,' she chirps merrily. 'He's very charming.'

'I believe that, otherwise Gaby wouldn't go out with him, would she?'

'No, she wouldn't,' Lilian continues happily. 'But it's a secret anyway. Her dad would go mad if he knew.'

'Don't you think he'd be pleased for Gaby?'

'I don't know.' She hesitates.

'What is it, love?'

'I don't know,' she repeats.

'Is something not right?'

'I don't know, Dad, but I think he's married –' She looks up at him.

'Really? Why does she go out with him then?' he asks. She shrugs. 'Is it because he's famous?'

'Maybe. He buys her things.'

'How would that make you feel?'

'Special?'

'Would it?'

She shakes her head. Then she takes his arm. 'I've missed you, Daddy.'

He melts. He kisses her hair. 'I love you, sweet.'

'I love you too, Daddy,' she says very quietly.

Chapter 43

'Hey, you two, you're wet though. I'll run you a bath, Lil.' Dannii rushes to the bathroom. In passing she flicks on the kettle. She comes back with towels. Lilian wraps one round her head. Lukas slings his over his shoulder. 'What's all this?' He walks over to the table, looks at the shopping and laughs. 'How long are you planning to stay, love?'.

'Just a few provisions. Got you some clippers for your beard.'

'What's this?' He holds up a box containing shampoo-in hair colour.

'Your roots are showing, love. I worked out you're a blonde,' she says. He looks at her, box in hand.

Lilian giggles. 'Aren't you going to grow it out, Dad?' Dannii snorts. Lukas throws the box back onto the table and walks towards the door.

'Where are you going?' Dannii asks.

'See if Sick Boy's home,' he growls, door knob in hand.

'He's gone to the pub to watch the match.' She passes him a mug of coffee.

'You're joking!'

'Did you expect anything else?'

Not really.' He takes the mug and drinks.

Dannii passes another mug to Lilian.

'Thanks.' Lilian blows on the hot liquid. 'Can we go too? To the match,' she asks quietly.

He turns to her slowly. 'Mancunia versus Merseyside?'

'Yes, Dad. Jayz may be playing. I'd like to watch.' She gets up and puts her mug on the tray.

Lukas looks at her, then sits down on the bed and buries his face in his hands. A moment later he breathes in deeply, drops his hands and stares at Dannii. She clasps her mug and returns his gaze. Then he turns to Lilian. 'Of course we can, sweet,' he says quietly. 'Is he the boyfriend you told Dannii about?' Lilian looks at Dannii sharply. Dannii smiles and nods. 'How did you two meet?' Dannii goes to the bathroom. Lilian squints after her. 'She's OK, love.'

'Are you two going out, Dad?'

He hesitates. 'Sort of, Lil.'

'What does sort of mean?'

'Yes, what does it mean?' Dannii leans in the door frame, arms crossed, a hint of a smirk on her tight lips.

He looks from one to the other. 'We haven't known each other long.' The smirk disappears from Dannii's face. He feels foolish, sat here on the bed, being outstared by his two beloved females. He clears his throat, gets up and paces up and down. These two women that he loves so much need to see him as a leader, not a punchbag for whatever life throws at him. 'We're in this situation together. Somehow we're involved in something possibly much bigger than we're able to ascertain right now, even you, Lil.' He turns to his daughter, eyebrows raised.

'Our lives have been uprooted as a result of the decisions we had to make during the last week. Remember gut feeling?' Lilian and Dannii nod in unison. 'When you follow it, like when you need to make decisions quickly, things sometimes happen very fast. You *feel* rather than *think* things; we act intuitively in extreme situations.' He looks from one to the other.

Dannii's shadow of a smirk is back.

Lilian frowns. 'You didn't answer my question, Dad. Are you two actually –'

The door flies open and Mark bursts in. 'Are you coming or what, you sad buggers, drinking, what, tea? The mighty Liverbirds have just scored. Manc shite looking well dodgy. Come on, let's go, we're in Blackpool on our hols.'

There is no quiet pub anywhere in the country when Merseyside play Mancunia at Fairfield Park. Especially not in Blackpool. Miraculously they find a free table in a corner at the start of the second half. Mark hollers at the bar where a bunch of Merseyside supporters are in full home strip. Lukas guesses he is on his fifth pint of lager. He elbows Mark in the side. 'Try and keep it down, you berk,' he hisses.

'Ey you! I bet she's heard it all before,' Mark hollers.

Lukas grabs him by the collar. 'I mean the beer, idiot. Now, try and internalise this, quickly,' Lukas hisses in his face. 'I've told her a story, what she needs to know only. She doesn't know about the match fixing and the blog. She thinks Dannii and I met by chance at Frank's hospital bedside. She has no idea about Briggs.'

Mark hollers his team's name.

'Listen!' Lukas pulls his collar, hard. 'Briggs's daughter is shagging fucking Leroy Callaway. Or rather the other way round. Briggs doesn't know this, of course. Gaby's shit scared of him finding out. And, by the way, my own daughter is apparently dating Jason Entwistle.'

Mark stares at him. 'How?' he asks, stone-cold sober.

'Fuck knows. She's just told me. I'm a mess.'

'I bet you are, mate. Listen. I know nothing. I'll just keep playing the rude drunk. Try not to put my foot in it. Sorry about earlier, by the way,' he hisses. 'We got to sort this fucking shite out. This has gone far too far. We can't have your kid involved – bastards!'

Lukas nods. 'Later.' He pats Mark's shoulder. 'Jägermeister, double,' he shouts at the barman and knocks the shot back in one. Then he orders lager for himself and Dannii and a coke for Lilian, plus several packets of crisps and nuts.

'What's it like?' he asks as he sits back down.

Lilian looks disappointed. 'Jayz is on the bench.'

Lukas takes the top of his pint. 'He's new, love, he's just learning the ropes.'

'He's bloody good, Dad.' His daughter scowls at him.

'Of course he is, love, he signed for Mancunia for how much?'

'Eleven mill,' Dannii says. Lilian looks from one to the other, straw in mouth.

Lukas swallows hard. 'At the age of what, nineteen. Not a bad start to a career. How did you two meet?'

'It was this friend of Gaby's. We were out shopping at Leonard Louis's –'

Lukas notices that her voice bends up at the end of the sentence in that horrible American fashion, as if she is asking a question. Dannii looks at Lukas stone faced. He returns the look. 'How come you're shopping at Leonard Louis's, love?'

Lilian points at the screen. 'There he is, Dad!' The camera is on the Mancunia bench. Several players are in shot, including Jason Entwistle, slouching and looking sullen, hands deep in pockets.

Lukas repeats his question.

'Hm?' Lilian turns to him. 'Just window shopping, Dad. You really sound just like Mum.' She scowls again.

Mark sits down at the table. He tries to nudge Lilian in the side. She pulls a face and moves away. 'Hey, love! I just heard the good news, but what yer doing going out with a Manc shite?' Lukas glares at him.

'What's it to you, you –' Lilian takes Lukas's arm.

'Only joking. He's a smashing goalie, just signed for the wrong team.'

'Whatever.' Lilian shrugs.

'So, does he lavish it on you when you go out?'

'Not really. We don't go out. Mum won't let me.' Lilian looks sideways at Lukas.

'But he's your boyfriend. Isn't she proud?'

Lil shrugs. 'She's just being Mum.' Lukas suppresses a smile.

'Hang on, let me get this straight. You're going out but you're not seeing each other? How does that work? Aren't you like "in lurve"?' Mark says it the Barry White way.

'Yuck, no!' Lilian shouts.

Mark raises his eyebrows. 'But shouldn't you be seeing each other occasionally, when you're seeing each other?'

'Dad,' Lilian pleads.

'OK, OK, Lil, but Mark has a point. How often have you met Jayz?'

'Once or twice –' Lilian looks at her nails.

Mark chirps in, 'Once or twice and you call that going out?'

'He's under constraints,' Lilian says quietly.

'What, love? Can't hear you, it's bloody loud in here.'

'He can't just go wherever he wants,' Lilian shouts back. 'He's famous.'

Heads turn to look at them, despite the din.

At this point the referee blows the whistle and Wallace limps off the pitch. Lukas isn't sure how he got injured, but young Entwistle has been warming up and they all have missed it.

Mark punches the air. 'Cum ed, lad! Bring the boy on. Come on laddie, let them in for the Liverbirds.'

Lilian beams. She obviously hasn't registered Mark's last outburst.

'Mark's certainly got his own way to break the ice.' Dannii breathes into Lukas's ear, brushing him with her lips. He gets goosebumps. Then her thigh vibrates against his. She pulls out her mobile, looks at the screen and frowns. 'Houston, we have a situation,' she says quietly and shows him the phone.

'Fuck,' he says, loudly and hands the phone back. 'Is that from J-P?'

Lilian is watching as Jason Entwistle takes a goal kick.

'Not directly.'

'Why now, in the middle of a match?'

'That's the way it sometimes happens. There's a bookies next door. You need more cash, don't you?'

'You're ruthless, woman. This one's a bit close to home, don't you think?'

'Yes,' she says. 'Do it anyway.'

Mark turns round. 'Will you two shut up. Scousers are winning.'

Lukas glares at him, nods in Lilian's direction and makes a cut-throat gesture. Mark holds his gaze. Lukas notices his expression harden. Mark turns back, his jaw working. 'Come on the Liverbirds,' he shouts.

Lilian elbows him in the side and giggles. Mark pretends to be dying.

'What do I do?' Lukas whispers.

'Penalty to Merseyside. Put some on a red card too.'

'Anyone in particular?'

She shakes her head. 'That would rock the pattern.'

Lukas nods. He feels sick and excited at the same time. At the bookies next door he puts twenty pounds on Merseyside to score next through a converted penalty, and ten pounds on a Mancunia sending off. When he returns to the pub The Liverbirds are attacking. Emilio Cortez runs rings around the Mancunia defence. He takes a shot and Entwistle almost spills the ball, having to parry twice. Lukas takes Dannii's hand and quickly passes her the betting slip. Entwistle now shouts at his defence. Leroy Callaway storms up to him and hollers right into his face.

'It's not his fault,' Lilian shouts.

'Lousy defence, love.' Mark leans over to her. 'Especially that donkey Callaway. Well past his best.' Lilian scowls at him. 'Never mind, love, it's all swings and roundabouts. Next time you'll batter us.' He laughs.

Callaway has Entwistle by his shoulders; he talks at the boy, foreheads touching.

'See that?' Dannii whispers and squeezes Lukas's hand. Lukas nods slowly. Entwistle looks shaky as he takes a long goal kick which ends up at the feet of a Merseyside defender, who lobs it forward. Hampson is onto it. He weaves through midfield and passes it long, back into Cortez's path, who has made a fantastic run. The pub erupts with shouts of offside.

'Look at bloody defence complaining. Go for it, Emilio-boyo.' Mark shouts.

Cortez runs straight at Entwistle and nutmegs him. Entwistle goes down and wraps himself around Cortez's legs. The striker falls inside the six-yard box.

'Penalty!' Mark hollers, on his feet.

The referee points at the spot. Then he reaches into his pocket and shows Entwistle the red card.

'No!' Lilian screams.

Mark puts his arm round her. 'Clear penalty, love. He would've scored anyway.'

Lilian batters Mark's chest as he holds her tight. She starts to cry and buries her head against his Merseyside shirt. Entwistle leaves the pitch equally in tears, swearing and shaking his head.

'What's he saying?' Lukas whispers to Dannii.

'Fucking bastard, I think. I wonder who he means.'

'You don't think this could be just coincidence?' he wonders.

'She shakes her head. 'Sadly, no.'

'Crap,' he hisses.

Hampson steps up to the spot. Callaway has taken up position in goal. He doesn't even move as Hampson buries the ball deep into the net.

'Don't be disappointed, love.' Lukas puts his arm round his daughter's shoulder. Her arms hang limply by her side.

'I'm not disappointed, Dad. I am mortified. He's going to wreck his career. He keeps making mistakes.'

'Isn't that just part of learning?'

'I guess so,' she sniffs.

'You like him, don't you?'

She nods slowly. 'Can we go to Yorkshire Fisheries like we used to, Dad? I'm starving.'

'I think I'll head over to Wetherspoons, if you don't mind,' Mark says.

Dannii saunters up to him and takes his arm tightly. 'You're coming with us,' Lukas hears her hiss. 'You could do with some solids.' She turns him round and marches him up the promenade.

The brown plastic seat covers still squelch like they used to as Lukas sits down, although they must have been replaced many times since he last visited. They manage to find a table in the crowded restaurant, having ordered cod, chips and mushy peas at the counter. Lilian sits down next to Lukas, and a waitress places pots of tea and rounds of bread and butter next to the condiments on the table. The food arrives quickly. Mark makes two chip butties and passes one to Lilian, who bites into it greedily.

'Where's mine? Where's his?' Asks Dannii and points at Lukas.

'You can make your own, love, and he's too fat.' Mark munches. 'Sorry mate. You should be on the lettuce.' He guffaws.

'And you should be at the AA.' Lilian throws her half eaten chip butty back on Mark's plate.

Mark laughs. 'Just kidding, love, and yes, you're probably right.'

They eat, Lilian reluctantly. Lukas lets Dannii have half his fish.

'So what's he like, your beau, apart from being clumsy in goal?' Mark sips his tea. 'Ouch!' Dannii must have kicked him under the table, Lukas deducts.

'He's nice,' Lilian says. Lukas nods. 'He's shy.'

'I've noticed that,' Lukas says more to himself than to his daughter.

'Have you met him?' Lilian perks up. Dannii rolls her eyes.

Lukas could kick himself. 'I met him very briefly, a while ago.'

'Where, Dad? Why didn't you say so before?'

'I was working on a possible report about education projects in big organisations. I got an appointment at Mancunia, and was shown round by their education chap. A few of the players were there. I'm sorry I didn't mention it before, Lil, but I only saw him very briefly.'

'What did you think?'

'He's bloody tall.'

She giggles. 'Yes, he's as tall as you, Dad.'

'He's taller. I had to look up to him. And he seemed a bit sad.'

'Hmm. He gets like that sometimes.'

'You said you only met him once or twice – ' Dannii says.

Lilian nods. 'A few times.'

'And was he sad then too?'

'Sort of. He thinks a lot. He's very intelligent.'

Lukas winks at Dannii.

'I bring him out of himself though,' Lilian continues. 'I make him laugh. When we were at the Turing we had a right giggle.'

'The Turing?' Lukas leans forward. 'Did you see a show?'

'No, the Alan Turing hotel. They sometimes have parties there.'

'You went to the Turing with the Manc shite? You insane, girl?' Mark scowls.

'Whoa, Mark.' Dannii grabs him by the sleeve and pulls him off the bench. Lukas hears fabric tear.

'What are you doing, woman? This is me best coat.'

'I'll buy you a new one. Come on, we're going to Wetherspoons.'

'No, I want to hear this. Bastards!'

'No you don't. It's none of your business. Now shut up, not another word.' Dannii puts her face right up against Mark's. He rolls his eyes and she ushers him out of the restaurant by the elbow.

'Why is he so upset?'

'Love, there are some allegations.' Lukas is unsure how to continue.

'Allegations of what, Dad? I don't understand.'

Lukas prays for the right words, the words that will turn his daughter to him, not away. Words that will make her feel that she can confide in him. 'It's probably just gossip.' She looks at him blankly. He smiles. 'So you made Jason giggle, you charmer?'

She nods. 'He's sweet. He's so shy. He needs to grow up.'

'Why do you think that?'

'I don't, but Leroy says he does. He told me to make a man out of the boy. It was really funny.'

'Is that what he said? That's hysterical.' Lukas laughs and swallows at the lump in his throat. 'So you're supposed to educate Jayz? That's why I thought you went to the Turing theatre. It's a good way of getting to know someone, experience the theatre or a show together.'

She nods eagerly. 'That's a good idea. He might not be allowed, though. 'Cos people recognise him.'

'You could always ask him. He might fancy it himself, doing something outside the fold, so to speak.'

She seems genuinely excited by the idea. 'I think it would be fun, better than sitting in a hotel room, watching sports.'

'Is that what you did?' Lukas asks. She nods. 'Just you and him?'

'Yes, the other lads had hired a couple of suites. They were quite rowdy. I think they were drinking lots of beer and shots.' Then quickly adds, 'We weren't. Jayz doesn't drink and I don't like the taste either. We had cola. Jayz wanted to watch the footy.'

'And you made him laugh.' Lukas feels like he is probing too much but she seems eager to talk.

'Leroy kept coming in bringing us more cola. He kept laughing at us, saying we looked like an old couple at opposite ends of the couch. Why don't you get comfy? he kept saying. Eventually we got a bit sleepy and Jayz put his arm round me. He kept calling Leroy names every time Leroy left the room. Jayz can't stand him. Says Leroy won't let him play his own game and that he treats him like a little boy.'

'Maybe Jayz needs some guidance; he's only young. And after all Leroy is the captain.'

'Maybe,' she admits. 'So after that we decided that when Leroy came in next we'd pretend to snog to shut him up.' Lukas tenses. 'I said pretend, Dad, like a conspiracy.' She grins cheekily.

'And did you? Pretend?'

She nods. 'Leroy did a real double take. Said that he hadn't expected to see what he saw.'

'What happened then?'

'Nothing really. I went home shortly afterwards. But we had a good giggle about it first.'

Her innocence is not an act, Lukas decides. 'Lil, listen to me.' He takes her hands. 'Whatever happens, I want you to know that I will listen to you, whatever you need to talk about. And'—He strokes her fingers—'you do know about contraception, don't you?'

'Dad!' She pulls her hands away. 'Just because you and her – ' She nods towards the exit.

Lukas suddenly realises that he and Dannii haven't discussed the topic. He swallows and continues. 'Sweet. Lil. At some point you'll need it. You react like this now and that makes me very happy, because technically you're a minor and Jayz is of age.' She tuts. 'Exactly. Dad splitting hairs. You're only two and a half years younger than him but you're a lot more mature.'

'Dad! I don't want to sleep with him. We're more like mates.' She looks angry and despairing at the same time. 'We just did it because of Leroy.'

'OK, love.' Lukas takes her hand again. 'All I want you to know is that I'm here if you need me.'

'Do you love her?' Lilian asks, studying his eyes.

Her directness startles him. He nods slowly. 'Yes, Lil, I think so. We haven't known each other very long but we've been through quite a bit together and you do get to know people when you're in tricky situations.'

'You love her – in that way?' She pulls a face.

He smiles. 'Yes, even in that way.'

She shudders. 'Mark is right, Dad. You're too fat. How can she fancy you?'

'Hey,' he growls. Like water of a duck's back, he wishes. 'I'll try and do something about it, OK. Until then, parents have feelings too, remember?'

'I'm sorry, I'm just imagining – '

'Don't imagine! *I'm* trying not to. 'Cos I'm finding it impossible to even bear thinking about my little girl in the clutches of some footballer.' He pretends to glares at her.

'I'm not in the clutches of anyone.'

'Good. Long may it stay that way, sweetheart. Will you promise me'—He strokes her hand—'that you'll tell me if that changes.'

She thinks then nods slowly. 'I will, Dad, I promise.'

He gives her a hug.

'Shall we join the others or do you want to go back to the hotel?'

'It's 8.30, Dad, and it's Saturday night in Blackpool.'

'I take that as a no, then.' He laughs. 'You'd better ring your mum and tell her you're staying over.'

Mark and Dannii are deep in conversation in a corner of Wetherspoons. She slides her finger across the screen of her phone and shows Mark something. Mark nods. 'You're dead right, love,' Lukas hears him say. He'd just had to do some decisive talking when Lil had passed him the phone with Liz shouting at the other end. Lukas looks from Dannii to Mark and back. 'Anybody need a drink?'

'I'm always on for one, mate. Carling,' Mark says and looks up at Lilian. 'I've calmed down, love, don't worry.' He pulls on Lilian's sleeve for her to sit down.

Lilian sits down next to Mark.

'Chippendales' tribute on in a mo, apparently.' Lukas frowns, drinks in hand, and looks down at Lilian.

'Seen it all before, Dad, if that's what you're worried about. Mum's got a few of their DVDs.'

Mark laughs.

'And what does Ron think about that?' Lukas says, drinks still in hand.

'Can I have my pint please, dear baffled, recently of Glossop?' Mark jokes. Dannii smirks. Lukas hands Mark his beer, absent-mindedly.

Lilian shrugs. 'He's taken her once or twice.'

'To see them, I suppose you mean?' Mark's thumb points behind him. Dannii hits him. 'What?' Mark mouths at her. She shakes her head at him firmly.

'He says he understands why a woman could find them sexy,' Lilian continues.

'Or a bloody poofter. They're all gay anyway.'

'Will you shut up!' Lukas snaps at him.

'That's what Ron says, too, that they're gay,' Lilian remarks. 'That's why he doesn't mind Mum watching them, he says.' She checks her phone.

Mark sups his beer. 'Suppose it probably does wonders in the bedroom,' he mutters.

Lilian turns to him and puts the phone on the table. 'Can you think of nothing else?' She looks round the table. 'All of you? Sex, sex, sex, you're pathetic.' Mark guffaws. 'Especially you.' Lilian turns to him. 'You homophobic basket case.' Lukas laughs out loud.

'Homo – what?' Mark frowns.

'Homophobic. Bet you don't even know what the word means.' She empties her glass and slams it down on the table.

'Uh oh, mate, one cola too many,' Mark says to Lukas.

Lilian ignores him. 'And you two – carrying on like, allegedly, teenagers – sad. Anyway, since it's sex you think about all the time, I'd better go to the loo before the action starts, 'cos here they come.' She gets up and struts off towards the toilets, cheering the Chippendales tribute act who step onto the stage to raucous applause, mainly from the female audience members.

Mark follows her with his eyes. Then he turns round. 'Go!' he says.

Quickly, Dannii reaches for Lilian's phone and slides the screen to unlock it.

'What are you doing, love?' Lukas looks at her.

'There are a number of ways and opportunities of getting a phone number; this is by far the easiest,' Mark shouts across.

The dance act has begun to loud disco music.

'But this is incredibly not on,' Lukas shouts back and reaches for the phone in Dannii's hands.

She turns away. 'Got it!'

'You can't just – this is my daughter's phone.' He grabs her arm. Dannii elbows him away and types something into her own phone. Then she clears the screen on Lilian's and puts it back on the table.

Lukas grabs her by the arm. 'I can't believe you just did that.'

Dannii snatches her arm away. 'It's useful to have his number and Mark is right for a change, this is the easiest way to get it.' She looks directly at him.

'For fuck's sake,' he mutters and looks away.

'Having it isn't a crime; it's what we do with it that matters.'

'Going through someone's phone, behind their backs, is not OK,' Lukas shouts.

'Getting fucking beaten up and framed for GBH is fine then, yes?' Marks shouts across. 'Bout time you took care of number one, mate, rather than clinging on to some elusive moral high ground while everybody is shafting you left, right and centre.'

Lukas leans forward. 'It's nothing to do with her, moron.' He hits the table.

Dannii takes his hand. 'It could be everything to do with her, Luke. The boy could be right in the middle of it. The allegations that I've known all along to be true, suggest that the company Jayz keeps might be directly to do with what you're trying to prove. She's been at one of the parties, for god's sake! And the boy's brother might well be involved in some way with what happened to Frank. In my view, and Mark agrees, that warrants being slightly unorthodox in how we research.' She looks at him and blinks.

'I don't care what *he* thinks,' Lukas mutters, nodding in Mark's direction, and drinks his beer down in one. Mark laughs, gets up and goes to the bar.

Dannii grabs Lukas by the collar and pulls him close. 'Gandalf the Great, holier than thou, you,' she says in his ear.

He shakes his head but feels her breath on his hairline. 'Gollum, traitor, you!' He brushes his lips against her neck, and feels her squeeze his thigh. She pushes him away.

Lilian stands on the other side of the table, hands on hips, head slightly tilted and looks at them with utter disdain. 'You two! Honestly. One blink and you're at it. Someone could have had my phone – ' She plonks herself down and puts the phone in her pocket. 'You're missing the show. It's great. Well sexy. Right up your street.' Lilian gestures towards the stage at the half-naked dancers.

They watch the artificially bronzed, twisting bodies until Mark comes back with more drinks. 'Look at these poofters. Can you believe it?' He laughs loudly and sits down.

Lilian takes his shoulder and shouts in his ear. 'Bet you're loving every minute of it, aren't yer, luv?'

He shrugs her off and scowls. Lilian starts clapping in rhythm to the music, along with the crowd who are becoming more and more animated.

Lukas leans towards Dannii. 'Give me a clue how to lose some weight, please,' he says into her ear, his hand stroking her thigh.

She looks at him. 'Are you serious? This isn't my cup of tea, you know.' She nods at the stage.

He shakes his head. 'I just hate to think I'm squashing you every time I get near you.'

'You're not. I like to be engulfed.'

He sits up straight and stares at her. 'Engulfed?' She nods and smiles. 'That sounds like a bloody beached whale situation.'

She laughs and shakes her head. 'It makes me feel protected to have you close and yes, you're heavy, but not in an unpleasant way. Just another way that you take my breath away.' She holds his stare, smiling. 'You're like some primeval force.'

'What?' he asks, stunned.

She laughs. 'Maybe that's what you could try, the caveman diet.'

'Now you are taking the piss. Would you stop, please.' He tries to kiss her but she cranes her neck to see the dancers, who are about to bare it all. By now everybody is standing and clapping, including Mark and Lilian.

'They're about to drop their kecks, love. Wouldn't miss it for the world.' Dannii gets up. 'Come on, it's only a bit of fun.' She drags him to his feet.

Reluctantly he watches the gods on stage gyrating their hips, grabbing their loins and displaying Hollywood smiles to Hot

Chocolate's "You Sexy Thing". Applause, music and temperature are at boiling point. The dancers line up in a row, their legs wide open, clad only in the tiniest of G-strings. In the middle, the lead man, the most muscular of the lot, tilts his head down. The others follow in perfect synchrony. Frankie Goes To Hollywood sings about wanting to come. Lukas knows the song, and guesses what's going to happen. He remembers there are a few seconds of drums and music only before everybody shouts come. That would be the moment. The crowd are bopping up and down, even Dannii is moving with the music. Lukas steps up close behind her and puts his hands on her hips. She presses against him and turns her head to smile at him. She must feel him in her lower back as he pulls her closer. She intensifies her movements against him as she dances to the beat. He kisses her neck as the vocals drop out of the song. The place has reached fever pitch. Even Lukas's feet have taken up the rhythm, in time with hers. Only two or three more bars of music, then the whole place erupts.

Everbody makes the final shout except Lukas, who holds Dannii tightly, her head tilted back against his shoulder.

As the place erupts in hysterical screams of approval at what is happening on the stage she turns round and kisses him passionately. He keeps his eyes open to at least catch a brief glance of the action. Lilian looks around grinning but the smile freezes and she turns away.

'Did you see them?' Dannii says in his ear. 'You've got absolutely nothing to worry about.' She pushes herself against his hips.

'I've got everything to worry about, love. Lil just spotted us.' He releases her and smiles. 'We'd better stop this. I'll engulf you later.'

She pulls at his collar and laughs. 'I wasn't taking the piss,' she says seductively. 'I enjoy being dominated by you.'

He raises his eyebrows. 'Seriously?'

'Not in that way.' She laughs. 'No chains and handcuffs, definitely not.'

'Phew.' He smiles.

'I'm not expressing myself very well here. I guess what I'm trying to say is'—she moves closer to his ear—'I enjoy surrendering completely to the man I love. The fact that you're so big and strong – it's a fantastic turn on not to be able to move when you get going like a fucking steam train, and I love giving myself to you.'

'Wow.' He studies her eyes. 'Have you ever felt like this before?'

'Before you?' she asks quietly. He nods. She slowly shakes her head.

'Will you two stop.' Lilian's hands are on her hips.

'Yes, stop or get up on stage.' Mark laughs.

Lukas turns round, smiling, looking at Lilian with the same expression he's just looked at Dannii with. Lilian's eyes widen. She looks him up and down. 'Dad, are you OK? You look so – happy.'

Lukas laughs and reaches for his pint. 'Yes, love, I'm happy. Did you enjoy the show?' He sits down and drinks then realises he's still holding Dannii's hand. He releases her as she sits down next to him.

Chapter 44

'I don't want to sleep on my own, Dad,' Lilian mopes as they walk back into the hotel lobby.

'Hey, Lil, no one's suggesting you do.' Lukas puts his arm round her shoulder.

She pulls away. 'But if you and her –' She nods in Dannii's direction.

A noisy hen party enters the hotel, dressed in scanty bunny outfits, straps disappearing between rolls of flesh.

'I'm off,' Mark says and follows the screeching gaggle to the bar.

'Can I sleep with you, dad?'

'Of course, darling!' Lukas looks at Dannii.

'Well, I'm not sleeping next door to 'God's Gift To Women', on my own. No way.' She says, hands on hips.

'Why don't we all sleep at the top, I'll take the couch, ok?'

Lukas glances towards the bar, where Mark is enjoying a great time on his knees, surrounded by bulging bunnies. Lukas puts his arms round his two ladies and escorts them towards the lifts.

He can't sleep. He lies on the couch fully clothed and boiling hot. The windows don't open and the air conditioning doesn't work.

Lilian fell asleep straight away and Dannii snores gently in the bed next to him. He stretches out his hand but can't quite reach her. Her long blonde hair is draped across her face and he can just make out her lips, slightly open. He is burning up with desire for her. This afternoon he'd let himself go, had shouted at her in desperate concern over his daughter. Now he wants to make it all better, make all the trouble disappear, apologise to her, kiss her and stroke her until they both forget about everything but their embrace. He imagines getting up and bending over her to kiss her softly. He imagines her responding to his kiss and pulling him towards her.

Lilian stirs in her sleep. His thoughts are invaded by visions of Leroy Callaway's gleaming smile, bare-chested, his muscular torso rippling and running with sweat. This vision has his arm around Lilian, who stares up at him adoringly. All the while the Chippendales tribute act gyrates in the background to Frankie Goes To Hollywood.

Lukas pulls himself out of the nightmare. He feels feverish. His forehead is cool, but he is sweating profusely. Sick with the thought of Lilian involved with men, let alone with men like Callaway, his body is tight and confused with a mixture of lust and disgust. He needs to calm down and think, logically. He picks up his shoes from beneath the bed, then tiptoes towards the door and grabs his coat. Carefully, he closes the door behind him.

The floor below is slightly cooler, though the window in the spare room is just as tightly shut as in the one above. Lukas sits on the bed and switches on the TV. He must've slept after all, as it's half past midnight. No SKY TV. He'd hoped for all night news or some documentary. Instead he arrives at the pay TV channels earlier than expected. A screen informs guests of two free minutes viewing time before a charge is made to the room bill and to press Select to go ahead. Lukas presses Select. Entangled bodies, just as he expected. Graphic close-ups alternate with mid-distance shots, taking in the full range of movements that the actors and actress are performing. The film is accompanied by a soundtrack of exaggerated moaning and dirty talking, dubbed badly into English. Lukas stares at the screen, blankly. The film does not affect his overall condition positively at all. He switches the TV off quickly, before the free time runs out.

The moaning continues in his head. He goes to the bathroom and throws cold water over his face. As he towels himself off he tries to focus on something else but the sounds don't cease. He quickly double-checks the TV and realises that the sounds are real, coming from another room.

Lukas steps into the corridor. Mark's door is ajar. He carefully pushes it open and tries to work out what he is looking at in the dimly lit room. He assumes it is Mark, on his back on the bed, covered in bulging bunnies, at least three of them, one riding each end of him, with a third doing something to, but thankfully obstructing, his middle. A fourth bunny staggers around the room, swigging from a champagne, or more likely Lambrini, bottle. Quickly, he pulls the door to.

He needs a drink. Urgently. His throat is parched. He walks downstairs but doesn't fancy the remains of the hen party.

Outside, the cold wind hits him forcefully and his head clears a little. Walking down the promenade he tries to summarise the events today, but can't concentrate properly. Images of Leroy Callaway and the

Chippendales tribute keep floating through his mind, as does the scene he has just witnessed, spurred on by his own frustrated desire. He tries to turn his thoughts to Dannii, to focus on her, rather than on the filth that seems to be all around him. He spots a young couple making out in a doorway next to a man urinating into a pile of vomit. He swallows hard and moves on quickly. He walks into a crowded pub. A barn of a place, plastic glasses only. He orders Stella. The beer is horrid but cold and he downs as much of it as possible. People bump into him. Everybody seems to be off their heads, old and young alike. There's a brawl by the door; the bouncers step in. Someone gets evicted, someone else gets a final warning. Girls with runny make-up stagger around, unstable on their impossibly high heels, too drunk to keep their impossibly short skirts down. Around the edges of the room couples snog, neck and possibly do more, it's too dark to tell.

Lukas finishes his pint and orders another, and a double vodka chaser for his churning stomach. The place is mayhem. Next to him a group of youngsters do Jägerbombs by the tray. One of the lads brings his straight back up and staggers off in the direction of where Lukas guesses the gents to be. He won't use the toilet, he has already decided. A boy standing next to him nudges him and points at a girl hanging onto the bar. She is of the high heels and short skirts brigade. The boy laughs a dirty little laugh and says something lairy that Lukas doesn't understand. Lukas looks into completely vacant eyes. The boy still grins at him widely. He reeks of marijuana. Lukas turns away. He orders another double vodka.

'Can you get me one of those, love? I've run out of cash.' The woman at his side has impossibly long lashes and unfeasibly big tits. He fails not to stare at her cleavage. He downs his double and orders two more. 'You want anything with it? Tonic?' he hears himself say.

'Just some ice, please, lovey, cool me down a bit.' She flutters.

'Sorry, no ice.' The barman slams the drinks down, grabs Lukas's twenty and slips a fiver's worth of change back into his palm.

'Well, I'll have to stay all hot then,' she moves closer, reaching past him for her drink. 'Chin chin.' She raises her drink. Lukas forces his stare off her bust and looks her in the face. She smiles at him through gappy teeth and bright crimson lips. 'Aren't you going to drink with me?' She pouts.

He touches her plastic glass with his, being jostled towards her by the crowd behind him. His drink partly spills onto her ample cleavage. 'Sorry, love,' he mutters and just about stops himself from trying to clean her up. He feels impossibly out of control. She giggles and jiggles against him. She drinks and grabs his crotch simultaneously. 'Who's a big boy then?' She squeezes and tugs at him. 'And so happy to see me.' She clutches his hand and pulls him round the corner of the bar.

He downs his vodka. Next thing he knows she has her tongue down his throat and he responds, pushing her against the wall and grinding his hips against her. She must've looked to be struggling as two bouncers pull him off her. 'We don't do bed and breakfast,' one of them states firmly as he escorts Lukas to the door.

'Leave him! He's OK, really. He didn't mean any harm,' the woman shouts at the other bouncer, beating his chest.

Lukas doesn't hear what the man replies. He's already outside the building, relieved to feel cold rain pouring down on his head. He looks around to get his bearings. What on earth has come over him? In his mind's eye he suddenly sees Dannii's kind face and instantly throws up violently. He walks away, then pauses and turns his face up to the lashing rain. He is sick again. Shakily, he makes his way back to the hotel. Mark's room is silent, door closed. Next door Lukas makes it to the toilet just in time. He strips off his wet clothes, his head spinning. He feels like he's been part of a bizarre Irvine Welsh Brit flick for the last few hours. He turns on the shower, as hot as he can bear it. The scalding water hits his face and body like burning needles. He can't stop himself from touching his aching body and finally shouts his relief into the steaming shower head.

Later street lighting creeps through a gap in the curtains. He checks his watch at half past five; he has slept for three hours. He pulls on his wet clothes, only to take them off again a minute later as he gets back upstairs to where Dannii and Lilian are still sleeping soundly. With just his underpants on he slips back onto the couch and sighs deeply.

She kisses him softly.

He stirs, and pushes himself up on one elbow. 'Where's Lil?'

'Gone for a run.' She strokes his hair and kisses him again, ever so softly. His lips, his nose, his forehead, his eyelids. Butterfly kisses. He reaches for her, eyes still closed. 'Don't stop, I'm all dented,' he mutters.

'I know and I won't,' she mutters back. 'You smell like a distillery.'

He pulls her close, onto the couch, and runs his hand over her side and hip and down her leg, and realises she's completely naked. He groans and kisses her with more urgency than she's just kissed him. His hand moves in and up between her thighs. She gasps and utters a little cry.

'Wow,' he growls. 'How – ?'

'It's you,' she pants.

'You must be joking.'

'No. Honestly. You're completely irresistible.' She shakes her head, breathing hard. 'You're so incredibly sexy. You turn me on so much.'

He laughs loudly. 'How – you're taking the piss.' He looks her in the eye, watching her pupils dilate. His heart beats wildly.

'Your smile. Makes my knees buckle. You don't smile enough.' She kisses him unbearably fleetingly.

'Wow!' he says.

She strokes his face, letting her hand drift down to caress his chest. 'And your voice. Drives me insane.' She kisses him again. He breathes, lost in her eyes. 'The way you growl, so deeply.' He laughs. She plants a trail of kisses down his chest. 'The way you say wow.' She mutters, now much further down.

'Wow,' he growls.

She looks up at him. 'Yes, just like that.'

The door crashes open and Mark spills into the room. 'Oh sorry, fuck, real sorry.' He laughs hysterically.

Lukas puts his arms around Dannii, as if to shield her from view. 'Can't you knock, you twit?' he shouts, shaken. It could have been Lil.

'Can't you lock the door?' Mark lifts the Do Not Disturb sign off the back of the door and waves it about.

'Can't you! I saw you last night.'

Mark laughs. 'Oh well – ' He shrugs.

'Do you mind leaving?' Lukas hollers.

'Where's your daughter?'

'Out jogging,' Dannii says, turning her head towards Mark.

'Oh hello, love, didn't see you down there,' he guffaws. 'How long has she been gone, Romeo, have you checked your watch? Is she running a marathon? It's ten o'clock gone. Never mind youse, I'll go catch her when she comes back and take her to brekkers, so you two can have another forty winks or whatever.' Mark laughs, hangs the sign on the handle, waves goodbye and leaves them.

'What did you see in his room?' Dannii asks eagerly. He tells her about the four "bunnies".

She laughs. 'You're joking!'

He shakes his head then pulls her up to him. She wraps her legs around him and he groans as she kisses him deeply. The way she rotates her hips drives him crazy. He breathes heavily.

'Hm, a proper orgy, then. Interesting. I wouldn't have thought he had it in him,' she says as she gyrates.

He grabs her face, gently but firmly. 'How can you hold a conversation while doing what you're doing?'

'Am I putting you off?' She bites and licks his fingers.

'No,' he growls. 'On the contrary. I'm just full of admiration.' He wraps his arms around her and lifts her up, then gets to his knees and turns her onto her back.

She gasps then laughs. 'How often have you practised that move?'

'I haven't. Comes naturally. Instinctively. Now shut up.'

Her laughter turns into a deep moan and she greedily pulls at him. He moves slowly at first, grinding himself against her. She flushes and moans in time to his quickening rhythm. He feels her quiver and tense around him, and forces himself to slow down, to make maximum contact with her body when he is closest. Then she suddenly shouts and he feels her contract, bucking under him, losing control. He kisses her deeply and urgently and she moans into his mouth in ecstasy.

He lets her recover a little, but stays with her, his own passion undiminished, unfulfilled. She strokes his face, saying his name over and over, and he smiles down at her broadly, because now he knows how much she likes his smile. He starts to move when he feels her tighten around him once more. They both sweat in the heat of the sticky room. His sweat drips all over her face, but she doesn't seem to mind, as she licks him off her lips. Now she kisses him, bites his lips, licks his teeth, taunts his tongue, sucking on him. He hears himself groan, pushing, and grinding faster now, he looks down at her squirming beneath him. She has pulled her legs up so high and he remembers something from a long time ago. He takes her legs. She wants to put them over his shoulders, but he smiles down at her and shakes his head. He places her knees in his armpits. She looks puzzled.

'Relax,' he says and smiles.

She touches his face and smiles back. He lowers himself slowly, his weight pushing her knees close to her chest, tilting her pelvis up. He pushes deeply into her, slowly and deliberately. She shouts out loudly and looks at him utterly surprised. He still smiles at her, so completely in love with her, wanting nothing more than to give her total ecstasy. His hands find her face, her hair, he caresses her as he continues to move slowly. She whimpers uncontrollably and shouts out again after just a few more thrusts. Tears fill her eyes and she keeps repeating his name, rolling her head from side to side, her fingernails digging into his back. He moves some more and she cries out again in just seconds. Now she is hitting his shoulders.

'What are you doing?' she mouths, tears stream down her face but she's laughing at the same time. He does it once more and now she begs him to stop. He lets her knees go.

'Please, Luke, please please fuck me,' she whimpers. And he does. Hard and fast and greedy, at his own pace. She moves with him though she must be shattered, but for now he doesn't care. He feels her contracting around him one more time, and tells her that he loves her and shouts as he lets himself go.

Then he holds her in his arms. She sobs and laughs and shakes simultaneously as the tears run down her face. He kisses them away.

'What was that?' she asks when she is able to speak again.

'Female G-spot, love.' He smiles.

'How come you – know about that?

'*The Joy Of Sex,*' he murmurs into her hair.

'That old, fat bloke giving it to that beautiful young girl?'

'Precisely,' he mumbles. 'Am I showing my age?'

'It's a timeless classic, love.'

He looks her in the eye. Flushed and exhausted, she is more beautiful than ever. He brushes the strand of hair from her face. 'Did you enjoy it?'

She laughs and rolls her eyes. 'How come I didn't know that?'

He kisses her. 'Because even you don't know everything.'

'Oh yeah? What else don't I know?'

He studies her eyes. 'I was propositioned by a prostitute last night.' He lies back.

She is up on one elbow. 'Really? What happened?'

Lukas scratches his nose. 'I couldn't sleep. I was imagining Lil at those parties, what could've happened – and that slime ball Leroy. Jayz hates him. Apparently, he bullies him. So I was totally wired. I went for a walk and ended up in this barn of a pub. The place had deteriorated beyond what I'd normally find acceptable, everybody off their heads and fornication going on in the corners.' She laughs. 'It was completely mad. Next to me these kids were doing Jaeger bombs, some stayed down, some didn't, you know what I mean.'

'Yuck, why did you stay?'

'There was something primeval about the place, a certain fascination.' He clears his throat. 'Suddenly this bird's right in front of me, breasts right in my face, and asks me for a drink, says she's run out of money. Guess what?'

'You bought her one.'

'I bought her one.'

'You berk!'

'I know. Next thing she's squeezing me.'

Dannii's eyebrows move up. 'Really?'

Then she tries to snog me.' He strokes Dannii's shoulder. 'And the weirdest thing was – I was incredibly turned on by it all. Unbelievable.'

She frowns then smiles. 'You've been through a lot recently. Makes you react weird.'

'Didn't know what came over me. He laughs. 'Then the bouncers pulled me off her. Threw me out. Then I chucked up.' He looks at her long and hard to judge her reaction. 'The scary thing is, I don't know what would've happened if they hadn't pulled me off her.'

'Surely you'd have come round – '

'I would bloody well hope so.'

'So would I,' she says quietly.

He wraps his arms around her tightly. 'I'm so sorry, I just had to tell you.'

'You did the right thing. You don't want to bottle stuff like that up,' she replies, her voice muffled.

'I'm such an idiot.'

'Weird things happen sometimes.'

'I suppose. I ought to learn from that experience.'

'Yes,' she says firmly. 'Don't let it happen again.'

He holds her closer. 'Are you engulfed enough?'

'Adequate.' She kisses him on the nose.

Chapter 45

'What kept you so long?' Lilian asks.

'Your dad didn't have a very good night. He needed some rest.' Dannii says.

Mark laughs.

'He looks alright to me.' Lilian chews.

Lukas sits down. 'Sorry to keep you waiting,' Lukas says. 'You OK, love?' Lilian nods. 'What time do we want to leave?' He looks at Mark, who shrugs his shoulders.

'Anytime you're ready, mate.'

An hour later they are back on the road. Lukas is glad to leave Blackpool; the trip has shaken him up. Last night he'd completely lost control. For the moment he believes he has regained his composure, enough of it anyway to have been able to explain to Dannii what had happened, and keep her trust. Nevertheless, it troubles him deeply, how quickly he'd arrived at the point of doing something extremely stupid and entirely unacceptable, whatever the circumstances.

The way forward is clear in his mind, regardless of any facts that may still lie undiscovered; his daughter is in a situation that is completely intolerable. Her friendship with Jason he could condone, but her proximity to people he believes to be deeply involved in corruption and debauchery he cannot.

Saying goodbye to Lilian proves difficult for him and painfully brief. They drop her where they picked her up the day before. Lukas gives her a quick, tight hug and implores her to get in touch through Pavel if she needs something or even if she just fancies a chat. She promises to do so. Then she is gone.

Upon their return Glossop looks dreary. The hills are hidden in cloud and drizzle, and the whole place emanates Sunday night blues. Mark drops Dannii and Lukas at the B & B.

'This room is a bloody awful place to call temporary home. Even his flat was better.'

'Maybe we could swap him?' She sits next to him and runs her fingers through his hair.

'Did you ever have it longer?'

'Long enough to go curly.' He smiles at her.

'Really? I can't imagine that.'

'At some point I used to have quite a mane.' He laughs. 'Blonde, red, depending on the time of year. Nowadays mostly grey. Didn't you see the photo in the *Evening News*?'

She shakes her head. He takes out his wallet and finds the cutting. She takes a look. 'You look like a completely different person.'

'I *am* a completely different person,' he says, mostly to himself.

She digs through the shopping and gets out the hair dye. He watches her move.

'Take your top off,' she says and he pulls jumper and T-shirt off. Carefully, she massages the paste into his hair and beard. He asks her what colour it is and growls when she says dark brown.

'Stop growling,' she says. 'You know what happens when you growl.'

He keeps his mouth shut. He can taste the smell. 'Are you going to time me?' he says when she's finished.

'Yes.'

He lights the fire and sits down on the bed. 'Bloody clammy in here.'

'What are we going to do tonight, Luke?'

'Get pissed? Only kidding, but what else is there to do?'

'I'm not sitting in this room all night.' Dannii folds her arms. Lukas nods. 'Besides, I'm starving. And I need to update the blog.'

'So you need Wi-Fi?'

'Ideally, yes.'

He walks into the bathroom and checks his hair.

'Be patient! Have we lost Mark for the night?'

'Looks like it,' he growls.

'Stop that.' She slaps his naked back.

'Is this stuff *supposed* to be turning purple? I don't want to end up looking like Elvis.'

'It always does that. I've used every colour under the sun.'

'Really?' he says, absent-mindedly, observing the dye run into his forehead.

'And all piercings have healed. I'm a new woman.'

'Piercings?' He focuses. 'Where?' She grins. 'Really?' He looks at her, wide-eyed.

'All gone now. What about you? Any skeletons in the closet?' she says, hands on hips.

'Depends what's acceptable in your closet.'

'No cross-dressing fetish as I suspected the other day?'

He laughs. 'Definitely not. I can't find stilettos big enough. Am I done?'

'Another two minutes.'

He leans on the sink and looks at himself in the mirror. She touches his back. His eyes move from his to hers. 'You know what Mark said about us, the blogger and the beast?'

'Yes, I overheard.' Dannii rests the side of her head against his back. 'What nonsense. How do you define beauty? If you're talking about character and ethics then you're definitely the beauty and I'm the beast.'

He frowns. 'You know exactly what he meant. Can I wash this out now?'

'Put your head in the sink.'

'Reminds me of last night,' he mumbles and obeys.

She massages his head gently. He growls. 'Stop it,' she tells him.

'I can't help it, not with what you're doing now.'

She turns off the water and pats his hair dry. Lukas stands up straight, towering above her in the tiny bathroom. She hugs his midriff. 'Stop beating yourself up. You're loved.'

He rocks her from side to side and buries his face in her hair. 'I suppose sex is out of the question?' he mutters, drawing in her scent.

She raises her head and looks straight at him. 'I'm starving.'

'Later I'll probably be drunk.' He smiles.

She pulls his head towards hers. 'You managed a couple of nights ago – and you were reeling.'

'I was on a roll.' He rubs his nose against hers. She bends back giggling to evade his kiss, without a chance.

She eventually slithers out of his arms towards the floor. 'Dry yourself off, I'm parched.' She smiles back at him, over her shoulder.

Lukas sighs and turns towards the mirror. His beard has grown surprisingly full. His new clippers sound tired, and he hopes they'll last until he's trimmed both sides equally. He quickly shaves both cheeks to leave long sideburns and a goatee and is tidying up his neck when she sneaks up on him.

'Let me do that. You don't want to cut yourself,' she says quietly. 'Sit on the loo, so I can reach.'

He sits down and cranes his neck back. She stands very close and looks for a suitable starting point.

'You need to hurry. The batteries are rubbish.'

She shaves him, slowly and deliberately. The machine's vibrations tickle his neck. He tries not to swallow; the clipper could easily nick his skin. He feels completely at her mercy and incredibly vulnerable. What did she say? She likes that feeling of surrender? Now he knows what she means, he's no option but to trust her completely. A low moan escapes his throat; he can't stifle it.

She puts the clippers down and kisses his neck. She tugs at his raw skin with her lips, then licks him and her teeth bite him gently. He can't stop moaning. He is well past caring how she's managed to lose her jeans, now that she sits on his lap. He keeps his neck craned back and exposed like prey surrendering to its predator, his eyes closed as she mounts and rides him wildly at her leisure and pace. After a little while he lifts her up and carries her to the bed.

Twenty minutes later they're on their way to the Wheatsheaf, Old Glossop. Dannii spotted a flyer advertising the pub's Sunday roast on the B & B's noticeboard. They walk through the dark park up the hill, past the Queen's Arms.

'Have you been up here before?'

'First night, with Mark. We had to leg it from the Commercial, it was full of coppers all of a sudden.'

'Looking for you?'

'Apparently it's popular with the police.'

'But you haven't been up as far as the Wheatsheaf?'

'No.'

'Better be good.'

They find space in the bar area. Lukas buys drinks and by the time he gets back to the table the menus have arrived. There's a blackboard advertising specials and roasts. The place is heaving with families, wet dogs and walkers in muddy boots. The inevitable television shows the last few minutes of Sunday afternoon football in the background. Newcastle vs Chelsea, Newcastle in the lead by a goal to nil.

'If this stays that way, Mancunia will go top,' Dannii states.

He nods. 'So yesterday's blunder doesn't really matter.' They squeeze together on the padded bench that surrounds the room. A multitude of small tables and bar chairs provide obstacles for anyone navigating their way to the bar. In the opposite corner a flat-capped villager feeds the dregs of his ale to his King Charles spaniel. The dog's forlorn eyes catch Lukas's; it looks at him with utter disdain.

'No, it doesn't at all. But the change of goalie to Entwistle spiked the betting patterns. He's getting a reputation.'

'For spilling them,' he says.

'Hm,' she says.

'Not good.' He observes.

'Do you think they have Wi-Fi in here?'

He looks around, sees kids playing on iPads and a couple at the bar watching another match on a smart phone.

The waitress walks over to take their order. Dannii says she'll have the same as him so he orders two roast beefs and two prawn cocktails and asks the waitress if they have Wi-Fi. She offers to get them the code.

'Nice place,' Dannii says.

'Hm,' he growls and she elbows him in the side. He laughs, puts an arm round her and kisses her on the cheek.

Chapter 46

'You mentioned the look in Jason's eye,' Dannii says.

'Yes, I've seen that look before. A long time ago.' Lukas scratches his trimmed beard and looks round the room. 'It's a long story.' He hesitates. 'It's my story.'

She smiles. 'Will you tell me? I feel I know so little about you.'

'And you've told me yours, so I tell you mine?'

She gets up. 'I'll go to the bar.'

'Is that a bribe?'

She laughs.

They've eaten well. The pub is warm and cosy. Lukas is glad to relax. With her. Alone. Yes, they need to talk, need to get to know each other better. They've learned only snippets about each other, here and there, and although she told him her story, he still doesn't know her. He desperately wants to trust her. He tells himself not to convince himself that he needs her. But he welcomes and craves the closeness and friendship she gives him, seemingly so effortlessly.

He wonders where to start to tell her about himself. The fact that he's never worked in all earnestness, that he's been a scrounger, that he's winged it all his life. That he's been a spineless wonder, not being able to put his foot down or make decisions, until recently.

'I don't know where to start.'

She sits down and brushes a strand of hair from her face. He smiles at her.

'OK. Meet Lukas Novak.   Recently of Glossop. Originally of Oppeln, Upper Silesia, then Germany, now in Poland.'

'Wow! A Slav. I can see it now.' She looks at his face closely.

'What do you see?' He squints.

'The cheekbones, the eyes.'

'Hold on, Miss Genealogy. Quarter German and a bit of something else.'

'I would've guessed German, initially.'

'Is that supposedly a compliment?'

'Yes.' She grins.

'I don't think I'm Germanic enough to be German.' He laughs.

'Meaning –?'

'Efficient. Organised. I don't think I qualify.'

'I can't possibly comment; I haven't seen your sock drawer.'

'That's lucky for you,' he laughs loudly. 'What made you think I'm German?'

'Your looks, but also your presence. You've an incredible aura of superiority about you. In a good way. And it's not just your height.'

'You're joking! Me?' He sits on the edge of his seat, looking at her incredulously.

'Yes, you. You fill the room when you walk in.'

'And that's a German thing? Or just another dig at my size?'

She squeezes his leg. 'When have I ever dug at your size? It's not solely a German thing, but it contributed, along with your looks and your muddy accent, to make me think that perhaps you're German, or maybe Swedish.'

'Why on earth Swedish?'

She shrugs. 'Just a thought – when did you come over to the UK?'

'It's a long story,' he says absent-mindedly.

She smiles. 'Try me.'

He clears his throat and takes a gulp of beer. 'I was born in Poland. I guess you can tell that by the accent.'

'I wouldn't say it's Polish, necessarily.'

'That's because we spoke mainly German at home. My Polish has always been a bit rusty. It's what we spoke out on the streets. Other kids called us "Niemiecki", which means German. We were German-speaking Poles, a strange sort of upper class. Adolf didn't agree.' Lukas laughs and drinks. 'After the war, the Polish in Silesia were different people. Many were Jewish and had disappeared. The German Poles were driven out by the Russian. In fact, they ran like rabbits. Fathers killed their families and committed suicide, rather than let them fall into the hands of the Russian.'

'So all that is true, the rapes?'

'Absolutely. Monsters. From the furthest eastern plains. Sent to the front line to do exactly what they did.'

'But why?'

'Revenge for what Germany did to them. You must've seen documentaries?'

'Was your family in one of those refugee treks?'

He shakes his head. 'These were the mostly pure Germans, trekking back to the Fatherland, so they hoped. Some absolutely horrendous stories.'

'I bet.'

'My mother is half Jewish. My parents had to disappear. They got engaged in 1938 just before leaving Poland. My mother, Ilena, was underage and had been my father's student. He was only a few years older than her.' Lukas notices her wry smile. 'They wanted to make a commitment to each other, just in case they got separated. Father is from a relatively wealthy family. His father was a well-published teacher and philosopher. Father followed in his footsteps. By the time they left he was already published with a Zeitgeist newspaper column.'

'Is he still alive?'

'They both are.'

'Ilena and – ?'

'Piotr Ilich. As in Tchaikovsky.' Lukas laughs. She nods. He fears she didn't get it but tells himself she did. 'They emigrated to Britain in 1938 and took with them enough of the family's assets to set up comfortably near London. The rest they hid. When Father left for England he knew he wasn't going to see his parents again.'

'What happened to them?'

'They were stoic that this was their home and they weren't going to budge. They were gone after the war, without a trace.'

'Your parents went back? You said you were born over there.'

'Yes, upon arriving in Britain my father was immediately taken on by one of the major newspapers as a political analyst. They finally married in 1943, when my mum turned twenty-one.'

'She was sixteen when they made the pledge?'

'Hm, I guess she was.'

She smiles smugly. 'Let that be a lesson to you, Dad.'

He squirms. 'It's never too late –' She squeezes his thigh. 'Different times,' he mutters, vaguely.

'Carry on, love,' she says softly.

'My two sisters were born towards the end of the war. Father felt he needed to do his bit and volunteered to serve in the English undercover army. He ended up in Russian captivity after infiltrating the German Wehrmacht. Though he fought for the British he was still half German and he only returned to Britain in 1947, having fallen seriously ill with pneumonia. They basically thought he was going to die, so they let him go home to see his family again. It took him a long time to recover.

'In 1950, after receiving compensation for his imprisonment, Father relocated the family back to Silesia. Now it was in their favour being part Jewish. Their property was returned to them – it had been used as a war hospital. My folks kept the house in Britain and Father still worked for the English papers on a regular basis, but he wanted the children to experience life back home.

'Markus and I came along as an afterthought. He was born three minutes after me. Our middle name is Valentine as we were born on February 14th.' Lukas takes a big swig and finishes his pint. The lump in his throat is back, bigger than before. He gets up, but she pulls him back down and signals to the lad behind the bar.

Lukas takes a deep breath. 'By now Father had resurrected his teaching career and when he wasn't teaching he was sitting writing. He'd become one of the most acclaimed philosophy writers of his generation, concentrating on his experiences during the war and his imprisonment. Poland was not the only damaged nation. His books fell on open ears worldwide.'

The drinks arrive and Lukas tips the lad a pound.

'Tell me more about Markus.'

Lukas swallows. 'Markus and I schooled at an international school in Poland and were sent to private school near London after we reached secondary level. Father thought that the Polish education system would be steering us towards a too communist approach to life.'

'Where did you go?'

'Only bloody St Christopher's.'

'You're kidding!' Her jaw drops.

He shakes his head. 'Dad apparently had made provisions for a few spaces before they returned to Poland.'

'My God, he must've been loaded.'

'And must have had connections.'

'Funny handshakes?'

Lukas looks at her. 'You know, I have no idea. I've asked myself that question often. I certainly am not, cross my heart.'

She laughs. 'I wouldn't have had you down as a mason.'

'Anyway, Markus and I couldn't have been more different. He had dark hair and I had a reddish mop. He was lively and outgoing, I was shy and withdrawn. He turned out extremely attractive, whereas I turned out – well, you know. We were definitely not identical. But we were inseparable. Like we were two halves of a whole. There are photos of us, two little cherubs, curly hair, black and ginger-ish, and smiles, his outgoing and genuine, mine shy and unsure.

'He played the piano, didn't even need lessons. He was improvising and singing, whereas I couldn't hold a tune in a bucket. I wanted to play like him. He laughed when I practised and pulled me off the piano stool. We play-fought until we were out of breath. He usually won and when he didn't, he let me win. I often cried in frustration, so he'd play me a song to make it better. He was never nasty but I still felt inadequate.

'When we turned five, we were taken to see *Peter and the Wolf*. Afterwards he composed his first song, about a clever duck that stays in the pond when the wolf appears. It sounded just like Prokofiev. In our early teens, I struggled with Beethoven, while Markus played Lennon and McCartney off by heart after listening to a song on the radio only once. I hid behind his back and thrived on his presence. Everybody was drawn to him, everybody loved him, and I was his brother, so they loved me too. He was my social secretary, which turned out to be useful when I became interested in girls.

'Markus and I hit Britain in the middle of Beatlemania. He immediately started a band. He was surrounded by girls from day one, charming, extremely good looking, good natured, athletic and tanned. Whereas I was spotty, fat, ginger and born with two left feet where dancing was concerned. But I was Markus's brother. I gave advice to the jealous and comforted the brokenhearted. Markus didn't mind. A girl on each arm and several in tow he paraded around town, strangely aloof. At the time of us turning fourteen his band were starting to get gigs. At the age of fourteen I lost my virginity to one of the brokenhearted.

'And then, one night, Markus touched me. I knew by now what that kind of touch meant. He'd never done it before. I told him to stop and he did. The next day he was different. There was something in his eyes that I hadn't noticed before. We were still a team and he was bigger and cooler than ever. But we never talked about what happened that night. I was embarrassed and he seemed to stand above it.

'He became a star, quite quickly. He wore the clothes, the flares, the make-up. He'd always admired David Bowie and emulated him by re-inventing himself every few weeks. And like Bowie he retained the rights to his songs. By the age of seventeen he had a record deal and by nineteen he was touring the UK and Europe regularly. At twenty-two he opened for The Police at CBGBs in New York, moved to the city and fell in love with a drink and drug-fuelled lifestyle.

'He visited rarely but when he did he was his old self, charming and with the irresistible innocence he'd possessed as a child. We went to the local like in the old days, met old friends and told old stories, but it was obvious that something was troubling him. It was in his eyes, something intrinsically sad and forlorn. I thought he was lonely and tried to talk to him about life in New York but he just waved it away.

'He told me to leave it and that I wouldn't approve. I was stunned about this assumption, after all, we'd always been a team. But I didn't probe any further. He suddenly fell round my neck. 'I love you,' he sobbed.

'I held him. I told him I loved him too, he was my little brother and we were a team. He smiled weakly with tear-laced, hollow eyes. He died two weeks later, jumped of Brooklyn Bridge. The friend he was with said Markus suddenly just climbed onto the railing and jumped. I went over to sort out his affairs. He'd left a letter. He told me how much he loved and missed me, that he was sorry for everything and that he hoped I'd be happy. He wrote how much he'd always admired me for my strength and confidence and how he'd felt inferior as I was always so much more grown up than him. 'The girls were just for show,' he wrote. 'I just wanted to impress you and make you love me.' I was stunned. He'd always been the bigger of the two of us. I felt shocked that he hadn't been able to confide in me, but then I'd clammed up too, at a time when talking would've been of the utmost importance.

'I met up with his friends, expecting to find a down and out motley crew. Instead I found passionate artists and musicians, writers and activists. There were drugs, sure, but it was not a shooting gallery. I learned that he'd been an enigmatic loner, a people magnet that went home alone. The women loved him, the men did too, but mostly Markus had been completely androgynous and standoffish. He'd had short affairs and one-night stands, but no one ever got close.

'Then, two weeks after, the search for his body was called off and his will was read. He left everything to me. Physically he didn't have much, but he left me the rights to his music. Virtually instantly I was inundated by lawyers acting on behalf of publishing houses. They offered astronomical sums to buy out my brother's rights. I refused. If they offered this much, then Markus's music must be worth a lot more. I've been living off my brother's compositions ever since. And I've been carrying a heavy guilt.'

Dannii squeezes his hand. 'Why, sweet?'

Lukas breathes out heavily. 'He was abused. At St Christopher's. In the bed next to me. And I turned a blind eye. I didn't do a fucking thing. Fuck,' Lukas groans. He looks at the ceiling but cannot stop the tears. 'I am a fucking fraud and a bloody coward.'

'Jesus!' Dannii pauses. 'Who did it?'

'Our bloody music teacher. The one person Markus truly loved and respected. I finally reported it after Markus died. The bastard was still teaching. God knows how many others he fucked up. It all blew up then. Others came forward.' Lukas sighs. 'God forgive me, Dannii, 'cos I can never forgive myself. I should've acted earlier. Markus deserved to see the bastard hang. I let him down so badly. He knew that I knew, I'm convinced of it.'

'You said Markus touched you?'

'Christ, yes. Why, I will never understand.'

'He loved the teacher and he loved you.'

'What are you saying?'

'Maybe he thought that's what he had to do to show his love. Touch you like the teacher touched him.'

'That's absurd!'

'Is it? Confusing, maybe.'

'Are you saying he liked being abused?'

'Just think, if the abuse was his first sexual experience it would have been a strong influence on the way he handled love and sexuality. We all confuse love and sex and that's without having been abused.'

'That doesn't make it any easier.'

'We all make mistakes, Luke.'

'Some mistakes can't be forgiven. He'd still be alive if I'd acted earlier.'

'And why didn't you?'

Lukas squirms. 'I don't know. I couldn't make sense of what the teacher was doing at Markus's bed.'

'How often did it happen?'

'A couple of times.'

'Was Markus in distress?'

'He didn't seem to be.'

'But you thought it wasn't right what was going on.'

'I didn't know what to think. Just like when Markus touched me.'

'When did you decide it was wrong?'

'Straight away I knew it was weird. I guess I didn't know it was abuse until I grew older.'

'So at the time, you were just confused.'

'Hm.'

'Go easier on yourself, Luke.' Dannii takes his hand. He is unable to hold her gaze. Then she speaks, quietly. 'He was right about you. You possess an intrinsic air of authority.'

'Then why do I feel so apart?'

'People are scared of your assured calmness; they think you're so self-confident that you'll always take the lead.'

'Nothing could be further from the truth.'

'I believe you. Just because you have this presence doesn't mean you necessarily are very confident.'

'Hm, quite.'

'You could try an experiment, though. You could pretend you are what people think you are.'

'And that would be convincing?'

'Nobody knows if you feel insecure. You might as well pretend you're not.'

'Hm.'

'And stop growling.'

Later, outside, she takes his arm. 'So you're loaded.'

He laughs loudly. 'No, I'm not. And I don't want to be either.'

'But you still get royalties?'

'Yes. Are you asking how much I'm worth?' He puts his arm round her.

'I'm not a gold digger.' She smiles. 'I make enough myself.'

'Yeah, dubiously. Seriously, most of the money is being invested as it comes in. It's not a regular amount, it changes every month, according to sales and radio play.'

'I know that, Luke. I've got albums out there too.'

'I pay myself a salary from an endowment I started. The rest I initially locked away and later put into trust funds for the kids.'

'And you? You're a man of leisure, I presume?'

He laughs. 'That's what my ex-wife thought, that I'm not successful enough, don't bring in enough dough. She never knew about Markus's catalogue and his estate. It all happened before I met her. Now, *she* is a gold digger, and in my heart I knew that when I met her. She would've married me for the wrong reasons.'

'How could you keep quiet about Markus?'

'I've never told anyone the full story, apart from you.' He pulls her close. 'Back to your question: I did my stint in the papers, but I'm just not ruthless enough. I've done some independent investigations. My mate's a publisher and he finds places to accommodate what I write. Done a few newspaper columns.'

'Great!' She smiles.

'Could do better. I don't have the cut-throat attitude though and I do like to tell the truth.'

'That's why you didn't make it in the papers then.'

'Precisely.' Lukas's phone beeps. 'Mark wants to see us. In the morning.'

'Good. You've got a prior engagement tonight.'

He pulls her closer and buries his nose in her hair. 'Go easy on me tonight, love. I'm not sure quite what mood I'm in.'

Chapter 47

'Sit down, you two.' Mark puts a a tray with coffee and biscuits on the table and sits down opposite Lukas. Dannii pours. Mark bites into a biscuit. 'Two things.' He chews. 'One: plan of action.' Dannii and Lukas nod. 'Two: we're swapping accommodation.'

'Why?' Lukas asks.

'You two need a proper base. This isn't my home anyway, so I might as well be in the B & B. Get your stuff in a bit and we'll swap keys.'

'Thanks, Mark. Didn't realise you could be as in tune,' Dannii says.

Mark smirks. 'You don't know a great many things about me, love.'

'I bet,' she says, and leaning over she kisses his cheek. Lukas swears he can see Mark blush.

'Plan of action.' Mark drinks. 'I've already spoken to Mitch this morning. He'll do what he can to hack the boy's phone, but he's asked to do it in his own time and at his own pace. Is that OK?' he asks. Lukas sits back in his chair and folds his arms. Mark continues. 'I know, you're not OK with this, mate, but Snow White here will stop sleeping with you, won't you, dear, if you don't comply with our wretched little plan.' Dannii laughs.

Lukas manages a smug smile. 'You owe me one.'

'Told you it would work, didn't I, hon?'

Lukas looks at Dannii questioningly. She shakes her head.

'So'—Mark leans forward—'What are we three going to do? Sip liquids and wait?' He looks at Dannii, then at Lukas. 'Ideas, anyone?'

Lukas clears his throat. 'I want go back to Dolly Green. On my own. To speak to Stan Entwistle.'

Mark nods. 'Good idea. See if he's clean.'

'Snoop around a bit more. Apologise for the other day.'

'Take Linda some flowers. She's anybody's for flowers.'

'You should know.' Lukas laughs.

Mark ignores him. 'And you, love, you could make this place into a little love nest.'

'Chauvinist!' She turns to Lukas. 'I'll do some updating.'

Mark drums his fingers on the table. 'OK. Can I have the boy's number?'

Dannii unlocks her phone and writes Jason Entwistle's phone number on Mark's hand.

This time Lukas has rung ahead and Stan Entwistle is expecting him. A defiant Linda had insisted that they received the permit before his visit when he introduced himself as the licensing department officer on the phone. He eventually told her that the permit needed an extension and he had to see Mr Entwistle in person to discuss it. He parks the BMW in the same place as before and enters. Hidden behind his back he carries a large bunch of flowers.

Linda points and shouts as soon as she lays eyes on Lukas. 'It's you! Again. Where is he? Is he with you?'

Lukas makes a calming gesture to shush her. Then he pulls out the flowers. Her demeanour changes instantly. 'Oh, aren't they beautiful. Are they for me, hon?'

'Yes, love. I came to say sorry for the other day.'

She grabs the flowers. 'Oh, how sweet. You shouldn't have.' She flings herself around his neck, kisses him on the cheek and presses herself against him. He notices that her breasts have a rubber-like feel. 'It's him that should be apologising, not you. That Billy the Bullet. Your mate.' She frowns at him when she lets him go.

'He's not my mate, love. I don't know him.' He smiles.

'So why are you here then?'

'I just came to say sorry, and I'm here to see Mr Entwistle.'

'Are you the permit man after all?'

'I was incognito last time. We do that sometimes.' He lies and winks at her.

She winks back. 'I'll let Stan know you're here.'

'Ta, love.' He smiles.

'Stan!' She screeches at the top of her voice. 'Permit man to see you.' She turns back to Lukas. 'I finish at five,' she whispers, conspiratorially.

'I'll bear that in mind.' he whispers back and winks at her again.

Stan Entwistle appears. 'D'you want to come up to my office?'

'Sure.' Lukas walks across and up some stairs. He shakes Entwistle's outstretched hand and smiles.

'Mr – ?'

'Luke. Lukas Novak. And I'm not the permit man.'

Entwistle laughs. 'You're not? What's this all about?'

'Linda. I needed a way to get past her.'

Entwistle gestures for Lukas to sit down on a worn couch, taking an old armchair himself. 'You're refreshingly direct, Luke. Why did you have to find a way to get past Linda?'

'I was here the other day with a mate. To cut a long story short, it came to an altercation and I want to apologise.'

'I heard about the scuffle. Linda claims she saw an old beau of hers. Someone who used to box here before I became a partner.'

'That's what she said,' Lukas states.

Entwistle looks at him. 'Was she correct?'

'I don't think so. My mate says he doesn't know what she's talking about.'

'Probably right. She sees ghosts occasionally. Why the scuffle?'

'My mate gets a bit shirty too quickly, sometimes. I apologise.'

Entwistle laughs. 'Don't we all.'

'I do have a question for you though.'

'Shoot.'

'The lads he fought with. Do they box here?'

Entwistle hesitates. 'Occasionally. Why?'

'What's the significance of their tattoos?' Lukas point at his neck.

'You haven't come here to ask me about tattoo designs, have you?' Entwistle smiles wryly.

Lukas leans forward. 'I don't know how to put this, but two men in their late teens with tattoos like theirs were seen at the scene of a GBH in Cheetham Hill last week. I just wondered if you could shed some light.'

Entwistle gets up. 'You're police?'

Lukas shakes his head. 'No. Just happened to be a friend of mine who got beaten up.'

'And all you have are the tattoos?' Lukas nods. Entwistle looks at him for a while. 'What are the police doing?'

'Chasing after the wrong man.'

Entwistle laughs. 'Nothing new there. So you've decided to take matters into your own hands?'

'I'm just making some enquiries.'

'And what brings you here?'

'I spoke to Eddie Ryley, who mentioned that boys with tattoos like Mike Tyson's can be found at your club.'

Entwistle stops dead in his tracks and turns around to face Lukas. His eyes are dark and hard. 'You spoke to Eddie Ryley. He used to box here, too, in the dark old days.' Entwistle walks up to Lukas. His voice shakes slightly and he speaks quietly. 'I don't want anything to do with Eddie Ryley, or the police for that matter.'

Lukas gets up. 'I understand.' He studies the many cuts in Entwistle's eyebrows and on his cheeks, old boxing injuries.

'I've put all nonsense behind me. I've worked hard to convince everyone that this club is legit, which, by the way, it is. I don't want anyone sniffing around here, dragging the police, Eddie Ryley or his mental brother along with them. Understand?'

'Completely.' Lukas holds his stare and stretches his spine. 'Me neither. Especially not the Ryleys.' He laughs.

Entwistle squints up at him. 'Nothing to laugh about,' he says quietly. 'They are evil bastards.'

'Why would they implicate your place?'

'As you know, there are a few boys who come here that have Tyson tattoos. Mike brought them down initially. They don't come very regularly.'

'Mike?'

'You want a drink?' Entwistle asks.

'Why not.'

Entwistle pulls a bottle of Jack Daniels and two tumblers out of a filing cabinet. He pours two generous measures and passes one to Lukas. 'My uncle used to be in charge here. Allegedly all sorts of dodgy stuff went on and the place almost got shut down. I think my uncle got framed for something in the process. He died a few years ago.'

'I'm sorry to hear that,' Lukas says.

'Me too. Never knew him that well. He wasn't around much when I was here, but he was family. I wanted to take over. The place meant a lot to me. I pretty much grew up here and I needed to do something good with my life. I'm sure you read the papers. After I finished boxing I took a bit of a nosedive. For a start, if you don't train you tend to put on weight and I matched that with a lot of Guinness. In Georgie Best's words, I spent it all on drink and women and the rest I squandered.' Entwistle laughs. Lukas chuckles with him. 'So I needed someone to finance this place and my uncle's lost little brother had just come out of the Navy with a healthy pension and lump sum of compensation for something that happened in Iraq. It also turned out that my uncle had left him quite a bit of cash. So we did the place up. Mike is Uncle Tony's younger brother. They call him Mr T, just as in Tyson, Mike Tyson.'

Lukas pauses for thought, then finishes his whiskey. 'What about your little brother? Doing well at Mancunia?'

'So, so. He's let some in recently.'

'Got to be nerves. He's still young.'

Entwistle puts his glass down. 'I guess so. He's got to learn the hard way. I did.' He laughs and gets up. 'So what about the tattooed lads?'

'It must be a coincidence. I'm sure there are more Tyson tattoos walking around Greater Manchester.' Lukas smiles. 'But if you hear anything –' Lukas jots his new cell phone number down on a scrap of paper.

''Course I will. And thanks for coming by and letting me know. I'll have a word with Mike about the lads.'

'Cheers, I'd appreciate that.' Lukas stretches out his hand. Entwistle shakes it and smiles.

'Alright, love?' He walks straight into her office.

'Hiya!' She grins widely and crosses stockinged legs. The flowers are in a vase on her desk.

'Fancy a drink then?' Lukas smiles and stands too close to her.

She looks all flustered and giggles. 'I'll just get me coat.'

He tells her he needs the loo, then rings Dannii. 'If there are any beans to spill, she'll spill them,' he tells her.

'Hey.'

'What?'

'No double vodkas, right?'

He laughs. 'Absolutely not! Just a bit of acting – as you suggested.'

'OK, Romeo, but take it easy!'

'I absolutely promise you that,' he insists.

'And I absolutely trust you, you know that, don't you?'

'Yes, I do.'

'And I absolutely adore you. You know that, too.'

'And I absolutely love you, Wonder Woman. Now let me go,' he whispers.

'Good luck,' she whispers back.

She is waiting for him inside and he swears she's pulled her cleavage down further. She grins at him inanely and flutters her eyelashes. 'Hi,' she mouths, silently.

'Come on then, love, let me whisk you away from here.' She giggles and grabs his arm. He leads her from the building and towards the car.

'Wow!' she exclaims. 'That's a posh car for a pen pusher.'

'It's Billy the Bullet's,' he states.

'You're having me on. Really?' Lukas laughs. She turns to him, frowning. 'You're taking the piss. Bad boy!' She hits him with her handbag.

He holds his hands up. 'Hey, sweetheart, don't kill me. I'm just about to take you for a drink.'

'Oh yeah?' She giggles. He opens the door for her. 'Hey, this is posh. Can you put the seat back a bit for me?'

'Of course, love. This is a fully reclining seat, and a fully reclining driver.' He leans over her to adjust her seat while she giggles inanely. As he expected, she grabs hold of him and pulls him towards her. 'You're a right so and so,' she whispers in his ear. 'I wouldn't mind giving you one.'

He grins at her broadly. 'We need a drink first though, don't we?'

'What a lovely smile you have,' she says and touches his cheek.

He sits back and fastens his seat belt. 'Where would you like to go?'

'There's a nice, cosy place just down the road. The Blue Bells.'

The Blue Bells turns out to be another barn on the local council estate, not the quaint real ale pub he'd hoped for. She obviously lives round here as everybody watches them when they walk in. She says hi to the lot, then drags him into a quiet corner. He gets the drinks, a Guinness for himself and a double brandy and lemonade for her. There's no need for him to start a conversation, as she blathers on about the club and everything that's wrong with it. Badly run. Filthy. Stan this and Stan that.

'What about Mike?' He gets a word in edgeways.

'Mike? Oh you mean Mr T? Never there.' She shuffles close to him and whispers. 'Wouldn't trust him as far as I could throw him.' He feigns surprise. She shakes her head. 'Tony was a bad egg. Mike is too. And he moves just like Tony. Tony hid all the betting money, you know. Then Mike comes back from wherever, badly shot up. I don't think he was in the Navy. The Navy, in Iran? There's not a bloody drop of water in Iran, it's all desert. Me thinks'—she grabs Lukas by the collar—'Mercenary,' she whispers and spits brandy in his ear.

He nods conspiratorially. 'I think you may be right, love. Another drink?' She nods eagerly.

'You haven't touched yours,' she says, frowning, when he returns with her drink.

'I'm driving. And I've been listening to you, love. Fascinating!' He takes a sip.

She giggles and drinks. 'Stan pretends he's on the straight and narrow now.' She nods importantly. 'But I don't believe a thing he says. Once bent, always bent.'

'Was anything ever proved?'

'Didn't need to be. I know what I know and I see what I see.' She points at her eye.

'And what do you see, love?'

'There's always been something fishy going on here, with Tony and that Billy the Bullet. You can't tell me it's all changed.'

'What if it has?'

'You can't kid a kidder.' She has finished her drink again.

He necks his pint and goes to the bar.

'Double brandy and lemonade, pint of Guinness?' the landlord asks.

'Make it a triple.' Lukas looks him straight in the eye.

'You'll take good care of her, won't you, mate?'

'I promise,' Lukas says. 'I'll drive her home and make sure she gets in safely.' The landlord nods and puts the drinks down on the bar.

She seems distracted when he rejoins her. Or maybe a bit drunk. He sits back down. She looks at him absent-mindedly and sips her drink. 'I used to go out with Alvin Stardust, you know.'

'Did you really?' He wonders whether she needs the triple.

'Georgie Best was my bestest mate. Those were the days,' she says, dreamily.

'Was Billy before or after that?'

'After, you silly. He was my downfall.' She looks at him, tears in her eyes. He strokes her arm.

'Did he know Mr T?'

'Who, Billy? No, Mr T wasn't around then. Not until Tony died. Maybe Tony had a face job, like Billy.' She giggles. Lukas doesn't find the thought far-fetched at all. She grabs his collar. 'He's not a good man,' she whispers. 'I think he grooms those boys.'

'Which boys?' Lukas looks deeply into her eyes.

She taps her neck slowly. 'You've lovely eyes. Bedroom eyes.'

He grins. 'You're not so bad yourself, love.' She puts her head on his shoulder. 'Which boys, Linda? What's with their necks?'

'Tattoos. They wanna be in his gang, his gang,' she sings quietly.

'Mr T's gang?'

She nods. 'Grooms them for crime and what not. T stands for Tyson.'

He puts his arm round her and rocks her gently for a few seconds. 'I'm going to take you home,' he says softly.

'Are you going to make love to me?' she mumbles and smiles.

'Not tonight, love. You're too tired.'

'Aw! You're so considerate. Not like the others.' Lukas fears she's almost asleep.

He drags her to her feet and looks her in the face. Her eyes are closed and her lips pursed. He smiles then leads her across the room. Some of the other customers heckle, in a nice way. Lukas just smiles back. Linda raises her right hand and shows them two fingers.

He pours her into the car and realises he's no idea where she lives. Swearing, he returns to the bar and asks the landlord.

Lukas finds the house easily. Not only is her front garden the only one that is kept at all, but it boasts an array of plants and flowers rarely found in a top-class garden centre, let alone on a council estate. She must be very popular not to have her greenery stolen or vandalised.

He lifts her out of the car. She giggles sleepily. He checks her coat pockets, finds her keys and tries to remember if she'd had a handbag. The door is secured by several locks and it takes him a moment to find the right keys. All the while she hangs round his neck like a wet blanket. Luckily, none of the neighbours seem to have spotted them. Finally, the door yields. Inside, the house is spotless and tastefully decorated, though a little kitschy. He helps her through to the living room and makes her sit down on the couch, then finds the kitchen to pour her a glass of water. When he returns she's stretched out. He spots a blanket on one of the armchairs and spreads it over her, then kisses her on the forehead. She seems fast asleep. He pulls the door closed behind him. As he walks back to the car he is certain that tomorrow she'll add him to the long list of bastards that she has undoubtedly gone out with in her time.

Chapter 48

'How was it?' Dannii asks.

'Bloody slippery out there. It's icing over. Not the right time to be in a Beemer.'

'I mean your date.'

'Drunk after two and a half doubles.' Lukas laughs. 'I took her home and left her on the couch.'

'Probably best not show your face round there for a while.'

'Hm. I think you may be right.'

'What did you find out?'

'Not a lot, but enough to be having a conversation with Mark,' Lukas says. She nods. He looks at her. 'What's the matter, love?'

'I saw them earlier. Boys with tattooed necks.'

'You're joking! Where?'

'The road that leads up to Old Glossop. I was coming back from the Wheatsheaf. I had lunch there. Updated the blog.'

Lukas swears and dials Mark's number. The phone rings for ages. Lukas puts it down. He swears again. He looks at her. 'They're on to you.'

Now Dannii's phone rings. 'It's Mark,' she mouths.

Lukas takes the phone off her and answers it. 'I was just trying to ring you.'

'And I was trying to ring you. We need to meet at once.'

'Yes, we do. Hang on, my phone's ringing.' Lukas looks at his phone. 'I got to take this; it's Pavel. Don't go away,' he says into Dannii's. Then he answers his own.

'Pavel. You OK?'

'It's Mitch here, Joseph's son. Pavel is with me.'

Lukas frowns. 'Joseph?'

'Mark, love,' Dannii mouths, impatiently.

'Mr Novak, you need to listen to what I found and then I want nothing more to do with it.'

'OK,' Lukas says slowly and switches on the phone's speaker.

'Take this email address.' Dannii writes it down and a password. 'Log into that account ASAP. I'll email Dropbox links to that account. Links to mp3 files. Can you download and play those on a different device than the one we're speaking on now?' Dannii nods.

'Yes.'

'Good. Text me from the phone you're speaking from when you've done it. Don't text me from the download phone. I'll delete everything once I receive your text. I got to go. Pavel says hi. You never got any of this from me, by the way.'

'Absolutely not.'

'In fact, you don't know me.'

'No, I don't.'

Father's son.

'Good luck and be careful. Regards to Dad.'

Lukas speaks into Dannii's phone. 'Your son says hello. You hear any of that?'

'Yup. Wi-Fi. I'll see you in the Wheatsheaf.'

'Dannii had lunch there to update the blog. On her way back she saw some tattoos heading that way.'

'Someone's onto us,' Mark says. 'I saw them in town on a scrambler. Not the same ones I kicked the other day. These are bigger.' Lukas swears. ' They won't know us then, will they? See you up there ASAP. Best to be in a public place, just in case.'

'Just in case what?'

'Get your backsides moving, now! And wrap up, it's freezing.'

'They tracked us somehow.'

Lukas nods. 'Just like when they turned up at Frank's.'

'And we still don't know who "they" are and how "they" do it,' Dannii says.

'Quite.' Mark leans back. 'Could you get on with doing what the boy said? I'm dying to get out of here.'

'We should get some drinks.' Lukas looks around the restaurant section. They are the only customers in the seating area. The pub is cold and they've kept their coats on. 'Order some food.'

A waitress appears at the table. 'Round of sandwiches, love,' says Mark. 'Cheese and ham for all.' She nods and walks off. Lukas goes for drinks.

Dannii taps on her phone. 'Almost got it.'

A few older men are watching the cricket on the TV in the far corner. As Lukas pays, the door opens and he feels the mood change behind him. The same tension he felt at the Ryleys and on their estate. Edginess. He smells smoke and a hint of marijuana.

'There you go, mate.' The barman hands him his change. His eyebrows furrow as he looks at the customers behind Lukas. He hears a gruff voice order Stella.

Lukas walks back across as the sandwiches arrive. 'Great, I'm starving.' He rubs his hands and sits down.

'Mate, if you hadn't noticed – ' Mark hisses.

'How stupid d'you think I am?' Lukas hisses back and bites into his sandwich. 'You got it, love?' he mumbles.

Dannii nods, takes a sandwich herself and grins at Lukas. 'They've no idea who they're looking for, do they?' she says through clenched teeth.

Mark shakes his head. 'Unless there's CCTV at the club and they recognise us.' He turns his chair slightly to watch the men from the corner of his eye. 'These are the ones I saw earlier.'

'How do we get out of here?' Lukas takes a swig of his cola.

'We just leave through the front door, mate. Shit. No, we don't. Don't look. Keep chewing, for fuck's sake. The law's just moved in. Double cross.' Mark swallows. 'Smile. Here it goes. Luke, they know you. Go to the gents, quickly. Don't turn right, go straight ahead into the cellar. There's a door, takes you outside and to the front of the pub. Go! Leg it! Don't wait for us. Back of my place in five.'

Lukas gets up briskly, and just hears Mark tell Dannii to go through the kitchen. He turns his head away from the two plain clothes officers that survey the bar area. He squeezes past the tattooed men, towards the gents, straight ahead and through the open cellar door into the stillage area. The door to the outside is open, he moves quickly through it, past empty crates and barrels, crosses the smoking area and jumps over the wall. The drop is much greater than he expected, but he manages to catch and steady himself. After telling himself not to do something like this again in a hurry, he turns left into the shadow of the wall. It has started to snow. Big, fluffy flakes give Lukas some cover as he runs down the hill. He doesn't look back, but concentrates on putting as much distance as possible between himself and the pub. As he moves round the corner into Wellgate he hears a trail bike start up and guesses that it is in pursuit of him. He runs along a stream, crosses a footbridge and ducks into a corner. The bike passes on Manor Park Road, parallel to Wellgate. It seems they're guessing he's in the park. In their wake he crosses the stream by the Queen's Arms and takes a muddy footpath behind the old post office. He hears the bike criss-cross the park and hopes that Dannii also has found an alternative to the direct way back to Mark's flat. Lukas follows the side of a cricket pitch, and eventually ends up on York Street, which leads him to High Street West. Now without cover for a few hundred yards, he crosses Manor Park Road quickly. The sound of the bike grows nearer rapidly. He realises it is speeding towards him down Manor Park Road and breaks into a run. He hears the siren as he turns right into the garages behind Mark's flat.

Mark's BMW faces him, engine running, doors open, ready to go. To his right he spots Dannii making her way across the neighbouring allotments. Mark emerges from the back of the flat and flings a rucksack into the boot of the car. Lukas hears the siren stop and the bike pass on the High Street. He lowers himself into the passenger seat as Mark revs the car up gently. Dannii dives into the back, with hardly time to close the door before Mark makes the wheels spin on the gravel.

The BMW's nose just pokes out of the driveway. They survey the scene. To the right, a police car hovers at the Shirebrook roundabout, hardly visible through the snow. Mark pulls out slowly and turns left.

'Crap,' says Dannii.

'Yes, I see them in the mirror.'

'Are they following?' Lukas turns round.

'Sure are,' Dannii remarks. 'Your Bloody Grand Theft Auto car.'

Mark laughs. 'They're in a Corsa; they haven't got a chance.'

The police car follows at a distance as Mark creeps up the hill towards the Snake Pass.

'No bikes, love?'

'No bikes. Those were our boys though,' Dannii remarks.

'Oh, deffo. Lightweights.'

'Look, Mark,' Lukas says and points ahead. Dannii swears.

'What are we going to do?' Lukas turns to Mark.

Mark looks back at him and smiles. 'You trust me?'

'You're not driving across the pass in these conditions. It's closed,' Lukas says. Mark laughs. 'Are you insane? It's started freezing, there's leaves everywhere and now it's snowing on top. I could hardly control the car earlier.'

'That's because you don't know how to drive it properly.'

'You arrogant twat. Stop the car!' Lukas grabs Mark's arm.

Mark shakes him off. 'Touch me once more and I'll slap you.'

'Will you two stop it!' Dannii shouts. 'You'—she kicks the back of the passenger seat—'Trust him. And you'—she kicks the back of the driver seat—'Drive!'

Mark floors the accelerator and swerves round the barrier blocking the pass. 'Police?' He looks in the mirror.

Dannii surveys the road behind them. 'Can't see them any more.'

'They're not going to follow us up here, not in a Corsa.' Mark takes the first hairpin carefully.

'They're going to send backup,' Lukas grumbles.

'Yes, from the other end.'

'We're stuck on this road until we reach the Bamford turn-off.'

Mark takes another hairpin. 'It's starting to stick. How far is Bamford?'

'About twelve miles. Do you have a map?'

'Glove compartment.'

Lukas opens the compartment door. 'Shit, what's this?'

'What does it look like?'

'Looks like a gun.'

'Then it's probably a gun, mate.'

Lukas pulls out the road atlas. 'You're insane.'

Dannii leans forward and looks at the speedometer. 'Twelve miles at this speed will take half an hour.' She puts a hand on Lukas's shoulder.

'Too long,' Mark says. 'We'll go faster once we're over the tops.'

Lukas takes Dannii's hand. 'Easy, Mark. There's big drops to the right.'

'I know, thanks.' He speeds up on a straight stretch. The car swerves slightly.

'BMW,' Dannii remarks. 'Rear wheel drive. Crap on snow and ice. Well done, the Bavarians.'

Lukas laughs. 'They drive it quite successfully over there in winter.'

'They got winter tyres, sweet.' She squeezes his hand.

'So do I,' Mark says.

'Really? You astonish me.' Lukas looks at him.

'Wow! Look. We're on top!' Dannii points ahead. The Dark Peak lies dormant, covered in snow.

Lukas reads the map. 'Bleaklow to the left, Kinder to the right. It's Bleaklow where they say those planes are. Must go up there sometime.'

'What, you're wanting to go for a stroll now?' Mark laughs.

Dannii slaps his shoulder. 'Just you drive, moron.'

The BMW picks its way steadily down Snake Pass. The snow lies thicker but the winter tyres negotiate the road safely. In Ladybower Forest ice and leaves occasionally make the car skid.

'We're halfway to Bamford.' Lukas's finger taps the map.

'Took fifteen minutes. We should be OK,' Mark says.

'Where's the next police station?' Dannii asks.

'No idea, love.'

'D'you think they'll be at Bamford?'

'Don't know, hon. There's two roads, one to Sheffield, one to Bamford. Which one?'

'Sheffield road gives us few options until the branch to the M1. There's a turn off at Strines but that road's tiny.'

'It's too steep. It'd be impossible in these conditions. I cycled it once. I wouldn't go down there today.'

'OK. Carry on, mate.'

Lukas returns to the map. 'Bamford road. Leads to Hope Valley. Right to Hope, Castleton, Winnats Pass.'

'Impassable,' Dannii says.

'Debatable, love.'

'Bradwell, Great Hucklow. Edale. Left, Hathersage, then Sheffield.'

'Bamford it is. Everybody OK with that?'

They both agree and Lukas closes the map.

'We're almost at Ladybower,' Dannii says. Mark sings the chorus of "The Dam Busters March" and laughs.

'Clever dick,' Lukas remarks.

When they reach the car park sign Mark pulls in, switches the main beam off and flicks the ceiling switch that controls the interior light.

'What are you doing?' Lukas asks.

'Time for stealth.' Mark grins at him in the dark then gets out and opens the boot.

'What's he doing?'

Lukas shrugs. 'You OK, love?' He reaches for her.

'Yes.' She smiles reassuringly, and pats his hand. They hear Mark rummage around at the back and then at the front of the car.

'The bugger,' Dannii says. 'He's changing the plates.'

Lukas laughs. 'This is ridiculous. What have we actually done to be in this position? An alleged GBH and a blogger that tells the truth? And now we're snowed in on Snake Pass with a wannabe Jack Reacher changing the plates on our Gangsta six series. Whatever next?'

Dannii squeezes his shoulder. 'Don't jinx it, love.'

Mark gets back in the car. Lukas looks at him. 'Plates,' Mark says.

'You really think they spotted our plates in Glossop?'

'Can't be too careful. Now listen, you two. We're going to drive across that dam really slowly. See the traffic lights on the other side? That's the Bamford turn off, as you well know. Visibility is fairish, so we can be seen if anyone's waiting. But it also means that we can spot them, if we peel our eyes. I want you to blank out those traffic lights and look beyond them for anything suspicious while I try to get us across quietly and safely. Same goes for the Bamford road. The road follows the shore for a bit. There are some lay-bys. Have a good look when we get closer.' He looks round. 'And stop bloody holding hands.'

Dannii pulls her hand back, puts her elbows on the front seats and rests her chin on her arms. 'Go, Reacher,' she says as Mark puts the BMW into gear.

They creep downhill and onto the dam. The wind is stronger, more noticeable now in this exposed position. Lukas squints through the whirling snow towards a point beyond the crossroads, where the road bends left and uphill towards Sheffield. The traffic lights change from green to amber to red and he notices some blue, too, occasionally. 'Police lights,' he says. 'Beyond the traffic lights. Must be parked at the Ladybower Inn.'

Mark slows down. 'Pub's still out of vision'

'I see them,' Dannii says.

Two cars descend the Sheffield road and stop at the lights. A barrier, similar to the one the Glossop side of the pass, blocks the way. The cars stop, then turn down the Bamford road.

'Long way round for them tonight,' Mark says.

A few cars wait at the lights on the Bamford road to turn right towards Sheffield. The BMW has crept up to the barrier.

'I can see them now,' Mark says.

'What are they doing?' Lukas asks. 'We're out of view to them.'

'Until we turn right or go past them. They know we're coming, so they just need to wait.'

'Mark, they're behind us, too,' Dannii says quietly.

Mark squints in the mirror. 'Got the Range Rover out. How far d'you reckon?'

'Not sure. I can see the lights reflecting in the reservoir. Wind's really picking up, it's hard to see.'

'OK,' Mark says. 'We'd better go after these cars.'

Three more vehicles from Bamford stop at the lights. A lorry makes its way down the Sheffield road to turn left to Bamford. When the truck passes the Ladybower Inn, Mark turns right. He laughs. 'Totally snookered the bastards.'

'Well done,' Lukas says.

'Don't think even the van noticed us. It's becoming a real blizzard.' Mark switches on the headlights. 'Spot anything on this road?' Lukas shakes his head.

'The other police car's gone through the lights,' Dannii says.

'They'll rendezvous. Hopefully they'll have a few pints,' Mark says.

Lukas turns to him. 'D'you think that'll be the end of it?'

Mark shrugs. 'Don't know. Best to get a bit further away before we start looking for a B & B. Where to at Hope Valley? Left or right?'

'See what's there first?' Dannii suggests.

Traffic is light but slow. The first snow plough meets them at Bamford station. Mark waits halfway up the railway bridge to let it past.

'Police!' Lukas says. 'At the crossroads.'

'Bastards,' Mark hisses. He drives the BMW down the bridge, switches off the lights and takes a right just beyond the station.

'Can we get through here?'

'No idea, mate.'

The road narrows to a bridleway. Iced-up puddles crack under the weight of the car. Then the bridleway rejoins the main A6187 beyond a bend.

'Bingo,' Marks says.

'Lucky,' Lukas says and jumps when his phone rings. 'It's Pavel.' He picks it up. 'Hi, son. You're OK?' Lukas listens. 'Fuck no, son, none of that's true! You need to believe me. Full stop. Delete them. Sorry, we didn't have time. Yes, he's here.' Lukas listens. 'You're right. I'll be in touch.' Lukas listens. 'Don't worry. I will.' He ends the call.

'What is it, sweet?'

'What's going on?'

'We're on the news,' Lukas tells them.

'You're joking!' Mark says.

'You jinxed it,' Dannii says.

'Switch all phones off,' Lukas says, quietly. 'Now. Mitch thinks we've been compromised.'

Mark reaches into his pocket, takes out his mobile and hands it to Lukas. 'You do it. Edale or Castleton?'

'You'll never get over Winnats,' Dannii says.

'Wanna bet?' Mark ignores the Edale turn off.

'Take the batteries out as well, Luke.'

Lukas opens Mark's phone.

'National or regional, mate? And why?'

'Regional. Pavel says he doesn't know about national. He missed it. You, or rather a William Unwin, ex-boxer, is wanted for assault at Dolly Green Boxing Club a couple of days ago.'

Mark laughs out loud. 'That's the bloody pot calling the kettle.'

'William Unwin?' Dannii asks.

'It's all in the name, love,' Mark guffaws.

'And much worse,' Lukas says quietly and turns to Dannii. 'I'm wanted for alleged sexual assault on an unnamed woman, who works at the same club.'

'You didn't,' Mark shouts. 'Swear that you didn't do anything to her.'

'No, I didn't.' Lukas still looks at Dannii. 'I swear.'

'That's what you said in Blackpool.' Dannii sits back and crosses her arms. Lukas can't see her eyes in the dark but he feels the daggers, nevertheless.

'What exactly did you do in Blackpool?' Mark growls.

'Nothing. And I definitely did nothing earlier today.'

Dannii leans forward and points a finger at him. 'You said you found it hard to control yourself in Blackpool, you said you almost lost it and that you kissed.'

'She kissed me, and I told you so you'd understand. I trusted you and now you throw it back into my face.'

'I want to trust you.'

'Then fucking do,' Lukas says. Dannii swears under her breath. 'Mind over matter, woman.' Lukas grits his teeth. She hits his shoulder. Hard.

Mark turns to him. 'You probably deserved that, mate.'

The BMW creeps through Castleton. The village is deserted, though the pubs seem to be doing good trade. The road has been cleared to one lane to the end of the village. A sign informs them that Winnats Pass ahead is closed. Mark guides the BMW through the mountain created by the snow plough, switches off the headlights and continues towards the pass slowly, in second gear.

'This is not going to work,' Dannii says.

'You're repeating yourself, love. It's getting boring.'

'Idiot. Plural. Both of you.'

Lukas turns around. 'They still don't know who you are, love.'

'So bloody what?' She sulks.

He turns to Mark. 'They know who you are, William Unwin. And Stan must have reconsidered reporting the other day's scuffle after whatever Linda told him earlier today. I'm surprised she sobered up so quickly.'

Dannii tuts.

'It's got to be Briggs. He's made the connection,' Mark says.

'Maybe there was CCTV in the club after all.'

'Maybe. It's no use speculating now. We're on the run and they know you and me are together. And Briggs now knows that I'm still around and not somewhere in the Caribbean on blotto blotto beach, where I should rightly be.'

'But he's surely not still after you.'

'He is now, after today, thanks to you poking your whatever in. And he can guess that I'm after him, 'cos he knows exactly what he's done to me. So an assault charge would be just the ticket to put me away for a few years and out of his way. This new development plays right into his hands. Now he can bring the big boys in to try and catch us, hence the attention we're getting.' Mark stops the car by the Road Closed barrier, just outside the entrance to Speedwell Cavern. 'Move that thing, will you?'

Lukas steps out into three inches of snow. The wind bites his cheeks and howls up the steep pass ahead. Drifts are forming on both sides of the road. Lukas walks to the barrier, lifts it and turns it sideways. Mark inches the car past him, towards the pass. Lukas places the barrier back in its original position and gets back into the car. 'This is crazy, Mark.'

'Where else are we going to go? They'll have locked the bottom end of Castleton down by now. That's where we switched off the phones.'

Dannii turns round. 'Yes, they're there. At least three cars.'

'They'll see our tracks.'

'This blizzard will do its job.' Mark turns the BMW's nose into Speedwell Cavern car park.

'What are you doing, parking up?' Lukas frowns.

'Thinking a cavern tour, mate.' He backs the car back out and up the hill. 'Would you move, love?' Dannii moves aside. Mark puts his arm round the passenger seat and turns round. The BMW's wheels bite into heavy snow. 'Should be OK, unless there are leaves underneath. Or ice.'

'No leaves here. No trees,' Dannii remarks.

Mark reverses the car up Winnats Pass patiently. Through a thickening curtain of snow, Lukas watches the police lights down in Castleton. 'They're not following.'

'They'll be thinking nobody could be this stupid,' Dannii says.

'They'll be waiting at the top,' Mark says. 'What are our options there?'

Lukas opens the atlas. 'Right to Rushup Edge and toward Chapel and Stockport. Left to Sparrowpit, then down to Chapel again or on to Peak Forest and eventually towards Derby.'

'Don't fancy Rushup Edge. West facing. Will be icy.'

'Left then, more options.'

'OK. Here comes the steep bit.' The BMW's back wheels temporarily lose traction and spin. They slip downhill a few yards. Mark straightens the car. 'I'm not even going to try.' He gets out and opens the boot. A moment later he gets back in. 'Could you open your door, love, and tell me when I'm on it?'

'On what?' Dannii asks.

'Just do it, love. You'll work it out for yourself, clever girl.'

'Idiot.' Dannii opens the door to a flurry of flakes. Mark lets the BMW roll forward inch by inch.

'Stop,' Dannii says.

Mark gets back out and crouches down by the right back wheel, then moves onto the left one. 'Car sox. Dog's bollocks. Swedish, of course,' he says when he gets back in. 'Watch this.' He puts the car into reverse. The wheels bite instantly and the BMW ascends the one in four gradient effortlessly. They pass Winnats Head Farm. 'Time to watch out for our friends, darlings.'

Both Lukas and Dannii are already facing backwards, the junction with the main road just behind them.

'Let me get out.' Lukas opens the door. He stays close to the wall and quickly closes in on the junction. Ahead and to his right Rushup Edge looms in the dark beyond fast drifting snow. He edges towards the main road, looks around the corner and spots a farm to the left. Red and blue flashing lights reflect in the snow in front of it. The car itself is hidden from view. He turns and spots similar lights in the distance, creeping up towards Rushup Egde. He hurries back and jumps in. 'They're coming from both directions. There's the turn off to Mam Tor, but we'd risk being seen.'

'Mam Tor's a dead end,' Dannii says.

'We need to hide the car somewhere, love,' Lukas says.

Mark asks calmly where the Mam Tor road is.

'Reverse left, your right, then straight ahead on the main road, three hundred yards, then turn right.'

'Is that overlooked by the guy behind me?' Mark inches the car backwards into the main road.

Lukas points ahead. 'Not once you're over that bump there. Then the road falls away very sharply.'

Mark puts the BMW into first. 'Any movement?'

Lukas observes the flashing lights behind them. 'No. Thank god for this blizzard. The others are miles away, struggling on the Edge, look. Get going.' Mark moves the car forward at walking pace.

'Can't see the lights behind us any more,' Dannii says.

'You can't see them, they can't see us. What idiots to keep their lights on.' Mark laughs.

'They probably didn't expect us to make it up the pass. Turn right.'

Even with snow sox the car struggles to reach the turning circle at the end of the road, in what must be a foot of snow.

'Open the gate,' Marks orders.

'That road is collapsed. We'll end up back down there in the valley,' Dannii insists.

'I'll just drive it round that bend to hide it. No one will think it's there. Open the gate.'

Lukas gets out, opens the gate and watches the BMW inch down the road, leaning sideways at quite an angle. Then he sees the car's nose suddenly dip forward. The whole vehicle slides from view and makes contact with something hard and unyielding with a sickening crunch. Panicked, Lukas rushes to the edge. The car rests virtually vertical against the edge, its bonnet crumpled and its windscreen in the snow further down the hill. A couple of yards further to the right and it would have ended up back down in Castleton.

Lukas climbs down and helps a shaking Dannii out of the car. He watches Mark reach into the glove compartment, then clamber out, laughing. Lukas can't suppress a wry smile. 'What a fantastically well hidden car, mate. No sign of it, not even from the car park,' he hollers through the blizzard.

'Thanks. I knew you'd appreciate it,' Mark hollers back.

Dannii pushes Lukas away. 'Bloody idiots! What do we do now? We can't sit in there.' She points at the car. 'It could slide further any second. And we can't go down there.' She points down at Castleton.

'Calm down, love. We'll think of something.' Mark rubs his hands.

'Better think of it fast, before we freeze to death,' Lukas says.

'There's only one place for shelter near here. The cave.' Dannii says.

'What cave?' Mark asks Dannii.

'Blue John. Over there and left.' She points towards the turning circle.

'No way,' Mark says. 'I'm claustrophobic.'

'There's a shop, I think. Follow me.'

'Hang on, love.' Mark opens the boot. He throws Lukas a torch and pulls out his rucksack. 'Let's go.' He climbs onto the car boot and Lukas helps him up. They walk into the blizzard. Lukas closes the gate behind them.

Chapter 49

The path to the cave is invisible under a foot of snow. Dannii walks ahead, torch in hand, her scarf wrapped round her head. Lukas follows blindly, stepping in her footsteps. Mark brings up the rear. Lukas only notices the small shop and ticket office when they stand right in front of it. Desperate for shelter they huddle against a wall. Lukas looks back at the path. Their footsteps have already been erased by the blizzard. 'What next?' he shouts into the gale. Mark raises a hand and waves them on. He stops by the door of the shop. Lukas watches him bend down, manipulate the lock and open the door. They hurry inside.

Lukas closes the door. 'How did you do that?' he asks. Mark lifts up a set of lock picks.

'Bloody hell, not much warmer in here than outside.' Dannii shines the torch over the shop's well stocked shelves and picks up a cave leaflet.

Mark walks up to a stand displaying maps. 'Ordnance Survey, Peak District, this'll do.' He pops a map into his rucksack.

'You're not just taking that, are you?' Lukas walks up to him.

'You bet I am. It's an emergency.'

'Luke'—Dannii puts her hand on Lukas's arm—'Just for once–'

Lukas raises his hands. 'OK, OK. Just don't ransack the place.'

Next to the map stand is a small outdoor pursuits area. Dannii takes a compass and a Swiss Army knife and pops it in Mark's rucksack. Lukas walks round the back of the shelf unit. 'Look at this. Ropes and stuff,' he says. Dannii joins him to look at the goods.

'Shh! Hear that rumble?' Mark whispers.

Dannii shakes her head. 'All I hear is the storm,' she whispers back.

'There. Torch off.'

Lukas fumbles with the switch. 'What is it?'

'Chopper.'

'In this weather? They must be mad.' Dannii says.

'It's gone. Grab what you need and let's go. They mustn't spot us in here.'

'Go where?' Lukas asks. 'Not the cave – '

'Yes, the bloody cave. Come help me with this,' Mark replies.

'I thought you were claustrophobic.' Lukas takes the rucksack Dannii hands him. 'We'll be like rabbits in a hole.'

'No time to argue, mate. We're not staying here or outside. I'm going to try and open the gate to the cave. Don't leave anything lying around that might point to our presence. Close the door properly. And hurry!'

Dannii puts a skein of rope round her body, and a couple of harnesses, protection and carabiners, hats, gloves and several chocolate bars in the rucksack. Lukas bags three large bottles of water. 'Should we not at least leave some payment, love?' He closes the rucksack and flings it over his shoulder.

'You can make a donation later, when we're through this. Now come on.'

Lukas checks the floor for fallen items as Dannii drags him out into the blizzard. He closes the door behind them.

Mark waves through the snow storm, beckoning them to hurry. Now, through the howling gale, Lukas hears the helicopter hovering in the distance. The huge iron gate to the cave yawns open. They rush inside. Mark locks the gate behind them and shines the torch along the wall. Fastened to it at regular intervals are small metal cages, each holding a light bulb. 'Help me with this.' Mark crouches down, inserts his fingers through the holes of the cage and unscrews the first bulb. Lukas loosens the second and Dannii, who has moved further into the cave, takes care of the third. 'That's deep enough,' he says and operates a switch on the wall. The cave lights up, further down the tunnel. 'We'll take out a few more as we move down. Now let's go.'

'Mark, look.' Lukas has spotted an emergency box on the wall, containing a spade and a pickaxe. 'Useful?'

Mark scowls. 'Maybe.'

'What is it?' Dannii walks back. Lukas points at the tools. 'Take them and let's go,' Dannii says and marches ahead into the depths of the cave system.

'Where exactly are we going, love?' Mark says, from the rear.

'Watch your step, this floor's slippery. I did some caving here years ago.'

'Of course you did,' Lukas says, to himself.

'I remember something about this system. I want to check out if my memory serves me right.'

'How exactly does it involve the rope?'

Dannii laughs. 'I'm not sure it will, Mark. Could be useful though.'

They walk down some steps, further into the cave along a winding passageway. Lukas keeps knocking his head on the low ceiling. They pass stalactite and stalagmite formations in a vast chamber. Mine shafts go off it at various levels. A life-size model of a working miner hangs in mid air, positioned near a vein of Blue John stone.

'Amazing.' Lukas looks round the cavern.

Mark stands next to him. 'It's warmer down here, somehow.'

Dannii pulls out a map of the cave system. 'We're here.' She points at the map. 'We want to be here.' She moves her finger a couple of inches.

'What's there?' Lukas asks.

'As I said, I used to do some caving and potholing here. Long time ago. I remember being in Peak Cavern and Speedwell down the road. And then in here. The guys I was with said all the caves are connected. This cavern is especially interesting, because its natural cave systems have been linked by mining extensively for Blue John stone from as early as Roman times. And here'—she taps the map—'I seem to remember being told that the cave went on, but was blocked up at some point in the sixties, when they modernised it as a tourist attraction. They said people kept wandering off down there, getting lost for days and re-emerging from Peak and Speedwell caverns.'

'So you think it's a really good idea to unblock this exit and nosey in there in the hope we'll emerge somewhere?' Lukas frowns at her.

'Why are you being so sarcastic?' Dannii frowns back.

''Cos it's a crazy idea. The whole situation of us being down here is insane.'

'You got a better suggestion where we should be, hypothetically, I mean?' Mark says calmly.

'We should have—' Lukas starts.

'Should have, would have, stop it!' Dannii stamps her foot. 'We all agreed we'd take this turn and that. It was team work to get this far and we had no option but to go into the cave. If we'd stayed in the shop they'd find us by morning at the very latest. Walking any distance in the blizzard was a no no. Besides, it's ten degrees warmer in here, and that's not even taking into account the wind chill factor out there. We'll be safe and sheltered overnight, but I suspect by morning someone will have sussed that we could be in here, even if the shop and the mine itself stay shut because of the weather.'

'I think you're absolutely correct, love.' Mark nods.

Lukas surveys the ceiling, hands on hips. 'I don't like it.'

'What don't you like? Being trapped like a rat?' Dannii asks.

'Yes,' Lukas hisses.

'I thought you bloody Germans never turn around but rather go through brick walls head first than admit you're wrong.' Dannii copies his stance, hands on hips.

Mark guffaws. 'German, you? You bombed our chippy.'

Lukas ignores him, and shoots daggers at Dannii. 'I'm not that bloody German, so convince me.'

She glares back. 'Convince yourself. Talk me through it. Take charge, big boy.'

'You,' Lukas growls.

'Don't do that!' she hisses.

'We can't go back. There's nowhere to go,' he growls. 'We can wait here and hope nobody comes for us.'

'Correct. Chance of success?'

'Fifty, fifty.'

'Much less,' Mark observes.

Lukas glares at him. 'We could go and find this blocked-off exit.'

'Good idea, Luke.' Dannii smiles. 'After all, my memory could be playing tricks on me.'

'Where are we now?' Lukas looks over Dannii's shoulder. He wants to touch her but doesn't dare.

'There.' She points at the map. 'I guess it's another quarter of a mile.' They continue down more steps into another dome-like cavern.

'Has anyone kept track of how far we've come?' Mark asks.

'And how deep?' Lukas adds.

'We've walked approximately three-quarters of a mile,' Dannii says. 'I've counted one thousand five hundred footsteps, give or take. We've descended one hundred and sixty steps of approximately twenty centimetres each, which means we've descended about fifty metres, taking into account the descending tunnels as well. All approximate of course.'

'Well, I'll be gobsmacked. Didn't realise you were so good with numbers, hon.' Mark laughs. Lukas just looks at her.

'So where exactly did you say we are?'

'Give me the map.' Dannii stretches out her hand as Mark digs it out of his rucksack. She crouches down and puts the map on her knee. She places the leaflet with the cave outline on top of the map and rotates it, so the cave entrances on both maps line up. 'Of course they're not the same scale,' she says and places the compass on top of the maps. 'Ah! The entrance tunnel doesn't enter the mountain at ninety degrees, as it suggests on the cave map. Look at the compass indication on it.'

'Didn't realise a compass worked underground,' Mark ponders.

Lukas crouches down and looks over her shoulder. He strokes his chin. 'Looks more like a sixty-degree angle.'

'Precisely.'

'Rotate the map to the left a bit,' Lukas says. She does as he suggests. 'And we are?' he asks.

'Here.' She points at the map.

'And you think we've done three-quarters of a mile? Is the OS map in kilometers?' He looks at her.

She turns to him and catches his eye. 'Yes. One blue square is one square kilometer.'

'So a kilometer and a bit is about this far.' He points at the map.

'Yes.' She says.

'Which puts us where?'

'Approximately one hundred yards from the entrance to Speedwell Cavern.'

'Above or below?'

'Not sure. Either.'

'That's a really scary thought,' Mark says quietly.

'You think we've passed Treak Cavern?'

'I think we've gone underneath it.'

'Of course you could be wrong and we surface in the cellar of the Royal Oak in Castleton,' Mark guffaws. 'Wouldn't that be lovely?'

Dannii looks at him sternly. 'We could well be totally elsewhere and not get out at all, so don't tempt fate.'

'Sorry, I thought you knew where you were.' Mark shrugs.

'It's an educated deduction, rather than a definite triangulation.'

'You sound like a maths prof, love,' Mark says.

'I am a maths prof.' Dannii returns to the map.

'Is she?' Mark mouths at Lukas.

Lukas nods and grins, then surveys the chamber they are standing in. 'Where's this blocked exit, love?'

'I think it's over there.' Dannii walks to the furthest and lowest part of the chamber. 'Here. Just before the official tour turned back towards the exit the guide pointed at this wall and said the cave continued but had been blocked off for safety.'

Mark walks up to her. 'It's a rock face.'

Dannii ignores him and turns to Lukas. 'Shine up there, Luke.'

Lukas lets the torch beam wander up the wall. His eyes follow the yellow disc until it disappears. 'There's a gap.'

She nods. 'The cave goes on. They just erected a wall to stop people getting lost.'

'It's just a bloody rock face.' Mark insists.

'Look at it properly. It's sandstone. It's corroded. Here.' She takes Mark's hand and runs his finger along the gap between two sandstone bricks.

'Blimey,' Mark says. 'There's writing, too.'

'Graffiti,' Dannii says. 'They've probably blasted it dozens of times.'

'Smooth surface.' Mark caresses the sloping wall with the palm of his hand.

'The onset of stalactites.'

'Wow,' Lukas says, next to her. She looks at him and holds his gaze. He nudges her with his body and grins.

'I'm going up.' Dannii moves left to where wall meets rock and runs her hands over the stone.

'No chance.' Mark laughs.

'Wanna bet?' Dannii finds a hold and takes one step up the wall.

Lukas positions himself below her. 'You forget she's renaissance woman, mate.' He looks up at her anxiously.

Dannii lifts herself up a further step. 'Bloody slippery,' she says.

'Careful, love – ' Lukas raises his arms.

'I'll be OK. It's only a few yards up.' She reaches high and pulls herself up. 'OK, I can see over the top.'

'What's there?' Mark cranes his neck.

'Darkness.' Dannii hauls herself onto the top of the wall and switches on her torch. 'It's a drop, the same height as on your side. Wall blocks a tunnel. I'll fix up this rope and then you come up.'

'Then we come up. Just like that.' Mark laughs.

'I'll go back and sort the lights,' Lukas says. 'If we leave them unscrewed they'll be on to us soon. We're OK for time, aren't we?'

'What about the missing shovel and pick?' Mark queries.

'They're more likely to spot the lights.'

'Go easy, Luke, no rush.' Dannii frowns. Lukas taps his forehead and walks back towards the exit.

Mark and Dannii are nowhere to be seen when he returns. The cave feels different in the dark. A few times he feared he had gone wrong, and he'd forced himself to focus on the fact that the path is a loop. When he passed the model he knew he was close. Now he hears Mark's and Dannii's voices.

'Oi! I'm back.' Lukas hollers.

'We're over the other side, 'Mark calls.

'Luke, I've thrown the harness back over. Have you worn one before?' Dannii shouts, and he shouts back that he hasn't.

'Piece of piss, mate,' Mark shouts, then laughs.

Dannii shouts instructions on how to get into the harness, which he follows carefully.

'OK. What now?'

'Climb the wall,' she shouts. 'I'll belay you from here.'

'And I'll hold on to her, or she'd take off if you fall.' Mark laughs.

'Luke?'

'Yes?'

'Try not to fall.'

'OK.' Lukas moves to the left, where Dannii had started climbing.

'Use your feet to push yourself up and your hands to steady yourself,' she shouts.

Lukas takes the torch in his mouth and finds a foothold for his right foot. He leans into the wall and reaches up to find a finger hold. With his left hand against the tunnel's side he pushes off the floor and immediately feels the rope tighten.

'Good,' Dannii shouts. 'We're pulling as hard as we can to help you.'

Lukas grunts and moves his left hand further up the side wall while searching for another foot hold. Lactic acid is already setting his right calf on fire, and he knows he won't be able to keep this up for long before his muscles will seize up. The small ledge in the corner, where the tunnel wall meets the man-made wall, is too far up to reach with his foot, so he pulls himself up on the hand hold and feels her tighten the rope. He jams his left foot into the the corner, missing the ledge. Groaning, he hoists himself up further and this time his foot finds the support. He pushes up and grapples to the right for a hand hold to stop himself swinging too far over. Dannii pulling the rope tight now brings him dangerously close to losing his balance. His body tilts awkwardly to the right. He's about to fall when his hand finds a rock to push back on.

'Stick to the left,' she shouts. 'You're almost there.'

He bends his right knee, pushes it up into the wall, and slides his right foot slowly down until it finds another hold. The wall seems to be sloping more at the top. Having steadied himself he follows some pointing with the fingers of his right hand. His left finds a hold high up against the tunnel wall and he yanks himself up a further yard. Now he can see the top and torchlight beyond it. He tilts his head back and shines his torch up at the ceiling.

'Well done!' Dannii shouts. 'I can see your torch.'

Lukas breathes hard. Sweat runs down his face and into his eyes. His calves are on fire and he has grazed his knee. With one final push he hoists himself up onto the wall and looks over the top.

'Piece of piss, mate, you're right.' He laughs. 'Now what?'

'Take a breather. Someone's done this before. There's a metal hook. I've pulled the rope through it. Walk backwards to the edge. Lean into the rope,' Dannii tells him. Standing on the edge of the wall Lukas leans his body backwards. 'Walk down the wall.' As he descends, Dannii lets the rope out. When he is down, she pulls it out of the belay device and walks up to him. 'Well done,' she says and touches his face. 'Scary?' She smiles. Lukas laughs. She pats his shoulder. 'Pull that rope down. Let's see what's ahead.'

Chapter 50

The tunnel ahead is in a much worse condition than the passages of the Blue John Cavern. Rough stone and rock line the ground and they pick their way carefully.

'So what's the plan now, love?' Mark enquires.

'I don't know,' Dannii says. 'To be honest, I'd hoped this wouldn't just be another tunnel.'

'What had you hoped for?'

'There's something up ahead.' Lukas points the torch into the distance. 'Looks like a T-junction.'

Dannii walks ahead. 'Yes,' she says.

'It's just a recess.' Mark shrugs.

'I don't think so. Light the ceiling, Luke.' She shakes her head. 'The floor.' She kneels down. 'There's some old candles here.' She sweeps the floor with her hands. Lukas crouches down, picks up the box of candles and puts them in the rucksack. Then he helps her move the rocks. 'There's something there. It's cold. Feels like metal bars.'

'Step back.' Mark hands Lukas the torch, takes the pickaxe, inserts the flat end between the bars and pulls. 'Bastard,' he hisses as he turns the pickaxe towards the floor to get more leverage and pushes down on it. 'Not a chance.' He exhales.

'Give it here.' Lukas steps into the recess and grabs the pickaxe handle. He inhales deeply and pushes down with all his might. The grid jumps out of the manhole with a loud, metallic clang.

'Bloody hell, mate!' Mark says quietly.

Lukas smiles, drops the pickaxe and squeezes against the wall to let Dannii move past him. She runs her hand across his chest and shines her torch down the manhole. 'Metal steps. Good,' she says and disappears down the hole.

'How deep?'

'Ten yards, I'd say.'

'How come you're so strong?' Marks looks over Lukas's shoulder.

Lukas shrugs. 'I've always been that way.'

'You should be a boxer, you'd have them all.'

'Didn't have them all at Guide Bridge, did I?'

'True, but then you were looking after the lady.'

Lukas grins.

'Another door,' Dannii shouts up. 'Wooden. Padlocked. Very corroded.'

'Is there room for two?' Mark shouts.

'No. I'll come up. I don't think you'll be able to unlock it, Mark. I think it needs more brute force.' Dannii sticks her head out of the manhole. Lukas helps her up and pushes the pickaxe through his belt.

He breaks the padlock with the same lever movement as before and opens the wooden trap door. 'Water,' he shouts. 'A boat! Speedwell?'

'Yes!' Dannii confirms it. 'Bingo. This is Halfway House. The passing place for the boats.'

'There's no oars, crap,' Mark swears.

Dannii smiles at him wryly. 'You've never done the trip, have you?'

'No. Should I have?' He scowls at her.

'Look at the width of the boat. Then look at the width of the canal. Notice something?' She winks at Lukas.

'No room for oars. How the – ?'

'You lie down on the front of the boat and walk on the ceiling.'

'You're having me on.'

'No, I'm not. And yours is the first shift.'

The canal shaft ends after fifteen minutes travel. Another boat is moored at a second jetty, for the return trip Lukas presumes.

'Take the boat back, you two.' Dannii disembarks.

'You're joking!' Mark spits.

'Do it, mate. No loose ends. I take one, you take the other.' Lukas flings the rucksack onto the jetty and lies down on his back.

Mark unties the other boat. 'What are you going to do? Have a fag?'

'I'm going to see what's beyond this fence. Looks like a drop. Switch the light on, moron. It's somewhere near the jetty. Safety switch,' Dannii says.

Lukas has already set off down the tunnel and just about sees the cave light up in all its glory. He ties his boat up at Halfway House, below the hatch that let them into the cavern less than an hour ago. His clothes are drenched with sweat and dripping water.

Mark walks the other boat to a standstill next to his. 'Bloody hell, me back's killing me.'

'I'll take the trip back.' Lukas joins him.

'Cheers, Hercules. She really gets off on your welly, doesn't she.'

'Yes, she does,' Lukas groans as he gets the boat going.

Mark laughs. 'Wanna tell me more?'

'Not really, except I don't think anyone's ever taken care of her properly. She's always fended for herself, always been the tough one. I don't think she's ever trusted anyone enough to let herself go completely.'

'And she's letting herself go completely with you?' Mark mocks.

'You truly are a moron. She's extremely strong mentally, but also very vulnerable.'

'Oh, true love, is it now? You're having me on.' Lukas just grunts in reply. 'Anyway, on to more important things – when are we going to listen to what me son sent?'

'No signal here,' Lukas pants.

'I'm just dying to know what's going on.'

'D'you know a Michael Jackson, Tony Jackson's brother, also called Mr T, after his middle name, Tyson?' Lukas grunts.

'You're having me on. Tony Jackson's brother? Michael Tyson Jackson. How's that for a name? Someone is pulling your plonker.'

'That someone is Stan Entwistle, and Jackson is his co-boss at Dolly Green, apparently ex-military.'

'Bugger me, I never new Tony had a brother.'

'Either that, or Tony is still alive and had a face job, like you.' Lukas turns his head. 'Are we nearly there? My abs are about to pop.'

'Tony still alive? That means he's totally conned Briggs,' Mark says with a sneer.

'And he'll be after you, 'cos you shopped him in the trial.'

'You're right. Crap,' Mark swears. 'What's Stan said?'

'That Mr T is Tony's brother, served in Iraq. Navy, allegedly. That Tony hid the cash. Mr T picked it up and used it to rebuild the club. Linda says he's a bad ass. Says he grooms boys. They wear the Tyson tattoos, 'cos they belong to his "gang". Lukas breathes hard. 'I got to stop talking for a bit,' he puffs.

'We're here anyway, mate.'

Lukas rolls over and grabs the jetty. Mark jumps out and ties up the boat. He sits down on the wooden bench erected for waiting tourists.

'Give me a sec.' Lukas rolls onto his back to catch his breath. He stretches out his legs and flinches.

'Mate, both scenarios are possible. Yes, he could've had a brother and yes, it could be the return of Tony. Did you tell Stan that tattoos have done over the old boy?'

'Yes.'

'How did he react? Hi, love.'

Lukas lifts his head, watches Dannii get into the boat and sit down to face him. She hands him a bottle of water and a chocolate bar. He drinks greedily, takes a big bite and hands it to Mark, who pulls a face. Lukas swallows. 'Stan was concerned. Wants to run a tidy ship. Not like when Tony was there.'

'He said that? If Tony *has* returned and Stan doesn't realise then he's thick as shit.'

'We can assume that he isn't the brightest button,' Dannii says.

'How old was he when Tony was there? When you were there? Did you even see Stan in those days?' Lukas props himself up on his elbows.

'Now you mention it, no,' Mark says. 'I saw his kid brother, though, your son-in-law, Jason. Stan must've already been semi-pro, probably already at All Saints, Audenshaw.'

Lukas frowns. 'So he might not have known Tony well. He mentioned that T is his uncle's "lost" brother. Is Tony impersonating a fictitious sibling?'

'Where did you get your nose job done, Mark?' Dannii asks.

'Nose job? Complete reconstruction more like. Bridgewater Hospital.'

'Police job?' Lukas sits up.

'Referral. They paid for part of it.'

'So, imagine this scenario. Briggs puts Tony away to distract from the fact that he's betting heavily at the club. He uses you to do the dirty work and testify against Tony. Tony's sent down for a while, is released and disappears. D'you know how he died?'

Mark shrugs. 'Alleged knifing. In the face. There was a funeral.'

'Could have been staged. I'm not suggesting we dig up any coffins, but if Briggs and Tony had a deal and if Mr T is Tony reincarnate, then it's just possible he had surgery at the same private hospital that the police, and incidentally, Premiership footballers, use.'

'Far-fetched, mate.'

'But plausible?'

'Entirely.'

'The alternative, if we do have two Jacksons, is that Tony is indeed dead, and that Mike has taken over, and is a bit dirty. This would be the end of the lead.' Lukas shrugs.

'Whereas with theory one, there is a connection. Between Dolly Green, Briggs, betting, fixing, Premiership football, tattooed teenagers and beaten-up old men. And me, the blogger,' Dannii says. 'And Jean-Pierre, and why he employed me in the first place. It's too good a conspiracy theory not to be true.'

'Who's Jean-Pierre?' Mark asks.

'I'll tell you later.' Dannii looks at Lukas. 'Is Stan a pawn or a liar?'

'It doesn't really matter what Stan is. I'm going straight down to Moss Side with a set of these.' Mark jangles the lock picks.

'He could be a pawn, or stupid, or a bit of an actor, or just a bit torn. I agree with Mark. Stan's persuasion doesn't really matter right now. The important fact is that Stan, or Mr T, must've been instrumental in getting you two charmers wanted for assault. And what that means is that either Stan or T, or both of them, are much happier to see one or both of you out of the way of Dolly Green.' Dannii looks at her watch.

'Nice summary.' Mark grins.

'We should stay here, try to get some sleep. I rigged up a rope to get us down into the main cave. Have a look down.'

'I'm not sleeping here, love. I'm not sleeping at all. I'm freezing. I want to get out of this bloody hole.' Mark spits into the water.

Dannii looks at him. 'This is possibly the last bit of timber we've got to sit on in this place. We should use it to keep warm. Further on it'll be damper and colder. We could get wet through.'

'What's ahead, love?' Lukas asks.

'Hopefully Peak Cavern. I went caving there ages ago. I'm hoping not too much has changed.' Dannii laughs. 'Sorry, not funny, in our situation.'

'I think it's hilarious,' Mark mutters.

'If we find the right branch we'll start to climb and eventually come out at some disused mines near Rowter Farm.' Dannii opens the map. Lukas moves to sit next to her. 'I think about here'—she taps the map —'Or there.' She taps another place, half a square away.

'Hazard mine, disused,' Lukas reads.

Mark laughs. 'Sounds fantastic. How will we know where we are?'

Dannii looks at Lukas. 'In the absence of GPS it would be better if we came out in the light, don't you think?'

Lukas nods. 'Absolutely. We'd be on top. Should see something.'

'Like a bloody blizzard?' Mark says.

'How far? Couple of miles?' Lukas looks at the map.

'Yes,' she says. 'But in a lot more difficult terrain than we've had so far. I might have to go ahead and suss out some branches of the cave. We mustn't get lost.'

Lukas squeezes her hand. 'We'll stick together.'

She smiles. 'We'll see. Let's rest for a couple of hours first.'

'For Christ's sake,' Mark says, pulls his knees up and lies down on the bench.

Chapter 51

Lukas wakes up holding Dannii. Mark sits and stares at them. 'Can we get going now? Have you finished your cuddle?' He scowls.

'What's the time?'

'Gone midnight.'

Dannii stretches. 'Let's go.' She picks up her stuff and gets out of the boat.

'Shall I turn the light off?'

'No, we'll need it to get our bearings down there.'

'OK. Ready?'

'Yes, go!'

Lukas leans back and abseils into the void.

'This is Bottomless Pit. Hundreds of feet deep.' They walk past a lake and stalagmites. The electric lighting hidden high up in the rocks and below the water's surface lends a spectacular view of the cave.

'There's a few branches.' Lukas directs the torch beam into the unlit corners of the dome-like cavern.

'We need to find all of them.'

'Here.' Mark points at a diagonal slash in the rock.

'How many candles have we got?'

Lukas opens the box. 'Nine.'

'Put one by each branch. Here's another, behind this boulder.' Dannii disappears behind a massive rock. Lukas hands her a couple of candles.

'Do you have a light?' She smiles at him.

'I don't smoke, you do.' He moves close to her and kisses her softly.

'Are the candles still OK?' Mark joins them. 'Honestly, you two.'

Dannii glues a candle to a rock just inside the passage. 'Could be this one. Look at the flame flickering. There's definitely movement of air. Go over and check yours. Let's follow this wall, Luke.' They walk on a narrow ledge round the lake.

'No flicker,' Mark shouts across.

'Good. Carry on.'

Mark disappears into the shadows. 'It bends round towards a passage,' he shouts. 'I need another candle.'

They find another three branches beyond the lake. 'Slight flicker on this last one,' Lukas observes.

'But it's in the wrong direction. I think this leads to Titan. Biggest cave in the Peak District,' she says. 'There's miles and miles of it.'

'Great. Let's stay well out of it.'

'We'll check the three non-flickerers first. Meet back here in half an hour?'

'I'm not happy with this,' Lukas says. 'You're the only one with any caving experience.'

'I'm not asking you to take risks. Just have a look. If there's any tricky climbs or descents come back and report. Same with water and narrow gaps. No diving or squeezing through tight holes.'

'Fat chance of that,' Mark mutters.

Dannii turns to him. 'You know, for someone who's got your training and expertise, you're quite a chicken-shit, when it comes to get up and go?'

'Piss off. Give me a torch.'

Dannii slaps her torch in Mark's palm. 'Time check.'

'Seventeen minutes to one,' Lukas says.

'Back here at quarter past. Luke, take the torch.'

'What are you going to do?'

'I'll take a candle. In a plastic bottle.' She opens the Swiss Army knife, cuts an empty plastic bottle in half and glues the candle in the bottom. 'Go, you two! What are you waiting for?' Mark disappears down the nearest passage.

'I'll take this one here,' Lukas says.

'Take care not to dislodge anything else.'

Inside the cave the floor is rocky but firm. There are markings on the walls that could be pickaxe strikes. A short distance later the passage ends, so Lukas makes his way back to Dannii and Mark in the domed cave. 'Dead end, man-made,' Lukas says.

'Mine ended in a lot of water, mate.'

'Mine's a natural crack with lots of little side passages. I reckon the rock's more porous over there.' Dannii points towards the passage behind the boulder.

'You think that one could be passable?' Lukas asks.

'It has to be. I remember descending to Peak Cavern. We were told that from Peak there's a way through to Speedwell. There was no mention of having to go via Titan, which is further south, but also links up with Peak. It would be a huge diversion to go through Titan.'

'We'll take the first passage,' Lukas says.

'Mark, belay me up the cliff, please. I'll switch the light off.' Dannii walks away.

'Please? Are you learning manners after all, hon?' Mark laughs and follows her.

01:30

'Best we just use one torch from now on.'

'This isn't a mine shaft.'

'No, it's natural. Watch your step.'

02:30

'Wow.' Lukas puts an arm round Dannii's shoulder. She shines the torch into a massive cave; the beam hardly reaches the wall opposite. Huge stalactites loom ominously above them.

'This is Peak cavern.' She smiles at him. 'We'll make it.'

'The first bit of good news in hours,' Mark mutters behind them.

'Peveril Castle is now above us . We should head south-south-west. Any link to Titan will be over there.' Dannii points and looks at the compass. 'Let's head the opposite way.'

Ten minutes later they've crossed the cave. 'Just look at this mess!' She says and shakes her head.

'Civilisation, thank fuck.' Mark stands between remnants of a fire and a pile of decaying plastic food containers.

Relieved, Lukas laughs. 'People leave litter everywhere these days, don't they?'

'Even on Mount Everest.' Mark slaps his shoulder.

Lukas turns to Dannii. 'How much further d'you think, love?'

'Another mile maybe. We'll be ascending soon. This is the tricky bit.'

03:30

Dannii enters a diagonal crack in the wall. Lukas notices protective climbing devices and chalk marks all around the entrance to the passage. He runs his fingers over small protrusions – holds for boulderers and climbers.

'Stay close, Luke!' Dannii shouts from inside the passage. He follows her onto sloping ground. 'Use your torch,' she says. 'This is too dangerous not to see properly. But watch for the batteries fading.' Lukas directs his torch beam towards Mark's feet.

'Thanks, mate,' Mark says. I'm not really wearing the right shoes for this adventure. They're coming apart.'

Lukas concentrates as they scramble up rock and scree. More than a couple of times Mark slips, swearing loudly. Lukas shines his torch into one of the many cracks in the wall. Another huge cave looms below to the left. He wonders how safe the ground is that they're walking on. A regular climbers' path, he tells himself, it's got to be safe.

04:00

'Can we stop for a minute. I'm absolutely goosed.' Mark sits down on a rock.

Lukas switches off his torch and lights a candle. 'Let's rest.'

Dannii sits down next to Mark. 'You OK?'

Mark's trousers are ripped and he is bleeding from one knee. 'It's nothing. I just need a rest,' he says quietly.

Lukas passes a chocolate bar to Mark. 'Here. Eat. And drink some water.'

Mark wets his lips. Lukas takes the bottle off him and drinks in deep gulps, then sits down on a rock and leans back against the wall. 'I've had enough of this bloody cave.'

'You've said it,' Mark mutters.

'You'd rather be out there in the blizzard?' Dannii chews.

'Nope.' Lukas closes his eyes.

05:30

He is woken by his own snoring. The candle is dying. He checks his watch. They've been here for over an hour. He looks at Dannii whose temple rests against the wall. She's fast asleep under her woolly hat and hoodie. Her gloved hands cradle her face. Next to her, Mark's head hangs forward, his jaw on the buttoned-up collar of his crombie, his trousers torn and bloodstained, the soles of his shoes almost off. Lukas pulls his collar up and puts his head back against the wall.

'Luke.' Dannii's soothing voice shakes him. 'It's six-fifteen. We should get going.' He opens his eyes and gets up.

Mark is standing in the narrow passage, stamping his feet.

'There's a spare hat, Mark.'

Mark shakes his head. 'I'm OK. Feet are soaked, though.'

Lukas smiles. 'And you told us to wrap up warm,' he says.

'Come on.' Dannii leads the way. 'Bit of climbing ahead, I'm afraid.' The passage narrows and steepens further. They haul themselves up the jagged rock. Lukas has to twist and turn to squeeze his shoulders through the narrow gaps, unsure if they are climbing rock or compacted boulder rubble. 'Step carefully. Some of this is quite loose.'

'It's also covered in bloody slime.' Mark grunts. 'Bloody shoes!'

'I'm right behind you,' Lukas says.

Mark laughs. 'That's what I'm worried about.'

'Hands and knees,' Dannii says.

'Bloody hell! I'm going to wreck me crombie.'

'I'll buy you a new one.' Lukas hears the smugness in Dannii's voice. He kneels down, and bends his arms to even get close to fitting through the next gap. In the end he lies flat on his stomach and pushes himself through the tunnel. He struggles to blank out the fact that he's stuck in rock, a long distance under the earth's surface, chased by childhood fears of being trapped or buried alive. He rests for a minute.

'You OK, Luke?' Dannii sounds anxious.

'Just taking a breather. You through?'

'Yes.' Her light shines towards him.

'Does it get any narrower?'

'No, you're OK.'

'Just,' he says to himself and struggles on.

'We're getting close now,' Dannii says.

Lukas looks over Mark's shoulder into the tunnel ahead. It seems to become wider as it slopes up. A hundred yards on, they emerge into a small chamber. Dannii shines the torch along the walls and floor. Through large gaps it reveals the same huge cave Lukas spotted before.

'There doesn't seem to be an exit.'

'Love, please. We've come all this way –' Mark groans.

She shines the torch into the cave below. 'It's too far down.'

'What are we standing on?'

'Some kind of ledge.'

'Is this man-made?'

'Holy crap!' Mark peers down into the cave.

'It looks like it. This floor here – it's so smooth.'

Lukas walks ahead. The wall blocking their way seems to consist of several massive blocks of rock, wedged together. 'Is this rock fall, love?'

'Difficult to tell.' She runs her hand over the stone. 'I don't remember this.' She shines the torch up at the ceiling. 'Looks like it's growing out of the ceiling.'

'What do we do?'

Dannii directs the beam towards the left. 'I don't think even I could get through those cracks.'

'Have you seen *The Descent*?'

'Don't! I'm surprised you didn't mention it before.' She moves the light about quickly.

He stares beyond her and grabs her shoulder. 'There,' he says and points straight at his worst nightmare. 'There's a passage, I think,' Lukas says quietly.

They move closer to the obstructing wall. Near the left of the chamber the ground falls away sharply towards the gaps and the cave below. Halfway down the wall, slightly below them, is a gap. Dannii shines the torch into the hole, then looks round at Lukas anxiously. 'It's tight.'

Lukas swallows. 'Try it,' he says. He watches her go down on her knees and peer into the gap. Then her hands, head and shoulders disappear.

'Jesus, this is going to mess up our clothes, big time,' Mark says, hands deep in pockets.

'There's a way through. There's a chamber and a further ascent ahead.' Dannii's voice is muffled. Lukas watches her pull her legs in, then she twists and disappears from view.

'Christ, this bloody cave.' Mark looks around.

'Shut up,' Lukas barks and stares into the crack.

'I'm through,' she shouts. 'It's tight alright. You've got to twist somewhat. It's doable. Who's next?'

'Go on,' Lukas says quietly.

'Crap,' Mark says.

'Can you hear me, you two?'

'Mark's coming through,' Lukas hollers. He watches Mark crouch down in front of the hole.

'I'll talk you through it, Mark,' he hears her shout. 'Put your arms forward and your head and shoulders into the gap. Then push with your feet.'

Mark follows her instructions, swearing. His torso slowly disappears into the crack.

'Fuck, it's tight.'

Lukas swallows.

'Look to the left. Slide yourself down towards the edge.'

'You must be joking.' Mark's voice sounds small and croaky.

'Just do it,' she shouts. 'You're not going to slip.'

'You're not fucking kidding. It's too fucking tight.'

Lukas watches Mark's torso twist. Then Mark pulls his legs in and disappears from view. Lukas looks down at the gap. His knees weaken. Not surprising, after the exercise they've had tonight. Walking a boat, for miles. Climbing and abseiling. Not really his usual regime. No wonder he feels a bit wobbly. He crouches down and directs his torch beam into the gap. About a yard away are Mark's feet, twisted sideways, soles hanging off.

'You got to turn yourself on your back, Mark,' Dannii shouts.

'How am I going to do that, woman? I'm stuck as it is.'

'Go further forwards.'

'What, into the void?'

'If that's what it takes, yes.'

Lukas hears cursing. How on earth is he going to fit through this hole? He knows in his heart he's too big. Towering a good head above Mark, he must be a few stone heavier than Mark ever was. His shoulders are wider, his chest much deeper. Mark is of medium build, he himself a giant.

He peers into the hole. To the immediate left the rock opens into a triangular gap. If he could get his chest into it and move sideways, rather than entering the passage head and shoulders first, he might find more room for himself. He watches Mark's feet move further away from him, then Mark turns over slowly, groaning.

'Mark, you're doing well,' Dannii shouts. 'Now walk your hands to where I am and pull your body round. There are plenty of cracks to hold on to.' Mark grunts and swears, then his legs disappear from view.

Lukas's side of the cave falls silent.

Then he hears Dannii, muffled, from a distance. 'Well done, Mark.'

'He's never going to fit through there, love,' Mark says, not quietly enough.

Fear creeps up Lukas's back. He walks up to the gap and turns away again, trying to control his breathing and his fear. He tells himself to be rational but knows full well he is too big to fit through the passage.

A strong movement in his bowels overcomes him suddenly; he knows he has to go right now.

'Luke,' she shouts.

His voice catches, he clears his throat. 'Give me a minute.'

'Take as long as you need.'

Lukas moves back into the tunnel, pulls down his pants and crouches in a recess. He groans as his body relieves itself in such an undignified way. He digs in the rucksack for paper and wipes himself with the leaflet of Blue John Cavern.

'Dannii, ' he shouts back at the gap.

'You ready for this, Luke?'

'As ready as I'll ever be. I need to lose the rucksack.'

'Hang on.' He hears Dannii grunt. Then the end of the rope appears in the passage. Lukas just about reaches it and pulls it through.

'Take your coat off,' Mark shouts. 'In fact, take everything off. And start off on your back.'

Lukas's throat is dry. He strips down to his T-shirt, puts his coat in the rucksack and ties it to the rope. 'Pull,' he shouts and watches the rucksack disappear.

He sits down with his back to the rock and takes a deep breath. Hips raised he pushes his head into the gap, switches off the torch and stuffs it in his trouser pocket. The stone's edge digs into his back as he squeezes his shoulders into the hole. To his right is the triangular space he spotted before. He exhales and manoeuvres his chest past the sharp edges of the entrance. To his surprise his torso fits into the chamber. He pushes on backwards, his hands against the ceiling, his right foot still outside, in mid air. Then he bends his knees and pulls it into the hole.

'Luke, are you there?' Dannii sounds closer now.

'I'm in,' he says and grapples to his left, tryingto shift in that direction. But the passage decreases in height. 'I can't go left – it's too low.'

'Move in the direction of your head,' she says calmly.

Lukas shunts backwards. The ceiling lowers further, and his forehead is flat against it. He pushes hard until the back of his head rests on some kind of edge. His right arm free, he reaches for the torch in his pocket and turns his head. Beyond him is the vast cave. His head sticks out of the side of a rock face. He moves the torch out into the void and looks left. She is right. The gap is wider there. Beyond the narrow bit. He pulls out further and places his hands on the edge of the rock above, then wiggles left into the narrowing passage. He lies on loose rock gravel, which aids his progress, but the gap is getting narrower and narrower and he finds it difficult to breathe. He stops and tries to fill his lungs.

'How are you doing? Talk to me!' Dannii demands.

'OK,' he gasps. 'Tight.'

'Don't forget to use your legs. Bring them with you.'

He'd pulled his legs up to the left. This was a mistake, he now realises, as it forced his right hip to rotate up. He straightens his right leg and pushes his knee sideways. He moves his bottom in a crab-like fashion and has some success until his hips grind against the ceiling and the pressure on his groin becomes unbearable. He stretches his left leg further. Suddenly he is able to straighten it and hook his heel round an edge. But he won't be able to move his torso any further to the left without serious pain.

'I can see your foot,' Dannii shouts.

'Dannii!' he gasps. 'Tie the rope – ' He struggles for air.

He feels her tie the rope round his ankle. He tries to pivot and bring his right foot round, but the pressure on his midriff is excruciating. There is only one way to go, and it is further backwards, into the void.

He pushes back and feels the rope tighten. His hips won't budge left. He swears and backtracks until he can reach and undo his belt buckle. He squeezes left, gains a couple of inches and relights the torch. The rock face above his head is jagged and broken. With his free hand he feels for hand holds. He pockets the torch, reaches out and up and finds a ledge to hook his fingers around. Then he pulls himself out of the hole until his ribcage is free.

'Make sure you tie that rope onto something solid,' he hollers at the top of his voice.

'Already done,' Dannii shouts back. 'How are you doing?'

'I'm hanging in thin air.' Lukas shuffles his hips sideways, sweating profusely. No way is he going to get his midriff through the narrow gap to the left. 'Need to go out further,' he hollers, panting. 'Need to be quick. My arms are going.'

'What are you holding onto?' Dannii shouts.

Full of lactic acid his screaming muscles are seizing up; he has no time to reply. After a deep breath he yanks himself out of the hole until his hips are free, drives his roped leg through the gap to the left, forces his right leg to follow and grapples for another hand hold with his left hand. He finds nothing but smooth rock and feels himself slide backwards. 'Pull,' he screams.

The rope tightens agonisingly slowly. He is slipping, close to losing his right hand hold as well. He reaches inside the gap, groping for a hold, his movement full of panic. He hooks his fingers into a crack just at the moment the rope yanks his legs a few inches back into the rock.

'Stop,' he bellows. The cliff edge digs deeply into his bottom and genitals. Pulling on the rope with his legs, he squeezes his midriff back into the gap and finds another reverse handhold on the ceiling to his left. His T-shirt has worked its way up to his armpits. He pulls it off impatiently.

'Luke! Let us know when you need a pull.'

'OK.' He presses his torso further into the gap. It's not as wide as he had hoped and the rock is covered in jagged miniature stalagmites that dig into his flesh. He looks towards his feet and into Dannii's torch light, which illuminates the way ahead. To the left the gap narrows. This is the widest part and his hips are relatively free, but his chest is compressed uncomfortably. Small pieces of rock burrow into his skin, as he wills himself towards the exit. Progress is centimeter by centimetre, then millimetre by millimetre, then he is stuck. He tugs hard on his leg but can't move any further. He pants for air.

Dannii's face appears next to his feet. 'You OK?'

'Can't breathe,' he whispers. 'No further.'

'Bring your right leg round,' Dannii tells him. He moves his right foot, then feels her tie the rope round both his ankles. 'Straighten up! We'll pull you through.'

Impossible, he wants to shout, but can't make a sound. Panic rises in his chest, and he aches to claw his way back into the void, just to get some oxygen. The back of his head tingles with fear. He feels sick and light headed. He forces himself to hold his breath, to stop hyperventilating .

'Luke.' She hits his legs. 'You hear me? Straighten up! Focus!'

'We'll end up dislocating your hip if you don't shift,' Mark shouts.

Lukas shuffles his hips and rotates to the left. The jagged stalactites above him cut into his skin, and he is certain they are drawing blood, just like the deeply embedded gravel under his shoulder blades. He tugs on the rope to signal he is ready. 'Hurry up,' he croaks, convinced she can't hear him.

The rope tightens.

'Push against the ceiling, as hard as you can and pull with your legs, count of three,' she shouts. He puts his hands up wide against the rock. 'One,' Dannii shouts. He knows this is going to hurt. Convinced he is bleeding already he knows this is going to be bad. He just hopes he's not going to break his ribs. 'Two!'

Lukas focuses. Push and pull as hard as possible. Into the pain. 'Make it quick,' he shouts.

'Three!'

The rope tightens abruptly. His joints stretch, knees and ankles popping. He flexes his muscles and pulls hard against the rope. His hips move an inch away from him, distending his spine and squeezing his torso further. His ribs, like springs, are compressed to breaking point. He gasps for air. Suddenly the pain is much sharper and completely intolerable. Panic grabs hold of his heart; this needs to stop now, no matter what. He screams and pushes as hard as he can, his ribs compressing further. He feels them creak, his vision going with the pain. In a final, desperate effort he tenses his chest and shoulders, and rears up against the unyielding rock.

Then there is movement. A rumble, dust and debris in his eyes and mouth. And shouting. He turns his head away and hard, as cold stone grates against his cheekbone. His legs are being yanked sharply, his ribcage still stuck. Completely winded and close to passing out he bucks his taut torso up and down. The weight on his chest shifts and changes for the worse. He fights unconsciousness and crumbling rock; sharp edges cut his flesh deeply, as he is being pulled through the rock collapsing around him. He attempts to turn his torso sideways and finally the weight on his chest shifts. He screams and breathes and coughs, feeling a harder, faster pull. His legs lift, he grates over some kind of edge and then his bottom hits the ground. Through a reddish haze he looks back at the shifting, tumbling rock, illuminated by candlelight. Then he just lies there, panting.

'Jesus, mate,' Mark says quietly.

Dannii crouches by Lukas's side. He makes to wipe his eyes, but she holds his wrists. 'Don't.' She turns to Mark. 'Water.' Lukas hears the bottle click open. Water pours over his face. His vision clearer now, he makes to get up. 'Don't,' she says again.

Mark holds him down now. 'Pour here.' The water on his torso makes him shiver. 'He's going into shock. Put his legs up!' Mark urges.

'I'm not going into shock.' Lukas struggles to sit up but Mark pushes him down and presses something against his chest. 'Do his arms,' Marks says.

Lukas lifts his head to watch Dannii, in her vest, pour water on his left arm, which is caked in mud and blood. She dabs at him, then dries him with her shirt. 'Now try to sit up.'

Lukas sits up slowly and gasps for air. 'My ribs are bust.' He tastes blood as he groans.

'You wouldn't breathe like that if they were broken,' Mark says.

'This is going to hurt – ' Dannii pours water over his back and shoulders. He flinches. 'Slate splinters. What happened to your T-shirt?'

'You look like the Incredible Hulk,' Mark says.

'Came off.' Lukas grimaces and clenches his teeth as Dannii works on his back. Something seeps into his eyes, clouding the cave red once more.

Lukas hears her tear packaging. He groans as cloth makes contact with open wound.

'Lift your arms,' Mark tells him. He obeys. Mark wraps something around his torso. 'That's all we've got, love.'

Dannii looks at his face. She frowns and dabs at his cheekbone.

'How's your legs?' Mark unties Lukas's ankles.

'Fine.' Lukas shivers, his teeth chatter.

'He's going into shock.' Mark squints at him.

'Fuck you!' Lukas struggles to his feet. His red world spins instantly and he leans heavily on Mark's shoulder. He rubs his eyes and swears as his stomach lurches. He turns away from Mark, holds on to the wall and throws up. He groans as he heaves once more. The pain in his ribcage is excruciating.

Dannii steadies him. 'Luke, did you hit your head?' Her voice comes to him as from a distance. He shakes his head and then his knees buckle.

'Fuck! Told you he's going into shock.'

'Put him down – carefully.'

Lukas sinks into a soft cloud of cotton wool. He stretches out and moans with relief. Mark covers him in something shiny and for some reason lifts up his legs. He doesn't want his legs up and makes to kick out, but he's too tired. And Dannii, she just looks down at him and smiles. She strokes his face and it doesn't hurt; the pain is on the other side, a big, heavy burning pain. He tries to smile back.

'Open your mouth,' she whispers. He obeys. She feeds him something that takes away the taste of puke and blood. He sucks on it and tries to swallow, but his mouth is too dry. Now she raises his head and puts the water bottle to his lips. He drinks greedily, choking and coughing, and once more his ribcage explodes with intolerable pain. And then he just lies there.

'Will you go and work out how we're going to get out of this fucking hole, please, woman?'

She gets up. 'How long will he need?'

'Another five. Don't be long. Look at him! The Hulk meets the Silver Surfer. I wouldn't want to have to wrestle him.'

Lukas hears her footsteps quickly fade away. He feels more together now. His body is warming up and as the blood pulses back to the surface of his skin he feels his multiple injuries. 'How bad is it, Mark?' He lifts his head and looks at himself, wrapped in a space blanket.

'I'm not going to pussyfoot around. You almost had it in there. The whole bloody lot collapsed around you.'

Lukas touches his chest and winces. He looks at his cut and seeping hands, then turns his arms to look at his torn elbows.

'Nice carpet burn.' Mark smirks.

'You can let me go now. I'm OK.' Mark releases his legs. Lukas sits up. 'Five seconds longer and I would've passed out.' He sips water and looks up at Mark. 'You look like a tramp. Sorry 'bout your crombie.'

Mark laughs. 'Don't talk to me about looks until you've consulted a mirror.'

'You're up.'

'Hey,' he says, as she crouches down by his side. She smiles, tears in her eyes. He touches her face. 'That bad?'

'I'm just relieved to see you in sort of one piece.' She sniffs and laughs. 'I've good news. We're almost out. We'll surface in a disused mine.'

'Hazard mine,' Mark says.

'Yes. And there's nothing but blue skies and sunshine outside. It's a beautiful morning.'

'The first day of the rest of my life,' Lukas mumbles as he watches his blood seep through the bandages.

Chapter 52

'You're not good, mate, I don't care what you say. These dressings are inadequate. We need to get you sorted. Come on, let's get out of this hole.' Mark gently pushes him forward.

Lukas follows Dannii up the passage. He can't bear to wear the fleece, to feel fabric against his wounds. Two space blankets wrapped around him, his skin burns red hot and amplifies the pain from his cuts and abrasions to an intolerable level. It's like he's been rolled in brambles. But he'd risk hypothermia without the blankets, so he grits his teeth and gets on with the climb. His legs shake as he plants his feet insecurely on the wet rock, and more than once he has to steady himself against the wall. Then sunlight hits him with a vengeance, the fresh air almost knocking him out. He takes in big, painful breaths of winter ozone. Tears sting his eyes.

They emerge into a snowdrift which completely fills the small quarry. Lukas shrugs off the space blankets, tears off the blood-sodden dressings and throws himself face down into the powdery snow. He closes his eyes and groans with relief as the snow cools his wounds.

'Yes, mate,' he hears Mark say. Lukas turns his head. Mark is talking into an impossibly small mobile phone and studying the map. 'We need transport. Blankets, towels, food, drink, medical supplies. Bandages.

Tetanus. Morphine and glue. No, conscious. Tried to take the mountain apart.'

Dannii crouches by Lukas's side. 'Take the dressing off my back, please,' he whispers. She carefully removes the padding. Lukas groans.

'We'll be at SK 158 810 in – ?' Mark asks her.

'Thirty minutes minimum,' Dannii replies.

'Hear that? OK. Hurry. Ta. Out.' Mark closes the phone. 'How are you, mate?'

Lukas pushes himself up. The snow beneath him is bright crimson. He swallows hard. 'OK,' he groans and lies down on his back.

'Do you feel together?'

'Yes.' Lukas grimaces.

'Let's have another five before we make a move. They'll be at least an hour.'

'Who are they?' Dannii asks.

'My associates.'

'What d'you do for a living, Mark?'

'Security. All aspects thereof.'

Dannii pulls a beanie over Lukas's head. 'Luke, can you get these on?' She passes him some gloves. He sits up, pulls the mittens over his injured hands and rests his forearms on his knees.

Dannii hands out the last of the chocolate. Mark declines and gestures towards Lukas. 'Cheers, love. We should get going,' Lukas says. He struggles back to his feet, ties the blood-sodden space blankets round his waist like a skirt and follows Dannii out of the quarry. Icy wind tears at, but also chills, his injured skin. He follows Dannii's gaze back into the quarry. The place where he rested is a blood bath.

'It's melting,' Dannii says and looks at his chest. 'You're still bleeding, love.'

Lukas peers down at narrow rivers of dark blood trickling from his cuts and seeping into his trousers. His belt is open, the buckle missing. He follows Dannii down the hill. Beyond her, Peveril Castle looms against magnificent blue skies that frame the Castleton hills and Kinder Scout in the distance. To his left, the craggy edge of faraway Mam Tor reminds him of the distance they covered underground, overnight.

Dannii's eyes follow his gaze. 'Mam Tor. That's where we started.'

Lukas nods. 'Unbelievable.'

'You know it's called the Shivering Mountain?'

'I didn't, but it's quite fitting, don't you think?'

She laughs and continues downhill. 'Good to have you back, Luke.'

'Good to be back,' he mutters and follows her gingerly.

They walk along a rough bridleway, passing more disused mines. Directly in front yawns a massive limestone quarry, skirted by a rough road. Broken asphalt shows through melting snow. Temperatures couldn't have been too low last night, otherwise the road would have iced over. In the distance Lukas spot farms and a village. He turns to Mark. 'What's that down there? Hope?'

'Bradwell. Hope's beyond that hill.' Mark points left.

'We're not going as far as that, are we?' Lukas squints at the hamlet, shielding his eyes against the glare of the morning sun's reflection.

'Would I do that to you?' Mark grins. 'Are you in pain?'

'I'm OK like this, but I can't bear to imagine what it's going to be like when I put a shirt on.' Lukas touches his temple and looks at his fingers. Red pus rather than blood.

'We'll sort you out. They're bringing supplies. The ooze will dry up in this wind. Your back's still pretty bad. Full of splinters that need to come out.'

'Great. Bleeding badly?'

'Thick and slow. Dark blood, deep wounds. You're going to mess up the car.'

'Where are your mates coming from?' Lukas touches his back just above his pants. The blood on his fingers is syrupy and almost black.

'The depot I took you to after MacFarlane.'

'That's near where you live?'

'Yep.'

'Nice house?'

'Adequate. Thirties semi.'

Lukas can't imagine Mark in a thirties semi. He can't imagine Mark in any kind of homely setting. The shabby flat seems to fit him down to a T. A shabby flat and most of his time spent in the pub.

'Girlfriend?' Lukas asks. Mark guffaws. Lukas looks at him. 'What does that mean?'

'It means it's none of your business.'

'But my business is in the public domain?'

'Your business is my business, mate.'

'Yet you won't tell me about you?' Lukas says, sharply.

'Isn't it enough that I save your bacon almost daily?' Mark scowls.

'Will you two stop bickering, dammit,' Dannii hisses. 'As soon as we're in the clear, you start again.'

'Didn't realise we're in the clear,' Lukas mumbles.

'We're in the clear, any minute now.' Mark squints at him.

Lukas glares back. 'Thanks.'

'For what?'

'For saving my life.' Lukas grabs Mark's collar and shakes him. 'I almost fucking died, you twat.'

'I know you almost fucking died,' Mark gasps. 'It was fucking close. Seconds. Now would you kindly let me go?'

Lukas drops Mark. Tears sting his eyes. He looks up at the sky and roars loudly at the heavens.

'We stop here.' Mark sits down on a rock in a small quarry by a crossroads and a cattle grid. 'We don't want to be in view of that farm.' He looks at the map and laughs. 'It's called Paradise Farm. Wonder why.'

'Sit down, Luke,' Dannii says. Lukas obeys. She picks up a couple of handfuls of snow and rubs them on his back then repeats the process.

'Is it stopping?' Lukas asks.

'It's not as bad. How long, Mark?'

'I reckon another twenty minutes. They won't hang about.' He turns to Lukas. 'By the way, yes. Occasionally.'

'What?' Lukas frowns at him, wincing.

'I do have a girlfriend, occasionally.'

'The same one, occasionally, or different ones?'

'Both. It's difficult to combine work, drink and girlfriends. They tend to think I'm a secretive bastard and a drunk.'

'Well, you are,' Dannii says.

'Cheers, typical woman talk.'

'Maybe you should find yourself a woman who gets blind drunk every night and doesn't divulge how she earns a living,' Lukas says.

'No way, mate. I couldn't cope with that.'

He hears the bike first. Scrambler, two cylinders. The car behind it is identical to the BMW Mark wrote off approximately twelve hours ago. The biker dismounts, walks up to Mark, takes his helmet and gloves off. 'Youse look like shit, mate.' They shake hands.

'Cheers. This is Rick, folks.'

Dannii helps Lukas to his feet. The biker named Rick walks up to Lukas, looks him up and down, then straight in the eye and squints. He is just as tall as Lukas, but of more athletic build. 'Another giant.' Rick smiles a wry smile. 'You OK?'

'Sore,' Lukas says.

'Well, apart from that. All in a day's work,' Rick says. 'I hear you breathed in and the mountain crumbled around you.' He narrows his eyes. 'Doesn't surprise me.' He taps Lukas's shoulder gently with his fist. Lukas draws a sharp breath.

'Come on, men of our stature stand above this kind of thing. Anyway, we got a nice, warm car for you and some lovely drugs to cuddle you up in a happy cloud.'

A much younger man, also clad in leathers, gets out of the BMW, keeping the car idling and retrieves a helmet from the back seat.

Rick gestures behind him. 'My associate for the day, Dave.' Dave gives a slight bow.

'And this concludes our business, lady, gentlemen.' Rick turns to Mark and points at the car. 'Supplies are in the back seat. Try and bring her back in one piece, please.' He nods at Lukas, then at Dannii, pulls on his helmet, gets on the bike and kickstarts it. Dave swings his leg over the pillion seat. The scrambler performs a tight turn by the quarry and disappears down the road in a flurry of snow.

'Get in and let's go.' Mark opens the driver's door.

The back seat of the car is covered in a plastic sheet. A couple of bags with supplies sit in the floor space behind Mark. Some blankets are stored on the back shelf. Lukas groans as he squeezes into the car and sits down on the sheet. 'Pull the seat forward, will you, mate?' Mark adjusts the passenger seat, while Dannii gets in next to Lukas. As soon as she shuts the door Mark puts the car into gear.

'What's there, food-wise?' Mark turns left when they get to Bradwell. The heating on full makes Lukas feels drowsy. He guesses his blood sugar is low and the lack of sleep plus the trauma of almost being killed inside the mountain is catching up with him. His head keeps dropping forward. He is about to give in to it when Dannii takes his arm and shakes it. 'Not just yet, sweet. There'll be plenty of time for sleeping and recovery. We need to sort you out first. Mark, there's sandwiches.' Dannii passes one over to him.

Lukas's throat is suddenly parched and Mark's sandwich smells divine. He takes the can Dannii has opened for him, drinks greedily and too fast. He sighs and belches loudly. Dannii passes over a sandwich which he devours in two bites.

Past Great Hucklow Mark turns right onto the A623 towards Peak Forest. The road is in sunshine and has been cleared and gritted.

'Decision, decisions. Didn't I say that just yesterday?' Mark laughs. 'Where to now?'

'What about your place?' Lukas mumbles through his sandwich.

'Sorry, mate.' Mark shakes his head. 'I'm sure it's been compromised. Briggs will have worked out where I am a long time ago.

And if he hasn't it'll be the only place completely safe for me. I don't want anybody or anything to jeopardise that. We don't know where all this is going to end and I want to be able to do my gardening safely, once all this is over.'

'Gardening?' Lukas pulls the plastic sheet around him and reaches for a blanket from the back.

'I like roses. And I've got a great lawn.'

Lukas raises an eyebrow at Dannii, who smiles and shrugs.

'What's that?' Mark looks into the mirror.

'Nothing.' She is still smirking.

'By the way, have a look in the medi-bag. There should be a tetanus shot. He needs that.'

Dannii finds the small ampule taped together with three miniature syringes. 'Got it. Where do I inject?' She retrieves the pre-loaded ampule from the packaging.

'Buttock. You can't miss it, it's big enough.'

'Very funny,' Lukas growls and pulls the blanket and the plastic away to bare his right side. He struggles to get his wet trousers open and groans as he twists and turns to get them down. Dannii quickly plunges the needle into his buttock.

'We can stop at my place,' she states.

'I thought you were of no fixed abode.' Lukas sits back.

Dannii digs around in the medi-bag. 'I'm not, officially. I rent, under a different name.'

Mark laughs. 'We're all incognito, except you, mate. By the way, hon, it might be a good idea if you dug the gravel out of our hero's back. Sooner the better.'

'Yeah, I'm just looking through the bag. Tweezers?'

'Iodine, dressings and morphine,' Mark says.

'Do you need morphine, Luke?' She looks at Lukas.

'Yes, he does. I once dug a cartload of shot out a mate of mine without it. Believe me, he wants morphine,' Mark says into the mirror.

Dannii passes one of the small syringes to Lukas. 'How do I do this, intra-venously?' he asks.

Mark guffaws. 'Not unless you want to be hooked for the rest of your life. Just inject it into fatty tissue – you've got enough.'

'Stop it!' Dannii hisses.

Lukas takes the top off the syringe, stabs himself in the abdomen, pushes the plunger, pulls the needle out and waits.

'So where am I going?' Mark says.

'Sale. Brooklands station.'

'We'll go via Stockport and the airport.'

Dannii peels the plastic off Lukas's back. 'Crap,' she says. 'It's stuck. It's going to bleed again if I pull it.'

'Just do it, love,' Lukas says quietly.

Mark turns on the radio. 'Finally! ModPop Radio, in range once again. Can't get that west of Gorton.'

Lukas takes in the rhythm of the song that Mark taps out on the steering wheel. The song makes him feel warm and cosy all over. Dannii pulls the plastic off his back and he feels the warm trickle of sticky blood seeping out of his wounds. The pain nags at him in a friendly way now. He knows it's for the best. He'll be fine, whatever. 'Pretty surrender,' he sings quietly along with the tune on the radio. 'Your sting is so tender.'

'Oy, mate! This is my favourite tune – would you mind?' Mark shouts.

Lukas smiles. 'Markus,' he says quietly. He feels an acute pang in his chest and chuckles. He's so close to him now, experiencing what Markus felt like, knowing what the song is all about now. Dannii's hand strokes his hair.

'Yes, Markus. With a K. My all-time hero. How d'you think I chose my temporary name? You're wrecking his song.'

Lukas laughs. He can't stop. He puts his cheek against the headrest in front of him. Tears roll down his cheeks as he laughs and laughs. And says his brother's name over and over. He feels Dannii hold him. 'He's off his head,' she says.

'Get to work, hon. Be quick.'

'He's Luke's brother,' Dannii says and Lukas feels her prod his back.

'Who is?'

Cold steel against his skin and then a short, sharp pain.

'Markus.'

Now Dannii dabs something on his back.

'What, my Markus? Hero of my life?'

Lukas laughs loudly.

'Yes.'

Lukas hums along to the tune.

'You're having me on, woman. How?'

'We're twins,' Lukas mumbles.

'Rubbish, mate. You're nothing like him.'

Cold steel again. He braces himself against the pain. 'I know. Beauty and the beast.' He visualises Markus, smiling.

Mark clears his throat. 'Listen, mate, I'm really sorry about that. I didn't mean to embarrass you.'

Lukas pulls air through his teeth sharply, as Dannii removes another splinter. 'You didn't mean to, but you constantly do.'

'Hey, I'm allowed to, I saved your life.'

Lukas laughs drunkenly and sings Markus's song.

Chapter 53

He wakes up in a cloud of cotton wool. Someone just said his name. He remembers being in the car. Another Beemer. He remembers Markus's song and hums, swaying. The car is now stationary, idling, its back windows steamed up with the dampness of their clothes. The headrest still supports his cheek. Dannii's gone, Mark is still in the driver's seat. Lukas hears him mutter to himself, something about hurrying up and bursting for a piss.

'Where are we?' Lukas croaks.

'Hi, mate, you're back with us. We're at Dannii's house.'

Lukas turns his head and winces. 'Where is she?'

'Opening the garage.' Mark puts the car into gear and pulls forward. Dannii opens Lukas's door. 'Hi.' She smiles at him broadly.

He smiles back and whispers. 'Hi, love.'

'Shall we try and get you out of there?'

He makes to swing his legs out of the car and grimaces. 'Bloody hell!' he groans through clenched teeth. He takes a deep breath and gasps with the pain of his bruised ribs. His hands clasp the side of the car door and he wills himself out and onto his feet. 'Whoa.' Out of balance, his hands reach behind him.

Mark grasps his shoulders. 'Easy! Steady on, old boy.'

Lukas pants. Out of control again; he hates it. Weakness, in himself, he despises. Fuck self-pity, grit your teeth and get on with it. Rick was right. A man of his stature should know how to pull himself together and show backbone. Again, he feels sick to his stomach. He looks down at himself. His torso is covered in a gluey paste of congealed blood and pus, except in two places where his flesh has been slashed and gapes open. 'Fuck,' he says.

'Give yourself a break,' Mark says quietly.

'Come.' Dannii takes his arm and leads him into the house.

'Lie down,' Mark orders him and spreads two large towels on the floor. Lukas groans as he struggles down onto his back in the middle of Dannii's bathroom.

'Heating's on max,' Dannii says as she crouches by his side. Lukas moans when she starts to clean around the deep cuts in his abdomen. She leans over him and kisses him gently on the lips. 'Thank god your lips are intact,' she whispers. 'And the other vital areas too, as far as I can tell.' She puts her hands on the zip of his pants.

'Hm.'

She smiles. 'You want more morphine?'

'Please,' he says. She administers the shot into his side. 'It's fantastic, you know.'

She laughs. 'I bet! That's why people get hooked. I've never tried it. You're one step ahead of me.' He chuckles and winces. She swabs his tummy. 'Now you know what Markus felt.'

'That's what I thought in the car, when his song was on. I felt incredibly close to him, although for him it must have been more extreme. He injected properly.'

'Do you know that for sure?'

'Yes. Oh, love, I wish you could've met him.'

She kisses him again. 'You've risen to the level of superstar in Mark's estimation. You, the brother of his god!' Lukas laughs loudly. It hurts his ribs and he swears.

'What's this? The giggles? Do I sense more class A drugs have been consumed?' Mark puts the tray on the toilet seat and hands out mugs and biscuits. 'I'll take mine to the spare room. I'm going to sleep. When you're done cleaning, glue him up with the stitch glue. Dries in seconds. Iodine him and put some dressings on. Bandage the whole torso so he can't shuffle it off. Can you get him to bed alone?'

'We'll be OK,' Lukas croaks. 'Thanks, mate.'

'Night-night Lucky Luke. Laters.' Mark walks away whistling "Pretty Surrender".

Lukas eases himself into the bed, chuckling. 'I'm as high as a kite, love. It's fantastic.'

'Don't tempt me.' She kisses him. 'Get some sleep. I'm going to tidy myself up and get some shopping in. I'll get you some clothes. XXXL, I assume, and what jeans size?'

'Thirty six, thirty eight. Shoes forty-eight.'

'Really?'

'Yes, really. I love you, woman,' he mumbles.

'I love you too,' she whispers and kisses his forehead.

Lukas just about hears her before drifting off to sleep.

When he wakes it's dark outside. The TV or radio is on somewhere in the house. He hears female humming. A daylight lamp in the shape of a crystal rock sits in the corner bathing the room in a cosy glow. Lukas looks around, groggily. He seems to be in the master bedroom. Whites, creams and natural colours predominate, the furniture overwhelmingly IKEA, mostly oak. He swings his legs out of bed and gasps with pain. The morphine has worn off and the pain is as sharp and acute as it could possibly be. He touches his torso gingerly, applying light pressure, and winces.

On the bedside table he spots a box of Ibuprofen and a large bottle of still water. He takes two tablets and drinks greedily. As he pushes himself up to a shaky stand he notices a pile of clothes and a toothbrush on top of the only chair in the room. There is a tracksuit, XXXL. Beneath it a pair of jeans, a T-shirt and a check shirt, socks and underwear. A pair of trainers, size 13 are on the floor. He shuffles out of the door and towards the bathroom.

'I'm up,' he shouts.

The house is filled with the most appetising smell of roast chicken, he reckons, or maybe some more exotic bird, which would explain the gamey hint.

'Are you OK? Do you need help?' Dannii's head appears at the bottom of the stairs.

'I'm fine, love. Give me a few minutes to sort myself out. Smells fab. Where's Mark?'

'Gone to rob a hospital. Do you want a drink?'

'I need one. What have you got?'

'Wine?'

Lukas groans. 'As long as you promise to carry me back to bed.'

'Anytime,' she shouts.

'Only if I can't walk any more, I mean,' he mutters to himself and shuffles into the bathroom.

The right side of his face is a mess. Both cheekbone and forehead are cut, he's lost a bit of his scalp, and his right ear and shoulder have had a right battering. She's put flannels out, nice white ones. He runs water in the basin and dabs at his face. The bleeding has stopped and he wipes away at thick scabs and ground-in dirt that cover his wounds. At least in some places his wounds clean up, in others they start to seep again. He repeats the process on his torso and arms. The bandaging round his midriff is holding up. He turns round and looks at his back in the mirror. Dark spots are visible through the bandage, but dry to the touch. He pulls off his filthy trousers and underwear, and washes in the basin, then puts on the T-shirt and tracksuit and follows the aroma of food down to the ground floor.

Chapter 54

'How d'you get the sound files onto your iPad?' Lukas stuffs a large forkful of bird into his mouth. 'This is spectacular.'

'Careful, Luke, pheasant can be full of little bones. Honestly, bloody greedy.' She shakes her head. 'I duplicated the files into a different Dropbox account, my own, just before we left the Wheatsheaf. When I was out earlier I went to McDonald's – they've got free Wi-Fi – and downloaded them onto my iPad, et voila!'

'Have you listened to what's there?'

'No, I came straight back to cook for the starving minion.' She takes a sip of wine.

Lukas wipes his mouth. 'Shall we have a listen?'

'Yes. There's three files.' She walks round the table and sits down next to him. Lukas pushes the empty plates away and takes a gulp of wine. 'Fingers crossed.'

Dannii touches the iPad. 'For what?' She gets cut off by Leroy Callaway's gruff voice.

'*Hey, Jayz, thanks for helping out this morning. And don't think I didn't see you looking at those little boys, my man. Guess it's not such a long time ago your uncle had his wicked way with you.*' Laughs. '*Turned you into a—*'

'Stop!' Lukas taps the screen. 'His uncle?'

'His uncle.' Dannii swirls the wine around and looks at him intently.

'Tony Jackson. Or his long-lost brother. Bloody hell!' Lukas taps the screen to resume playback.

'*Turned you into a right little spineless poofter, hasn't he? Anyway, the reason why I'm ringing: that—*'

Lukas taps the iPad, sits back, winces and breathes out heavily.

'He's gay.' She smiles at him.

'At least there's a good chance he is.'

'*– why I'm ringing: that reporter this morning mentioned this blog that's spreading nonsense about our little soirees and other issues that are nobody's business. Whoever writes this shit needs to be taught a* *lesson, you get where I'm coming from?'* Lukas nods. *'Anyway, I thought of you and your connections at your brother's club, maybe there's someone there that could help? I know you want to be going straight, ha, get it? But you wouldn't want anyone to know about your, well, tendencies? Have a think. And Jayz, next game I need you to do the business, OK? We can't substitute you all the time, you're supposed to be the up and coming star. Just do it, bro, OK?'*

Lukas taps the screen. 'Blackmail.'

Dannii nods. 'Poor kid. When was this? When were you there? The reporter is obviously you.'

'Day after Boxing Day. They've a youth academy. For underprivileged kids.'

'Mark is going to love this.' Dannii finishes her wine and gets up to fetch the bottle.

'You bet. What a bastard.'

'Anyway, he admits to the soirees and match fixing; I think we're in possession of Leroy Callaway's P45.' She returns with the wine.

Lukas shakes his head. 'Except we acquired the recordings illegally. Won't stand up in court.'

She pours the wine. 'Couldn't you write a nice little piece about it?'

He takes his glass. 'Or you?' Lukas drinks.

She laughs. 'That's exactly what I've been doing all along and everybody's calling me a nutter.'

'Isn't that what you wanted, genius?'

'Yes, but now people want to teach me a lesson.'

'Just imagine what they'd do to me if this ends up in the papers. Vladi wouldn't touch it with a bargepole.'

'Shall we listen to the next message?' She sits back down, close to him. Lukas taps the screen.

'Jason. Listen son. I got your message. Look, don't panic. I can imagine…'

Dannii puts her hand on Lukas's arm. 'Bradshaw?' Lukas nods. 'Moses Bradshaw.'

' – panic. I can imagine what you must feel like, especially with all the stuff you've been through, but once you join a senior team there's a hierarchy we need to adhere to, otherwise the team won't work. Callaway's a good man. OK, he sometimes speaks out of turn, but he's had it tough too, in the past, you're not the only one. He's a good leader. I want you to trust him and do what he says. He needs to be able to rely on you to follow his orders without question on the pitch, otherwise the team won't function. If he tells you to do things that, as

236

you suggest, have consequences, well, he's the captain and sometimes things go wrong. The decision of how we play is first and foremost mine, that's true, but once you're actually on the pitch, he's much closer to the action. So I want you to follow his lead, under all circumstances. As I said before, I won't have players talk about other players behind their backs, especially not the captain. You, the team, must build on him, you're like a pyramid. But, Jason, thanks for having the confidence in me to confide. There's nothing wrong with mentioning things if you're worried about something. I won't forget what you said and if at any point in the future something happens that makes me change my mind I will take action. But until then, please follow your captain. I'll see you at training. Bye, lad.'

Dannii finishes rolling a cigarette. 'Blimey.' She looks up.

'He doesn't want to know.' Lukas leans back, winces, then puts his hands behind his head slowly.

'Turns a blind eye.' Dannii holds his gaze and slowly licks the Rizla paper, seals the cigarette and puts it between her lips. Lukas instantly desires both, the nicotine and her lips. He catches himself licking his own.

She smiles. 'Do you want one?'

'I might have a drag.' He rocks on his chair.

'Don't you want me to go outside?'

'Don't be daft, it's your house. As long as you don't chain-smoke. Go on, light it.'

'Junkie.' She holds his gaze and lights the cigarette.

'What's that smell? You two been doing drugs again?' Mark wrinkles his nose when Lukas lets him back into the house.

'It's a roll up. I've got your drugs right here.' Dannii takes a six-pack from the fridge.

'Oh, beauty. You wonderful woman.' Mark cups Dannii's face and kisses her the mouth. Then he flings a newspaper onto the table, cracks open a can, gulps several mouthfuls of lager and burps loudly. 'Have a look on page six.'

Lukas opens the tabloid. 'Since when do you read trash like this? Bloody fascist rag.' On page six Lukas spots a very rough CCTV photograph of himself and Mark standing near the office at Dolly Green Boxing Club with Linda and Carl. The picture has been taken from above and to Lukas they are both unidentifiable, except for body stance. Next to it is a photograph of himself, the one that was published in *Metro* on the day of his escape, and a picture of a blue-eyed Mark in his

Billy the Bullet days, Lukas deducts, much stockier and sporting a bleached blonde mane.

'Bloody hell, Mark, you look like Adrian Street. Is that make-up you're wearing?'

'Cheers, mate, I'm flattered. Yes, it is. I was "themed" at the time.'

Dannii yelps. 'What's with the blue eyes, Mark?'

Mark points at his face. 'Contacts. As a disguise. Give me a mysterious aura.'

'Cunning.' Dannii snorts.

Lukas drops the paper onto the table. 'No picture or mention of you, love. The article has nothing to do with reality. Anyway, if this is all they got on us then they haven't a clue.'

Mark looks at the iPad on the table and jabs a finger at the screen. 'Have you been listening?'

'We have.'

'And?'

'You first.'

'OK I'll make this quick. It's good old Tony, without a doubt. Had his face fixed. Bingo. Let's listen.' Mark taps on the iPad's screen. 'Why isn't it working?'

'It's gone to sleep.' Dannii states.

'Wake the bugger up then, woman!'

'Hang on, you're saying that Mr T is definitely the reincarnation of Tony Jackson?'

'Yes. I took photos of the file.' Mark gets out his phone and shakes it. 'There's X-rays and before and afters.'

'So is plastic surgery common in witness protection?' Lukas smirks at Mark.

'Apparently, yes, and in villain protection as well. It absolutely stinks of police, quite literally. Ha, get it? Briggs, Stinky?' Mark creases, drinks deeply and crunches up the can.

They repeat the first two messages.

'Bet you're relieved, mate.' Mark scowls.

Lukas looks at him. 'Yes, I am, about the possibility that Jason's homosexual. I'm not at all happy at how he's being bullied, or how his manager tries to brush his concerns under the carpet.'

Mark puts his elbows on the table. 'He admits to stuff though. At least we know we've been thinking in the right direction. Is there another message?'

'Yes. We were about to listen to the last message when you got back.' Dannii taps the iPad again.

'*Hey, Jayz. Me again. Thanks for the tip about that guy at your brother's stable. I've got our guardian angel at CID dot com onto the where and when. By the way, why did you bother the boss with all that rubbish about me telling you how to play the game? I'm your bloody captain and if you don't play as a team you won't play for the team at all, is that understood? You're treading on very thin ice, my mate, all things considered. If you ever spill any of this anywhere else I'll break your fucking legs, like, in a nice way. Ha! I mean it. You'll never play football again. So don't you be going off to third parties spilling the beans. It's nobody's business but the team's. The boss needs to be able to rely on us, buddy, OK? I know, you're still learning, and I want to help you, but you need to do your bit, OK? Talking of parties, Jayz, you know it's my birthday next week. We've booked the Turing. Bring that little girlfriend of yours, will you. She really brightens up my day. And that mate of hers, that Gaby, she's well up for it. Have I got a special surprise for her! Anyway, buddy, you know I love ya, we all do, so please be cool, my man. Over and out.*' Leroy blows a couple of kisses into the receiver.

Lukas gets up too quickly. 'When did he leave this message? When is this bastard's birthday? Why don't we have any access to the bloody internet?'

'I do.' Mark flips open his phone and passes it to Dannii. 'You do it. I can see fuck all on that tiny screen.'

Dannii squints and types. 'January seventh. Today.'

'Today! The party's tonight? I need to speak to Lilian immediately. She's in danger.' He fumbles for his phone.

'Leave that off!' Mark barks and reaches for the handset. 'You heard what Mitchell said.'

Lukas snatches his hand away. 'I don't see why it should be my brand new SIM that's compromised. You're merrily using your "official" phone lately. It's more likely to be Dannii's, otherwise they'd be onto Pavel and Mitch as well.'

'That could well be the case,' Mark hisses.

'Stop it!' Dannii says. 'Lukas is right. Most likely me that's compromised.'

'Would you at least go round the block then.' Mark scowls.

'Can I at least get me shoes on?' Lukas snaps back and stomps off upstairs. 'Roll me a fag, woman,' he hollers.

'I'll go with you,' Dannii shouts after him. 'You stay here and hold the fort, you bloody grouch. And do some bloody thinking,' Lukas hears her say, gruffly. He flinches as she slams a door.

Chapter 55

'Can I switch on now? It's already past nine.'

'Let's go a bit further, love.' She takes his arm as they rush past Brooklands station. 'How are you feeling?'

Lukas takes a drag of the roll up, immediately feels sick and throws it away. 'A bit broken. Can't breathe right.' He puffs shallowly.

'Is that why you've started smoking again?' she asks.

'No, it's because of that idiot. And now this – '

'Yes, I know. Just teasing.'

'Thanks for these, by the way.' Lukas tugs on his hoodie.

'Warm enough?'

'Hm.' He hurries her along, absent-mindedly.

'Good,' she whispers and slows down.

He puts his arm round her shoulders. 'Are you OK, love?' She shakes her head and clears her throat. He lifts her chin. 'Are you crying?' She sniffs, then hugs him tightly. Lukas grimaces and clenches his teeth.

'I almost lost you in that fucking mountain. Have you any idea what you looked like?'

'I know what I felt like.' He kisses her forehead.

She grabs his face with both hands and glares at him. 'First, you swing into a void unprotected. You should've seen yourself as I could, through the gap. If you'd fallen, you'd have broken your back in the whiplash. We'd tied the rope around a rock, but it's no bungee. It doesn't stretch more than an inch. You'd have snapped like a pea pod. And I could see it happen.' He takes her head against his chest, urging himself to be patient, rocking and shushing her gently. She hits his chest with her fists. 'Don't you bloody shush me, you bloody great big oaf! Next, you swing back feet first into the biggest pile of rubble I've ever seen and dislodge the lot. The whole shebang collapsed around and above you. And all you have is a few scrapes – bloody hell!' She beats his chest, crying.

Lukas grabs her shoulders and bends down to look her in the face. 'Hey, Dannii!' She looks up, reluctantly. 'What else could I have done?'

'Nothing,' she says quietly. 'Apart from turn back.'

'Which wasn't an option.' He hugs her and rests his chin on her head. This time she lets him. This time she hugs him back, wraps her arms round his waist and strokes his injured back.

'I was scared,' she whispers. 'So scared.'

Lukas kisses the top of her head. 'I'm sorry, love, to be such an oaf.' He says sorry until she starts to beat him again.

'You're not a bloody oaf. Don't ever say that!'

'But you just said it yourself.' He grabs hold of her wrists impatiently to stop her hitting his injured chest.

She struggles against him. 'You're not an oaf,' she insists through clenched teeth. 'You're not stupid. You're just big and strong and clumsy and I love you.' She gives up struggling. He raises her hands to his face and kisses them. 'Don't listen to what Mark says,' she whispers. Lukas breathes into her hair, thinking of Lilian. 'He's a foot and a half shorter than you. From his perspective, of course you do look – wide.'

'And from yours?' He focuses.

She beats him only once this time. 'Stop milking it!'

'Sorry, but I haven't felt like this in a while. Before you came along, I mean. In fact, not for an awful long time – '

She touches his face, the good side. 'Did she never talk to you, nicely, or intimately?'

He laughs. 'Who, Liz? Not really, once we were married. It became apparent very quickly that I wasn't good enough at anything.'

Dannii just looks at him, her hand cupped round his cheek. He notices the drizzle and looks about. They stand in front of the station. People walk around them, probably assuming them to be parting lovers waiting for the next train to Manchester. Dannii smiles up at him. He touches her cheek in return and bends forward to kiss her gently. 'My poor man,' she whispers. 'Don't you know how lovely you are?'

He chuckles, their noses still touching. 'If Mark was here he'd complain about feeling queasy,' he whispers.

'Yes, but not in those terms,' she murmurs back.

'Absolutely not.' He kisses her once more and reaches inside his pocket.

'I've got to make this call, love. I'm tired of all this phone nonsense. Who'd track this fresh SIM anyway? By the way, does anybody know where you live?' Lukas switches the handset on.

'All my paperwork goes via Frank's. I've no phone line.'

Lukas takes her hand. 'Bills?'

'Included.'

'Who's the landlord?'

'Who d'you think?'

He smirks at her. 'You're kidding.'

She shakes her head. 'Nope.'

'Jean-Pierre.'

'Yep.'

Lukas laughs. 'And? Do you trust him?'

'As long as I don't step out of line, yes. After that I wouldn't trust him as far as I could throw him.' She squeezes his hand.

'Good. Electoral register?'

'I've made someone up.'

'Council tax?'

'Same person.'

'OK.' Lukas's phone bleeps. 'Shit.' He puts the phone to his ear, listens, then snorts as he finishes the call.

'Was it Lilian? Bad news?' Dannii looks anxious.

'No and yes. Stan Entwistle. Accusing me of betraying him – you come in here all full of yourself and pretend to be concerned. Then you try and get off with my secretary and force your way with the poor woman after getting her pissed. And your mate previously assaulted my staff and friends. That's why we reported you, etcetera.'

'Hm,' Dannii says. 'You left your number.'

'I did.'

'Don't you think Briggs might be tracing your phone after all?'

'Maybe. Depends who registered the incident. 50/50 chance I reckon.'

'You'd better ring Lil quickly.'

'Then I need to text Stan back.'

Lukas finds Lilian's number and dials. He swears when the call goes straight to answerphone. 'Lil. It's Dad. Listen. This is urgent and I can't be long. I've reason to believe you're in danger, hanging out with Leroy. I believe he's having a birthday party, tonight. Love, I don't want you to go. You or Gaby. Please, take this seriously. I also believe Jason is being bullied. You said he didn't like Leroy. I believe it's much worse. I believe Leroy's making him do things on the pitch that Jason's not happy with. Love, you've got to take this at face value, there isn't time to explain. Lil, please, have a word with Jason. I don't mind you being mates with him. Please say that if he needs anyone to talk to, I'm happy to talk to him. Nothing to do with any story. I think he needs a friend, so you be his friend and let him know I'd be there for him if he needs to talk. Please darling, I'm not interfering with your stuff, but this is really serious and – ' Lukas is interrupted by a beep that signals the end of the available message space. 'Shit.'

'You said what you needed to say. She's grown up enough to understand. Now, the message to Stan.'

'I fear she's already there.' He pulls himself together, navigates back to the answerphone mail box and types. '*Stan, you're very much mistaken. I never laid hands on Linda. Quite the opposite. I got her home safely. I guess it's my word against hers. Maybe you should ask her again. You're right about the other assault. I apologised to you already. But I suspect those boys more than ever of committing a serious crime, orchestrated by your partner, Tyson. I believe someone is playing you big style and you'll be framed and left to pick up the tab. I suggest you start asking questions. I'm sorry I can't speak to you in person. You can trust me. I'll be in touch. Lukas.*' Lukas sends the text. 'Was that OK?' He turns to her.

'Yeah, straight on the schnecker.' She kisses him on the nose.

'I'm keeping the phone on, love. Lil needs to be able to get in touch if there's a problem. This might compromise our whereabouts and your home. Is that OK with you?' Lukas slides the handset into his pocket.

'Let's hope it's fifty per cent in our favour. And the phone's not traced.'

Lukas puts his arm around her shoulder. 'What are the odds on that, love? After all, you're the betting expert.'

'I wouldn't be so cocky if I were you, Novak. I don't think the odds are too good.'

'What kept you so long?'

'So Leroy spoke to T.' Lukas ignores Mark and sits down at the table.

Mark crushes two empty cans. 'Looks that way.' He opens a further beer.

'Does Tony have the nous to find out my alleged address?' Dannii pours more wine. 'Like Luke, by chance, on PayPal?'

Lukas takes a sip but doesn't really want it.

Mark shakes his head. 'You haven't been listening properly, you two. Too wrapped up in your private fumblings. No, I don't think Tony would've gone through all that trouble. Remember your mate, the other Pole?'

'Vladi.' Lukas stretches his aching ribcage.

Mark nods. 'Took the snapshot of Leroy and Stinky at the casino. There's the connection. We said it then, I'm saying it now. In the third message Leroy mentions their guardian angel at CID finding a location. Couldn't be more obvious. Briggs found your supposed address, hon, I'm convinced of it. And Leroy passed it on to Tony Jackson.'

'But there's a link between Tony and Briggs, too.' Lukas burps. He's been unable to concentrate, thinking about Lilian. An idea has entered his mind. He can't grab hold of it but it nauseates him nevertheless. Similar to how he felt in Blackpool on his lone night out. He pushes his glass away.

'Yes, from the old days,' Dannii continues, oblivious to him. 'And now it looks like Briggs allows Tony to stage a miraculous resurrection. So whether they're all in it together or whether it's Briggs and Jackson, or Briggs and Leroy, doesn't really matter. It sounds like the latter to me, though. Leroy didn't know Tony previous to asking Jason for help from Stan's stable. But there's a possibility that Briggs is back in contact with Tony directly. This'd be one level higher, management level, off the record level. There's currently nothing pointing in that direction, but it's entirely conceivable. I'm convinced Briggs engineered the comeback for his old crony. He made him a lot of money, after all.'

'I've got to lie down, I feel dreadful.' Lukas gets up and sways, his balance upset once again. He leans heavily on the table. 'We've reached some kind of conclusion, but there's something else I can't lay my finger on at the moment. I'm bloody worried about Lil and the booze isn't agreeing with me tonight.' He burps again.

'You alright, mate?' Mark asks.

Lukas shakes his head and feels bile rise in his throat. 'Have you any indigestion tablets, love?

'I've got something better.' Dannii opens the fridge's icebox and lifts out a bottle. 'I've got Aquavit.'

'Christ.' Lukas runs a shaky hand over his sweaty forehead and looks at her. 'Do you mean to kill me, woman?'

She laughs. 'Kill or cure, sweet.' She pours a generous measure into a shot glass and hands it to him. 'Down in one, y'know the drill, Pole!'

'I sure do,' Lukas mumbles, necks the shot and groans. His ears pop and his throat and stomach explode. He slams the glass on the table, exhaling noisily. 'Another,' he says, breathless. Dannii grins and refills the glass. Lukas drinks the second shot in two gulps. 'Jesus. What is this?'

'Linie. Norwegian. Forty-seven per cent.'

'I thought so.'

'Does the trick, doesn't it?'

'Hm. Hope it stays down. I'm off.' He looks at Dannii.

'She'll come up and tuck you in once she's done the washing up.'

'You could've done that when we were out, you lazy git!' Dannii snatches the can from Mark's hands and pours its contents into a glass.

'OK?' She sits on the side of the bed.

'Yes, fine.' Lukas props himself up to take the weight of his ribcage. 'Bloody pathetic! So bloody worried.'

She smiles and takes his hand. 'Aquavit working?'

'Seems to be.'

'What had you so upset earlier?'

He watches her stroke his hand. 'I can't put my finger on it.' He wiggles his fingers and makes her smile. 'You said something about management level. It was before that.'

'About who found out the address and who passed it on to Tony?'

'Yes. You said there's no connection between Leroy and Tony, otherwise Leroy wouldn't have asked Jason to find someone to carry out the attack.'

'Hm,' she says. 'Do you think there's a link after all?'

'There's a link we're not seeing, somewhere – I'm convinced of it.'

'Stan?' She's moved on to stroking his arm.

'Stan has got to be holding something back. I don't believe that your uncle disappears, then his previously non-existent "brother" turns up years later and you wouldn't spot it's the same person. How old is Stan?'

'Mid-thirties?'

'And when did Jackson start Dolly Green?'

'No idea.'

She gets up and walks to the door. 'Oy, Bullet, when did Tony start Dolly Green?' she hollers down the stairs.

'Early nineties, I think,' Mark hollers back.

'When were you there?'

'Are you two decent? I'm coming up.' Another can pops open downstairs. Seconds later Mark appears in the doorway. 'My god, the Taj Mahal.' He looks around the room. 'So this is what a lady's boudoir looks like. Nice.'

'Answer the question, moron.' Dannii snaps.

Mark leans on the end of the bed. ''Bout 2005-ish?'

Dannii frowns. 'No good asking us. Can't you remember?'

Mark looks at her. 'It was about that time. I was suspended in 2007. Tony was sent down a year later.'

Lukas shuffles into a more upright position. 'So you were out of the force when you gave evidence.'

'Yes. I was knackered.'

'D'you remember Stan at all?'

'Not really. He was rich and famous by then. Was spotted at Dolly Green when he was in his teens and moved to All Saints in Audenshaw. Came back to take over the joint after Tony died. To save it, so he said. Was all over the papers. Reformed character, my arse. I only saw him a few times when I was there. During high-stake fights. He was off his head most of the time. Mind you, so were we all.'

'So he was aware of what was going on?'

'Nobody could have been stupid enough not to know what was going on, mate. It was pretty much invite only.'

Lukas scratches his chin, looks at Mark, then at Dannii. 'Did we ever establish what Jackson did before he started the club?'

'Professional footballer,' Mark says.

'What?' Lukas sits bolt upright.

'He played for Coventry Wanderers. When they were still good. Won the league and the cup. Can't remember the year, but I was about eight.'

'Jesus, Mark.' Dannii crosses her arms.

'Jesus, what, love?' Mark looks at her, blankly.

Lukas hollers. 'She says Jesus, Mark 'cos we're trying to put together an investigation into match fixing and corruption in football. And the most corrupt character we've come across, a guy you scammed with and who staged his own death, just happened to be a professional footballer in his prime. Which you knew all along, yet you only mention it now, in passing? How dare you tell me I make mistakes. Fucking hell!' Lukas swings his legs out of the bed, roars and stands up.

'Sorry, mate, but you never asked.' Mark shrugs.

'Did I have to? Isn't it so bloody obvious that there's more, much more to this? We've only just seen the tip of it. Briggs, looking after footballers now, betting then, in your heyday, and protecting Jackson, the crook. How long have they known each other? What about the Coventry days?'

Mark shrugs.

'Bradshaw,' Dannii says quietly.

Lukas turns to her sharply, adrenaline rushing through his broken body. 'Bradshaw?'

'Moses started his career at Coventry.'

'What? At the same time?'

'Don't know. I'd have to check.'

Lukas's phone rings.

'You left it on?' Mark frowns.

Lukas ignores him, pulls the phone from his jacket pocket and looks at the display. 'Lil,' he whispers and presses the green button.

'Lil,' Lukas shouts into the receiver. He can hear loud music and distant shouting. 'Lil!'

'Mr Novak?' Someone shields the receiver from the noise beyond.

'Jason! Is that you, Jayz? Where's Lilian?' Lukas shouts. The background noise reduces slightly. 'Jason. What is it, son?'

'Lilian,' the boy sniffles. 'She's out of it. She's taken something.'

'Is she OK? Jason?'

'Yes. She's been sick. But the others – Mr Novak, it's just not right. She told me you left a message. She told me what you said. I'm not a grass, but it's just not right.'

'Jason! What's going on? What's not right?'

'Lil's friend, Gaby, and her mate. She's in there with the others, The Clan, like. There's no way she'd want to do – it couldn't be,' the boy sobs.

'Jayz. You at the Turing?'

'Yes. Top floor.'

'You stay there, son, and you protect my daughter or I'm going to have your balls, you understand that?'

'I'll try,' the boy sniffs.

'No, Jayz. You promise me now that you will protect her until I get there, understood?'

'Yes, sir.'

'Take her out of there if you can, safely, otherwise sit tight. I'll be there in twenty.'

'OK.'

Lukas ends the call. 'Car keys,' he barks at Mark and stretches out his hand.

Mark shakes his head. 'No way! You're pissed. I'm coming with you.'

Lukas grabs him by the collar and lifts him off his feet. 'Listen, you little shit, I don't have time for this. Car keys. Now!' He shakes Mark who keeps as still as a mouse in a cat's fangs. 'Now, Mark! I'm not going to ask again.' Lukas puts Mark down, sees the sudden glint in his eye and parries Mark's punch with his left arm. He grabs Mark by the throat and hits him hard on the temple. Mark's legs collapse. Lukas pushes him onto the bed with his left, shaking his hurting hand. 'I've fucking had enough.' He drops onto Mark to rifle through his pockets, and quickly finds the car keys and mobile phone. Then he turns to Dannii who cowers in the corner, wide-eyed. Lukas hesitates. 'D'you know where Briggs lives?'

She shakes her head slowly.

'Fuck.' Lukas opens Mark's phone and rings the only number in the recent calls register.

'Yes.' A neutral voice, almost bored.

'This is Mark's mate, who you saved this morning.' Lukas hurries. 'Where is Mark?'

'Out of it. Listen, I don't have time – '

'What?' The voice says calmly.

'I need to know DCI Richard Briggs's address, it's an emergency.' He waits while the man gets him the information he needs. '28 Woodland Gardens, Sale,' he repeats.

'Good luck. Ring if you need anything else.'

'Thanks.' Lukas closes the phone and slips it into his pocket. Mark groans on the bed. 'Listen, love, I'm sorry – ' He turns to face Dannii.

'Go. It's that way.' She points and gets up. 'I had no idea he lives so close.'

Lukas touches her face fleetingly, brushing his lips against hers just as briefly.

She grabs his hand. 'Be careful, please.'

He gently pulls his hand away. 'I'll call you, as soon as I know more.' Then he pockets the pain killers, hurries downstairs as fast as his bruised ribs allow, grabs his jacket and opens the door to the garage.

Chapter 56

Lukas calmly eases the BMW out of the garage and checks the glove compartment. The gun is hidden under a road atlas. He makes sure the safety catch is on and drops it in his jacket pocket. He puts the car into gear and accelerates out of the driveway towards Brooklands station.

On Brooklands Road he opens the BMW up further and checks the time. Seven minutes have passed since he spoke to Jason Entwistle. Seven minutes, during which his daughter's fate could well have changed for the worst. Lukas puts his foot down, turns right at the end of Brooklands Road and into Woodland Gardens. Why do roads have such flowery names when there are no brooks, let alone woods anywhere close? Lukas studies the house numbers. Even on the right.

He calculates that Briggs's house will be towards the end of the cul-de-sac. He slows to a crawl and watches another vehicle in front of him. It pulls into a driveway which could well be Briggs's. Lukas switches off the lights and allows the BMW to roll slowly towards the parking car. The driver's door opens and Briggs steps out onto his driveway.

Lukas slides out of the car. Crouching, he hobbles towards the DCI, who walks towards his home through a carport, past another parked vehicle. There Briggs stops and searches for his keys.

Lukas swiftly moves behind him. 'Briggs,' he whispers, his right hand on the gun in his pocket.

Briggs visibly jumps and turns around quickly. 'Who is it?' His voice quivers slightly and he reaches into his coat.

'Put your hands where I can see them.' Lukas produces the gun, steps closer and turns his face towards the street lights.

'Is that you of all people, Novak? Jesus, you scared me. What's happened to your face?' Briggs says, under his breath.

'I walked into a door. What do you think, moron?' Briggs moves his hand towards his coat pocket. 'Don't!' Lukas hisses.

'What you going to do, big boy? Shoot me?'

'Give me your phone!' Lukas waves the gun about.

'Why should I?'

''Cos your daughter's in grave danger. Give me your phone, so you don't do anything stupid.'

Briggs laughs. 'She's upstairs, in bed, you oaf.'

Lukas takes a step forward, slips his gun into his pocket and grabs Briggs by the throat. 'No, she isn't. She's in the Turing hotel, being fucked by Leroy Callaway.'

Briggs gasps for air. Lukas reaches inside the detective's coat and feels for a gun. It sits in a holster underneath Briggs's left armpit. Lukas squeezes Briggs's throat a bit more to discourage resistance and removes the weapon. Briggs tries to say something.

'You're going to tell me you've just come from there, aren't you?' Lukas eases his grip round Briggs's throat, then lets him go.

Briggs nods. 'I have,' he croaks.

'Phone.' Lukas stretches out his hand. Briggs pulls a mobile from his coat pocket and hands it over. 'And the other one.' Briggs tuts and removes another handset from his inside pocket. 'Let's go,' Lukas says and grabs Briggs by the arm.

'You're insane. My daughter's inside, asleep. I'm going to call for help.'

'Shut up or I'll knock you out! I'm telling you, she's being abused by your own mate and his friends.'

Briggs looks at him as Lukas drags him to the car. 'I don't believe you,' he whispers through clenched teeth.

Lukas opens the passenger door, pushes Briggs inside and leans heavily on the car roof. 'She's being fucked by The Clan, if that makes more sense to you, Guardian Angel of the CID, Manchester.'

Briggs looks at him, wide-eyed. 'Who on earth have you been speaking to?' he whispers.

Lukas slams the door shut. He reverses fast and swings the BMW around the corner and onto the main road.

'Slow down, you lunatic!' Briggs touches his bruised voice box. 'What makes you think our Gaby is at the Turing? As I just said, I've just been there checking on security.'

Lukas laughs. 'You've just made sure that boys can be boys, without repercussions.' He turns towards Manchester and floors the accelerator. Fourteen minutes since the phone call.

'I don't know what you mean, Novak. Would you please slow down.'

'Negative,' Lukas growls. 'My daughter is with Gaby. I want her out of there.'

'Gaby doesn't even know your daughter.'

'You rotten liar! You told Gaby that I'm a thug, responsible for the GBH on Frank Staines. You wanted to destroy my daughter's trust in me by feeding this lie to Gaby, who dutifully passed it on to Lilian, as you planned. Luckily, my daughter's cleverer than you anticipated and didn't believe your little story. The girls have been mates for a while, chasing after footballers, for pity's sake, with your little girl being the ringleader. They're currently attending Leroy Callaway's birthday party, your daughter apparently on her back, under duress.'

'Bollocks! You're making it up.' Briggs looks at him.

Lukas gets a full blast of the man's breath and gags. 'I received an anonymous phone call. Do you even own a toothbrush, man?'

'Yes.' Briggs sneers. 'I also own a breathalyser, Novak. You've been drinking.'

'Yes. I've been drinking. Heavily. I'm also on morphine. It's amazing.'

'You're insane!' Briggs gets hold of the door handle.

Lukas flicks the central locking switch. 'No, Dick. Can I call you Dick? I'm not insane, I'm just extremely pissed off. With everything. Especially you. So you'd better be careful.'

Briggs sneers. 'Who called you, Novak?'

Lukas laughs. 'Didn't I just tell you it was an anonymous call?' He slows down at a red light below the M60 junction, checks for traffic and jumps the lights.

'You're going to have my colleagues on your tail in no time.'

'In which case you'll do the talking.'

'Whose car is this? Unwin's? Or Miller's or whatever he calls himself these days?'

'Who's Unwin?'

'Oh, come on, Novak. It's his gun, too, isn't it? The gun alone would be enough to put you away for a while, you know?'

'Probably. It is, however, the only felony I've committed and you know it.'

'Drunk and drugged driving? Kidnapping and assaulting a police officer?' Briggs titters. 'It'll be a while, Novak, or can I call you Luke?'

'In the light of what's going on at the Turing any jury would be lenient. And, after all, it's your daughter, so I'm doing you a favour, getting you there. You can call me Novak, Dick, or even fucking polak, if you prefer.' Lukas floors the accelerator. 'Anyway, what I've been dying to ask you for quite some time now: why are you after me? Why this mad goose chase?'

'You're a suspect in an attempted homicide – would you please slow down, you bloody idiot? Besides, you ran.'

'I don't believe that's the reason you're following me. You don't send hit men to arrest suspects.'

Briggs turns to him. 'Hit men? What on earth are you talking about?'

'MacFarlane?' Lukas looks at Briggs. Briggs returns his stare. Lukas notices the glint in his eye. 'It was me at the end of his phone, Dick, when you called MacFarlane after the attack at Guide Bridge station. Don't deny it, Briggs, I heard your voice and I have your number. The number of your special phone. Here.' Lukas takes out his mobile and fumbles through a number of button.

'Give me that!' Briggs reaches across. 'Keep your bloody eye on the road, moron.'

Lukas laughs and pulls his hand away, the BMW swerving wildly. 'The innocent cyclist your heavies beat up is OK, by the way, thank you for asking. We dropped her at MRI,' Lukas lies. Then he holds down the green call button. In his pocket, Briggs's phone first vibrates, then rings.

'You bastard.'

Lukas laughs. 'It's you who's the bastard, actually. I still don't know why you're after me, though I have a theory.'

'And what's that?'

Lukas looks over at him and smiles. 'You want me to lead you to the blogger.'

Briggs laughs. 'Why would I want to know the blogger? What's so important about him?'

'He spreads muck about your prodigies,' Lukas says. Briggs laughs. 'Muggers told him to stop pointing fingers at people.'

'Who did?' Briggs glares at Lukas.

'Tony's boys did. The ones who attacked old Frank. Mistaking him for the blogger. And you weren't even interested when Frank told you in hospital that they had a message.'

'Who said that?'

'I have my sources, too, Dick. You leave traces, even you. We all leave traces – ' Lukas jumps the lights at Old Trafford, home of world-famous Manchester United, at sixty. He looks neither left nor right.

'Bastard!' Briggs lashes out and hits him in the side. Lukas jumps and roars with pain from his ribcage. 'Ha! What's the matter with you? You're not injured, are you?' Briggs hits him again.

Lukas grabs Briggs's wrist, twists and pushes it against the DCI's face and smashes his head against the BMW's doorframe. Briggs shouts and immediately recoils, groping for Lukas's arm, blood running from his left eyebrow. Lukas seizes Briggs's face with his left hand and pushes his fingers into the man's eye sockets. Briggs howls and grabs Lukas's wrist. Lukas pushes him back into the seat. 'Sit still or I'll injure you badly, I promise. I've knocked several people out recently and I'm beginning to get a taste for it,' he lies.

Briggs touches his injured face and swears.

They enter the end of Deansgate roundabout at fifty and turn left immediately towards Salford. It's been twenty-five minutes since the phone call. 'We're late,' Lukas growls. 'Because of your bloody interference. I'm holding you responsible if anything's happened to either Lilian or in fact to your own daughter. I'll have you charged with neglect. You protect these people. What on earth is going on in your head?' Lukas slams his fist on the wheel. He skirts past a few waiting cars and jumps the light at Salford station. And now there are sirens behind him. He sees blue flashing lights in the mirror, a long way off. He laughs and pushes Briggs's shoulder. 'Replay of last night. Boy, was it fun! Do you know what it feels like to almost die? When you know it's going to happen and you realise you don't have any time left to ponder what it's going to be like? No?' He hits the DCI's shoulder again. 'It's a sobering experience. Everybody should experience it some time. Enough to drive you to the edge.'

'Apparently,' Briggs says, under his breath.

'Are you going to answer my second question before we get there, although in my opinion you haven't answered the first?'

'What?' Briggs turns to him.

'About what the fuck is going on in your head to protect criminals?'

'Fuck you!' Briggs sneers and looks behind. 'You're done for, Novak. Any minute now.'

Lukas grabs his collar. 'At least have the decency to worry about your daughter, even if you don't give a damn about your own soul.' He pushes Briggs again, hard, and hears the man's skull crack against the window pane. Briggs swears and holds his head.

In the mirror Lukas watches the blue flashing lights catching up fast. He skirts the final corner, flicks the central locking switch off and accelerates towards the lay-by outside the entrance to the Turing Hotel. The patrol car cuts off his path by the stairs that lead up to the lobby. Lukas rushes round the car. He opens the passenger door and drags Briggs out and up to his feet. Then he pushes Briggs forward and hisses into his ear. 'Your turn.'

Briggs holds up one hand towards the traffic officer geeting out of the patrol car. 'It's OK, officer.'

'Sir, is that you? Are you OK?' Lukas grabs Briggs's arm and pulls him towards the hotel. The officer approaches quickly. 'Sir, you're bleeding.'

'It's OK,' Briggs barks. 'Stay here with the car.'

Lukas lets go of Briggs's arm and runs into the lobby. 'Come on,' he shouts, breathless and holding his side.

Suddenly Briggs appears next to him. 'Lifts are over there.' He runs ahead and presses the call button. Lukas limps in after him. Briggs presses the top button. 'Penthouse suite,' he says. 'Limited access.'

'Hello?' A fuzzy speaker sounds.

'Briggs.'

'Who?'

'Briggs, you arsehole!' he says. Lukas grins. The doors close. Briggs turns and looks up at him. 'So, you almost died? You didn't happen to go down that cave, did you?'

They reach the top floor in seconds. A uniformed police officer steps aside to let them leave the lift.

'Where's the party?' Briggs barks.

'Penthouse suite, sir.'

'I fucking know that, moron. Where is it? It's not going to be the only fucking suite on this floor, is it?'

'Through those doors and turn left. Suite uses the whole wing.'

'Come on,' Briggs marches off.

'I thought you were here earlier, checking on security,' Lukas keeps up with him, breathing hard.

'Bashed your ribs, did you? This is for earlier.' He elbows Lukas in the side. 'I was. Downstairs. Talked to the big guy in charge.'

Lukas is too winded to respond. He pops a couple of pain killers into his mouth. They turn left. Several heavy-set men in black stand along the corridor.

'Can I help you?' The nearest one turns to face them. 'Boy, oh, boy!' He laughs. 'Been in the wars? You want some more?' He takes a rubber truncheon from his belt and slaps his palm with it.

'I'm Briggs, you moron. Where's the party?' Briggs touches the man's chest to push him aside.

'I don't care who the fuck you are and the party's over.' The man makes to hit Briggs from behind with the truncheon. Lukas grabs the security guard's wrist and pulls his arm back sharply until he hears a crunch. The guard screams and goes down to his knees clutching his shoulder.

Briggs bends down to him and shouts. 'DCI Briggs, moron, Greater Manchester Police. Where's the party?'

'I'm afraid they left, sir.'

Lukas looks up at the second guard. 'Carl.'

'Thought you was the law.'

'I'm not.' Lukas points at Briggs. 'He allegedly is.'

Management level, need to know only.

'How come moron number one at the lift didn't tell us they'd left?' Briggs barks.

'They left down the service lift,' Carl says calmly.

'Why?' Lukas asks and opens a door.

'Dunno. Privacy?' Carl shrugs.

'Dad!' Lukas spins round and walks into the room. 'Dad, over here, quickly.'

Lukas hears music, presumably in the next room. 'Briggs!' He runs over towards her voice. She is on the floor, bent over someone. He crouches down by her side and touches her back. 'Lil, are you OK?'

'Dad.' She turns round. 'Oh, god! What happened to your face?' She is pale underneath smeared make-up.

He looks down beyond her. Jason Entwistle is unrecognisable, his face a mess of blood and dark pulp, his shirt torn and covered in blood and vomit. 'Fuck! Briggs!' Lukas bends down to Jason and takes his wrist. 'Jayz, son, Jayz.' Lukas feels for a pulse.

'He can't hear you, Dad,' Lilian sobs quietly.

Lukas turns to her. 'You OK?'

She nods. 'What happened to you?'

'Oh, shit,' Briggs says, behind him.

'Call an ambulance!'

'You've got my phone.'

Lukas takes out a phone and throws it at Briggs. 'Help me turn him, love.' Lukas manoeuvres Jason to his side and moves the boy's arm to prod him up into the recovery position. The arm bends in the wrong place and Jason groans. Lukas puts it down gently. 'It's broken,' he says quietly. 'Hold him like this, on his side.' Lukas checks inside Jason's mouth for obstruction. 'What happened, love?' He turns to face his daughter.

'They clocked that he rang someone,' Lilian sobs. 'Then – '

Lukas puts his hand on her arm. 'Where's Gaby?'

'Through there.' Lilian points to the next room.

Lukas gets up and walks towards the doorway. He hears Briggs talk outside. He hesitates, then pulls out his own phone. He takes a photo of Jason in the recovery position and one of Lilian supporting the young goalie.

Carl and another guard walk into the room. 'What's going on? Need help?'

'Out! Or I'll break your legs,' Lukas hollers.

The two men retreat to the corridor. Lukas moves towards the music in the next room. A noise filters through the din as he approaches. It sounds very much like whimpering.

He stands in the doorway, filling it. His fingers absent-mindedly play with the gun in his pocket. His stomach tightens as he identifies two bodies on the bed, amongst sheets and pillows. The room is pretty dark, so he can't see too much detail. And he can't hear too much either, past the music blaring from the television. One of the girls on the bed looks at him, the whites of her eyes and her beach-blonde hair strangely illuminated by flashing music videos. She sobs behind smeared make-up then looks up at him and mouths something. He lets the gun slip from his hand, lifts his phone and takes a photo.

The girl he assumes to be Gaby Briggs lies naked and contorted on the messed-up sheets. The other girl is cradling Gaby's head in her lap. The blonde withdraws further when Lukas crouches down, letting go of her friend's head.

'No, no more, please – ' she sobs, wide-eyed.

Lukas holds out a hand and shushes her gently. 'I'm not one of them, love.' She bursts into tears. 'Briggs!'

'I'm here.' DCI Briggs stands behind him.

Lukas looks up at him surveying the scene, his eyes darting to and fro between the two girls. 'I told you not to go with him,' Briggs whispers, as if there was nobody in the room besides his daughter and himself. 'I told him to keep his grubby hands off you.' Briggs takes a step towards the bed. 'Made sure he knew who you were and to leave you alone. That's the least he could have done – '

'Dad – ' says the blonde.

'You're Gaby?' Lukas asks quietly. The blonde nods.

'Haven't I told you not to wear that wig?' Briggs raises his voice. 'Makes you look like a whore.' Gaby bursts into tears and tears off the platinum wig.

'Your father is an idiot, love.' Lukas touches Gaby's arm. 'What's your friend's name?' He tries to catch her eye.

'Vicky.' Gaby looks up.

Lukas sees despair in her eyes. 'Can I have a look at her?' He moves closer.

Gaby pulls her legs up to her chest. Lukas gently puts the duvet round her shoulders. 'They gave us drinks. I was sick, and Lil, too.'

Lukas nods and checks Vicky's pulse.

'Dad?' Gaby looks up at her father. Lukas follows her gaze. DCI Briggs stands in the room like a pillar.

'Dick? We need help. Why don't you check if the ambulance has arrived?'

Briggs walks towards the door. He suddenly stops and looks back. 'Bastards,' he hisses and walks away.

Lukas covers Vicky and switches off the TV. 'Gaby, love, I'm going to check on Jason.'

'What's happened?' Gaby asks.

'He's in a bad way.'

Lukas rejoins his daughter. 'Won't be long now, love. Hang in there.' Lilian smiles at him, weakly. He opens the door. 'Carl,' he shouts. The big man steps into the room looking worried. 'Come here.'

'What's been happening?'

'That's what I want you to see. I want you to see what you're protecting.' Lukas takes Carl's arm and leads him to where Lilian holds Jason.

'Jesus!'

'This is my daughter. Her drink was spiked. She threw up, luckily. You know him?' Carl shakes his head. 'Jason Entwistle, Stan's brother, promising young goalie. Beaten to a pulp by his teammates, for not playing ball. Probably the beginning of the end of his career.'

'Good Lord!'

'Come.' Lukas pulls Carl towards the other room. 'Look!'

'Oh my god!' Carl looks at Lukas.

'One girl threw up. The other one didn't. Can you imagine what went on here, can you?'

'This is unbelievable. How can this be allowed to happen?'

'Because morons like you don't ask questions. You just follow orders.' Lukas looks him straight in the eye.

'But this is Mancunia FC – '

'Bad bastards everywhere, Carl.'

'Mr T needs to see this.'

Lukas laughs. 'Don't you realise Mr T is Tony Jackson resurrected? He endorses this kind of shit. Always has, apparently.'

'I never knew Tony—'

Lukas interrupts him. 'D'you know DCI Briggs?'

'Not until I met him just now.'

'Never seen him at Dolly Green?'

Carl looks at Lukas with doggy eyes. 'Honestly. If I'd known this was going on I would've done something.'

'You lead the security group?' Lukas pulls Carl aside as an ambulance crew arrive. 'Over there, guys. Carl, I need to go.'

'Yes. I lead the group, but for the very last time. Your name's Lukas, right?'

'Lukas Novak. Stan has my number. You should talk to him. He won't like this either. And tell your mate I'm sorry about his shoulder.' Lukas pats Carl's arm.

'This needs to stop.' Carl pats him back. 'Good luck with your daughter. Shame about young Entwistle. I hope he's going to be alright.'

Chapter 57

'You're not a very compassionate man, are you, Dick?' Lukas stands next to Briggs. Gaby and Vicky are being treated by the ambulance crew. Jason has already been taken to Salford Royal, accompanied by Lilian, who needs checking out.

'Or are you just scared?' Lukas whispers. 'This is all of your own making, Dick. Your own daughter, for Christ's sake!'

'I'm going to have his balls,' Briggs says through clenched teeth.

'No, you're not, and you know it. Why don't you stick to the truth for once? You're far too deep in each other's pockets.'

'What the fuck is this?' a brash voice barks behind them. Briggs shrinks. Lukas turns round and looks with interest at the man who has just entered the room. Shaven head, Yul Brunner style, plus a fake tan. Not at all the hulk Lukas was imagining. But then, as far as he knows, Tony Jackson never was a boxer. The tattoo on the man's neck is similar to the one Mike Tyson sports on his temple. Lukas looks at the scar down the man's tight cheek and reminds himself to look up an image of the Tony Jackson who won the double with Coventry Wanderers in 1975. 'Fuck, Briggs, is this what you're protecting?' the man barks.

'No, Tony, this is what your lot have been protecting, and not for the first time,' Briggs sneers half-heartedly.

'Don't you fucking tempt me.' Jackson steps right up to Briggs. Lukas grins. Jackson is taller than the DCI, but Lukas still towers a good head above him. Briggs scowls past Jackson. Jackson turns round slowly. 'I thought I could detect a landmass behind me.' He looks Lukas up and down. 'Novak, the gentle giant, I presume.'

There is something in the man's demeanour that stops Lukas from commenting. He holds out his hand. 'Correct. Pleased to meet you.'

'Fuck off.' Jackson spits and turns away.

Lukas has never in his life felt a bigger desire to kill someone. 'Did you fuck Stan too, Tony?' He says, quietly.

Jackson rotates on his heels. 'Didn't you hear me, twat? Fuck off or I'll stick you.'

Briggs puts a hand on Jackson's shoulder. 'Tony.'

Lukas is aware of the ambulance crew watching them. He looks past Jackson at Briggs's anxious expression. 'You knew, didn't you. You knew all along and you never said a word.' Lukas pushes Jackson aside and squeezes past them. 'You two deserve each other. Why don't you get married?' He laughs. 'Oh, I forgot, you're already firmly in bed with each other.' Lukas walks towards the corridor.

'Novak,' Briggs shouts. Lukas spins round and extends his fist in the direction of Tony Jackson, who brandishes a flick knife and is already alarmingly close to him. Upon his face making contact with Lukas's fist Jackson collapses on the floor. Briggs looks at Lukas. 'Blimey.'

Lukas walks towards Briggs and stands very close to him. 'Promise me you'll drop it.' Lukas growls at the inspector.

'I promise if you do.' Briggs holds his stare.

'Everything? You'll let me be?'

'Your promise first,' Briggs hisses.

'It's not for me to press charges,' Lukas says, vaguely.

'OK.'

'I can go home. No more tapped phones or monitored emails. You leave me and my family and friends alone.'

'Yes.'

'Even Unwin?' Lukas glares at Briggs. 'Promise, Dick.'

'Even Unwin.' Briggs says through clenched teeth.

'Cash and credit cards reactivated?' Briggs nods. 'Go and see to your daughter.'

Briggs stretches out his hand. 'Piece and phone.' Lukas reaches into his pocket and passes Briggs his possessions.

Chapter 58

'It's over.' Lukas closes the door and hugs Dannii tightly.

'Oh my god, Luke! What happened? Where's Lil?'

'What d'you mean, it's over?' Mark sports a black eye.

Lukas puts an arm round Mark's shoulders. Mark pushes him away. 'Fuck off. It'll be tongues next.'

'Listen, mate, I'm really sorry for hitting you.'

Mark smirks. 'I would've done the same under the circumstances. Very impressive punch.'

'I just used it to floor Tony Jackson. Felt bloody good.'

'Bloody hell, mate, you've made an enemy for life. Where was this? At the Turing?'

'He tried to knife me from behind. Briggs of all people warned me.'

'Jesus! What was Tony doing there?'

'He supplies the security for Mancunia's soirees, but wasn't enamoured by what he saw behind closed doors. Neither was Briggs.' Lukas sits down at the table.

'By the way,' Mark squints. 'What did you just say, it's over?'

'He's dropping all charges. Any more of that Aquavit, love?'

'He's dropping the charges?' Mark sits down.

'Against you, too.'

'You've made a deal with the bastard?'

Lukas smiles smugly. 'Let's just say it became apparent in conversation that Briggs knew about Tony abusing Jason. And Stan, incidentally.'

'You're joking.' Dannii puts the shot glasses and Aquavit bottle on the table. Lukas helps himself.

'Have you got witnesses?'

Lukas necks the shot, groans and leans back. 'I do. Ambulance crew. And Carl. Remember him?'

'The big bruiser from Dolly Green?'

'Yes. In charge of Tony's security outfit. Hired by Briggs via Tony. Carl had never seen Briggs before in his life, until tonight. Or so he says. Was appalled by what was going on.'

'Fantastic! Would he testify?'

'Didn't get that far. I suggested he have a quiet word with Stan. Doubtful Stan knows what's going on.'

'I bet that bastard Tony's got Stan in a blackmail headlock. The abused harbouring the abuser. Bloody codependency.'

Dannii puts her hand on Lukas's arm. 'What about Lil?'

'She got away lightly. Someone spiked her drink but she threw up. Jason stayed with her all evening, it appears. She's shaken and they're just checking her out at hospital. She'll be out in the morning. I'll take her back home. Would rather take her to mine, but Liz put her foot down, when I phoned her, as usual. She's not happy at all with what's been going on. She did agree, reluctantly, that Lil should spend time with me eventually. Lil told her about Blackpool and apparently we didn't get everything wrong. It was bloody hard for Liz to admit that. Kind of a peace offering on her part, I think.'

'Good. What about Briggs's daughter?'

'Gaby and her mate Vicky. A bloody mess. Briggs behaved like a twat, accusing her of dressing like a whore. He's a dick, literally.'

'Is he going to press charges?'

'No idea. He was totally shell-shocked.' Lukas laughs. 'I gave him back his phone.'

Mark laughs. 'How did you get his phone?'

Lukas pours another shot. 'At gunpoint outside his house, when I forced him to accompany me to the Turing.'

Mark slaps the table. 'If you weren't so bloody ugly I'd kiss you. But listen, whatever deal you've made with him, he's not going to stick to it. He'll hate you forever. You made him lose face.'

'I'll keep an eye out, Mark.' Lukas smirks.

'You better had, mate. You know what he's capable of.'

'What about Jason?' Dannii moves the bottle onto the window sill.

Lukas's eyes follow the removal of the bottle. 'They did him in. Literally. He looked as if someone had jumped on his head. How anyone can be so brutal – to a teammate.'

'Drugs. Crystal meth, most likely. Leaves the bloodstream quickly. Makes you feel invincible, and paranoid. And then there's the sex thing.'

Lukas looks at Mark. 'Is it not quite a dangerous drug?'

'Not if you just have it occasionally. It can't be traced after a couple of days. Ideal if you take regular drugs tests.'

'Drug's a bastard, Luke. Believe me,' Dannii says quietly.

'So the brutality could've been a paranoid over-reaction?'

'Absolutely, mate. Paranoid and invincible. Not a good combination.'

'Alcohol?'

'Compounds it.'

'How bad is Jason?' Dannii asks.

'Broken arm. Multiple head injuries. They wouldn't let me see him at hospital. The club's already closed the door.'

'Wonder what the official line's going to be.'

'It'll be a big one for the blog, that's for sure.'

'Do you think he'll play again?'

'How he could ever play with Callaway again I can't imagine.' Lukas reaches over for the Aquavit. 'Nightcap, anyone?'

'I think we all need it,' Dannii sighs.

Lukas opens the bottle and pours.

Chapter 59

'Welcome home!' Lukas opens the door to a pile of mail. The lock has been replaced and the splintered wood patched up. He silently thanks Vladi for his thoughtfulness.

Dannii picks up letters and junk mail. 'Wow! Look at these.' She runs her hand over the Victorian tiles. 'Didn't imagine you living in a house like this.

'What kind of house did you have me inhabit, in your mind's eye?' He buries his nose in her hair. 'Council?'

She laughs and leans back against him. 'I hadn't imagined anything. This is grand.'

He hangs her coat up behind the door. 'I bought Liz out. I felt very strongly this was my house. I've done a lot of work on it that she didn't agree with. In fact she didn't like it in the first place. She wanted something modern. I put my foot down.' Lukas opens a door. 'The kitchen is where I live.' He puts the BMW's keys on the table and opens a window. 'I did all this myself. These cupboards were hidden behind sixties plywood cladding. I ripped the whole lot out and shelved it. I also opened up the old hearth.'

'Nice drying rack.' She looks up at his underpants and long johns hanging below the ceiling.

He moves the pile of newspapers off the table and stacks them on the floor. 'What a mess.'

Her eye catches the Christmas tree and she laughs. 'Poor tree. Nice decorations.'

'Look at the needles.' He takes a brush from beside the hearth.

She puts her hand on the brush. 'No need to tidy up, not on my behalf. Show me your house. And then let's live in it together, just the two of us.'

'In peace and quiet?'

'Yes, in peace and quiet.' She strokes his face. 'This time yesterday we'd just survived the cave.'

He nods. 'I'll cook you Christmas dinner tonight.'

'Oh, fab. I never had any this Christmas.'

'Silesian Christmas dinner. It'll involve sauerkraut.'

'Hm, sauerkraut.' She snuggles against him.

'Come, let me show you the house.' He puts his arm around her and leads her upstairs.

'Vladi. Are you around?'

'Gosh, don't tell me that's you, Novak! Where've you been?'

'If I told you I'd been trapped in a mountain and held the chief of Manchester CID at gunpoint, you wouldn't believe me, would you?'

'Absolutely not. But it would make for a good story. The one you were after?'

'Part of it, yes. You in the pub later?'

'I could be in the pub straight away, if you wanted me to be.'

'I got to do a few things first. Half four?'

'At the very latest. I've missed you, old sport.'

'OK. Check list.' Lukas pours coffee.

Dannii towels her wet hair. 'The pic of Leroy and Briggs.'

'On my phone.'

'Needs backing up and printing,' she says. Lukas writes. 'Can the phones go back on?' she asks.

'Briggs gave me his word. Mine's on.'

'Does that qualify for the blogger too? He still doesn't know that I'm the blogger, does he?'

'No. Maybe best to be safe.'

'I agree. I'll continue to use the new SIM. I'll do my updating from the library, as usual. But…'

'But what?'

'I'll put you a decent firewall in here.'

'Thanks. I took pictures of the kids at the Turing, by the way.' He navigates to his photo folder.

'Jeez,' is all she says.

'Hm, quite. Next, connection between Jackson and Moses, Coventry.' Lukas writes.

'Yes. What I didn't tell you at the time, 'cos Scouse would've asked questions, is that J-P was at Coventry too. Just not sure when.'

'Tony, Moses, J-P. How does Briggs fit in? We need a CV for the DCI.'

'And we need to highlight negative play on the pitch. Get some leverage other than wrist slapping.'

'What d'you mean?' Lukas asks.

'There's apps that track the movement of players, how many passes completed and so on. Let's analyse how Leroy plays.'

'And trace the witnesses to the Turing incident. We need to find out who bats for which team. For example, can Carl be turned? What about

Stan? Briggs? Is there an early connection or did he only appear on the scene when Tony came to Dolly Green?'

'Mark?'

Lukas laughs. 'Mark. Still possible he's diddled us.'

'He'd certainly know more about the early days of DCI Briggs. Lots of loose ends. Write them all down.'

'I'm writing, love,' Lukas says, frowning.

'How are your ribs?'

'Been better. Funny you didn't ask that an hour ago, when you had me groaning in agony.'

'I thought I had you moaning in ecstasy, grump.'

'Hm. Bit of both.'

'Just a bit?'

'A bit of pain and a lot of fun.'

'That's better.'

'Anything for a bit of peace.' Lukas gets up and opens the freezer. 'It's only been twenty-four hours.' He takes out some food boxes.

'And aren't you doing well. Everything healing OK and no infection.' She finishes her coffee.

'Sausages and sauerkraut. I'm going to get Lil.' He kisses her head.

'I'm coming with you. Your computer can wait.'

'OK. By the way, we're meeting Vladi at four-thirty.'

'Cool. Where's the pub?'

'Just round the corner.'

'Trust you.'

'Indeed.'

'They won't let me see him, Dad!'

'Yes, I thought they'd be clamping down on security. Do you know how he is?' Lukas puts his arm round her as they walk along the hospital corridor. Lilian shakes her head. 'That reminds me, Dannii. We need to find out what the official line is about last night.'

'Internet and papers?'

'Before we meet Vladi.'

'What happened to your face, Dad?'

Lukas smiles and puts the BMW into gear. 'We were hiding in a cave a couple of nights ago.' He looks over at her. She frowns. 'We were on the run.'

'Again? Who from?'

'Not entirely sure, but they had helicopters.'

'So what happened?'

'I was stuck in a passage in a cliff face. The rock collapsed above me.'

'Are you OK?'

'I'm fine, love. Don't you worry. Looks worse that it is.' Lilian takes his hand.

'Liar,' Dannii says quietly, behind him.

'Liz.'

His ex-wife stands in the mansion's doorway and stares at him wide-eyed. 'Oh – my – god!' Her hands wander to her face. She cups her mouth.

'Dad was trapped in a cave and almost died in some rock fall.' Lilian says.

Liz grabs Lilian by the shoulder and pulls the girl away from him; all the while she glares at Lukas, who holds her stare. 'What on earth have you been doing, for Christ's sake?' Liz looks hard at Dannii, who steps up and stands close to Lukas.

'Liz, my friend, Dannii – Dannii, Liz.' He gestures from woman to woman. Liz looks Dannii up and down and frowns. Dannii huffs next to him.

'She's a genius, Mum.'

'Is she?' Liz gives Lukas a hard stare. 'What's going on? What's with your hair,' she asks.

'I'm on a story. It involved changing appearance and hiding in a hole.'

'A very unstable hole,' Dannii adds.

'In future, would you keep our daughter out of situations like yesterday, please.' Liz still holds Lilian's shoulder in a tight grip. The girl tries to wriggle out of it.

'You know that yesterday's nothing to do with me. Don't patronise me.' Lukas frowns.

Liz laughs. 'Me, patronising you? In front of your, whatever she is?'

Dannii steps up to Liz. 'I'm his girlfriend. Like it or not. I care for him. So you lay off him. He's not your doormat any more.' Dannii turns and stomps off towards the BMW.

'What a tramp,' Liz says with a sneer, and looks at Lukas sternly.

'She's not, Mum. She understands stuff.'

'You – are – grounded!'

'Mum!'

'Go inside. Wait until Ron gets home.'

Lukas laughs. 'And what's he going to do, play father?'

'More of a father than you ever were,' Liz hisses.

'That's not true,' Lilian shouts from inside.

Lukas's heart leaps. 'Look, love, I've moved on. I'm not who I used to be. You still look fab, by the way. And all this'—he gestures at the house—'is really beautiful and I'm so happy for you. But it's really not my thing. I enjoy making things happen these days.'

'I can see that,' she says curtly and gestures at his face. 'You're completely in charge.'

'It's called life and I'm enjoying its ups and downs. Don't think you can walk all over me any more, like you used to. I'd like for Lil to stay with me for a while once this is over.'

'Yes, please.' Lilian presses her face against the kitchen window.

'We'll see,' Liz snaps. 'I need to discuss it with Ron.'

Lukas takes a step towards her and tilts his head to one side. 'She's not his daughter. And she's sixteen. Shouldn't she have a say in the matter?'

'You drink too much, your friends are alcoholics and you have no direction in life. Your place is a mess and you don't have a job. I don't want her in that kind of environment,' Liz says through tight lips.

He takes her by the shoulders. 'But you allow her to socialise with the likes of Leroy Callaway? Is it the money or the fame that turns you on? Bit of both?' He tries to catch her eye, but she turns away.

'I had no idea what was going on. Honestly.' Now she looks up at him. He even spots a tear. He smiles and squeezes her shoulders. 'Neither had I,' he says softly.

'She's friends with that copper's daughter. I thought she was safe.'

Lukas nods. No need for his ex to know more about DCI Briggs. No need for her to know any more about anything. He wouldn't trust her, not after what happened in the run up to their divorce. 'Keep her safe.' He mouths close to her ear. 'Maybe the grounding isn't such a bad idea, but don't quote me on it.' He winks at her.

'You're different.' She holds his gaze.

'I told you that earlier.' He lets go of her shoulders. 'I'll be in touch.' He turns and walks towards the BMW.

'When did you get that car?' she asks.

Lukas laughs and raises a hand to give a little wave. 'Regards to Ron,' he shouts, then gets into the car and starts the engine.

'Lol,' Dannii says.

'Lol, indeed.' He beams across at her.

'You've well and truly outgrown her. Talk about suburban angst. Exactly the same as Gaynor and my dad. Small people.'

'No individualism, no drive for the new. And he has to take her to see the Chippendales to get anything going in the bedroom. Mind you, you haven't seen him.' Lukas laughs.

'Not attractive?' She puts her hand on his knee.

'It's incredible how irresistible ugly people can be if they're filthy rich. I mean, look at me!' He slaps himself on the chest and winces.

She squeezes his knee. 'Or Leroy Callaway.'

He turns to her. 'You don't fancy him? Don't you see him jiggle when he's running?'

'Yikes!' she says with a shudder. 'Couldn't think of anything worse. Anyway, I told you, you've nothing to worry about in that department.' She moves close and kisses his ear.

'Don't do that! We'll end up in the ditch.'

She laughs a dirty laugh. 'I'd like us to end up in a lay-by.'

He puts his arm around her. She slowly lowers her head towards his crotch, her hand on his zip.

'Dannii, please!' He laughs and looks for a turn-off. She giggles and continues her journey south. He pulls up in a disused car park. She is on top of him before he can even switch the engine off.

Chapter 60

The pile of papers on the table looks huge. 'Did we really need to get all the tabloids as well?' Lukas lifts *The Sun* off the stack to reveal '*The Sport*' below.

'Not really into page threes, are you?' Dannii boots up the computer.

'I prefer the real thing,' he mumbles, absent-mindedly. 'Coffee?'

'What was that?' She turns round.

He looks at her over the top of his glasses. 'D'you want coffee?'

'No, what did you say before that?'

'I said I prefer the real thing,' Lukas says, pragmatically and holds her gaze.

'They're all fake, you know.'

'Precisely.' He opens *The Sun* on page three and studies the full-page photograph, looking down his nose.

'And airbrushed.'

'Hm,' he grunts.

'Caveman.' Dannii turns back to the computer and switches on the printer. 'What are you doing?'

Lukas grapples below the desk with his chin on her shoulder. He kisses her briefly on the neck. 'I need a folder. It's down there.'

'You need a shave.'

'All of a sudden?'

'You're grating.'

Lukas retrieves a cardboard folder and kisses her ear. 'I think I love you,' he says. She reaches behind and squeezes his leg.

'Player line-up Coventry Wanderers, 1975. It'll blow your mind.' She passes him the printout.

'Dalton, Bradshaw, Willis, Jackson, Seaton, Pullman, Kovacs, Davis, Lee, Crawford, Courante. Bingo. Kovacs. Janos. Who was the other Kovacs, the one with the unusual tastes? Member of the original Clan?'

Dannii leafs through her notepad. 'Miklos.' She types it into the search engine. 'Janos's son, apparently.'

'Like father, like son?'

'Or the other way round?'

'That's what we need to find out.'

'Read this.'

He takes the sheet from her. 'Did you say you wanted coffee?'

She shakes her head and puts a hand on his shoulder. 'I'm ready for a beer.'

Lukas smiles and reads. 'Richard Briggs grew up in North London and joined the police force in 1968. Prior to taking up his post with Greater Manchester Police, he worked for Essex, Nottinghamshire and West Midlands police forces. He has had wide experience of policing inner city and rural areas and has held positions at Dudley, Birmingham and Coventry. Throughout his career as a chief officer, he has been a strong advocate of police reform and modernisation. He has experience of leading fraud and murder investigations and major complaint enquiries.

'Richard Briggs lives in Manchester and is married with one daughter. He holds an Honours degree in English from Birmingham University and a Masters degree in Human Resource Strategy from the University of Essex. He was awarded the Queen's Police Medal in March 2005.'

'Coventry. When?'

'Don't know. Can't find any reference to it. I'm obviously not searching right.'

'What's his year of birth?'

'1950. Wikipedia. He's one or two years from retiring. A lot of risk to take at his age.'

'Maybe he's a serious gambler. Maybe he has debts. Sold out his pension, who knows.

'Anything else?'

'Just more links. Have you found anything useful in the papers?'

He looks at her sternly, over his glasses. 'I've cut out all the page three tits and saved them for later.'

'Idiot. Look at this on the Mancunia website.'

'Entwistle in booze scare,' Lukas reads out then laughs. 'The lad doesn't even drink. Goalkeeper Jason Entwistle was rushed to hospital last night, following a player's birthday party at the Turing Hotel, Salford.' Lukas continues. 'It is believed that the promising young player fell over and hurt his face after consuming too much alcohol. An update on his condition is expected this afternoon in time for a press conference at 15:00 hours.'

'What a load of bull.'

'Was there anything about this in the papers?'

'No. Probably too early.' Lukas pulls up a chair.

'Or too dicey.'

'By the way, I thought it might not be a bad idea to follow Leroy on Twitter.'

'Let's go. What a bloody waste of time'

'He said sweet FA?' Dannii wrestles into her jacket.

'Precisely. Too much booze. Suspected broken arm. Too early to tell. Big cover-up, if you ask me,' Lukas says as they leave the house.

'Who are you ringing, sweet?'

'Mancunia,' Lukas growls. 'Hi. Lukas Novak. I visited the schools training session on Boxing Day and met Mr Bradshaw. I still have some questions regarding the programme. Can I make an appointment with him tomorrow? No, I don't want to speak to Mr O'Neill again. I appreciate Mr Bradshaw's a busy man, but I'm convinced he'd like to speak to me. I know he's at a press conference, but please make an appointment for me to see him tomorrow. You're not his secretary? Well, put me through to her then. Please.' Lukas rolls his eyes and waits. 'Hi. Would it be possible to see Mr Bradshaw tomorrow? I appreciate that. I'm convinced that he'd like to speak to me. No, it's not really about the education programme. Look, I don't know how to say this. It's important and personal. Something happened last night at a player's party. No, I'm not the press. It involves my daughter. I need to speak to him directly and confidentially. Please.' He waits. 'Ten am. Thank you. Yes, at the offices. Thank you. Bye'

Dannii looks at him. 'You're seeing Moses.'

'I'm seeing Moses.'

'You jammy bugger.'

The Globe is empty apart from Vladi, who sits in his usual spot, sipping lager.

'Prepare yourself,' Lukas says, under his breath, as they walk through the door.

'Novak!' Vladi slams his glass down, spilling most of its contents, and slides off the bar stool.

Lukas gives Vladi a bear hug. Vladi returns the embrace. 'Don't squeeze me too hard.' Lukas winces.

'Old boy, what happened to your face?' Vladi takes a step back but holds on to Lukas's shoulders. 'You look like a Bosnian hit man. And why shouldn't I hug you as tightly as I possibly can?' Vladi lets go of Lukas. 'And who might this be?' he says slowly.

'Vladi, this is Dannii. Dannii, Vladimir.'

'Well, well, Novak, you cunning old goat. What can I say? She is with you? Could this be possible? Does she speak?' Vladi circles Dannii like prey.

'She does,' Dannii says.

'Oh, posh.' Vladi nods.

Dannii crosses her arms. 'Not.'

Vladi ogles her closely. 'Not posh?'

Lukas takes Vladi's elbow. 'Come on, old friend, let's sit down and drink beer.' He smiles at the girl behind the bar. 'Two Krombachers please, and whatever the old fool is having.'

'Three,' Vladi croaks and clambers back onto his stool.

'So. You were trapped in a mountain, hence your appearance, or were you having me on? What's with the hair and the beard?' Vladi gesticulates wildly. Dannii suddenly gets the giggles. 'Is she alright?'

'She's a bit weird, to be honest,' Lukas squints and puts his hand on Dannii's knee.

She giggles and slaps his aching shoulder. 'It's a disguise.' Lukas grins and points at his face.

'Well, you had me fooled. Didn't recognise you at all when you walked through the door.' Vladi lifts his glass. 'Prost!'

Dannii snorts into her pint. 'Prost.'

'She has manners. Super.' Vladi drinks deeply.

'Prost.' Lukas smiles.

'So, to summarise, the night I phoned you from the casino, you ran, disguised yourself as Commander Azizullah, and ended up in Glossop, where you made the acquaintance of a homophobic Scouser with a violent streak. Since then you've rubbed noses with this beautiful lady, the Manchester underground, an ex-world-champion boxer and half the Mancunia FC team, who are all bent, according to you, and bust up one of their sex parties. You held the CID of GMP at gun point and you've been to Blackpool with your daughter for a night on the tiles. To top it all you've almost killed yourself in a rock avalanche. And all this in the last ten days. Does that sum it up correctly?'

'Pretty much.'

'You forgot the hooker,' Dannii says.

'Oh, do tell me more.'

'That's filed under "night on the tiles at Blackpool". Case closed,' Lukas says firmly.

'Whatever next?'

'I've had an idea.' Dannii opens her iPad.

'Go on, darling. Dazzle me!' Vladi leers.

'What's your logon details, love?' Dannii shouts to the barmaid.

'buymorebeer. All lower case,' the girl shouts back. Dannii snorts.

'We've been trying to establish an early connection between Tony Jackson, the co-pilot at Stan Entwistle's Dolly Green boxing circus and James Bradshaw, manager of Mancunia. This is the team Coventry Wanderers put out March 1975.' Lukas passes Vladi the printout.

Vladi reads out the names. 'What a line-up. Courante. Jean-Pierre. World-Wide Football Association bigwig.'

Dannii nods. 'And my supplier.' Vladi squints at her. 'He gives me tips. Amongst others.'

'She's the blogger, Vlad,' Lukas says.

'Heilige Scheisse!' Vladi gawks.

Dannii grins. 'He never rings himself. I get anonymous texts.'

Lukas continues. 'We've also established that the Kovacs listed is the father of Miklos Kovacs, who about ten years ago was part of a group calling themselves The Clan. We believe The Clan still operates today, with different members.'

'I remember. They got into the papers for throwing wild orgies. Someone even mentioned the "r " word. Never went to trial and the papers had to issue an apology. And you think they're still in existence?'

'Yes. The Scouser, Mark, was in the force at the time of the original Clan. He was on the edge of the investigation. He reckons someone tidied up after the boys and he thinks Briggs might be involved. Bit like now. We're trying to find a link.' Lukas drinks.

'You know what they called themselves in the old days?' Vladi leans forward.

'Who?'

'Bradshaw, Courante, Kovacs, Jackson and a few others? The Gentlemen's Club. Fancied themselves as playboys. On the back of Georgie Best. The only one thát would pass as a playboy was Courante. Jackson's always been a thug. Didn't he die, knifed or something? Bradshaw was just a workhorse, and Kovacs, well I suppose he had a certain eastern flair. Runs my favourite casino in town, amongst others. Rumour has it he supplies entertainment, leisure and relaxation to the glitz and glamour.'

'Why didn't you mention this before, you fool?'

Vladi shrugs. 'Never occurred to me there was a connection. It was all such a long time ago. No idea you'd stumble over Courante and Jackson. Anyway, they were just dandies. Nothing as serious as The Clan. They just wanted to be like old Georgie Best. Didn't Jackson die?'

Lukas smiles and taps his nose.

'I found it.' Dannii turns the iPad. 'I searched for Briggs and Coventry Wanderers, together. You'll never believe it. Briggs was on the Coventry Wanderers youth team. Never made it into the first squad. Joined the police force at eighteen. Must have got his further qualifications while already a copper. Anyway, Bradshaw came up through the youth academy. Briggs, Bradshaw and probably Jackson knew each other as teenagers. Courante and Kovacs appeared on the scene later, as signings.'

'Wow! Looks like Briggs went into the force but they remained mates, all this time. And Briggs was in the vicinity of young Kovacs, too, when he was in The Clan investigation. Mark said he thought Briggs was burying statements. He said that—'

'I said what?' Lukas and Dannii turn around. 'I've missed you guys.' Marks grins.

'I thought you had a job today.' Lukas frowns.

'Tomorrow. Thanks for dropping me off in my own car this morning, by the way.'

'You offered it to us, moron.'

'Of course I did, hon. Who's this? The other drunk polack?' Mark nods in Vladi's direction. Vladi snorts.

Lukas introduces them. 'You're going to be great friends. Play Russian roulette with vodka shots. Drink each other under the table.'

'Nice to meet you, old chap. Lovely shiner.' Vladi shakes Mark's hand.

Mark rolls his eyes. 'Got in the way of the Hulk here.'

Vladi cackles. 'You're the law, I understand?'

'That was the old days. I do security now.'

'You're a guard?'

'Fuck that, I own the joint! WestPoint Security, Warrington. Any chance of a beer, love?' Mark turns to the bar. 'Make it a round.'

'You own the firm?' Lukas looks at Mark.

'What did you think I am? An employee?' Mark draws inverted commas into the air.

'Why didn't you tell me?'

''Cos after all this time you still don't ask the right questions, Sherlock.' Mark scowls and drinks.

Dannii turns to him. 'And you're still an arsehole.'

'I love you too, sweetheart.' He turns to Lukas. 'How's your girl?'

'At her mother's,' Lukas says. 'She's fine. The Gentlemen's Club – mean anything to you?'

'Nope. Who are they?'

Gallivanting footballers in the 70s. We're looking at 1975. Coventry. Bradshaw, Courante, Kovacs, Jackson and Briggs.'

'What, Briggs, a footballer?'

'Youth team. Never made it to the first team.'

'Kovacs?'

'Janos. Father of Miklos. Apparently now supplies entertainment and leisure, owns a few casinos and nightclubs.'

'Bloody hell, mate! When did you find all this out?'

Vladi gestures in Dannii's direction. 'The power of the internet at the fingertips of a clever woman.'

Mark laughs. 'Hm, her fingertips. And all the places they might've been – '

Lukas grabs him by the throat. 'Don't!'

'Oho!' Vladi cackles. 'So this is the new Novak I've heard so much about?'

Lukas lets go of Mark and turns to Vladi. 'You can pack it in as well.'

Vladi lifts his hands. 'OK.' He clears his throat. 'So you've got half a story. You've established an interesting connection. Now what?'

'We need a link to last night. We think there's a connection, but we need concrete evidence. We do have possible witnesses. But if Jackson and Briggs keep on watching each others' backs we'll never get leverage.'

'Need to find out how they do the fix on the pitch also. I'll stir it a bit tomorrow, on the blog.'

'I've got an appointment to see Bradshaw in the morning. I'm going to ask him straight out what he thinks is going on.' Lukas takes Dannii's arm.

'You're not leaving us?' Vladi looks aghast.

'We've got Christmas dinner to catch up on, and I do need a good night's sleep.'

'And where am I staying? After all I've done – ' Marks asks.

Vladi grabs his arm. 'You can stay with me, old chap. It'll be fun.'

'Fun?' Mark frowns.

'Come on. Quickly.' Lukas pulls a grinning Dannii towards the door.

Chapter 61

Lukas lights the kitchen fire then puts a CD on. The quality of the recording is bad, as the original vinyl record had been played and scratched so much.

'What's this, sweet?' Dannii asks as she lights some candles.

Lukas peels potatoes. 'Christmas carols I grew up with. Mostly German, but some Polish. Pavel ripped it off an old vinyl.'

'Interesting instrumentation.'

'Carl Orff Schulwerk, mainly. Do you know Orff?'

'I know Carmina Burana.' She watches him peel then hugs him tightly and puts her head between his shoulder blades.

Lukas turns round. 'I want this to be special.' He brushes away a strand of hair from her face.

'It is. I haven't had Christmas dinner cooked for me, like, forever.'

'And I haven't cooked Christmas dinner for anyone, like, forever, too.' He kisses her hair and laughs. 'And no turkeys in sight.'

'What a bonus.' She squeezes him a bit too hard. 'Carl Orff, what?'

'Schulwerk. He invented a set of instruments for children in schools and kindergartens. To make music available from an early age. Recorders and xylophones. Old instruments too, cornemuses and so on.'

'How d'you know all this?'

'Boys from good families are taught classical music.' He looks at her and drops a potato into the pot.

'And you're a boy from a good family?'

'Yup. Only it was Markus who was the talented one. I was incredibly jealous. He just played and I had to practise note by note. Infuriating.'

She laughs. 'I know what you mean. I could just play, too. But when it came to playing printed music I had to drum it into myself. Repetition ad nauseam.'

He raises an eyebrow. 'Latin? Is there no end to your talents?'

'Nope.'

He lights a gas ring for the potatoes. 'Did you do any jazz?'

'I was in a big band.'

'I love jazz.' Lukas tips the defrosting sauerkraut into a pot and puts it on a small flame.

'Why not the microwave?'

'Doesn't taste the same.'

'These are special Christmas veal sausages. Got to be done in butter. Here, mash that and stick it in the oven.' He passes her the pot with the boiled potatoes. 'I need to do something upstairs before we eat. I'll be twenty minutes.'

'OK. I'll need another twenty at your computer too. You'll be bulletproof.'

'Excellent!' Earlier he had nipped into Boots and bought some hair bleach and blonde colouring. He applies the bleach to his hair and beard. Twenty minutes later he has cleaned the bathroom and restored his original colour. He puts his head in the basin and washes out the colouring then returns to the kitchen, bin in hand.

'What were you doing?' Dannii still sits at the computer, facing away from him.

'Cleaning the bathroom.' Lukas empties the bin. He opens a can of beer for her and puts it on the desk beside her. Then he kisses her on the neck.

She pulls up her shoulders. 'Eek! Your hair's wet.' She turns round. 'Wow!' He smiles. 'So this is the real you?'

'Hm.'

She touches his damp hair. 'Fabulous.' She strokes his face. 'Peter Schmeichel. Uncanny.'

'Or rather his dad. He's Polish, too.'

'Peter Schmeichel is Danish, sweet.'

'He is now, but not from birth. Peter Boleslaw Schmeichel was born in Denmark but his father's Polish and he held Polish citizenship until the 70s. His middle name is the name of a town near where I'm from, in Silesia. Used to be called Bunzlau.' Lukas puts pots and pans with cabbage and sausages straight onto the table.

'I didn't know that.' Dannii pours beer into the glasses.

Lukas puts a huge portion of sausage onto her plate. 'See, darling, you don't know everything. Here's a big chunk of Polish for you. Don't forget to take plenty of mustard.'

'That was delicious. Come here!' Dannii leans over and takes hold of his face. Lukas is still chewing but swallows quickly. She kisses him on the mouth. 'Hm, sauerkraut and butter.'

'Wait till the morning,' he growls.

'Too much information.' She laughs.

Lukas clears the plates and takes a bottle of Jägermeister from the fridge. 'This is necessary. Do you like the music?'

'Early Armstrong? Cheers.' She necks the shot.

'1928. Whatever happened to prost?'

'Sorry, you'd better pour another.'

'Do you want to move to the living room? It's more comfortable.'

'I like it here. We could sit by the fire.' She gestures to his old couch.

He feels the night's chill creep in from outside. The candles have almost burned down. 'It's a mess in here.' Lukas suddenly feels a lump in his throat.

'Luke, I love it in your kitchen.'

He shakes his head. 'It's all a mess. Like me.' He unexpectedly feels tearful and avoids looking at her.

'What's the matter, sweet?' she ask him. He feels cold, though his face is burning. 'Look at me,' Dannii says. He shakes his head. 'Look at me!' she repeats. He reluctantly looks at her without lifting his head. She puts her forehead against his. 'Tell me.'

'I'm afraid. Panicked.'

'Why?'

'I'm worried for you and me.'

She looks alarmed. 'Why?' she repeats.

'I'm worried for all fucking humanity.' He falls round her neck and feels like a childish fool.

'Let it out, Lukas.'

Lukas. The first time she's called him by his full name. He roars at her shoulder. She holds him. Tightly and tenderly. She strokes the back of his neck and he feels himself aroused despite the darkness inside him. He buries his face against her neck and tugs at her skin with his lips. She pushes him away to look at him. 'Why are you worried about us?' He leans forward and kisses her wildly. She pulls back. 'Lukas, why are you worried about us?'

His deep sigh is full of anguish. 'There is so much shit going on in the world, what hope is there? For truth, for fairness?' He slams his empty shot glass onto the table. She recoils. He stares at the glass, seeing the last drops of liquid seep through his fingers. 'If this is what people do to each other'—he feels her hand on his shoulder and looks at her— 'What hope is there for you and me?' He leans heavily on the table, glass still in hand. 'What's going on in people's heads, for Christ's sake? That fucking copper, what's going on inside him? That arsehole of a fucking footballer. How bloody compromised do you have to be to do that to your teammate, to those young girls, for the sake of what, pleasure?' He turns to her and spreads out his arms. 'Come on, give me an answer! What do you think? What d'you think it feels like to be so twisted that you can justify doing stuff like that?'

She looks at him silently. He sees fear in her eyes and clears his throat. He gently puts the glass down on the table. 'For god knows how many years I thought I'd chosen what I thought I wanted, but now I know I was just afraid of being lonely. The marriage gave me security despite it not being ideal, I thought. Then Liz destroyed it all and I thought I wasn't going to be able to carry on. I missed the kids so much. I had unbearably dark thoughts but I got used to being alone eventually and comfortable doing what I do with my pitiful, long day. Now suddenly everything's changed but I'm losing my belief in mankind. I thought there were rules in life. Simple Christian rules.' He swallows hard and sees her do the same.

'They need to be punished,' she says quietly.

He leans on the table. 'How?' he hollers and sees her flinch.

'It's your job to work that out.' She holds his stare.

He slams his fist on the table, making the glasses jump, and turns away. 'Impossible! If they stick together like they've done for years, there's no chance. This is way out of my league.'

'Stop finding excuses not to act.'

He flings himself around. 'You're part of it. You're at the very centre,' he shouts and points and glares at her wildly.

She walks towards him slowly. 'Yes, Lukas Novak, I can see now how afraid you are.' She stands in front of him, hands on hips, head tilted, brows furrowed. She pokes her index finger into his breastbone and runs it very slowly down over his stomach. 'You think they are better than you somehow, hm? You think that just because they play for Mancunia or they work for the police with three letters in front of their name that you can't reach them? These are small people, with few options. Manipulated by habits and mechanisms they established decades ago and can't get away from, like hamsters on a wheel. You may think they're in charge of what they do, but they aren't. Exactly the opposite. Driven by ego, debt, greed. By fear and adrenaline. Codependency. The abused harbouring the abuser. Fight and flight. They are prisoners of their own making.' He looks at her, incredulously. 'They unimaginatively make the same bad moves, the same mistakes, over and over again. But you, you have changed.' He swallows hard. 'You have choices. You are creative.' She takes his hands. 'Don't you realise that you're free, Lukas?'

'What about you?' he whispers.

'I can pull the plug tomorrow.' He just looks at her. 'Let's finish this, Lucky Luke. In style. Let's turn up the heat until the pot boils over.'

'Put a spanner in the works?'

'Yes! That's more like you.' She hugs him. 'Why are you worried for you and me?' She plays with an empty beer can.

'Do you want more?' he asks quietly.

'Do you have any wine?'

Lukas fetches a bottle of Rioja from the cellar then throws another log on the fire. He sits down by her side. 'I don't know you,' he says.

She plays with her glass. 'You think.'

'I don't know what I know or what I don't know any more.'

'You said you know what you don't want. And you said you didn't want to wait and fret. I said I felt the same and we went ahead. Are you backtracking now?'

'No. It's just I don't know what to believe any more. Maybe the life I want is unobtainable, in the long run. With everybody out there behaving like a total bastard.'

'Not everyone. Just the bastards,' she says. 'Not you. Not me. I hope you're seeing that clearly.'

He studies his glass. 'I am.'

'What are you doubting?'

'I'm afraid that it won't work out. You and me, and this whole thing we're involved in.'

'But we're in charge here. You're looking at the mountain as a whole. That's too much to get your head round.'

'One step at a time?'

'Exactly. You and me, this'—she draws a circle in the air— 'We both want this to work, don't we?'

'Do we? Do you really want to be with a fat, old bloke? What can I possibly offer you?'

'Oh, for Christ's sake, don't start that again! I want to be with you, Lukas.' She is frowning.

'Are you sure?' he asks.

'It's the same damn thing, isn't it? The same reason you're thinking you won't succeed in nailing these bastards. You think you're not good enough. To get them. Or for me.' He shrugs. 'What did you say? Sometimes it's time to leave behind what we've believed in, what we've learned from our upbringing, because we find it's no longer applicable to our lives?'

'Did I say that?'

She nods. 'I've a secret to tell you. I feel the same as you. I want security. For once in my life. And I too feel I'm not good enough. I've done drugs. I've slept around. I had piercings. You detest all that.'

'Have you ever had an HIV test?' He instantly regrets asking.

She scowls. 'Yes I have. Have you?'

'Why would *I* need one? I've never been promiscuous.'

'Not ever?'

'HIV wasn't around then,' he growls.

'It was starting to be. I could ask you just as bluntly about syphilis or herpes.' She drums her fingers on the table. He laughs nervously and stalls. 'The fact that you're asking means you don't trust me enough to tell you if I'm positive.'

He shakes his head. 'That's absurd. That's not my motivation at all.'

She sits back and folds her arms. 'Let's drop this. It is, after all, an important question. Though absolutely infuriating the way you went about asking it. What else do you want to know? No, I've never injected, I told you that. The other question?'

He looks at her and swallows hard. 'Are you on the pill?' He feels himself blushing, and runs his hand over his eyes. 'Sorry, I'm behaving like a twat.'

'Yes, you are,' she says quietly. 'I've had a coil fitted. Not so I can be promiscuous. I just didn't trust myself for a while. But I honestly can't remember how long it was before you – years. Believe it or not.'

He looks at her. 'I can't remember either. Feels like ages.'

She holds his gaze. 'Don't you think you could've thought of protection as well? Why is it always supposed to be the woman?'

'I was totally besotted with you.'

'And now you're not?'

Lukas twists in his chair. 'I still am, of course, it's just—'

'Your brain was in your underpants.' She laughs. 'No. It's because we've been trapped inside mountains and been chased by lunatics we've not talked about stuff like this. Not to mention the overbearing presence of Mark. Our life together has been incredibly hectic, so far. You get to know people much better that way than by long conversations.'

'Ideally I'd like a bit of both.' He drinks. 'Only a few days ago I thought that in a way it was so much easier when I was married and I didn't have to think about feeling safe. And then she left me and I woke up.'

'False sense of security.'

'You can say that again.'

'Security doesn't work.'

'I guess not. You take things for granted.'

'Are you turning into a new man, Novak?'

'No, I'm turning into a desperate, sentimental old fool, hanging on to the one and only thing that seems real and true in my life since Markus.'

'Are you looking for a promise?' She moves closer.

'I guess so. Something to make me feel safe. Ridiculous, isn't it?'

'No. I promise.'

'What?'

'Everything.'

'What does that mean?'

'I don't know.'

He takes her by the shoulders. 'In that case I promise you everything, too.'

'Trust, not security.'

He nods. 'Trust. Not security.'

'Shake on it?'

He laughs and shakes her hand.

'Come here.' Dannii sits down on the old couch and pats the space next to her. She opens her iPad. 'I've been doing some analysis.'

Lukas throws another log on the fire, picks up the bottle of wine and sits down next to her heavily. 'I never sit here, you know. Just another dumping ground.'

'Very comfortable.' She snuggles up to him. 'Look at this. This is the Match Stats app I was talking about,' she says. Lukas grunts. 'Do you remember the Mancunia Halifax game just before Christmas?'

'Yes, I was in the Hare with Pavel. He'd just found your blog. You were talking in code, implying Bradshaw knew the outcome of the match. It all went wrong when Wallace came on.'

'Do you remember what happened just before?'

'Callaway came on for Stevens, who was carrying a metatarsal injury, allegedly.'

'Well observed.'

'I was curious about your allegations.'

'They didn't come on together, did they?'

'Callaway came on first. About fifteen minutes before Wallace.'

'And he had a little chat with Entwistle during that time.'

'I didn't notice.'

'You probably didn't know what to look for. After the chat Jason was quickly taken off and replaced by Wallace. Wallace obviously was happy to play along with the fix. The game turned and Mancunia lost. Now, have a look at this.' Dannii taps on Leroy Callaway's name. 'Player stats.'

'Passes completed,' Lukas reads.

Dannii brings up a diagram of blue and red lines. 'The blue ones are successful passes.'

'And the red ones are not,' Lukas concludes.

'Precisely. Now watch. I'm narrowing the timescale of analysis to approximately the time when Wallace came on. You see, overall and until then Leroy's passes were OK. Now see what happens.'

'He's passing across goal a lot. And ultimately it was a mistimed pass like that which caused Mancunia's demise.'

'Precisely. It was this one.' Dannii puts her finger on one particular red arrow. 'Just before Halifax's goal.'

He ruffles her hair. 'Genius.'

'When were we in Blackpool?'

'Feels like weeks ago.' Lukas caresses her neck.

She looks at him sternly. 'Cut it out, Romeo!'

He forces his eyes back to the screen, but snuggles closer to her. 'It was last Saturday.'

'You're going to slide off this couch any minute now, aren't you, Novak?' She smirks. 'Here it is. Jason's initiation, so to speak.'

'Got himself sent off pretty much straight away.' Lukas takes the iPad from her and puts it on the floor. 'I trust you've analysed other matches, too?' He moves his face close to hers.

She touches his cheek. 'Yes I have. Similar patterns, though not as obvious. You're impossible.'

'Hm. Print them out. Can I take you upstairs now?' He kisses her softly on the nose.

She giggles and puts her arms around his shoulders. 'I'm very comfortable here.' She brushes her lips against his.

'So you keep saying,' he mutters, and pulling her closer returns her kiss.

Chapter 62

Lukas has just parked the BMW at Longford Park when his phone beeps. It's too early to be on his way, but he needs to think. He's had a good night's sleep, finally, and his body doesn't feel quite as broken as it has done since his near death experience. Last night, once the kitchen fire had burned down, he'd carried a sleeping Dannii upstairs to bed. When she sleeps, she sleeps and he'd left her that way this morning. She had all but sighed and turned over when he said goodbye to her. He had bought a breakfast barm and a coffee, which, on top of last night's meal, he now regrets. With the site of demolished Longford Hall to his left, he walks towards the leisure centre and checks his message.

Dannii has forwarded a tweet that Leroy Callaway posted last night. *'Thanks, everyone, for #KindBirthdayWishes. #fantastic. Where are you now, #MatchMaker? Love, #LeroyC #MancuniaFC'*. *'I'm going to have him,'* Dannii has added after the tweet.

Lukas frowns. Exactly how deluded is Callaway? Doesn't he realise he's left a trail of injury and mayhem? And what about his conscience? Callaway is married with children, always in the public eye and often in the tabloids. How does he justify his actions, in his own heart. Lukas can't imagine how heavy Callaway's burden must be, if he were ever to acknowledge it. Same for Briggs.

He revisits last night's conversation; how childish to have been so emotional. Yet he still doesn't comprehend how people can be so seemingly indifferent to right and wrong. Maybe what she says is true. Maybe the likes of Callaway and Briggs are driven by other forces than he understands. Maybe pressures rest on them that they can't circumvent, that they have created for themselves and are a slave to. His comment about true Christian values now seems naive. Like how someone shielded from reality would speak about the evils of the world. And it is true, he does feel naive and vulnerable in the light of his recent experiences. But then every reaction has a trigger action. Only when pressure, when leverage is high enough will people do something about their circumstances; he guesses this applies as much to the drug addict, finally checking themselves into rehab, as it does to a DCI nearing retirement age, monitoring his bank account.

How he'd love to have a frank talk with Richard Briggs. Still surprised at his own courage the night before last, he tells himself he had to do what he did, for Lil's sake. And Briggs was ultimately his only way into the hotel. His fists would've got him nowhere. So he chose Briggs, subconsciously and successfully. He should trust himself more often. And trust her.

He looks at his reflection in the window of the leisure centre. She says he is imposing, with an intrinsic air of authority about him. People see him as a calm, self-assured leader, apparently. He smiles back at himself. The wide smile that she likes so much. Fair enough, dressed all in black, he makes quite an impressive figure; his triple XL leather jacket weighs a ton but hides the bulk round his midriff. Doc Marten-style boots and 501s lend him a hint of a bouncer. Much more comfortable now with his original colour restored he watches himself run his fingers through his hair. Yes, he does have an air about him, he notices now, as he takes a mental step back. He puts on his sternest face and admits to himself that if he didn't know himself, if he did meet a man of his own appearance, he would possibly be intimidated.

She says he needs to trust, to believe, rather than feel. To admit openly to himself that in his core he believes he is a stronger, a better man than the Callaways and Briggses of this world, would have seemed arrogant, before he knew her. Whether the Callaways and Briggses have or have not made their peace with themselves and their actions shouldn't be his concern; they don't need his sympathy and he doesn't need to entirely understand their motivation. He just needs to know what their motivation is, so he can get leverage.

He stands up straight. She says he fills the room. He thought that always having to bend down to speak to people or to enter the average British building has made him develop a stoop. Or is he just trying to hide his size? He towers heads above most people. But maybe he just doesn't want to stand out, maybe he just doesn't want to be the first person people look at in a crowd. He feels better after the deep intake of oxygen, looks better with his shoulders back and his stomach in. He's being too self-analytical, too narcissistic, again. Too much of an old woman, indeed. He should pull himself together, be more of a man, get back to the car, see James Bradshaw and put a spanner in the works.

Mancunia FC's administrative offices are situated within the grounds of the imposing Diamond Park Stadium, next to the club's museum and merchandise store. The place feels more like a private home than an office; sofas and soft lighting give the interior a warm and inviting aura.

The receptionist points him down a broad corridor decorated with club memorabilia and historic photographs of players and managers. James Bradshaw's office is on the right, the manager's name embossed on the door in bold letters. Lukas switches off his phone, stands up straight, pulls his shoulders back and is just about to knock when the door opens.

'You.' Leroy Callaway looks surprised and apprehensive. He inches away.

'Me,' Lukas says and squints.

A second door, behind Callaway, is closed.

Lukas stops himself from clearing his throat. 'You'—he taps Callaway's chest—'Are not going to get away with what happened the other night. No matter how much nonsense you tweet.' He pushes Callaway aside brusquely and steps into the space between the double doors. He quickly opens the inner door without knocking and enters James Bradshaw's office.

'Oy!' Callaway grabs Lukas's elbow.

Lukas snatches his arm away, turns and laughs. 'Mr Bradshaw, would you please control your player.'

'Boss, he—'

'Out,' Bradshaw barks.

'Boss!'

'Out, I said, Leroy! I'm done with you,' Bradshaw thunders. Callaway swears and slams the door. Bradshaw exhales noisily.

Judging by the colour of his face, the man has high blood pressure, Lukas decides. He takes a step towards Bradshaw's desk and points behind him. 'I didn't—'

'You didn't have to,' Bradshaw interrupts and gesticulates towards a sofa. 'I've already spoken to him in no uncertain terms. Can I offer you anything?'

Lukas shakes his head and sits down. 'This needn't take long.'

The small, corpulent man nods and sinks down into another sofa. He puts his fingertips together as in a steeple and leans forward. 'I don't condone what went on at the Turing.'

'How much do you know?'

'I know you got your daughter out. She was with young Entwistle.'

'How is he?'

Bradshaw breathes in deeply. 'Can I trust that this conversation will stay completely confidential?'

'Of course.' Lukas pulls his shoulders back and cracks his neck.

'He's bad. Very bad. I doubt he'll play again in a hurry.'

'D'you know who's responsible?'

Bradshaw shakes his head. 'Leroy isn't owning up to anything. But he was in charge. It was his party. I'll get to the bottom of it.'

'Who told you I was there?'

'DCI Briggs.' Bradshaw chews his bottom lip.

'Do you know what he was doing there?'

'You brought him, he said. You forced him. Made a mess of his face. You told him his daughter was being abused by − ' Bradshaw nods towards the door.

Lukas gives a wry smile. 'I brought him, yes. But did you know Briggs was at the hotel earlier on that evening?'

'No. Why?'

Lukas crosses his arms. 'I may well know more than you think, James. So don't bullshit me.'

'Are you threatening me, man?' Bradshaw's face darkens a shade.

'No. But do you want to know what this whole situation looks like from my perspective?'

'Go ahead.'

'I know about The Gentlemen's Club.'

'Many do. We were quite famous.'

'Some of you became quite infamous.'

'Like who?'

'Tony Jackson.'

'Tony's dead.' The manager looks at him intently.

Lukas notices that Bradshaw is slightly cross-eyed. 'But is he?'

'What are you implying?'

'Can I be frank, James?'

'I wish you were, Lukas. I've a league to win.'

'Who's in charge of security at Leroy's parties?'

Bradshaw shrugs. 'I don't know of any special arrangements. I thought the hotel was looking after it. Are you saying an outside contract is involved?'

Lukas squints at Bradshaw. He finds it difficult to judge the man. 'Do you really not know or are you protecting a friend?'

'I'm protecting this club, Novak. I don't much care about individuals. What friend?'

'OK, let me rewind. Before the last party, did you think the allegations of what goes on at the parties were true?'

Bradshaw exhales noisily. 'To a certain extent, yes. I thought the papers were exaggerating though.'

'So did I.'

'Some of the girls get greedy. And imaginative.'

'Do you pay them off?'

'Yes.'

'You don't think we've another Clan scenario, do you?'

'You know about that?' Bradshaw frowns. 'No, I don't.' He gets up and paces the room, hands behind his back. 'Leroy might be rampant, and out of order as far as the other night's concerned, but he's not a pervert. Those guys were nasty.'

'Who did the mopping up then?'

'What do you mean? It went to the police.'

'No one was ever prosecuted.'

'I believe there was a lack of evidence and some very contradictory statements.' Bradshaw stops. 'What are you implying?' he asks.

'I want you to tell me who was on the investigation. I want to hear it from you directly, so I know you're following my trail of thought.'

Bradshaw breathes out heavily. 'Off the record.'

'Absolutely.'

'Dick was part of it.'

'Yes. I know. Thank you.'

Bradshaw's face reddens further. 'Why did you ask me then?'

'As I said, I wanted to hear it from you.'

'Are you trying to frame me?'

'No. I'm making you see what's going on behind your back.'

Bradshaw turns purple. 'I'm in charge here. And I'm a busy man. If you don't get to the point soon, Novak, I'll have you thrown out, like last time.'

'Calm down, James. I'm not saying you've lost control. I'm just saying it was Briggs who was in charge of security, not the hotel. He admitted to me he was there earlier in the evening to check that everything was OK. You've suspected there's drugs, haven't you?'

Bradshaw nods and picks at his fingers. Then he looks up at Lukas. 'You know we're probably going to win the Premiership, don't you?'

'I bloody well hope so.'

'I won't let anything stand in the way of it,' Bradshaw says quietly.

'You don't care about the individual.'

'The individual player is his own man. I demand he gives two hundred per cent for the club, as Leroy has. He's been the pillar I built this team on. But every man is also an individual. I can't control all the choices players make.'

'I understand.'

'If a player fails a drugs test, or develops a drink problem or a messy relationship, I quarantine them.'

'How?'

'You know those long, drawn-out back injuries some players seem to be so much more prone to than others?'

'Interesting.' Lukas pauses. 'Do you know who supplies them, James? With, as somebody put it, relaxation and entertainment?'

'What d'you mean?'

'Drugs and prostitutes, just like in The Clan's heyday.'

'I don't know anything about a drug supply now or indeed who was supplying those idiots then.'

'Yet it's the same person.'

'Who? I want a word.'

'Do you really not know, James?' Lukas raises his eyebrows. 'I don't care if right now you know who it is or not. That's between you and your conscience. But if you really don't have an inkling, then let me tell you, you've been left out of the loop and you are being played. And a man in your position, of your influence, must not be played by anyone, especially not their mate, right?'

Bradshaw's eyes dart around the room and stop when they meets Lukas's. 'You're absolutely fucking right, Novak. Who is it? Briggs?'

Lukas smiles lopsidedly. 'Why did you say that?' Bradshaw chews his bottom lip. 'You got to give me something, James. Why do you suspect Briggs is involved?'

'I've already said too much, Novak. And I won't have you blackmail me.'

'It's not Briggs, and I'm not trying to blackmail you. But as you know, my daughter was drugged and Briggs's Gaby was abused. Let me put it this way, Briggs didn't exactly behave like a loving father. You and I have just established that Briggs was part of the Clan investigation and I'm telling you he was in charge of security at the Turing. In both cases, dodgy stuff went on. The fact that you even mention his name in connection with drugs and prostitutes makes me think that you don't trust him completely and that you think he might be capable of being involved.'

Bradshaw sits down and looks at Lukas sternly. 'Novak, even if I wanted to, I couldn't tell you anything.'

'Funny handshake scenario, is it?'

'That's one way of putting it.'

'Jackson, too?'

'Yes.'

'Then you know he's not dead.'

'I suspected it.'

'He's back at Dolly Green, raising a new type of thug. Briggs hired him to supply security for the Turing. I suspect he also hired him to scare that blogger – remember him?'

'Yes. Did he find him?'

'Tony's guys put an old-age pensioner in hospital by mistake.'

'Shit.'

'That's not all. I'm being framed for it.'

'Who by?'

'Guess. I've been on the run. I almost got killed. Look at my face.' Lukas sees the man swallow hard. 'D'you know what your players call your friend Dick?' Bradshaw's face reddens. He shakes his head. 'They call him their guardian angel at CID. In other words, their mopper upper.'

Bradshaw jumps up and stares down at Lukas. 'He's a gambler,' Bradshaw barks and paces up and down. 'Massive debts. Hopelessly addicted. Always has been. Is that enough for you?'

'I figured as much, James.' Lukas gets up.

'You're infuriating, Novak.'

'Sorry.' Lukas laughs. 'It's Kovacs. Supplier of entertainment and leisure.' He smiles down at Bradshaw.

Bradshaw swears loud and long. Then he looks Lukas up and down. 'Do we still have an agreement?'

'Yes. But maybe it's time you took advice from your lodge. I don't envy you in your job. I find it hard to discount the individual.'

'You let me worry about my mess and sort out your own. What about your daughter? Don't you want to—'

Lukas shakes his head. 'She's learned her lesson. Maybe you could put us on the security list so she could go and visit Jason? She's fond of him.'

'He's gay.'

'Does that matter?'

'I guess not.'

'Did he ever confide in you, that he was being bullied?'

'Yes. I thought I put his mind at ease. I wish I'd done more now, believe me.'

'I believe you.' Lukas turns to face the door.

'Novak.' Lukas looks back at Bradshaw. 'You're different.'

'Different to what?'

'Most people.'

Lukas turns. 'Can I ask you another question?'

Bradshaw sighs. 'Is it going to take long?'

'Depends how worked up you're going to get. Do you fix?'

The man remains surprisingly calm. 'One day you and me ought to have a drink. When I retire, maybe.' He laughs.

Lukas laughs with him. 'Maybe. Are you going to answer my question?'

'Do I fix? Did I not tell you earlier that I will win the league?'

'You did.'

'Does that not answer your question?'

'I'm interested in the "how", not so much the "why".'

'I've agreements with many people, not just you.'

'And your squad follow your orders? What's their reward?'

'To win the league.'

Lukas smiles. 'This is where I don't believe you not knowing about Kovacs's role. He supplies rewards.'

'Not the rewards I dish out. Winning the league is the highest reward anyone could have.'

'In that case maybe Leroy rewards his mates further?'

'No comment. And circumstantial.'

'I agree. But a possibility.'

Bradshaw takes Lukas by the elbow. 'You've learned enough, Mr Novak. I need to get back to business.' He tries to turn Lukas towards the door.

'Thank you.' Lukas shakes Bradshaw's hand. 'You've helped me a lot. I won't break my word.'

Bradshaw looks at him seriously. 'Good luck. And I mean it. You understand I can do very little—'

'And maintain your integrity. I understand. Thank you for understanding my position.'

'I'd be as furious as you are.'

'It's a new emotion for me.'

'I believe you. At our first meeting you came across as a gentle giant. Now you're quite a force to be reckoned with.'

'It's the scars.' Lukas points at his face.

'No, it's not. And you bloody well know it.'

Interlude

With a sigh James Bradshaw sits down heavily behind his desk and stares at the telephone for a while. Eventually he picks up the receiver and dials zero for an outside line. At the dial tone he punches in six numbers. His index finger hovers above the seventh number for a short while. Then the manager of Mancunia FC slowly replaces the receiver.

Chapter 63

Lukas smiles as he switches his phone back on. Bradshaw has grown on him. He reckons the man is honest as far as his restraints let him. Just another human looking after his lot.

His phone beeps. '*Check the blog,*' she texts. Lukas navigates to the blog and stops dead as he reads in Mancunia FC's hallowed corridors.

He checks her previous message and copies Callaway's Twitter name. He quickly leaves the building, aware that he is still on Mancunia's property, gets into the BMW and drives a few hundred yards before he stops the car. He punches in Callaway's nickname on Twitter and presses the search button. Lukas quickly finds the message Dannii forwarded to him earlier. Following it is another tweet by Callaway. It contains just four words. *@MatchMaker, you are #dead.*' Lukas swallows hard. His new world has suddenly gone dark.

For a few minutes he tries to get his reaction under control. Then he laughs out loud. Two worlds, two different platforms of reality exist side by side. At least two; it could well be more. The information he is fed, through any media, is always going to sway him one way or another. Whenever anyone opens their mouth, they do so for a reason. Some people don't understand that their contribution affects others negatively as well as positively. In his opinion these people should keep their mouths firmly shut and put their brain in gear before speaking. Ninety-nine per cent of the information out there, the current television offerings, his pet hate, the daily soaps, Facebook – which he's avoided like the plague so far – all that information overload belongs in the mouth before brain variety, in his opinion. Someone wants you to buy their shit or vote for their brain-dead political party. Somebody else wants you to follow their fad, and as always it's those who shout loudest, those who are crudest, that get the most attention in the media, who generate and repeat mindlessly the crap that sticks out most.

Like Leroy Callaway. Lukas wonders if the man is aware how close he is to committing suicide by social media. Or whether he is just too stupid to realise that his little emporium built on corruption and greed is only fuelling his own delusions of invulnerability.

Lukas can't quite believe that Dannii actually posted the photograph he took of Gaby and Vicky at the Turing on the blog. But Callaway's reaction to her post is as much an admission of guilt as it is a severe threat to Dannii, if Callaway isn't just mouthing off, as Lukas hopes he is.

He tells himself to take a step back, react objectively. After all, he is in charge of his reaction to any situation. He could easily panic or just go to the pub and laugh at the evil world out there. Or he could stay in charge. '*I just read Leroy's latest tweet,*' he types to her. '*And the blog. Is that what you call stirring it a bit? Keep looking behind you. I'll be home in 15.*' Lukas puts the BMW into gear and drives slowly back to Chorlton.

The youths are hanging around on his corner again. Truants, no hobbies, no imagination, shouts his old, bitter self. They look at his BMW with interest. He is surprised the car wasn't keyed last night. But then he'd parked it in the driveway, which is exactly what he intends to do now.

One of the kids films Lukas driving past on his mobile and he makes a mental note of his face, just in case. He sees the boy pan down the road behind the BMW.

In the mirror, suddenly very close behind him, is a massive, white four by four. So close that he can't even see the badge on its bumper. He does, however, see its headlights flashing him fast and furiously. The four by four is offset into the road, forcing Lukas towards the kerb. With cars parked ahead on the left, Lukas is trapped. He pulls in, takes one long look at the glove compartment, then tells himself not to be so bloody stupid. He calmly opens the driver's door and gets out.

The four by four, a Chevrolet, blocks the road at forty-five degrees, almost touching the back bumper of the BMW. Lukas faces it with his hands on his hips. Stand-off in Chorlton-cum-Hardy. For just a brief moment he fears he is going to get run over.

Then Leroy Callaway jumps out of the Chevrolet and is on top of him in an instant, hollering. Lukas stretches out his arms to prevent Callaway from reaching his throat. 'Keep the fuck away from me, arsehole! You greased me up with the manager.' Callaway swings a right.

'I've done no such thing.' Lukas parries Callaway's fists.

'You gave that fucking photo to the MatchMaker.'

'What photo? Calm down, man.' Lukas holds the footballer by the shoulders, at arm's length.

'The two fucking whores. You took it!' Callaway struggles against him.

'Who says?'

'What the fuck does it matter? They all want it, you know? They're begging for it. Just because you can't get any – you're just fucking envious, like everybody else.'

'What, envious of you?' Lukas pushes Callaway away from him, making him stumble. 'You pitiful creature! You dive and cheat and you're a bully. You seriously think money can buy anything, don't you?'

Never has Lukas seen such hate in a human being's eyes; the grimace on the man's face hurtling towards him is animalistic to the core. Callaway roars as he approaches low and fast. Lukas predicts a rugby tackle to the midriff, and decides not to parry but braces himself for impact. Callaway slams into his broken chest with full force, screaming obscenities. Lukas goes down like a sack of potatoes. Callaway makes to kick him but Lukas rolls over fast enough to destabilise the footballer. He grabs Callaway's over-extended foot with both hands and twists it as hard as he can. Now it is Callaway who goes down, howling, to whistles, cheers and his name being chanted by the fascinated youngsters around them.

Suddenly Callaway is holding a knife. He tries to disguise it by the side of his body. Lukas kicks hard at the footballer's right arm, forcing his bruised upper body to flex towards Callaway to reach for the disarmed hand. He uses his body mass to push and turn Callaway's arm up behind his back. Then he yanks the howling footballer to his feet and kicks the knife away.

'You fucking arsehole broke my fucking leg. I'm going to fucking kill you.' Callaway seems to have trouble putting weight onto his right foot.

'Listen, you pussy.' Lukas pulls the man close to him, puts his mouth next to Callaway's ear. 'I could perform a citizen's arrest right here and now. You know, you wouldn't stand a chance,' he hisses, aware of the kid with the camera.

Callaway spits and kicks back with his bad leg. 'Fuck you! You're in fucking bed with him, that fucking blogger. I'm going to have you both, you're finished.'

Lukas laughs. Little does the man know how close he is to the truth. 'What blogger?' he asks and pulls Callaway's arm up higher.

The footballer whimpers. 'The one who posted the photo. That fucking arsehole's ruining our careers.'

'No, you're doing a fantastic job ruining your own career. He's just ruining your kind of fun. Good luck to him. Did I just read somewhere that you intend to kill him?' Lukas spots Dannii across the road, filming on her iPhone. Back from stirring it a bit at the library, he guesses. He turns Callaway and his line of vision away from her. Callaway howls and spits.

'Go on, Leroy. Get him off you!' one youth shouts. His mate is still filming.

'Yeah, go on,' another youth says, sounding less convinced.

Then Lukas hears sirens. He marches Callaway back to the Chevrolet and pushes him into the driver's seat. The footballer makes to get back out. Lukas kicks his injured leg and holds him down. 'Stay! Don't you hear the law?'

Callaway touches his leg and looks around quickly.

'You don't want them here any more than me, Leroy, believe me.'

Callaway suddenly smiles, but there is a spiteful smugness about it. 'It's you, innit? You're him! It's been you all along writing that fucking blog.'

'Piss off.' Lukas slams the door shut. He stays on his side of the road and hopes that she'll do the same. Behind him Callaway revs up the Chevrolet and passes him, clipping the BMW's ring rear wing. Lukas swears.

Dannii crosses the road, smiling. He signals for her to stop. She doesn't seem to understand and carries on walking towards him. Callaway has stopped his four by four ten yards away. Lukas swears he can see the man's eyes in the rear view mirror.

'I wish you hadn't done that.'

'What? I got it all on camera. Are you OK?' She tries to hug him but he turns away.

'I wish you hadn't come over here,' he hisses.

'Why not?'

'He's still bloody there.'

'He's too thick to make the connection.'

'Walk away from me. Walk to the corner.' He feels Dannii look at him but keeps his back turned. 'Please!' he says. Dannii tuts behind him. Then he hears her walks away.

'You.' Lukas steps up to the kid with the camera phone. The group of youngsters stand frozen by the roadside, a couple of them still eyeing the Chevrolet disappearing down the road.

'That was Leroy Callaway. You're in the shit, mister.'

Lukas laughs. 'What are you going to do with that video you took?'

The boy shrugs. 'Dunno.'

'You're a fan?'

'Dunno.'

'Are you, or are you not a Mancunia fan?' Lukas looks the boy in the eye.

The kid looks away. 'Yeah.'

'But?'

'That wasn't cool.'

'Oh, so not everything he does is cool?'

The kid shakes his head. 'He pulled a knife.'

One of the other kids walks over towards the knife. 'Oy!' Lukas shouts. 'Leave it where it is.' The kid turns around to look at him, grins and makes to pick up the weapon. 'Do you want your prints all over it? Law's on its way.' The kid kicks the knife further into the bushes.

'He always says violence is evil.'

Lukas turns back to the boy with the camera phone. 'Is that what he says?'

'He's a liar.'

'If you think he's not so cool why don't you tweet it?' Lukas asks. The boy grins at him. 'You could be famous.' Lukas feels for a note in his jeans pocket.

'What's it worth?'

Lukas pulls out a twenty. 'That's all I've got. Now shoot.' The kid grabs the note and runs off towards the main road.

Dannii gestures at him from the corner. He points towards the Globe. The sirens are deafening and must be almost on top of her. He takes a few steps towards the bushes, finds the knife, picks it up with his handkerchief, folds it up and puts it in his pocket. As the police car turns into the road, Lukas crosses the playing fields and enters the Globe through the back door at the same time as Dannii steps through the front.

'Oh, hello, love. Where did you leave lover boy?' Vladi cackles.

'He's behind you.'

Vladi turns round laboriously. 'Bit early for you, Novak, isn't it? What have you been doing? You're filthy again.'

'Broken Leroy Callaway's leg, most probably,' Dannii says.

'Tell me more,' Vladi demands eagerly.

'I'm furious with you.' Lukas ignores him and stares at Dannii. 'Can't you do what I say?'

The girl behind the bar puts two lagers down on the bar. Dannii downs half of hers and wipes her mouth. 'You should have been clearer in your signalling. You don't seriously think I'm in danger?' She laughs.

'You're not untouchable and you saw his tweet.'

'He won't make the connection that I am who I am, sweet.' She finishes her pint.

Lukas hasn't even started his. 'No, now he thinks I'm the blogger. And he'll make the fucking connection that we know each other. I think Leroy Callaway has just worked out his leverage.'

'What is it?'

Lukas drinks his pint down in one. 'You!' he says and slams his empty glass on the bar.

Chapter 64

'Fill me in please?' Vladi says.

Lukas composes himself and gives Vladi the lowdown on the morning's events. 'Police will see the dented BMW,' Lukas concludes. 'They'll think it's a hit and run. They'll trace the BMW back to Mark's firm and hopefully won't pursue it further. In that case no harm done. Where is he, by the way?'

'Left early. Said he had some business.'

Lukas sees Dannii typing on her phone and frowns. 'What are you doing, love?'

'Updating the blog. Tweeting,' she says without looking up.

'Can I see the film?' he asks her. She passes him the phone and he tilts the handset so Vladi can see too.

'Holy crap, Novak, nice moves,' Vladi chuckles. 'Is that a knife you're kicking away?'

'Hm.'

'Where is it now?'

'In my pocket.'

'Minus your prints.'

'Of course.'

'Enough to send Callaway down, I'd say. If that's what you're intending to do. Certainly nothing to incriminate you. Apart from self defence.'

'Give me that back,' Dannii says. 'Let me finish this. It should cause a Twitter storm. I'll make sure it's well tagged.'

'D'you know what she's talking about, my old friend?'

'I've a vague idea,' Lukas replies.

Lukas's phone vibrates, then rings. 'Stan.'

'I got to see you.' The man sounds nervous.

'What about?' Lukas asks.

'Not on the phone. It's important,' Entwistle says. Lukas tells him he'll be there in thirty.

'Please go home, love, and don't open for anyone. In fact, lock yourself in,' he tells Dannii.

She laughs. 'Don't be ridiculous.'

'I must say, old sport, aren't you being a tad over-reactive?'

'No. We've been through enough shit.'

'All sounds exciting to me, doesn't it, darling?' Vladi slaps Dannii on the knee. She laughs.

'Your own funeral would be an exciting adventure for you, Vlad, if you'd consumed enough.'

'Come on! She'll be fine. Your place is just down the road.'

Lukas turns back to Dannii. 'Please, Dannii, for once – ' He takes her head in his hands and looks her in the eye.

She wraps her arms round his shoulders and kisses him. 'I'll be fine. I love you, you old grump.'

He sees mischief. 'Please do as I say,' he says, maybe too firmly, and lets go of her.

'Control freak. Go away and beat someone up.'

He turns and walks out, craving a cigarette.

'What are you doing here? I guessed when I saw the car.'

'Nice to see you too, mate,' Mark replies.

Perplexed, Lukas sees Linda rush towards them. And Mark put an arm around her. 'We've made up. After all these years.' She beams and giggles.

Lukas smirks. 'Is this all in one morning's good work?'

'He brought me flowers.' Linda squeezes Mark round the midriff.

'And you like that,' Lukas says.

'Yours are almost dead,' she says, pouting.

'Haven't things changed round here.' Lukas says, hands on hips. 'Look at you two. Happy families.'

'Lukas.' Stan Entwistle walks towards him and shakes his hand.

'I'm glad you've forgiven us.' Lukas nods towards Mark. Entwistle slaps his shoulder.

'And me. I've forgiven you, too,' Linda screeches.

Lukas squints at Mark who still has an arm round her. 'What's going on here, mate?'

'Things are changing for the better.' Linda hops up and down. 'We're getting rid of the old crap.'

The situation reminds Lukas of a bizarre comedy. And yet another level of reality. 'When did this change occur?' He eyes Entwistle inquisitively.

'It started indirectly with your text, Lukas. And directly after what happened to Jason. Shall we go upstairs?'

'How is he?' Lukas asks.

'In a pitiful state, physically as well as mentally. His career could well be over. And I am full of vengeance. I want to help you, Lukas.'

'With what?'

'Last time you came you wanted to find out the tattoos' identity. I gave you some information.' Stan looks at Lukas as he produces the whisky bottle. Stale smoke hangs over the ashtray, rekindling Lukas's craving as Entwistle gestures towards the couches.

Lukas sits down. 'Do you want to revise what you told me?'

Stan pours two generous shots. 'I need to revise my life.' He looks into his glass. 'Again,' he says and necks the shot. Lukas sips at his and waits. 'Your mate'—Stan gestures towards the door—'walks in here this morning. I've just been to see Jayz and I'm not in the mood for a fight. Our kid is broken. His dream is over. But that's not all. He's broken inside and has been for a long time.' Stan runs a hand over his face and pours another shot. 'All this has got to stop. We have, I've been living a bloody farce for too long. It's a bloody miracle I did as well as I did, I'm telling you. And it's no surprise I crashed when I came back here, back to the lion's den. Fuck.' He finishes his second shot. 'I'm not a soft bloke, believe me. You know what I've achieved.' Stan looks up pleadingly.

Lukas sips his whisky and nods. 'Carry on,' he says softly.

'I'm not a nancy boy, for fuck's sake! But Jayz, Jayz – it's such a shame.' Stan Entwistle buries his head in his hands.

Lukas rolls his glass between his palms. 'Is it really so terrible?' Entwistle looks at him vacantly. 'You love him, don't you?'

'I'm not a new man,' Stan says, his jaws working. 'I come from hard stock. We don't do lovey-dovey shit between blokes.'

'Maybe not. But you do do adults raping children, and everybody keeping schtum for donkeys' years.' Entwistle stares at him wide eyed; he reaches for the whisky bottle, and spills drink all over the table. 'Here, let me do it.' Lukas takes the bottle from Entwistle's shaking hand and pours. Then he moves round the table and sits next to the boxer. 'Here. Drink.' Lukas puts his hand on the man's shoulder.

Entwistle drinks, spilling whisky down his chin, tolerating Lukas's touch. 'You know?' he says, very quietly. 'How?'

Lukas turns the boxer to face him. 'I met Tony at the Turing. It is Tony, not Mike, correct?'

'Yes. It's what I was going to tell you. But there's more.'

'I know he hurt you. Both of you,' Lukas says. Stan groans. 'You love Jason, don't you? Your little brother?'

Stan roars through tears and Lukas pulls him close and rocks him from side to side. Entwistle wails against his shoulder, pushing against Lukas, who holds him tight until the ex-featherweight champion of the world gives up the fight.

'Are you going to record this?'

Lukas nods. 'You sure about this?'

'Yes. In case something happens to me. Or Jason.'

'Do you think that's a possibility?'

Stan shrugs. Lukas switches on the voice recorder on his phone. Entwistle fumbles in his trouser pocket for a packet of Marlboro Lights, puts one between his lips, offers the packet to Lukas and gives him a light.

'Where is Tony now, Stan?'

'I don't know. He didn't come back after the Turing. We was waiting for him, we had fights on. He always supervises when we have fights. Wants to be in the building.'

'Does he still fix?'

'Sometimes.'

'Do you do anything about it?'

'No.'

'Why not?'

'I'm glad when he's peaceful.'

'Is he often not peaceful?' Lukas pinches the tip off his cigarette and puts the butt in his shirt pocket. He looks back up at Stan.

'When he doesn't get his own way.'

'How often is that?'

'Often. He manufactures confrontation – you know what I mean? He turns around what you say.'

'Does he get violent?'

'Not with me. With the boys.'

'The boys who box for him?'

'Yes.'

'The ones with the tattoos?'

'Yes.'

'How does this violence manifest itself?'

'He hits them. I don't know what else he does.'

'Does this hitting happen here?'

'Yes.'

'What else?'

'He takes the boys elsewhere, too. To do jobs for him.'

'What do you think is really going on?'

Stan looks at him. 'I think he abuses them, sexually.' He gently stubs out his cigarette.

'What makes you think that?'

'I see the signs.'

'What signs?' Entwistle looks at him pleadingly. 'You don't have to, Stan.' Lukas smiles.

'I see myself in them,' the boxer says quietly. 'Jason coped with it worse than me.'

'How did you cope with it?'

'I grew coarse and withdrawn at the same time. I self-harmed, still have the scars. Worst of all, I wouldn't trust my new mentors at All Saints. They sussed me out, though. I didn't tell them what was wrong with me, but they had enough of a handle on psychology to restore my faith in myself and what I wanted to do.'

'There's nothing wrong with you, Stan. You were the victim.'

Entwistle looks at him blankly. 'You never stop blaming yourself.'

Lukas thinks of Markus. The boxer is right. 'These boys, they seem to adore Tony. How do you explain that?'

'He makes them dependent on him. They want to please him. Be the best boy. It's sick.'

'How does he do that?'

'If I knew that I'd have stopped it ages ago. They just keep coming back for more.'

'How does he get them to attack an innocent old man?'

'He nurtures hate. They want to be bad for him.'

'Bit of a Fagin scenario. Part of his gang.'

'Hm.'

'Drugs?'

Stan laughs. 'Have you looked at the neighbourhood around here?'

Lukas smiles. 'I suppose so. Do you think Tony has anything to do with that?'

'Supplying the neighbourhood?' Stan raises his eyebrows. 'I never thought that far.'

'Did he offer you drugs?'

'Yes.'

'What did he give you?'

'Speed, coke, amphetamines. Weed, of course.'

'Where did he get the stuff from?'

Stan shrugs. 'I'm not sure. Everybody took it.'

'Did you ever see this man?' Lukas brings up Janos Kovacs's image on his phone and shows it to Stan. 'For the record, I'm showing Stan a photo of Janos Kovacs.'

The boxer studies the screen. 'Yes, I remember him. Weird bloke. Haven't seen him recently though.'

'Not since Tony came back?'

Stan shakes his head. 'Definitely not.'

'You never knew his name?'

'No. What does he do?'

'Have you ever been to the Central Casino?'

'Yes.'

'It's Kovacs's. He runs it. And others.' Lukas's phone bleeps. 'He reads Dannii's message. '*It's gone viral.*' Lukas puts the phone down and frowns. Stan smiles at him politely. 'So you don't know where Tony is now?'

'No.'

'You say he takes the boys away. Do you think he has a hideout?'

'I think that's possible.'

'But you don't know where it is. He never took you there.'

'No. It all happened here or at his house.'

'Where did you and Jason live?'

'With him.'

'Why?'

'He adopted us.'

'Jesus.' Lukas pauses, then necks his whisky. 'I didn't know that. When?'

'We were supposed to be given into care when I was ten. Dad fucked off and Mum drank. Tony's her brother. He gave me boxing. He also started abusing me straight away. For me it was a couple of years. For Jayz it was a lifetime.'

'Your mum said nothing?'

'She'd had it off him before. He fucked her up completely. She was in no fit state to do anything.'

'Is she still alive?' Stan shakes his head. Lukas pauses. 'And Jason was – how old?'

'He was only a baby.' Stan pushes his glass towards Lukas slowly. Lukas pours two more shots. Then he switches off the voice recorder. Stan lights another cigarette and picks up his glass with shaking hands. 'I'm willing to put my name against this. You'll do something, won't you?'

'Yes, I will.' Lukas looks at the cigarette packet.

'You need to speak to Jason. He wants to talk to you, too. It won't be easy for him.'

'Yes, I'll see him straight away.' Lukas wonders if Bradshaw has put him on the visitors' list so quickly.

Stan sips his whisky. 'I don't normally drink this much, not any more.'

Lukas smiles. 'Sometimes it's unavoidable. I don't smoke, by the way,' he says. Stan laughs. 'Do you have anybody here to give you a bit of protection? I mean, wherever Tony is, he won't suspect you've talked, unless he's watching the place and saw me come in. But he does have friends in high places and I've been making things difficult for a few of them recently. So, if someone spots me here – '

'I understand. Carl's reliable.'

'I thought so. He was at the Turing, too.'

'Yes, he said he saw stuff.'

'Good. Mark downstairs isn't exactly Tony's best mate either.'

'Yes, he explained earlier that Tony might want to have a word.'

'That's putting it mildly.'

'I do remember Mark from the old days. Or rather Billy. Wouldn't have recognised him though. And I didn't know he was undercover.'

'Why does he say he's here?'

'Make amends, he says. With Linda. He also says he owes the club?'

301

'He's loyal. Runs a security firm. It's good that he's here. But don't drink with him,' Lukas advises him. Stan laughs. 'Are you OK?'

'As I'll ever be. Thank you.' Stan puts his hand on Lukas's shoulder. Lukas pats it. 'Not so difficult, is it?' he says. Stan shakes his head. 'Can I take another fag?'

'Take the packet.'

'You're on the news!' Mark shouts from Linda's office. Lukas stops momentarily, then runs down the stairs and towards the office, hearing Stan close behind him.

'Wind it back, love,' Mark says. Linda presses play and Lukas watches Callaway's attack on him.

'Bloody hell, mate,' Mark says.

'You're famous,' Linda says.

Lukas gets a cigarette out of the packet.

' – unsure of the identity of the victim and the reason behind this vicious attack. Questions will be asked of the footballer, who has been in the news for a missed drugs test and allegations of fixing sex parties involving underage girls for his teammates and friends. In other news –'

'Bye bye, Leroy,' Mark sings.

Lukas's phone rings. 'Novak, you bastard. You broke my trust.'

'James, I did no such thing. Calm down.'

'Calm down?' Bradshaw screeches down the line. 'You – you orchestrated this, you – '

'No. He attacked me outside my home. He forced me off the road. He damaged my car. Then he knocked me to the ground.' Lukas hears Bradshaw breathe heavily into the receiver. Lukas continues. 'He must have followed me from your office, unless he got my address elsewhere.'

'Who filmed it?'

'Some kids on the corner.'

'It's on the blog.'

'I'm not surprised, it's all over Twitter. It's gone viral,' Lukas bluffs. He navigates to the Twitter app.

Bradshaw is breathing heavily at the other end of the line. 'Novak, you swear, you didn't set this up?'

Lukas scrolls up the Twitter messages. The relevant tweet has been retweeted tens of thousands of times. Lukas taps it. Almost instantly the video of his fight with Callaway starts to play back. 'James, I swear. I gave you my word. Trust me.'

'OK, Novak. I trust you. But no more surprises,' Bradshaw says and puts the phone down.

'James Bradshaw, ey?' Mark smirks.

'He's famous,' Linda beams and points at Lukas.

'I'm going to visit Jason. Will you watch this place?' Lukas asks.

'Sure, what d'you think I'm here for,' Mark replies.

'Is Carl about?'

'He's in the back.' Stan puts his hand on Lukas's shoulder. 'Give Jayz my best.'

Lukas smiles. 'I will, Stan. You keep your eyes open.'

Chapter 65

Back in the BMW Lukas makes three calls. First, he phones Lilian and asks for Vicky's surname and phone number. His daughter sounds remarkably together given her ordeal a few days ago. She is, however, worried about Jason, a concern Lukas shares wholeheartedly. He omits to mention that he is about to visit the young goalie. Best to go and see him on his own for now. Lilian doesn't mention Twitter or the news; Lukas deducts she hasn't been exposed to his latest escapade yet. And he is certainly not going to be the one who breaks it to her.

Then he rings Vicky, introduces himself as Lilian's dad and calmly explains that he was at the Turing, a witness to the aftermath of the party. Vicky puts the phone down. He rings again. She tells him to get lost in no uncertain terms though she seems to be sobbing. The next time he gets put through to her answerphone. He mentions how Lilian has been traumatised by the experience and that he can't possibly imagine what she, Vicky, must be feeling like. He suggests gently that he believes a crime has been committed, that Vicky should talk to someone, her parents, a friend or him. He leaves his number. Then he texts Lilian back and urges her to sound Vicky out.

The third call Lukas makes is to DCI Briggs. The detective picks up the phone in his usual, gruff manner. Lukas hears the man sigh loudly. 'What do you want?'

'Your thoughts on what happened the other night.' Lukas hears rustling. Then Briggs swears in the background. 'Is this not a good time to talk?'

'As good a fucking time as any,' Briggs barks. 'You took me hostage.'

'Come off it, Dick. That's not what I'm talking about. You know exactly what I'm asking you. I'm asking you to stop stalling and let me know your thoughts on what these "bastards", in your own words, did to your daughter.'

'She doesn't want to press charges.'

Lukas laughs loudly. 'Who says?'

'She does.'

'What about you?'

'If she doesn't want to press charges, she doesn't want to press charges, Novak.'

'Bollocks.' Lukas spits it out. He hears Briggs laugh. 'You think that's funny, Dick? Which side of the law are you on? You don't have to answer that, by the way.'

'Are you done?'

'No, I'm not. Your Gaby's mate, Vicky, you remember, the one covered in blood? She's pressing charges,' Lukas lies. Briggs laughs. 'And another thing, Dick. Have you seen the news? If not, watch it. Have a look at Twitter, too. There's a lot at stake for you. Search for Callaway, Leroy,' Lukas tells him. Briggs swears. 'And then you might experience the irresistible urge to phone me back.' Lukas ends the call and puts the BMW into gear.

Ten minutes later Lukas's phone rings. 'A penny for your thoughts, Dick.'

'Shut up, moron!'

'Hour and a half. Hospital coffee shop.'

'What the fuck are you doing there?'

'My daughter wants to see her boyfriend,' Lukas lies.

'Get rid of her before you meet me.'

'How am I going to do that?'

'Put her on a bus.'

'You are indeed an utter dick, Dick.'

Lukas leans in the doorway of Jason Entwistle's hospital room. In his coat pocket he activates the phone's voice recorder. Getting past security had been no problem and Lukas is relieved that the outfit is not another extension of Tony Jackson's reach, but a legitimate firm. Entwistle tries to sit up as Lukas enters the room.

'Mr Novak.' The boy looks surprised.

'Jason.' Lukas sits down by his bedside and puts his hand on the plaster cast on the boy's left forearm. 'We only met twice and I don't think you remember the last time.'

'Mr Novak, I'm scared.' The boy looks beyond Lukas, towards the door.

Lukas turns his head and follows his gaze. There is nobody else in the room. The door is shut. Lukas looks at Jason. The boy's face is bruised heavily, just like his own. 'What has you scared, Jayz?'

'He's been threatening me.' The boy starts to cry.

'Leroy? They let him in?' Jason nods and sniffs. 'Was it him that attacked you?'

Jason looks over Lukas's shoulder. 'Yes. For calling you.'

'Does he know it was me you called?'

'I called someone. That was enough.'

'He was gone when I got there. What's he threatening you with?'

'He says he'll end my career if I say anything. He says he'll tell everyone.'

'What will he tell everyone?' Lukas says softly. The boy shakes his head and sobs. 'Jason, I've just been to see Stan.'

The boy looks at him with large, frightened eyes. 'What did he tell you?'

'He tells me that he loves you very much,' Lukas says. The boy cries hard and silently. Lukas puts a hand carefully on his shoulder, making the youngster flinch. 'It's OK, Jayz.' Lukas waits a few seconds. 'Lilian's thinking about you, too.'

'He says he'll tell everyone that I'm a fucking poof.'

'You think in this day and age that'll shock anyone?'

'Why, does it show?'

'No, Jayz, it doesn't show. Callaway is a bully. A dangerous bully. Do you know why he's doing what he's doing?' Lukas asks. Jason shakes his head. 'To blackmail you into not implicating him in the attack on you.'

'But it *was* him.'

'He's in deep shit. That's why he's acting like a lunatic.'

Lukas momentarily sees hope in Jason's eyes. Then the young man's expression changes. 'I've done a terrible thing, Mr Novak.'

'Go on, son.'

'He asked me to find someone who could take care of the blogger, you know, scare him a bit. Otherwise he'd tell the lads I'm gay.'

Lukas narrows his eyes. 'When was this. Recently?'

'No. After you first came to the training ground. He said I should know people that could help solve the problem.'

'What did you do?'

'I panicked. I told him to ring Dolly Green and ask for Mr T.'

'You didn't ask him to contact Stan?'

'Stan wants nothing to do with violence and crap any more.'

'And you do?'

Jason shakes his head. 'No,' he says quietly. 'I've left all that behind. But he was threatening me. Same with the bloody fixing. Do this, do that, or else. I've been letting them in, Mr Novak, I'm a fraud.'

'Jayz, listen! You're being blackmailed. What's he threatening to do to you?'

'Just this morning he told me he would fuck me until I couldn't walk any more,' the boy says quietly.

Lukas wonders how literally Callaway meant that remark. 'He was here this morning?'

'Yes, early.'

'Did he threaten you before?'

'Yes. He told me he'd injure me enough to end my career.' Jason laughs bitterly.

'You've got to fight, Jayz. Don't let that arsehole win.'

'Do you think I've committed a crime by putting Leroy onto Mr T?'

'Possibly. But who's going to find out? It's his word against yours. If it ever comes to anything.' No need to mention to the boy that Mr T had been involved all along, at management level.

The boy looks unsure. 'You won't mention it?'

Lukas shakes his head. 'Listen, Jayz. Stan told me stuff, but I knew already. Things were said at the Turing after you were taken to hospital. Between Briggs and Mr T.'

'Mr T was there?' the boy whispers. Lukas nods. 'Did Stan tell —'

'No, Jason, I deducted it from the conversation at the Turing. You know that Mr T is the same person as Tony Jackson?' The boy stares at him, panicked. 'You know, don't you.' Jason stares at him with dark, hopeless eyes. Lukas holds his gaze. 'The big question is,' he says it slowly, 'how does Leroy know what happened to you?'

'I've no idea.'

'Did you receive some sort of counselling when you arrived at Mancunia? Stan told me he had some help at All Saints.'

'No, I never told a soul,' Jason says quietly.

Lukas's phone cuts through the moment. He looks at the display and reads Dannii's name. 'Excuse me, Jayz,' he says and picks up the call.

At first he can't work out what is going on. He says her name, once, twice, then he reconsiders. The line is noisy and Lukas sticks a finger in his ear to try and hear better. He looks at the boy in the bed. The lad makes to say something but Lukas shakes his head. He suddenly feels sick. He identifies the noise on the line as the sound of a car engine. A loud moan cuts through it which Lukas instantly recognises as Dannii. A man's voice barks brashly at someone to shut up accompanied by another man's laughter. A thud and a further shriek implies that Dannii has just been hit. Lukas's knees go to jelly.

The laughter clearly belongs to Leroy Callaway; Lukas remembers his distinct chortle. And the brash bark could well be Jackson's. Lukas is scared. He puts his hand over the receiver and walks over to Jason. The youngster looks extremely alarmed before Lukas even bends down to whisper in his ear that he needs to go urgently. The boy shakes his head violently, begs not to be left on his own. Lukas grabs the lad's hand and squeezes it hard.

Lukas runs through the corridors of the hospital with the handset pressed to his ear, listening to low conversation, too quiet to understand, and Dannii's occasional groaning. She's letting him know she's still there, he deducts.

Far too early for the meeting Lukas is relieved to see Briggs already waiting for him in the hospital's deserted coffee shop. Lukas runs up to him, a finger to his lips. He grabs his arm and presses the receiver to his ear. The inspector listens, then looks at him. 'Who's the woman?' he mouths. Lukas stabs himself in the chest repeatedly. The inspector's face turns into a grimace of rage. He swears, grabs Lukas's arm and turns him towards the exit. As they hurry across the car park Lukas switches the phone to speaker, taps Briggs's shoulder and points at the BMW.

On the A666 they lose the signal. Lukas swears and hits the wheel repeatedly.

'Where's your daughter?' Briggs barks. 'You said earlier she wanted to see Entwistle.'

'Changed her mind. Fuck, I thought you were implying she's in danger, too.'

'You lied to me,' Briggs slowly peels a mint from its wrapper and pops it in his mouth.

'Where would they take her?'

'No idea.' The inspector sucks on the mint noisily. 'But Bolton's not a bad direction.'

'You recognised the voices.'

'Did you?'

'I think so.'

'Callaway and Jackson. How do they know each other?'

307

'You tell me, Dick.'

'Hang on. I'd never let Leroy in at Jackson's level.'

'Jason put him in touch with Jackson. He just told me.'

'Why? Stupid boy.' The inspector opens the window and spits the mint out.

'Stupid boy was being bullied for his homosexuality. He was also threatened with violence if he didn't go along with the fixing.'

The inspector laughs. 'What fixing?'

Lukas hits the wheel. 'Come off it, Dick.'

Briggs glares at him. 'And who allegedly bullied the boy?'

'Your protégé. The one who beat me up. You watched the news, didn't you?'

'He's not my fucking protégé. He's a fucking liability of late,' Briggs spits out. Lukas laughs. 'Yes, I saw the news. He's flipped somehow. Why you?'

''Cos of what happened at the Turing, of course. He thinks he's going to get caught. Rightly so.'

'You're out of your depth, Novak.'

'He assaulted me. It's all over the news. He's abducting my girlfriend as we speak.'

'Why should he?'

''Cos this morning after the attack she crossed the road to see if I was OK. He saw us together.'

'Did you take pictures at the Turing?'

'Yes.'

'And how exactly did they end up on the blog?'

'You see, that's what Callaway implied this morning; he said it was me – ' Lukas stops dead in his tracks. The inspector has laid a trap and Lukas has walked straight into it. Mark would have a field day.

Briggs leans over. The benefits of the mint have long since worn off. 'And? Are you?'

There's only one way out of this. Only one way to save Dannii. 'Yes, I am.' Lukas says.

'The MatchMaker?' Briggs queries. Lukas nods and grins. Briggs beams back. 'Thanks for all the tips.'

'Don't mention it.'

'How do you get them? Tell me, Novak, or I'll put you away for passing on illegal gambling information. Interpol will be ecstatic to receive your name and whereabouts.'

'One thing at a time, Dick. You're a client and there's a management level above you, don't forget. Where would Jackson take a hostage?'

'What level would that be, Novak? And what hostage?' Briggs laughs. 'They'll just want to question her.'

'Bollocks! Why would they want to question her? She doesn't know a thing. They want me, and they want me to do precisely what I'm doing now. Coming to the rescue. I don't believe that in all those years you spent affiliated at Dolly Green you've never been aware of a hideout.'

'I haven't, I swear.'

Lukas comes off the A666.

'Where are you going?'

'What do you think?'

'What the fuck's he doing here?' Mark rushes up to DCI Briggs, grabs him by the collar and lifts the man clean of the ground.

'Let him go, Mark. They've got Dannii. Where is Jackson's hideout?'

'You're fucking joking! What hideout?'

Linda stares at Lukas, blankly. 'Who's Dannii?'

'Think, love. The old days.'

Stan points at Briggs. 'What's he doing here? I know him from ages ago.'

'He's been protecting Tony all these years.'

'Fuck off, Novak,' Briggs says.

Mark moves towards the inspector. 'Stop me someone or I'll kill him. You're on my turf now, Stinky. Bear that in mind.'

Briggs looks Mark up and down. 'You're a fucking loser, Unwin. Always have been, always will be.'

'Stop,' Lukas hollers. 'Hideout, love.' He turns to Linda.

'What about where he kept the cars?' She looks at Mark.

'Courtesy cars. For the big fights. Possibility.'

'Does he still have them?'

Linda shakes her head. 'No. Too expensive.'

'Where is it, for fuck's sake?'

'Sharples Park. 'Bout fifteen minutes.'

'What's the scenario?' Mark asks.

'Callaway and Jackson. Maybe some backup.'

'Where and when did they take her?'

'At my house, I presume, don't know how long ago. I bloody warned her and all.'

'Any new insights with Jason?'

309

'Boy's shit-scared. Somehow Callaway knows that Jackson abused the boy. He set his bullying up on it. Even threatened the boy with rape.'

'You're making this up, Novak,' Briggs barks.

'Why would he?' Mark says calmly and looks over at Briggs.

'He's just fishing for a story, for some far-fetched conspiracy theory.'

'No, Dick,' Mark says. 'Let me tell you what he's doing. He is slowly picking apart the web of lies and deceit you've been weaving for decades. If he weren't such a bloody thick polack, he'd have figured it all out long ago.'

'You're insane, Unwin.'

Lukas laughs. 'You told Callaway, didn't you, Dick? You've known about the abuse all these years and you kept schtum, apart from telling Callaway.'

'Keeping schtum is a felony in itself,' Mark says.

'Fuck you both. You're so far off the mark, you haven't a clue.'

'Then tell us the truth, Dick. Help us get to the bottom of it.'

Mark laughs. 'Forget it. You'll never hear the truth from this man's stinking gob, as long as you live.'

'I should've killed you, Unwin, when I had the chance,' Briggs hisses.

Lukas remembers that his phone's voice recorder is still on, and wonders how much recording time the average smart phone has. He clears his throat. 'Let me tell you what's happening, Dick. I'll give you the short version, because we're in a bit of a hurry. You've known for more than a decade that both Entwistle boys were being abused by their uncle. How you could live with this knowledge and why you didn't report Jackson is beyond my understanding, but doesn't really matter right now. It does tell us a lot about your character though. Don't give me that Masonic shit. I don't for one minute believe your lodge condones child abuse. What happened, in my view, is that when Callaway needed leverage to get young Entwistle to fix, you gave it to him. Entwistle was already a victim. It was easy for Callaway to capitalise on the abuse and the homosexuality. I believe he went as far as linking the two, convincing Jason that he's gay as a result of the abuse. Heck, even that Entwistle liked the abuse and wanted more. It was you who told Callaway, wasn't it?'

'Fuck you.'

'You did it, so Callaway could continue fixing matches for betting purposes, even with a new goalie in place. So you could continue gambling and winning.' Briggs looks out of the window. 'Don't forget

that I'm the MatchMaker and I know how much you lap up my tips.'
Mark glances at Lukas in the rear mirror. Lukas winks.

'You're way off the mark, Novak,' Briggs says.

'Time for a detour,' Mark says and turns left.

Chapter 66

'We don't have time for this, Mark.'

'Yes, we do. Where were you when she called?' Mark speeds up
Belmont Road towards Winter Hill.

'Hope Hospital.'

'Fifteen minutes from your house. We're fifteen minutes ahead
minimum.'

'You're grasping at straws. How do you know the Sharples Road
location is correct?' Briggs sneers.

'Oh, you have an opinion all of a sudden, Dick?' Mark spits out the
man's name.

The road narrows to a single track.

'It's the only information we have. In the absence of another phone
call.' Lukas tries to sound convincing.

'Have they made any demands?' Mark asks.

'I haven't actually spoken to anyone. She just made the call and left
the line open.'

'Why on earth did they take her?'

'To get at me,' Lukas says. 'Stop me sniffing around. Stop my
investigation. It's another step deeper into the shit for Callaway though.'

'He's flipped, as I said,' Briggs says.

'And on that note – ' Marks pulls into a lay-by.

Lukas gets out and opens the passenger door. 'Come,' he says and
gestures for Briggs to get out of the car.

'Where are you taking me?' Briggs tugs at his elbow which Lukas is
holding firmly.

'For a chat, mate.' Mark brings up the rear.

'I'm not your fucking mate, Unwin. In fact, I'm your worst enemy.'

'You're not wrong there, Briggs,' Mark says, nonchalantly. 'Up
there.'

'You got to be fucking joking,' Briggs spits the words out.

'It'll put your sorry little life in perspective with the rest of the world,
Detective Inspector,' Mark says.

Lukas doesn't fancy the climb himself but gets on with it, dragging the inspector up the hill to a folly.

'Rivington Pike,' Mark announces.

'Put your hands against that,' Lukas says.

Briggs obeys. 'And now you're going to fuck me over?'

Lukas retrieves the inspector's weapon and passes it to Mark. 'Turn round and face me.' Briggs turns slowly and looks up at Lukas. Lukas's fear for Dannii has temporarily given way to the utter contempt he feels for everything this man stands for. His urge to hit the inspector over and over again in the face until he resembles the pitiful mess Callaway left Jason in is compelling. Lukas sniffs up the contents of his nose noisily and spits out phlegm to the right of the inspector. Briggs pulls a face. Lukas narrows his eyes and speaks very quietly. 'The time has come.'

'The time for what?'

'The time for you to make up your mind which side you're going to bat on from now. The team you've been siding with is about to lose. Do you want to go down with them?'

'Fuck you. Nobody is going down.'

'First, Jackson. Rape and sexual exploitation of minors. You knew about it all these years and you didn't do a thing.' Briggs tuts. 'Second, Callaway. Pretty similar offences, plus GBH on a teammate, drugs and attempted GBH on me. Match fixing. Abduction, presumably for blackmail purposes, we'll find out later.'

'Won't come to anything.'

'Third, the attack on Frank Staines that you tried to pin on me. We'll see who's to blame in good course. You were aware of all these offences; you even facilitated some of them. Oh, I forgot, MacFarlane.'

'You're in the shit, Briggs. Your career is over.' Mark steps up and stares at the DCI.

'You've no evidence,.' Briggs hisses.

'You want me to name witnesses? So you can pressurise them? Think back to the Turing. There was a security guard and two ambulance personnel who witnessed our conversation during which you admitted knowing about Jackson's sexual abuse of the Entwistle brothers. The attack on Frank was first and foremost witnessed by Frank himself, second, Sean Ryley's boys saw the tattoos that did the old boy in dropped off on the estate. They're willing to talk,' Lukas lies.

'Sean Ryley?' Briggs looks up at Lukas.

'Uncomfortable? Join the club. Back to old Frank, he says you were uninterested in his description of the attackers when interviewing him in hospital. He thought that was odd. He also thought it odd that you kept mentioning me. You told him you were looking for me in connection with the attack. He insisted and kept telling you, that he was attacked by two youths with Tyson tattoos. Apparently, you didn't care.'

'Nonsense. The old bugger was confused. I wouldn't share details of an ongoing investigation with the victim of said investigation.'

'Just like you wouldn't grant the main suspect in a GBH case access to the victim?'

'What do you mean?'

'Security let Callaway through to visit Entwistle at the hospital and intimidate him further, although he's the lead suspect in the attack. Why was he let in?'

'I've no idea. Security must've blundered.'

'Nonsense. You never put him on the "no access" list.'

'Any man is innocent until proved guilty.'

Lukas rests both palms on the folly either side of Briggs's head and leans in closely. 'Dick, he raped your daughter, for fuck's sake. Her friend is willing to testify.' Briggs stares hard at Lukas. 'I'll deliver you to the gallows on the basis of the fact that you knew about Jackson's abuse, unless you do the right thing and stop protecting Callaway.' Lukas holds his stare. 'Come on, Dick. Do the right thing for once in your life. Redeem yourself. And if not yourself, then redeem your Gaby. He had your little girl.' Briggs stares back. 'For fuck's sake, what does it take for you to become human? Don't you realise what a mess you're in? Will you, for heaven's sake, stop backing the wrong side, stop making mistake after mistake after mistake?'

The DCI stirs and looks up. Coldly. 'I don't make mistakes, Novak.' He pauses. 'Give me a few minutes.'

Lukas removes his hands. He watches as Briggs paces up and down in the bracing wind on top of Winter Hill. In the distance Manchester sits in the mist. He fishes for his phone and checks that the voice recorder is still working. The phone has room for a further ninety plus minutes. With dread he notices there is no signal up here on Winter Hill.

Briggs gestures him over. 'You and me, Novak. Leave the moron out of it.' They start walking. Mark follows twenty yards behind.

'What I tell you now, Novak, you're to keep confidential. However, if you feel at the end of the day you need to get your revenge and string me up on a rope, I can't stop you.'

'Sure.'

Briggs clears his throat. 'I told Callaway to keep his grubby hands off her. Made sure he knew who she was and tell his mates to leave her alone. That's the least he could've done after what I do for him. Never trusted him one iota. All this business at the Turing came as no surprise. I just hadn't envisaged it would involve my Gaby.'

'What did you do for him, exactly?'

'I did it more for James, for old time's sake. You've worked out our connection?'

'Yes.'

'Callaway and I became partners. Business partners. I do him some favours and he gives me some tips. Just like you do, indirectly and impersonally, through the blog. Needn't go no further than business in his case. No need to marry the man. I trust Jim implicitly. We're in the same club and we virtually grew up together at Coventry. I work for Jim too. Not that he knows of Callaway's and my business association.'

'You play a dangerous game, Dick.'

Briggs laughs. 'I'm Jim's security department, making sure the great Mancunia FC comes out smelling of roses every time some slimy reporter writes some filth.'

'And you mop up after Callaway.'

'If you want to call it that, yes, fair enough.'

'Carry on.' Lukas checks his phone. Still no service.

'Are you listening to me or checking your bloody messages?'

'I'm listening. Please carry on,' Lukas says politely and puts the phone away.

'So when the boss is worried about a blogger spreading nonsense I investigate. It's not that I don't know Jim's up to something. He's friendly with some of the refs, but how he goes about it and what his own arrangement is with Callaway, I don't want to know. I know my side of the story and any more might tempt my conscience to wake up and act.'

'That would be a surprise.'

Briggs ignores the remark. 'Jim's the boss and the boss leaves decisions to his line manager, Callaway. I deal with the boss and the line manager, though in slightly different ways. The boss doesn't need to know about my arrangement with the line manager. It's not me who has to report to Jim, it's Callaway. Jim can't be having online allegations about match fixing at his club. Especially not after you turned up. I had to get to the bottom of who's behind the blog. 'I don't like the online thing, Novak; it leaves traces. It's caused me trouble in the past, but of course I read your blog more in depth from then on. I didn't really want to get my boys involved at this stage. Too risky for me and anyway, nothing had happened at this point. I did ask myself even then if it could be you that writes the blog. But you don't seem the type. I envisage a blogger to be someone who carries a laptop. All you carry most of the time is a pint of lager. It was really just a question of sticking close to you. If you weren't the blogger then you'd lead me to him, I was convinced. You were easy to find. Always in the same pub. All I had to do was follow you to Cheetham Hill.'

'You didn't know Frank's address before?'

'Did I fuck! You led me to him. And then Callaway's henchmen fucked it up. I didn't know then he'd gone to Jackson, of all people, via the boy, for Christ's sake. So of course I took charge of the case. They were quick, I give you that, but why did they do the old boy in? He obviously wasn't blogger material. Questions needed to be asked. Callaway would have to explain himself. And then you turn up again, like any good old criminal returning to the scene of the crime. An easy catch. And an easy decision. I decided to frame you to deflect off Callaway. No motive though. Not a problem. When we caught you we held you for a bit. Try and find out how much you knew. Work on a motive. I did the questioning of course.'

Lukas nods. 'That's all pretty much what I figured.'

'Are you expecting me to apologise?' Briggs sneers.

'No. Carry on.'

'You slipped through the net twice. The first time you were quicker than me. I let you run. No point mobilising the masses at this point. Besides, I thought it would put the fear of god in you.'

'You succeeded. It did.'

'The second time you foolishly tell me where you're going to be yourself. Guide Bridge station. At this point I still believed that you and the blogger were two different people. I thought you'd be meeting him. What doesn't tally now is why you made a date with yourself. Were you trying to confuse me into believing there was a blogger and it wasn't you?'

'I copied the mail to myself,' Lukas says slowly. 'I was meeting someone. I've been visiting this dating site.' Lukas scratches his head and tries to look embarrassed. 'I ran it through the MatchMaker account, didn't want the ex to find out. The woman on the bike, it was her I was supposed to meet. She didn't expect our first date to end in hospital. It brought us closer together, though. Now she's Callaway's hostage.' Lukas watches Briggs. 'There's no email address for her on the original mail as the contact was made through the dating site,' Lukas lies. The DCI gives him a long, hard stare. Briggs could well have cottoned on by now, Lukas fears, but hopes that his own poker face has caught the gambler out.

Briggs walks on. 'Dating site, ey? Anyway. That bloody MacFarlane messed it up with his two trigger-happy morons. Couldn't wait, could they? Had to go straight for you. Bloody mess, I did feel sorry for your girl at the time, believe me. And as it turns out, wrong place, wrong time it wasn't entirely. By the way, Novak, I hardly recognised you. Looked like some Balkan thug. You'd really gone to work on your appearance. And you had an accomplice. Couldn't make out the bastard, tinted windows. Could it be that idiot drunkard friend of yours, the other polack? Doubted it very much. Big beemer, looked official. Maybe some security outfit. I wasn't happy about you having help. And definitely not happy about what happened to MacFarlane. I couldn't see you being that ruthless though. Maybe it was your mate who messed him up. Alternatively, MacFarlane could've got himself into totally unrelated trouble on that estate.

'You were still on the run. Suited me down to the ground. At least you weren't receiving information from the fictitious blogger since the messed up rendezvous. I was monitoring your email account. I figured you'd still be spooked. The extra loops of the dealer-chasing chopper in Chorlton were my idea. As long as you were worried about the bill being after you for GBH on Staines you wouldn't have too much energy to go investigating football matters. And the MatchMaker was still trading. He posted that lunchtime. Good for everybody. I certainly was quids in. No idea it was you. How did you continue posting?' Lukas smiles enigmatically. 'Secrets of the trade, ey? I decided to put you on a long leash. Hopefully you'd make a few more mistakes and lead me to the MatchMaker. Then I'd cut you off. You logged on in Glossop. Glossop! End of the line. Put you nicely out of the way, I thought.'

'So how did it start, the being bent thing?' Lukas asks.

'What, this time?

'God, Dick, your conscience must be like an abyss, if you've even got one.'

Briggs laughs a bit too confidently. 'Simple, Novak. With a mistake. It always starts with a mistake. I gamble, Lukas. I'm sure someone's told you that by now.'

'I've heard it mentioned.'

Briggs grins at him lopsidedly. 'I won't ask. Anyway. Casino, bad luck, broke. Again. Wife and daughter expecting a holiday to the Seychelles. Them footballers, from Jim's new club here in Manchester, they've hung round the joint for a few months now. I don't like them, arrogant twats. And they're always with some thick tarts, bought, of course. That defender, Callaway, allegedly the captain – I don't do football, rugby's my sport – seems to be running the lot. Looks like a gangsta rapper. If he weren't a famous footballer he'd be a mug. Anyway, they're behaving like arrogant twats, which is exactly what they are. They earn their money by rolling around on the ground a lot, simulating and complaining. It's champagne all round. Then some of them disappear, including Callaway. I don't care where they've gone, don't really pay attention, I'm losing and I've lost a lot. Had a streak earlier and got cocky. Finally it's all gone with one heroic effort of everything on black.   Mistake number one. I'd never let it slip that far before. It's got hold of me. I don't drink, so my addiction has to be something else, right? I was kidding myself that this once I could pull it off. Wrong. It never happens when you need it most. Remember, no fast money.

'And that leads us to mistake number two. I've got to book that holiday, tomorrow. Credit cards and overdraft are maxed out, and I'm still paying for the last shopping spree. It's late and I got to go home and avoid questions. Quick trip to the loo. They're having it off with a couple of girls. Callaway's standing sentry by the door. He puts his arm round me, calls me detective. This guy is Moses's best mate, he shouts. No idea how he knows. Let go of me! I hiss at him. He pulls me into the room with the wash-hand basins. What the fuck is this? I ask. Callaway squeezes me and tells me they're having fun and Moses knows all about it and doesn't mind.

'Does he indeed? What about the coke? I ask him, seeing the lines above the sink and I shake off his arm. He says maybe it should be our little secret and it's mainly for the girls. He'd noticed I wasn't doing so well at the tables. He pulls out of his trouser pocket a silver money clip with about an inch of twenties and stuffs the lot into my top pocket. More than enough for two weeks Seychelles, all in. I look at him. He's got me. Mistake number three. I told him just this once, trying to sound menacing. The bastard winks at me, like I'm one of his whores. And that's when the lying and massaging the truth started again. I thought I could pull it off. Just no more mistakes.'

'And now you're in so deep you don't know how to get out.'

'Thanks to you, Novak.'

'Hang on, I didn't turn a blind eye to child abuse.'

'No, but you spotted the one thing that I can't mop away.'

'You're not just at my mercy but at Jackson's too.'

'It fucking seems that way. Thanks for pointing it out.'

'Why do you do it, Dick? How did you get so twisted?'

Briggs laughs. 'I'm a bad man. I know full well. What I do is wrong and immoral. Why do I do it? 'Cos I'm too far down the line. I've made mistakes in the past and instead of correcting them when I could I chose an easier way out. Jackson's abuse is the prime example. I should've reported it. But I didn't. Because of the club, because of –'

'The funny handshake scenario.' Lukas smiles.

'Yes. Then, suddenly, years have passed, other things happen. You forget about it. But not completely. Occasionally you remember and you think you should've done something, should've said something; it's almost like it's too late, you'd make it worse for yourself if you said anything now. It ate at me like a cancer. Then there was the betting. The boxing club. Good money. I knew Tony was fixing and everybody was betting on the fix. He knew I benefited from it massively. I couldn't do anything about the abuse now, I was in his pocket.'

'You still are.'

'He's dangerous these days. Wouldn't trust him as far as I could throw him.'

'Tell me about the gambling, Dick. About you and money.'

'There's no easy way when it comes to money. You get it two ways: the slow way, through honest work, or the fast way, through dishonesty. For a while I thought there was another way to get it fast, which was also the way into my troubles. Gambling, the pull of fast money. Who for? For her. The wife. I love her, really, but she has expensive tastes. And so has Gaby. She wants a rich man. Takes after her mother. And this is ultimately why I am where I am and why I do the things I do, Novak. Now I've an empire to protect and if I don't protect it I go down. And that won't do. I'm not going down. I'm telling you I'll be remembered as a hard but fair bastard.'

'Except fair is exactly what you're not. Hard, but not fair.'

'Give me a chance.'

'You have it now.'

Chapter 67

'How long were we up here?'

'Twenty minutes, mate.'

'Let's get off this fucking hill.' Lukas is suddenly awash with worry. The fact that up here mobile phone coverage is non-existent is particularly unnerving. As soon as they are back on tarmac his handset rings. 'It's her.' Lukas presses the phone to his ear as Mark speeds down the road back towards Bolton.

'Anything?' Briggs asks quietly.

Lukas switches the phone to speaker. After a while the engine sound stops abruptly and car doors are being opened. A gruff voice, that Lukas takes to be Jackson's, shouts to get out of the car. Dannii tells someone to fuck off.

'Shit, that's her phone,' Callaway says. 'Phone says Lucky Luke, the crafty bitch.'

'Give it here, Roy!'

There is jostling and a short, wooden knocking sound in the distance followed by shouting and cheering.

'Novak!' Tony Jackson barks in his ear.

'Hello, Tony,' Lukas says politely. 'Let Dannii go. She's nothing to do with anything.'

'She's got a nice arse.'

'Is that why you've abducted her?' He puts his hand over the receiver. 'Cricket pitch.'

'I think Leroy fancies her,' Jackson sneers. 'You wouldn't want anything to happen to her now, would you?'

'Of course not.' Lukas observes Briggs navigating on his phone. 'What do you want, Tony?'

'What d'you think? Bit of fun with your bird, Novak.'

'You can fuck right off,' Dannii shouts. Then she squeals.

'Seriously, Tony. Tell that moron to leave her alone.'

'Sharples Park –' the detective mutters.

'Let me see now,' Jackson says slowly. 'You've been threatening my client with exposure.'

'Your "client"?' Lukas turns round to Briggs who pulls a face like thunder. 'Who would that be?'

'Mr Callaway.'

'Mr Callaway? You must be joking. You saw the mess he made.' Lukas watches Briggs's jaws working overtime.

'Could've been anyone.'

Briggs pulls out his own phone and starts to type.

'Yes, but both you and me know it was him.'

'Irrelevant,' Jackson barks. 'I'll ring you back.'

'How can it be irrelevant, Tony? For fuck's sake – '

'He's flipped,' Mark says.

'Changed teams,' Briggs adds.

'But why? What would attract him to Callaway?'

'There's a cricket pitch near Sharples Park. Behind the colleges,' the inspector mutters.

'Why a cricket pitch?'

'Ball striking bat, on the phone. How near are we?'

'We're there.' Mark swings into Sharples Park.

They pass a school to the left and expensive housing to the right. Ahead looms a council estate. Mark turns left into a small lane which winds between meadows.

'Mossy Lea. Back of the school.' Mark nods left. 'Trust Tony.'

'Where is it?'

'Past the care home ahead. Used to be a big estate. They sold off the outbuildings, I think. Can't quite remember, bit hazy.'

'You were off your rocker then, Unwin. You still are now,' Briggs sneers.

'Listen, Stinky, I've pulled myself around, in spite what you did to me. I should have your balls, man.'

Briggs tuts.

'Could we leave it out and concentrate on Tony, please? How do you feel about Tony taking over your pitch, Dick? No doubt Leroy paid well?'

'Fuck off.'

'You're not happy, are you?'

'I'm not fucking happy at all, Novak. He's double crossed me, after all I've done for him.'

'You get what you deserve, mate.' Mark says. Briggs hits the back of the driver's seat, hard.

Lukas turns round. 'All this has got to end right here, Dick.' Briggs stares at him. 'Are you with us? At least until we get her out?'

'OK,' Briggs says.

'Then you can reconsider, if you wish.'

'I've texted Gaby. Told her to meet with Vicky and get their story straight. Told her to make a statement. Happy now?'

Lukas feels a lump in his throat and looks away quickly. 'You know you're doing the right thing.'

'Whatever,' the inspector replies and looks out of the window.

'There it is!' Mark stops the car.

'Looks like a smallholding.'

'With a couple of sheds for storage. Or garages?'

'That's Callaway's car,' Briggs says. '

'You been here before, Dick?' Lukas turns round.

'No.'

'Recognise that Merc?'

'Nope.'

Lukas opens his door.

'They'll be expecting us, Novak.'

'Yes, I think we can safely assume that.'

'You. Go.' Mark stands behind the corner of a shed, out of vision from the front entrance.

'I agree, Novak. You go in alone. I'll back you up if necessary.'

Lukas runs his hand over the bonnet of the parked Mercedes. 'It's warm.' He looks over at Mark, who scowls back. 'Dick?'

'No idea, really,' Briggs whispers.

'Kovacs?'

'I don't know. I'm not familiar with what he drives these days. Go in. When you open the door I'll move into the corner.'

The original door of the building has been replaced with a tatty plywood slab, a small window is covered with wire mesh. Lukas takes hold of the latch above the lock and pulls on the door lightly. It is not locked. Inside, a corridor. Partitions, more plywood, a single light bulb. A door at the back looks closed. Another door, to his left, is slightly ajar. Voices from the room to the right. Laughter. Callaway. Then a gruff voice telling someone to fuck off.

Lukas checks the time on the voice recorder. Still running. Still a good while left. He gently nudges the door to the left and peers inside. An empty rundown bedroom. He feels nauseous and tells himself to stay focused. His attention is drawn back to the room on his right.

'You can go to hell,' he hears Dannii shout. Lukas opens the door abruptly and stumbles in.

'You were quick.' Tony Jackson sneers. He is leaning on the window sill.

Dannii sits on a chair in the middle of the room, her arms behind her. She looks at Lukas. He assumes they've tied her hands. Beyond her a cluttered desk holds computer hardware. To Lukas's left Leroy Callaway lounges on a couch, smoking a joint.

'Fancy a fight, Roy?' Lukas looks down his nose at the man through heavy marijuana smoke.

'No, man, I'm good,' Callaway chortles. 'I'm enjoying myself.'

'If you don't mind, you two jokers, I'm going to take my friend home now.' Lukas makes a move towards Dannii.

Jackson laughs. 'You think we're letting her go just because you've turned up? We're only just starting with her.'

'Come on, Tony. This game's over and you know it. What are you trying to achieve?'

'You're going to clear my client here.' Jackson saunters up to him, hands in pockets.

'Clear him of what, exactly?'

'All the dirt you're dishing out.' Jackson paces around him like an animal stalking its next meal.

Lukas remembers the flick knife. 'And how am I going to clear him?'

'Take the allegations off the blog.'

Lukas feels a slight draught from the door. He assumes Briggs is in the building. 'I can't.'

'Why not?'

'Because you're holding my girlfriend.'

'Callaway would only be too happy to hold your girlfriend even tighter if you don't comply.'

'I still can't.'

Callaway gets to his feet. 'Why not, man? You owe me.' He puts his face close to Lukas's.

'I owe you? You selfish little git, you think the whole world owes you, don't you? When you're lying on the ground simulating, complaining about having been fouled, shouting abuse at the ref that you've been wronged, fucking up young girls to feed your ego, they all owe you, do they? You truly are a dickhead, Callaway, and I don't often swear. I can't sort the blog because I don't know how too. I'm virtually computer illiterate.' He turns to Jackson. 'Bit like old Frank Staines, who you put in hospital.'

'Cut the crap, Novak, or I'll lose my temper.'

'I'm telling the truth.' Lukas smiles.

Callaway glowers at him, full of hatred. 'You want me to give him a hiding, boss?'

'Shut up, Leroy. If I wanted him hit I'd do it myself, with pleasure.'

'He's telling the truth.' Dannii pipes up.

'Of course you'd say that, you stupid bitch.' Callaway steps towards her and slaps her in the face.

Even before he remembers giving his body the order to move, Lukas has swung around, rugby-tackled and pushed the footballer backwards, until Callaway's back and head hit the wall with a crack. He takes down with him the contents of a small shelf unit. Lukas swings his head back quickly and administers by far the harder of the two Glaswegian kisses he has delivered in his lifetime.

Callaway's nose shatters under the ferocity of Lukas's forehead, blood splashing onto Lukas's face. Then the footballer collapses on the floor. Lukas doesn't care if he has knocked the man unconscious. He wipes his face with his sleeve breathing heavily.

'You two don't like each other very much, do you?' Jackson pulls a small revolver out of his pocket. 'Now remind me, why you can't do anything about the blog? Leroy might be a wanker, but he's still my client.'

'Put the gun away, Tony. I'm not the blogger.'

'Then who the fuck is it?'

'Ask your old friend Jean-Pierre.'

Jackson's face lights up with surprise but he doesn't have time to answer. Loud footsteps from the corridor shake the floorboards. Sounds of a struggle end in silence. Then the door opens and Briggs is marched into the room by two giants, who are clearly twins.

Jackson laughs out loud. 'Now look who it is.'

'Fuck off, Tony. You switched on me,' Briggs spits.

'Looks like you switched on me too, Dick.' Jackson moves up to Dannii and presses the barrel of the gun into her neck.

'It's over, Tony,' Briggs says. 'Let the girl go.'

'Yes, I can clearly see it's over. Put the snitch over there.' He gestures at a chair in the corner.

Lukas tries to place the two men that hold the spitting and swearing inspector in a vice grip. It doesn't take him long to figure out how things fit together. On the floor Callaway shows signs of coming round.

'Tony, there's no need for this,' Briggs demands.

With relief Lukas watches Tony Jackson move the gun away from Dannii's neck and slip it into his pocket. With Briggs safely out of the way in the corner, the two heavies reposition themselves either side of Lukas.

'Hello, boys.' Lukas stares hard at Briggs. 'How's Sean?' He can't suppress a wry smile as the inspector's eyes light up.

The twin to his left elbows Lukas in the side and winds him. 'Shut up, moron. Who allowed you to speak?' The man's voice resembles that of the voice-over artist on American disaster movie trailers.

'Isn't that Leroy Callaway?' his brother nods at the man struggling to his feet.

'Looks like this one gave him an hiding,' the first twin laughs and elbows Lukas again.

Callaway looks around blearily. Blood oozes from his nose. It has coloured his teeth pink and drips down his chin. Lukas doesn't fancy him coming round completely, doesn't want anyone in this room to be subjected to the man's insanity. 'He's your way into a more affluent society, Tony, isn't he?' Lukas nods in Callaway's direction. 'I'd have thought Kovacs would have decent enough contacts but you like to aim for the stars, don't you?'

The first twin punches Lukas in the stomach. Lukas struggles to stay on his feet, overwhelmed with nausea. 'Or isn't Kovacs in on all this?' he asks. Jackson grabs Dannii's hair. Dannii yelps. 'The question is, why do you want to upgrade yourself? You wouldn't fit into high society,' Lukas gasps, doubled over.

'You really do want trouble, don't you?' Jackson pulls Dannii back by her hair until the chair is balanced on its back legs only.

'Answer the man.' The second twin uses his vice grip on Lukas's head.

'Not sure what the question is,' Lukas croaks, his neck creaking.

'Stupid bitch!' Callaway kicks Dannii's chair. Her head flies backwards as the chair tips over and hits Jackson in the groin. Lukas watches Jackson stumble backwards. On impact Dannii's chair comes apart. The vice round Lukas's neck momentarily loosens. Lukas takes the opportunity to push his kneecaps into the back of the second twin's knees. Instantly, the man's legs collapse. Lukas follows through with a hard kick to the man's calf then ducks out of the way of the first twin's outstretched hands, reaching for his throat. Lukas grabs the still dazed Callaway and turns him quickly towards the first twin's swing. Callaway's face collides with the man's right fist and Lukas drops him. Dannii rages on top of Jackson, hitting his face.

Lukas wonders about the gun in Jackson's pocket a moment too long. The first twin floors him in the same way that he had just taken care of his brother. 'Briggs,' Lukas shouts as he goes down. DCI Briggs just stands in the corner, observing the scene.

'Look what I found in the back.' Mark storms through the door and drops a plastic bag on the floor. Then he pulls out his gun and the inspector's. Lukas gets onto all fours.

'Stay down, mate. Dannii, move away from that shit, he's tooled.'

'Billy.' Jackson struggles to his feet. He frowns. 'Billy?'

'Put your piece on the floor, Tony.'

'You bloody bastard. I won't do any such thing.'

'Yes you will, Tony. Get in the corner with the DCI,' Mark orders the twins.

'It's Billy, boys,' Jackson shouts.

The first twin moves towards the inspector.

'Don't look like Billy to me,' the second twin says and follows his brother.

'It's his voice,' the first twin says.

'Never done me no harm,' the second twin adds.

Mark laughs. 'Who says there's no loyalty between crooks. Put your piece on the floor, Tony. I won't say it again. Nice bag of confectionery you've got here.' Mark kicks the plastic bag. It splits open and smaller bags filled with pills and powder spill out.

'Careful with that,' the first twin says.

'It's not ours,' the second twin says.

Lukas takes a deep breath, gets up and walks over to Callaway. The footballer is still on the floor, groaning. Lukas drags him to his feet roughly. 'Stop diving.'

Briggs pushes past the twins and towards Mark. 'Give me my piece.'

'Nope.' Mark keeps the guns pointing at Jackson. 'Listen, Tony. I'm going to say this only once more – '

'No point,' Lukas says.

Jackson reaches into his pocket. Lukas is upon him and removes Jackson's hand, holding the gun, from the man's pocket.

'You shouldn't have gone in with him, Tony.' Briggs pushes Callaway in Jackson's direction. 'He went one step too far. My Gaby was out of bounds. He betrayed my trust.'

'She bloody wanted it,' Callaway hisses.

'Shut up, twat,' Briggs barks. 'And now drugs, Tony? Sean Ryley's drugs?'

Jackson eyes Callaway. 'You messed up, you selfish little shit. Should never have taken you on.' He slaps Callaway's face and turns to Briggs. 'If you ever try and take me down, Dick, I swear I'm going to take you down with me. Now, fuck off, you oaf!' Jackson pushes Lukas hard. Lukas loses his grip on the man's arm. Jackson runs past Mark and out of the door. It slams shut behind him, followed by a metallic grating.

'Shit, he's locked us in.' Mark shoulders the door. Lukas watches through the window mesh as Jackson gets into the four by four and drives off.

'That's my fucking car, man. Shit.'

'Sit down, moron.' Briggs barks at Callaway. The footballer sinks into the couch and gets out his mobile, muttering to himself.

'Give me that.' Mark takes the mobile off him.

'Arsehole,' Callaway mutters.

'We've let him slip through the net,' Lukas says. Dannii moves up behind him. He takes her in his arms and kisses her on her forehead.

'By the way, I've bugged both cars. So don't beat yourselves up.' Mark eases a lock pick into the ancient Yale lock, moving it up and down while pushing on a tension wrench. The lock snaps open.

'Piece.' Briggs steps up to him and holds out his hand.

'Peace to you too, brother.' Mark reaches up, pick in hand and shakes Briggs's hand with two fingers. Lukas notices that DCI Richard Briggs suppresses a smile.

'What do we do with him?' Dannii nods in Callaway's direction.

'What's it to you, you stupid bitch. It's all your fucking fault anyway.'

'How's that, Leroy?' Lukas asks, hands on hips.

'They're all the fucking same. Bitches. Fuck around with us.'

'Oh, it's plural now, is it? It's womankind's fault that you rape underage girls?'

'Cunt,' Callaway mumbles.

'Stop me, someone, before I remove this moron's balls from the gene pool.' Lukas roars.

'Leave it, sweet.' Dannii puts her arm on his shoulder.

'Let him go,' Briggs says. 'He can catch a bus. We're in Wanderers territory here, he'll enjoy himself.'

Lukas walks over to Callaway, grabs his collar, drags him to his feet and to the door. 'Get out. I hope I never see you again, on or off the pitch. Shoot.' Lukas shoves him out of the building.

Callaway turns round. 'Fuck you,' he hisses and spits in Lukas's face.

'You two,' Mark addresses the twins. 'I'll take the bug off your Merc and then you buzz. Say hi to Sean.'

'What about them?' The first twin points at the bag.

Briggs picks it up. 'We'll pin that on our friend Tony. Tell me. You're just the runners, right?' Briggs smiles at the two men encouragingly.

'Correct,' the first twin says.

'We didn't know them were drugs or nothing,' the second twin adds.

'Course not.' The detective smiles. 'This is a delivery from Sean to who?' The twins look at each other. 'Where were you taking this after here?' The detective explains slowly. 'Remember you're just the runners, right?'

'The casino,' the first twin says. 'We was just cutting it in the back.'

'OK. Anything else?'

'Leroy took some too, earlier.' The second twin nods towards the door.

'OK. Now go.' Briggs takes out his mobile. 'I need two dispatches. Both to Bolton. Moss Bank Way area. I'm at Mossy something, end of Sharples Park. I need someone collect a huge pile of dope. The other is for a black male in the area, possibly at a bus stop, mid-twenties, six foot five-ish. Looks like that Mancunia defender. Suspected dealer. Let me know how you get on. Cheers.' He ends the call and winks at Lukas.

'He's got a fifteen minute head start. I must get going,' Briggs says.

'I'm coming with you,' Lukas says.

'OK, Novak. Though this is my jurisdiction now.'

'Understood. Do you have a tracker, Mark, or how does this work?'

'Yes. Works like phone GPS.' Mark hands Lukas a handset.

'Luke,' Dannii says.

'It'll be OK, I promise.'

'How can you promise? You're following a violent criminal.'

'We'll be back in no time, love.' Lukas puts his arm round her shoulder. 'Have a look at the computers before the law arrives, will you?'

'Just what I was thinking,' She says and he kisses her gently on the cheek.

'We should get going, Novak, unless you've changed your mind?'

Lukas lets Dannii go.

Mark hands him the car keys. 'I suppose you want to borrow the car, again?'

'You drive, Novak.' Lukas hands the detective the tracker and puts the BMW in gear. 'M62, this thing says. Join it from the 666. Eastbound.' Briggs takes out his mobile and calls in. 'Jeremy, we're in pursuit of a vehicle on the M62.' He gives out their car details. 'We don't want to be stopped, can you arrange that?' The inspector ends the call.

Chapter 68

The afternoon traffic is bumper to bumper, but flowing at a steady sixty-five. Rochdale, Milnrow and Shaw pass in quick succession, then the motorway widens to four lanes, climbing the Pennines steadily.

'Saddleworth,' Briggs states.

Lukas clears his throat. 'Did you work on the Moors murders at all?'

'Not on the original ones. I'm not that old. But I was present when the last grave was found.'

'You've been with Greater Manchester Police that long?'

'Yes. Seems like a fucking life sentence.' Briggs studies the tracker. 'We're catching up slowly. He's just passing Bradford.'

'Any guesses to his destination? M1?'

'We'll see. If he wanted north, he would've turned left by now.' Briggs shifts in his seat. 'I'm bloody annoyed with you, Novak. You made me believe you're the blogger.'

'I remember us arriving at that conclusion together.'

'It seemed to be the right conclusion. Logical.'

But incorrect.'

'Quite. Who is it? You know. And what's this about asking Courante? What's he got to do with it?'

Lukas thinks long and hard. Briggs is on his side for now, he believes. In denying the detective information Lukas risks alienating him again. He looks over at the inspector. The man catches his eye and holds it. 'Have we seen all the double crosses in our little tale, Dick?'

'You mean, can you trust me?'

'Correct.'

'What you have on me, Novak, would produce a very popular article in a national broadsheet. I don't know what you're worried about.'

'Just wondering.'

'You think I'll do another U-turn?'

'Yes.'

'You can think what you like, and go to hell.'

Twelve minutes later they pass the M606 exit to Bradford in darkness. Traffic has eased up and Lukas sits in the fast lane at ninety-five. He laughs suddenly. 'Just think about it, Dick, all this time they've been dealing right under our noses while we tried to find a blogger.'

'Right under my nose,' Briggs says.

Lukas looks at him. 'Both our noses. We both had the same goal. My motivation was a story, yours was keeping Jim's stable clean.'

'You found him and I didn't. And now you're rubbing it in.'

'No, Dick. Just think. They sidelined you. You never knew about the drugs. They kept you thinking you were part of the A-team but you never were. You never even made the first team back at Coventry, yet all this time you did the mopping up. Why? 'Cos you wanted to be part of the gang? And now they drop you like a hot potato and move on to bigger things.'

'What are you, a psychologist?' Briggs sneers.

'No, I'm a realist. And you're a fantasist. Maybe it's time you got real.' Briggs looks out of the window. Lukas continues. 'Don't you realise you've wrecked lives? For example, Unwin's, just to keep the status quo for these bastards? Heck, you're in danger of wrecking your own daughter's future. And all the while they're using you, you just don't see it.' Lukas slaps the steering wheel. 'You know what Unwin kept saying while he kept me dangling about his history? He said "mate, you call yourself an investigator?" He kept taking the piss out of me, calling me Sherlock. Said I was making mistake after mistake after mistake and not seeing the obvious. I could say the same thing about you, Dick. You just keep digging in the same direction, in hope of finding the single spud. And you end up deeper and deeper in the shit and find fuck all.'

'You done?'

'No,' Lukas continues. 'Just think. I'm not the MatchMaker and instead of putting your brain in gear you just keep asking who's the blogger. I'm not going to tell you. If you haven't worked it out by now then you don't deserve to know. I'm not surprised so many crimes go unsolved. Queen's Police Medal, my arse!' Briggs looks surprised. 'It's all over the net, Dick.'

'Everything seems to be all over the net these days,' the inspector mumbles.

'Is it Unwin?'

'I'm not even going to answer that.'

Lukas's phone pings. He reads the message and turns to Briggs. 'Computers are full of kiddie porn. Your boys are taking the lot.'

'Jesus.' Briggs pauses. 'Why did you go to old Frank's house, Novak?'

'Because his address was on the MatchMaker's PayPal account.'

'Someone was using his address.'

'Yes, Dick. Did you ever check it out?'

'Nope.'

'Are we catching him?'

Briggs looks at the tracker. 'He's just crossed the M1. We're getting closer.'

'If you're not the MatchMaker, then you didn't set up an online date through that account.'

'No.'

'You're not doing online dating at all.'

'D'you think I need to?'

'Not with your lady friend.'

'Thank you, Dick.'

'What was she doing at Guide Bridge?'

Lukas pauses. 'You tell me, Dick.'

'Never,' the inspector gasps.

''Fraid so.'

'What on earth is the Courante connection?'

'It's a very long story.'

The inspector's phone rings. 'Yes, I heard. Yes, it's him in the car ahead. We're still in pursuit. Let us have the first shot.'

'I hope you don't mean that literally,' Lukas says.

'He's past the M180. He's going to Hull.'

'When's the ferry, Dick? He's trying to leave the country.'

Briggs swears and types into his phone. 'Rotterdam six-thirty. It's almost six o'clock now.'

Lukas floors the accelerator.

'He's at the port.'

'Let's hope they're full.'

'I bet they're not, at this time of year.'

Briggs rings in. 'I need stand-by at Hull port. Rotterdam ferry. We'll follow him onto the boat. I know it's Leroy Callaway's car.' Briggs listens then laughs, ends the call and turns to Lukas. 'Apparently our friend Callaway reported his car stolen when they arrested him for possession at a bus stop in Bolton.' Lukas smiles and concentrates on signs to the port. 'He was in a brawl with some lads, apparently, kicking and spitting at them. Shouting that he was the greatest, Mancunia this, Mancunia that. Moses is going to kill him.'

'I hope Moses is going to kick him.'

'I agree, Novak.'

Lukas turns sharply and accelerates towards the green lane leading to the booths beneath the Rotterdam signs. The ferry looms ahead, bow doors open. 'Is he on?'

Briggs checks the tracker. 'Yes.'

Lukas stops at the booth. The attendant slowly slides down her window. 'You're too late.'

Briggs leans over and flashes his badge. Lukas takes in a lungful of the inspector's breath and gags.

'Go ahead. I'll let them know,' the attendant says and picks up a walkie-talkie.

Lukas speeds towards the ferry. The lines are being slackened as they approach and the passenger gangway has been closed but the car ramp is still down. Lukas accelerates up it and catches the BMW's exhaust on the top edge. He sees sparks in the mirror and grins. Ahead the white Chevrolet sits slightly askew on the half-empty car deck. Lukas pulls up next to it, tyres screeching. Briggs is out of the vehicle before it comes to a stop. He crouches by the bonnet, gun in hand.

Lukas gets out of the BMW and scans the deck for movement. 'Put the gun away, Dick. We'll just attract attention.' He looks at the bow doors closing slowly.

'Upstairs.' Briggs runs towards a door marked Exit A.

'Slow down! Where's he going to go?'

With a deep drone the ferry starts to move out of the harbour and into the Humber, towards the North Sea. Lukas hasn't really envisaged spending the night on a cross channel ferry to arrive in Holland eleven hours later. His thoughts are interrupted by his phone.

'Get the fuck up here, Novak! Top deck. Rear. Hurry,' Briggs hisses in his ear.

Lukas snaps out of it and runs towards Exit A. He wonders how many more times he is going to end up completely winded. By the time he reaches Level A and opens the door to the sun deck he sees stars.

Briggs is crouching behind a box for lifejackets. A strong easterly wind catches Lukas's face as he ducks down by the doorway. Rain drives horizontally across the deck. The ferry is still in the harbour, turning away from the quay, a huge vessel to get into motion. A couple of police cars are pulling up on the quayside.

Briggs clicks his fingers to attract his attention, then points across the deck. Lukas's gaze follows the inspector's outstretched hand. On the other side of the deck Tony Jackson is working away at one of the lifeboats.

'You got to be kidding,' Lukas shouts in Briggs's ear. 'Shouldn't we tell someone? Does the ship have police?'

'Yes, me.'

'You're going to arrest him?'

'I'm going to try.'

'Don't be stupid. He's armed.'

'So am I. Go through the cabin. Sneak up on him.'

'Are you insane?'

'I'll keep him occupied, don't worry.'

Lukas sees the back of the lifeboat move. 'Surely it takes more than one person to lower a lifeboat".'

'Go,' Briggs hollers.

Jackson must have heard him or maybe he just worries about being caught. He turns round, his eyes searching the wet deck. Lukas ducks into the shadow of the door recess. He opens the door behind him, slips back inside and quickly crosses to the other side of the vessel. When he opens the backboard door he hears Briggs shout over the din of the engine and the howling gale, 'Don't be stupid, Tony. Put the gun on the ground.'   Lukas pokes his head out and sees Tony Jackson waving his gun about. 'Fuck off. You don't order me anything,' Jackson shouts then backs into a recess behind the lifeboat.

Lukas quickly sidles along the railing towards him. He sees the flash before he hears the sound. Impossible. This mustn't happen. Another shot. And a scream. 'No!' Lukas lurches forward.

Tony Jackson seems suspended in air. The small gate in the railing, where the lifeboat is launched, is open. This must be a mistake and Jackson must have leant back against it. It should have been locked. Now Tony Jackson leans with nothing behind him but the Humber estuary.

Lukas seizes Jackson's collar but his feet fail to find proper purchase on the wet deck. He grapples for the railing but only reaches the other half of the lifeboat access gate, which swings open. Lukas tumbles forward, on top of Jackson, who silently stares at him, wide-eyed. Over Jackson's shoulder Lukas watches the gun as it falls ahead of them towards the murky waters of the Humber.

Interlude

Not much goes through his mind after he hits the sea; the shock to his system is complete and irreversible. The impact on the water's surface almost knocks him out. Seconds later, the cold leaves him paralysed, and sinking fast. What is below is as black as what is above. Unbearable pressure compresses his ears, his lungs. He kicks his feet and flails his arms in panic. The propeller, the fucking propeller! He opens his mouth to scream; his body breathes against his will. He coughs, then vomits under water. Suddenly, he is above the surface, icy wind slaps his face and his lungs explode in agony as they fill with air. A hundred feet above looms the deck he's just fallen from. Fifteen yards beyond his feet the ship's propeller chops away at the Humber; it is sucking at him and any second now will chop him to pieces. He kicks his feet out in the direction of the huge, slow-turning screw, arms paddling wildly.

Then something pulls his sleeve and drags him under once more. He thrashes about, swallowing more of the foul liquid. He gags and retches. Finally, he wills himself to fight against what is holding him below the surface.

Tony Jackson is bleeding from the mouth, his grin a grimace of hate and horror illuminated by the harbor lights. He releases Lukas's arms and wraps his hands around his neck instead. Lukas pulls with his left and punches with his right. Although the water brakes his punch to slow motion, Jackson's head still jerks back satisfyingly with the impact of fist on chin.

Lukas looks round. The ship's propeller is still no further away. He takes Jackson in a vice and tries to pull him away from the vessel. But Jackson kicks and struggles, so Lukas hits him hard on the temple. He reaches for the man's arms and drags him on top of his chest. Suddenly Jackson goes limp.

Lukas turns to see the quay wall still a good thirty metres away. Jackson's body pulls heavily on him, his own limbs unresponsive with the cold. He won't be able to move much longer and certainly won't be able to hold Jackson above water. But he can't let him go. The man must be held responsible for what he has done, for what the likes of him do to the likes of his little brother.

He screams in agony and frustration but utters nothing but a small cry. The waves lap at his open mouth as both air and Humber fill his lungs.

Chapter 69

'Hey,' he hears Dannii say. Someone pats his cheek. He sits up suddenly and retches hard. Dannii recoils. Lukas feels impossibly sick as his stomach cramps up painfully, again and again. He spits and gags, but brings nothing up. Dannii sits back down by his side. He swallows bile.

'They pumped your stomach,' she tells him. He lies back and moans. 'I got here an hour ago.' Lukas feels for her hand.

The door opens and Mark enters. 'You OK, mate?'

'Where's the flowers?' Lukas groans, his voice hoarse.

Mark laughs. 'You drank the Humber dry, apparently. Doesn't surprise me. This is DI Colston.' Mark gestures behind him.

'Mr Novak. You had a close shave.'

'Seems to be a regular thing for me at the moment.'

'I understand you were driving DCI Briggs earlier.'

Lukas coughs. 'Are you Jeremy?'

Colston offers a wry smile. 'Yes, I am.'

'Where is Briggs?'

'We don't know. Who shot first? We saw the flashes from the quayside.'

'Jackson did.'

'Are you absolutely sure? It's crucial that you're right.'

'I am. Is Jackson alive?' Lukas swings his legs out of the bed.

'Barely. Shot through the throat. He was lucky the shot didn't rupture an artery. Apart from that he almost drowned. Just like you.'

'He needs to be brought to justice. Do I have clothes?'

'In the bag over there.' Dannii points towards a holdall by the basin. 'So Briggs is still on the ferry.'

'We have divers looking for him.'

'He went overboard? I don't think so.'

'He got hit and went over.'

'And shot at Jackson in mid flight? He was crouching behind a bench full of life jackets when I left him.'

'He must have straightened up to take aim at Jackson,' Mark says.

'What makes you think so?' Lukas coughs and spits in the sink.

'To hold his weapon with good aim,' Colston suggests.

'And expose himself to Jackson?' Lukas pulls on a pair of jeans. 'I reckon Jackson's shot missed Briggs completely and he's still on board.'

'Then he would have seen you and Jackson go over. He would have raised the alarm. The boat would have stopped and the coastguard would have been mobilised.'

Lukas laughs and looks at Mark, who grins behind the officer's back.

'What's funny, Mr Novak?'

'Nothing. Just a cough. Jesus, I feel sick.' He holds his stomach and leans on the basin. 'So no one on board noticed that two or three men, give or take, went overboard?' Lukas pulls the hospital gown off and replaces it with a T-shirt and hoodie.

'It seems that way.'

'And you reckon if Briggs had still been on board he would have raised the alarm.'

'Of course he would have.'

'So what you're thinking is he was shot and went over opposite side to Jackson and myself. Which would have dropped him into the path of the ship's propeller, as the boat was still moving away from the quay.'

'That's quite likely.'

'The pull of the propeller was incredible. I could hardly put any distance between myself and the vessel. How likely do you think it is you'll find remains?'

'I really don't know. The search is fairly fruitless in the dark, with the waters being so murky.'

'I assume it was the coastguard that pulled me out?' Lukas asks. Colston smiles and confirms that it was. 'Do you need to question me further just now?' Lukas asks.

'No, you're free to go. We'll need to speak to you again as you're the only witness to the shooting. But for now go and rest.'

Lukas shakes Colston's hand firmly. 'What happens to Jackson?'

'When he recovers he'll be taken into custody and await trial. The evidence against him is overwhelming. And he shot at the DCI. You might have to give evidence.'

Nothing would please me more.'

Half an hour later, after strong insistence on his part, Lukas is discharged from hospital.

'We won't make last orders if we drive back to Manchester,' Mark comments.

'I'm glad you've got your priorities right,' Dannii says.

'We're staying here. I couldn't face the trip. I feel like I've swallowed a gallon of diesel.'

'You have, mate.'

'Let's find a hotel,' Dannii says. 'There's a Travelodge sign over there.'

'You think he's dead?' Mark puts a triple whisky down in front of Lukas. He pushes the glass away. 'I couldn't.'

'It's medicinal,' Mark insists.

Lukas grimaces. 'Get me a vodka and I'll try.'

Dannii laughs and goes to the bar. Lukas feels the bile rise in his throat. He knows he needs something to cut through it. Dannii hands him a double. He necks it and immediately rushes to the toilet. He leans heavily on the wash basin, breathing hard. Slowly the nausea is replaced by a warm glow in his stomach. He looks at himself in the mirror. Decision number one: he is going to get blind drunk tonight, if his body will allow him to. Decision number two: from now on he is going to do everything he has been too lazy, too afraid and too self-conscious to try. He laughs and returns to the bar.

'OK?' Dannii says. 'I was just about to get you—'

He takes her in his arms and kisses her passionately. She pants heavily when he is done and looks at him wide-eyed.

'I don't think they do bed and breakfast, that's why we booked an h-o-t-e-l.' Mark frowns and looks around the bar.

Dannii laughs. 'Are you OK, Luke?'

'I'm fine. Get me another, will you?'

'When did you last eat? Apart from plankton, I mean,' Mark asks him.

'This morning, before I went to see Moses. God, was that only this morning?' Lukas runs a hand over his face and leans forward. 'To answer your question: no. I don't think he's dead. I believe Jackson missed. Then Briggs shot at him. Shot to kill. Deliberately. Almost succeeded. He'd say it was self-defence. Which it probably was. Jackson tried to steady himself on the railing by the lifeboat. The access gate in the railing wasn't fastened properly. It swung open and Jackson lost his footing. I tried to grab him and pull him back in, but failed. We both went overboard.' Lukas downs the second vodka.

'Jesus, mate.'

'Just imagine Briggs, having promised allegiance to us. Both his problems go overboard in one fell swoop. Couldn't have worked out better for him.'

'I told you he couldn't be trusted.'

'And he's got your car. I left the key in the ignition. He probably hasn't even worked out yet he's got transport.'

'I suppose I should be extremely pissed off with you now, but for some reason I can't bring myself to be.'

'I'll pay you back, Mark. I wouldn't be here if it weren't for you. Do you have the number for Dolly Green?'

'Of course.'

'Can I borrow your phone please?'

'Stan,' Lukas says after a short palaver with Linda. 'How's Jason? Listen. Callaway's in custody for possession with intent to supply. The girls from the Turing are willing to testify against him. So am I for attempted GBH. What you don't know is that Callaway and Jackson abducted my girlfriend to put pressure on me not to publish the story. Of course I will! So tell Jason he needn't worry any longer and to concentrate on getting well. Where's Tony?' Lukas laughs. 'Tony's in hospital after a fall from a cross-channel ferry. Before he fell he got shot through the throat. Yes, he'll live and stand trial. For possession of narcotics and child pornography. Found at his hide-out, where he was holding my fiancée. He's going down, Stan. Will you report him for what he did to you and testify? For the sake of all youngsters?' Lukas listens, then smiles. 'OK, Stan, thanks.'

Lukas turns to Dannii and Mark. 'He's reported Jackson for sexual abuse on himself and Jason. He's going to go public and give me the story.' Lukas looks from one to the other. 'What are you two grinning about?'

'Fiancée?' Mark asks. Lukas looks at him, puzzled. Dannii walks up to him, takes his face in her hands and kisses his forehead.

'What was in those waters you took? You're positively weird,' Mark comments.

Lukas looks at him, then back at Dannii. 'Well?'

'I'll think about it, sweet.' She pats his cheek.

'Have you two got money? I don't. And I'm gagging for a fag.'

Chapter 70

As he sips his coffee Lukas looks down at the pile of papers on the table. With a sigh he sits down and takes *The Times* off the top of the stack. *The Mirror*'s front page displays a blurred photograph of Leroy Callaway having a go at him. *It was Callous-Ways!* reads the headline.

He'd moved them on to champagne after a few vodkas last night, though Mark had insisted on staying on lager. He had even managed a curry later on. He can't recall going to bed but remembers vividly how Dannii had woken him up this morning and soothed his hangover.

The Sun and the *Daily Star* don't hold back either. Leroy Callaway has indeed fallen out of favour with the tabloid press overnight, though the news of his arrest has not made the papers yet. Each paper also features a small article with the same dated image of a gruff, but determined looking, DCI Briggs on pages two or three, headlines ranging from *Man overboard! Possible illegal immigrant goes missing from cross-channel ferry* to *Fatal shooting of undercover officer – man vanishes after possible gunfight, boys in blue clueless.*

On their return to Chorlton he had taken the ringing house phone off the hook. With the answerphone cache full already he'd only bothered to listen to the first few messages. Requests for interviews, demands for his view of yesterday morning's events. Now they've descended on him in person.

'Have you seen the crowd outside?' Dannii makes for the coffee machine.

Lukas grunts. 'We'll have to stage another getaway.'

'To Glossop?' She laughs.

'Why not? It's a nice enough place, isn't it?'

'It's a lovely place. Seriously, Luke, I feel like a trapped mouse already. They don't even know the half of what happened yesterday.'

He looks at her over the top of his glasses. 'Quite. We're like a raft going down the Swanee. Especially me. Fast.'

'I've lost Mancunia's number along with my mobile.'

'You want to talk to Moses again?'

'I want to know what the official line is.'

'You can count yourself lucky if he doesn't come after you.'

Lukas scowls at her. 'I made myself clear yesterday.'

'That was before Callaway abducted me and before he was framed for drugs.'

'True, but—'

'You think Moses has the time or the desire to talk to you, of all people?'

'Why not?'

'All his trouble started with you, I believe.'

'He wanted to know the truth.'

She laughs. 'The truth? Moses? Luke, where have you been?'

'He seemed very reasonable to me.'

'He seems perfectly reasonable to everyone. That's why he is who he is and where he is. A different shade of the truth for everyone, and everybody's happy.'

'Do you have the number, love?' Lukas says, impatiently. Dannii snorts, then reads the number out to him.

Two minutes later he replaces the receiver carefully.

'And?'

He shakes his head and grins sheepishly.

'Told you so.'

'I suppose if I was in his shoes I wouldn't want to talk to me either.' He walks over to her and puts his arms round her. 'Shall we?'

'Shall we what?'

'Escape to the country.'

'As long as we can stay somewhere different from the B & B, please.'

He kisses her on the nose. 'I promise.'

Thirty minutes later they board the Metrolink Bury service at Firswood and get off at Piccadilly Gardens.

'Are people looking at me or am I imagining things?' Lukas asks.

'No one's going to recognise you from that blurred pic.' Dannii takes a copy of the *Manchester Evening News* from one of the platform sellers and holds up the front page.

'Twenty quid to tweet a clip,' Lukas reads out the minor headline above a photo of the grinning boy who he had bribed yesterday. 'Is twenty pounds enough to end a legend's career?' Lukas quotes from the paper. 'He was well out of order.'

'I hope he means Callaway, not you. Is your name mentioned?'

'Not yet.' Lukas walks towards the cash till on the station approach. 'Crunch time,' he says as he pushes his card into the slot. 'I don't believe it.' The machine releases his card and two hundred pounds in twenties and tens. 'The bugger told the truth.' Dannii smirks. 'New phone.' Ten minutes later he's purchased an old Nokia handset from a second hand phone shop and a pay as you go SIM card. 'I feel like a new man. Time for a hair of the dog.'

He orders a pint, takes a careful sip and licks the foam from his lips. Then he gestures at the TV. 'Look. Doesn't look any clearer on a big screen, does it?' The image changes and Lukas now looks at a newscaster. The sound is off but he recognises the street nevertheless. 'Bloody hell!' he says under his breath. The newscaster is interviewing a grinning youngster on the corner of his very street. The boy shows his phone to the camera.

'Look! Vladi, leaving the Globe in the background.' Dannii giggles.

'This is getting far too close to home. Look at him.'

'He's running away.'

'And ducking, so nobody spots him. Jesus.' Lukas downs his pint. 'I'm freaked.'

'And you were on the news just a few days ago with that alleged assault. Could be a right mess if someone puts two and two together.'

Lukas gets up and puts his empty glass down on the table. 'Come on, we'd better lie low.' He takes her hand and drags her towards platform one.

In a newsagent's he buys a baseball cap and pulls it down deeply over his forehead.

'You can't be serious,' Dannii says when he comes out. 'I love Mancunia? Couldn't you get a Callaway shirt to match?' He turns and walks back into the shop. 'She supports United.' He hands the cap back to the youth behind the counter and points his thumb back over his shoulder. He steps out of the shop wearing a New York City cap.

'You look like a Yank,' Dannii says. He rolls his eyes.

They board the next Hadfield train. Lukas is asleep by the time they reach Guide Bridge and Dannii has to shake him as the train pulls into Glossop.

Chapter 71

'We could just ask in the pub.'

'That might not be such a bad idea,' she replies.

'There was nothing in the estate agent's.' He looks at her as they walk through Manor Park. She looks tired, he notices.

'True.'

'Maybe not the best place to look.'

'Maybe not.' She sounds fed up. Monosyllabic. He hopes it's not him.

In the pub, she wants a lager shandy. He orders coffee for himself and returns to the table with her beer and two menus. '

'You're having coffee.'

'Yes. I'm knackered,' he says. She smirks at him lopsidedly. 'Do you have a problem with me having coffee?' He takes off his glasses.

She opens her menu. 'You don't have to prove anything to me, you know.'

He closes his. 'Prove what to you?'

She looks at him innocently. 'Normally you'd have a beer, wouldn't you?'

'Normally, what's normally?' he huffs. 'You don't know me "normally". And contrary to what you're saying, normally I only drink when my working day is over.'

'If you do work, that is.' She returns to the menu.

'I work every day. I do set challenges – what are you doing, Dannii? When did you have the time to develop these preconceptions of what I do or what I don't do, and what I'm like normally? You've only ever known me in times of extreme stress.'

'I could say the same thing to you,' she says.

'That's absolutely correct. But unlike you I haven't come to conclusions about you.'

The barmaid arrives with his coffee.

'And what conclusions have I come to, you think?' she asks him. The lopsider is back and he doesn't like it.

'That I don't work much and I drink beer for breakfast, for example.'

'And, do you drink beer for breakfast?'

'Only on holiday.' Lukas necks his coffee black and burns his mouth. The pain hits the back of his throat after scalding his tongue. 'I'm not going to retaliate and invent stuff about you, you know,' he lisps breathlessly.

'Like what?' Her face is set in stone.

He touches his lips carefully. 'As I said, I won't. You told me enough to make the toughest man run a mile.' He flinches at his own touch. 'But seems I'm just too old and fat to be bothered.'

'I thought you to be tougher than the toughest.'

He looks at her and curses his eyes, watering with the pain from his mouth. 'Bollocks,' he says. She tuts and looks away. She's run once before. He reaches for her shoulder. 'Will you get me a beer to cool down my mouth please?' he says quietly.

She rises and looks down at him, her nostrils flared. He is convinced she is suppressing a grin. 'You know this is that Liz Taylor talking in your head.'

'At least you didn't say I told you so,' he mumbles and lets her go.

'What are you having?'

'I'll have the pie.' She slams shut the menu and gnaws her lip. 'Shall we order before we have a good talk, Dannii?'

'Hm.' She gnaws. He swallows hard and watches her go to the bar.

'There's a cottage in the village for hire on a weekly basis. It's empty for a few weeks. We can have it even if we only need it for a few days. At least we won't get chucked out for the weekend.'

'Old Glossop?'

'Yes, up from the Wheatsheaf. Belongs to the landlord here.'

'OK.'

He takes her hand. 'Dannii, will you please tell me what's wrong. You've been trying to pick a fight, you've been unusually quiet and I won't be able to eat a bite if this wedge is still between us when the food arrives.' She looks at the Vintage Channel on the TV. The Human League sing about not being wanted, and the lump in his throat is getting bigger. 'Love?'

She turns to him. 'I had a missed call. On the train. When you were asleep. There's hardly any service, so the phone didn't even ring.' She sounds apologetic. 'It was Jean-Pierre.' She looks him in the eye. 'He didn't leave a message.'

He studies her. She looks like a little girl. 'Are you worried?'

'For him not to be in touch properly for years and now he rings at this time, with what's been going on?' She frowns.

'He's probably read your posts.'

'He's probably talked to Moses, or rather vice versa.'

'Are you going to ring him back?'

'No. That's not the way it works. I've got to wait for him. He's out of bounds.'

'Why?'

''Cos that's the way it is.'

He leans on the table and frowns at her. 'Do you seriously think you should carry on with the blog after all this? Don't you realise you might be incriminated?'

'Don't you tell me what I can and what I cannot do.'

'Christ, woman! I love you. I'm concerned. I don't want anything to happen to you. Remember. Peace and quiet?'

'Yeah, stop dreaming 'bout the quiet life, 'cos it's the one you'll never know.'

His fist hits the table before he can stop himself. 'That's you, that's never been me. You move on as soon as you're near completion. I'm the opposite. I have trouble moving on. I'm fucking scared of you, woman!'

'Join the club,' she says and gets up.

He grabs her hand in panic. 'Don't go.'

She looks down at him. 'I'm going to ring him back. There's no service in here. Time to break his rules. Time to move on.'

Lukas exhales noisily as she walks outside…

Interlude

…and picks up the Glossop Gazette on the next table.

'Murder on the Moors' reads the headline.

'Another mysterious death at the Superfortress crash site, the third in as many decades, freaks out locals and tourists alike. The body of Gladys Turner, the popular local librarian, was found by fellrunners on Higher Shelf Stones on Sunday morning. So far the cause of death is

unknown. Ms Turner's body remains at Tameside Hospital. The police would like to speak to the owner of a Manchester Central Library card which was found in her possession. The card number has been partially torn off but ends in the digits 140256.' Lukas folds the paper *carefully and puts it into his pocket.*

Chapter 72

'Mr Novak, it has been brought to my attention that you are concerned about corruption in football, the fixing of matches in particular. Is that correct?' Jean-Pierre speaks with a strong French accent. Lukas had just taken the top off his pint when Dannii put her head through the door and beckoned him outside. 'Let me make one thing clear, Mr Novak, I'm not going to give you solutions. I was merely alerted by an acquaintance about your research.'

Lukas laughs. 'An acquaintance? Dannii's just passed me the phone. Why so secretive, Monsieur Courante?'

'Let me stop you there. Sometimes it is to one's advantage not to spell things out. Or to mention names. You never know who's listening. Let me tell you that you're dabbling in a dangerous business.'

'Are you trying to threaten me?'

'No, Mr Novak, but then I have no interest in making life uncomfortable for you. Others might.' Lukas doesn't respond. 'You probably think you're on a knight errant's mission investigating this matter of match fixing. But believe me, you're putting yourself in danger and those around you.'

'You're not kidding.'

'Take this from someone who has no interest in you personally. I love the game of football, but as the name implies, it is a game and like all games the stakes can be high for those who gamble.'

'The seagulls are still chasing the boat?'

Courante laughs. 'They are, indeed, Mr Novak, more closely than ever.'

'Whose side are you on?'

'As I just said, I love football but I hate the game; it is, however, an irrevocable evil without which football would not exist—'

'At this level and exposure, you mean,' Lukas finishes the sentence.

'The game is like any other game; it is about winning and losing, about strong and weak, about clever and stupid. You're clever, Mr Novak, without a doubt, so why do you play stupid?'

'I'm getting a feeling I'm being played alright.'

'Curiosity killed the cat, Mr Novak.'

'You can't just ignore injustice and fraud.'

'Is that why you write your stories? To unselfishly expose? Are you too not making a living, looking for fame?'

'I'd hate to think so.'

'You tell yourself what you want. You play the game, too, and so does everyone else, as a matter of fact. Games attract cheaters and someone always ends up with a lot of money or a lot of debt. Mr Novak, I'm not having a go at you, I'm trying to help you, but you need to want to be helped.'

'I don't need steering in the wrong direction.'

'So far you have been getting lost repeatedly all by yourself. You have even been inside a police cell. I read the British papers; they can be merciless.' Lukas wanders how recently Courante read a British newspaper. With any luck it's not today. Anyway, the man doesn't want to argue. He wants to talk. 'Are you familiar with the Watergate scandal?' Courante asks him.

'Of course.'

'Think of me as the Deep Throat character. You're familiar with Deep Throat?'

'Of course. What journalist wouldn't be?'

'I will tell you things. But only this once. You listen and you make up your own mind. Deal?'

'Deal.'

'OK. Écoutez! You're looking for corruption in football. For evidence of match fixing. You're asking around, big managers, big players. People don't like that. Everybody has their own little empire. No one wants things to change, not for the worse. For the better, yes please; but journalists sniffing around usually means trouble, for everyone. People protect themselves. What do you think the biggest motivation is in football?'

'The game itself.'

'For you and me, perhaps, but then we are idealists. We love the sport. There are millions like us. Do you go to the opera?'

'Sometimes.'

'Then you know about show business, don't you? What you see is what you get, but not necessarily the truth. The opera houses are storytellers. But the opera house manager still balances his books. The game is a business. The football is the story. The game is money. Big money. There are lots of people who don't give a shit about football, if you pardon my English. And lots of people who spend all their money to see their team. And wives get beaten when their husband's team loses. You read it in the papers. And a young boy kicks a ball around at the other end of the world from you and gets famous in another country and very rich, very young and then people think that their personal happiness rests on this 17-year-old's shoulders every Wednesday and Saturday?'

'That's what's happening.'

'And what's also happening, whilst you and I enjoy the football, is the business. The game. Games attract people. Money attracts people. You have the knights, like yourself, Mr Novak. I was one too once, but I was also a pawn. You're a pawn now, something bigger than you is moving you around. You have the crooks, on the opposite side of the board. Always looking out for an advantage to make money, big money in football's case. Or fame. Fame is another motivation. Fame and girls. Money and fame makes you irresistible, Mr Novak. Look at some of these boys and the girls they take out. Doesn't it make you envious? Let me tell you, it makes the whole world jealous; a whole generation of girls want to be wags, as you call them, footballers wives. And what are they, really? Do I need to tell you?'

'You don't need to spell it out.'

'I'm glad you're listening to me, Mr Novak. It's a tragedy. The boys mean no harm other than to take advantage of their fame and money. Too young to be able to tell what's good or bad for them. And who tells them what's right or wrong? The parents? In Peru. The manager? If they're lucky and if they speak English. Their mates? Quite likely. The pull of the herd. But I digress. This is the way it will always be. Fame and money. Footballers and rock bands. Artists and divas. The perception and the reality. People will use it and abuse it. Don't blame the kids. The worm sits deeper. In big business.'

'Outside football?'

'It's all connected. This is all I will tell you. Where big money can be made big money will invest.'

'Where do I look next?'

'I cannot tell you this. You must follow your leads, you must – ' Lukas hears a commotion at the end of the line. 'Mon dieu!' he overhears a muted Jean-Pierre. Then the receiver is being grappled with.

'Novak?' DCI Briggs says, gruffly. 'I hope you've heard enough. I'm taking him to Brussels. European Court will be interested in what he has to say.'

Chapter 73

'Vladi, I need to borrow your car.'

'Again? Listen, Lukas. Casino's been shut down. Kovacs? He's been arrested, it's rumoured. Allegations of drug dealing. The whole chain's been closed for the time being. Anything to do with you?'

'No.'

'Anything to do with your story?'

'Possibly. Ripples.'

'Can I have it? Your story.'

'About?'

'Whatever it's about, I'll publish it.'

'There might be more than one story, Vlad.'

'I don't care. You're all over the news.'

'I know. By the way, I saw you skipping from the pub earlier.'

Vladi chuckles. 'It got too hot to stay.'

'Do you need much?' Lukas asks as Dannii unlocks her front door.

She shakes her head. 'I furnished it with his money.'

'Post?' Lukas picks the mail up from inside her front door.

'It'll all be junk but chuck it in the bag.'

'You know what his downfall was?'

'Pride?'

'The assumption that he was untouchable.'

He opens the door to the cottage and holds it open for her. She carries a holdall with her possessions. The cottage is warm and homely. She steps inside and dumps the bag on the floor. Then she looks at him.

He feels like he is looking at a stranger. 'Do you want to walk? Pub afterwards?' He smiles and tries to hold her gaze. 'For old times' sake?' She nods.

'Doctor's Gate?' she asks as they walk down Blackshaw Road.

'Yes. Would you like to go and see the elusive planes? Apparently, there's been a suspected murder up there.'

'Really?' She looks at him carefully. 'And you want to go up now?'

'Not now, some other day. We'll wait until the weather picks up.' He pauses and looks at her. 'That's if you're still here when the weather picks up.' She doesn't answer but turns and looks at him. He brushes the stubborn strand of hair from her face. Is she trying to smile? He can no longer tell. Lukas clears his throat. 'You know, at home going out with someone is called "going with someone", spending time, walking with them on the path of the journey of life.

She holds his gaze. 'Isn't that what we've been doing?'

He shakes his head. 'No, Dannii, so far we've mostly been running.'

Epilogue

Tony Jackson is sent down for GBH, possession, rape, indecent assault and a long string of other offences. He is currently serving a lengthy sentence at Her Majesty's Pleasure and the taxpayers' expense. Jackson's Tattooed and Faithful unfaithfully testified against him to avoid a similar fate.

DCI Richard Briggs retired from the force early after receiving a prestigious long service award, and a second chance by his wife after cleaning up his act and booking a holiday to the Seychelles. An anonymous tip by a hooded stranger enabled Briggs to convert it into enough dough to pay off his sizeable overdraft at a bookies at the other end of the country, and to pay for the aforementioned holiday.

Jean-Pierre Courante's appearance in the European Court of Justice never happened due to lack of interest in an investigation. He continues his job as a bigwig at WWFA.

Sean and Eddie Ryley still run Cheetham Hill.

Janos Kovacs's casino chain re-opened after a brief investigation and a fine, equivalent to a slap on the wrist.

Leroy Callaway was out of action for months with a mysterious back injury. During this time he appeared in court several times charged with various drug and sex offences. Mancunia FC's psychologists explained Callaway's alleged erratic behaviour as the result of the player's difficult childhood and his borderline dependence on recreational drugs. His manager's tearful testimony made the front pages of several tabloids and caused Lukas Novak to spend seven pounds fifty on a packet of Marlboro Reds.

After his recovery Callaway allegedly and successfully requested a free transfer to Kingston City Rovers.

Jason Entwistle made a slow but full recovery and resumed playing in goal for Mancunia FC's first team. Jason and Lilian Novak continue to be good mates.

Mark Smith, aka Joseph Miller, aka William Unwin, aka Billy the Bullet still runs WestPoint Security, by proxy, and Dolly Green Boxing Club alongside Stan Entwistle and Linda Tottington.

Dannii Staines lived temporarily with her Uncle Frank until he had recovered fully from his attack. She then moved him to sheltered accommodation near a rented cottage that she co-habits, at an undisclosed location in Glossop, the Gateway To The Peak.

The true identity of the mysterious MatchMaker was never officially established.

After having several articles published by Vladimir Tomasik across several platforms, Lukas Novak wrote three books that hog the top of the bestseller lists worldwide. *The Entwistle Story*, the touching life history of the Entwistle brothers, provokes a national outrage and (yet another) deep probe into child abuse at the hands of the powerful and famous. It finally not only set the proverbial casting couch on fire, but also burned it firmly to the ground.

Novak's *The Beautiful Game* illuminates football from a different angle; that of a young boy growing into a rising star, and is a semi-fictional account of what some critics call the Young Entwistle Re-Hash. Nevertheless, the book rocketed up both the fiction and non-fiction charts.

His own account of what happened during his investigation into match fixing was released a little later; inspired by his conversation with Jean-Pierre Courante, Lukas Novak decided to call the book *Match Games*.

Post Script

The is no access from Blue John Cavern to Speedwell and Peak Caverns.

There are only two Premiership football teams in Manchester: (In alphabetical order) Manchester City and Manchester United

* * *

If you have enjoyed reading *Match Games*, please consider leaving feedback on Amazon, and recommending it to your friends.

For occasional updates please join Bea's newsletter recipients at
www.beaschirmer.com

coming soon...

The HemiHelix Effect Episode 1
RUBBER BAND
Synopsis

Lukas Novak's life has just taken a turn for the worst. His wife wants a divorce and Lukas has had enough of being the underdog. He promises himself to start over. There is just the matter of the death of his old family friend Tibor, and his funeral to be taken care of.

But all is not what it seems at Fairhaven care home, Tibor's last residence. With ten deaths in just as many weeks, superstitious inmate O'Daniel smells a rat. Lukas asks questions but is sidetracked by Fairhaven's mysterious councillor Eda Enigma, who believes in the transference of spirits. Desperately seeking resolution in his own life and curious about her methods at Fairhaven Lukas enlists for a course of counseling.

Days later his research into a mysterious book with a call to invite his "Guardian Angel" into his life stretches Lukas's own sanity to its edge.

NaNoWriMo project 2014

Displacement

The HemiHelix Effect Episode 2

Lukas Novak travels to Poland on the trail of an errand given to him by his late uncle Tibor. The errand, or mission, as Lukas called it, leads him back into his family's distant and forgotten past, to a time when European history was at its darkest. Lukas needs to face up to the demons of the past and realise that not all he has believed in was real.

Lightning Source UK Ltd.
Milton Keynes UK
UKOW04f0625220215

246606UK00002B/50/P